"It's a cosmic battle roy. delivers a stunning conclusion that will leave you pondering its significance long after you've turned the last page. Five-plus stars to *Two 'Til Midnight*."

—*Publishers Daily Reviews*

"In *Two 'Til Midnight*, author Bernard L. Dillard does an amazing job of storytelling while integrating several of today's hard-to-discuss topics. . . . This book is not for the faint of heart."

—*San Francisco Book Review*

"Dillard skillfully weaves each character's part into the plot. . . . [He] has done an exceptional job creating a novel that will be enjoyed . . . This is highly recommended reading."

—*Reader Views*

"[R]eaders will find [that] the discoveries . . . and revelations in *Two 'Til Midnight* make for thought-provoking reading . . . with a plot that drives home lessons . . . Readers who stick with the myriad of characters . . . and [the] blend of super-natural influences, daily life challenges, and confrontations between Christian and secular worlds will find *Two 'Til Mid-night* an engrossing, multifaceted story."

—*Midwest Book Review*

"*Two 'Til Midnight* is an imaginative and engaging story . . . [T]he novel offers insightful glimpses into critical issues . . . Dillard excels, and so *Two 'Til Midnight* works well as a prescient tale about contemporary issues."

—*Self-Publishing Review*

BERNARD L. DILLARD

Bernard L. Dillard graduated from Morehouse College with a degree in English Literature. He is the author of *Lemonade: Inspired by Actual Events*, which, in 2013, won first place in Dan Poynter's Global Ebook Awards in the autobiography/memoir category. He is an associate professor of mathematics in New York City. He enjoys running, modeling, and watching indie films.

TWO 'TIL MIDNIGHT

a novel

BERNARD L. DILLARD

BERNERD PUBLISHING

New York

Copyright © 2019 by Bernard L. Dillard

BerNerd Publishing trade paperback edition 2019

Author photograph © Moebius Simmons, The Cocktail Office
Interior designed by Damonza
Book cover designed by Augusto Silva

Manufactured in the United States of America

Dillard, Bernard L.
Two 'til midnight: a novel / Bernard L. Dillard.

ISBN 9780578453484 (paperback) | ISBN 9780578469706 (ebook)

www.bernarddillard.com

To those weak in the faith

and

For civility

Moses answered Pharaoh, "You may have the honor of choosing when I should pray for you, your officials, and your people. Then the frogs will leave you and your homes. The only ones left will be those in the Nile."

"Pray for me tomorrow," Pharaoh said.

Exodus 8: 9–10

GOD'S WORD Translation

FOREWORD

As a person who labors in the same profession as this new novelist, I can offer admiration for his creativity, eclecticism, endurance, and success. He has accomplished much and, though I was his undergraduate professor, who is supposed to have surpassed him, he inspires and unwittingly chastises me, for I cannot list the diversity of achievements that he can. "Yet, do I marvel."

Such is the spring of his enthusiasm and dedication to his craft and the energy of his engagement in activities that undoubtedly drive him. Such perseverance reminds me of the title by the first college president for whom I worked and one Dillard surely reveres, *Lord, The People Have Driven Me On*, or Benjamin E. Mays' work that is an inspiration for those at Morehouse College, Dillard's alma mater. That hallowed place is where I first encountered the novelist. That title is a rubric for the second creative publication by this son of Morehouse, whose experiences are a major part of the reflections in his revelatory work, *Lemonade: Inspired by Actual Events*.

That memoir introduced me to a Bernard Dillard I had not known, though he remains one of my Morehouse sons who has periodically kept me informed of his professional activities. Proud of his drive to use hardships to give credence to a concept in which I earnestly believe – "It is not what happens to you in life that matters; it is what you do with what happens to you that matters," – proud of his joining me in the trenches of teaching, proud of his multidisciplinary academic bent, proud of his fending himself to several tangents of the arts, proud of his striving to bring others along through serving as an *exemplum*, I am most proud that he has asked me to offer a few words to introduce his novel.

Teacher that I am, and an open bookaholic, I approached his fictional world not with the eyes of the literary critic or reviewer but with great curiosity about the tome that he had kept me informed about as he fleshed it out. However, he never shared a draft nor divulged its genre, tone, or theme. Thus, I approached with the eyes of a reader who is intrigued by the title and the "stuff" of the work. Soon, I found myself hearing tingling echoes of James Joyce, Ishmael Reed, Kurt Vonnegut, John Oliver Killens, and others whose characters' wanderings I recall even though I have not returned to them recently. And jazz – "straight-ahead" – [what aficionado does not hear "'Round Midnight"] and melodic tones emerged for me as well, for the world his characters traverse invited me, sometimes with apprehension and sometimes with empathy, to move along with them.

None of these vibes suggest to me that Dillard sought influence from any of these or from any more contemporary writers. No, Dillard is moving in his own path, at his own pace, and toward his own vision of realities and beyond. Therefore, it is with pride and great expectations that I accepted his invitation to be an introducer to this tome. I await his subsequent ventures.

Dr. E. Delores B. Stephens
Professor of English
Morehouse College

ACKNOWLEDGMENTS

After six years of on-again, off-again research and writing, this project has finally gotten to a point where it can be consumed by the masses. Such often is the plight of self-published authors, who have no looming pressure or deadlines to meet with mammoth publishing houses and toe-tapping agents. What motivates and pushes are an internal passion and drive to accomplish what was started. Since writing is currently something I do "on the side," it is good to step out into the light on the other side of the writing tunnel and offer something tangible.

I am grateful to My Lord for helping me realize another dream. I thank you, Sir, for being my strength and my help. I am thankful for my family, mostly in North Carolina, which has always supported me in all of my endeavors, literary and otherwise. You appear to have gotten used to my quirkiness and have led the way in celebrating my unique giftings. To my church families in Atlanta and Baltimore, I appreciate your undying support and prayers. I realize, as John Donne offers, that "No man is an island entire of itself." Your love and encouragement keep me laughing and excited about what future blessings will unfold. To my Facebook friends, Twitter followers, and those on the Gram, your wait is finally over. Several of you have been asking, "So, when is the next book going to be ready? You can't just tease us with *Lemonade* and not give us anything else." Knowing an audience is waiting with bated breath is fuel enough to stick with the challenge and see it through. I hope you enjoy this one, too.

Finally, a special thanks goes out to a special contributor. About 25 years ago, I sat in a stadium-style classroom in Dansby Hall with several other eager English majors. We'd gotten through some of the earlier courses in the major and now had to confront this one: Shakespeare. Admittedly, all I had been exposed to up to that point was *Romeo and Juliet* and the famous question known for the work. Before long, the door in the rear gently opened, and the professor made her way down the twenty or so steps, leading to the hallowed teaching space. From where I sat – close to the front but away from the descending staircase – she appeared rather short. In fact, the textbook, with its 600 or so pages and weighing in at about eight pounds, seemed almost as big as she.

Height quickly became a nonfactor as she dove into discussions of salient themes in Shakespeare's work. The poor textbook, if it were a living creature, would have sulked because of abandonment. Once it hit her desk, it was rarely opened. Lectures were crafted and presented without it. I remember how she explored themes like unrequited love, appearance vs. reality, and greed as she quoted line after line after line from the plays, all from memory. To witness her in action was a sight to behold. She kept the educative bar high, and we knew it wouldn't be lowered. In all, I sat under her tutelage in three courses: this one and the two survey courses in English literature. No doubt, the training I received helped to strengthen my writing and sharpen my critical eye. In retrospect (and totally unplanned!), the way the protagonist in this novel presses her students beyond surface explanations, and the playful reference to Shakespeare elsewhere in the work are probably my subconscious nods to a professional mothering by Dr. Delores Stephens.

I remember her disappointment with one of my decisions as I approached graduation. I'd kept my GPA a secret, only for her to discover, as department chair, that my grades in the English major courses qualified me for membership in its honor society, Sigma Tau Delta. I declined the offer, much to her chagrin. Hopefully, over two decades later, my invitation for her to pen the novel's Foreword relays to her that I am still wedded to the pursuit of knowledge and that I am deeply grateful for the literary standard of excellence she modeled for my fellow English majors and me.

Thanks, Doc!

TWO 'TIL MIDNIGHT

11:58

1
COUNTDOWN

HE WAS SHAKEN awake coincidentally. It didn't have anything to do with the fact that he really *was* up against the clock. He hadn't even felt himself dozing off, let alone dwelling in the deep trenches of sleepville. The car's soothing interior and the sound of the deafening rain must have been the tag-teaming culprits, lulling him into that Sandman-ushered space. And now, they were late. When she exited the car, she said she'd be right back and that she already had an idea about what she'd change into. So the amount of time this was taking was absurd. Even if she had to steam the dress, this was taking way too long; ten minutes had become twenty. "What in the hell is she doing in there?" Tario stated to himself. He shot Davida a text, claiming that they were six minutes away. But the truth was that they hadn't even left yet. Now that the downpour had calmed to a drizzle, he'd just make his way inside to see what the holdup was. Soon, the car's engine was off, and he performed unequal jump-strides from the curb to the front door, careful to avoid the patches of water.

He cracked open the front door. "Dr. G?" After a short silence, he repeated. "Dr. G?" As he entered the house, she still didn't answer. The floor creaked. Making his way through the hallway, he noticed the umbrella propped against the wall. The hallway fed into the living room. Nothing there either. A quick transition into the kitchen revealed nothing but an empty glass in the sink. Nothing too out of the ordinary, except for the slip on the kitchen floor. *Yo, Dr. G trippin'*, he thought. *I know we in a rush, but she just throwing stuff everywhere.* Other than that, the kitchen was spick and span.

Finally, his ears saved him. He heard water running in her bathroom. He'd never laid eyes on her bedroom before, so the thought of entering naturally made him feel guilty and like he was trespassing. He called for her louder, now that he stood right next to her door. "Dr. G?" He had to walk softly so that he didn't see anything he wasn't supposed to, especially if she was sitting on the toilet or praying. Or worse, sitting on the toilet and praying. "Dr. G?"

Filled with consternation, he inched toward the bathroom door and touched it, preparing to turn. In an instant, the knob turned and the door swung open away from him.

Garnet was rushing as fast as she could when she was startled. "Tario, sweetie, what are you doing in here? I thought you were going to wait in the car."

Embarrassed, he said what he thought made sense. "It was getting late, and I just wanted to come in and make sure you were alright. I called your name I don't know how many times, and you didn't say nothing. I was hoping didn't nothing bad happen."

A text from Davida popped up on Tario's phone: *So wya? Jmy and them still doing praise. Tell Ms Gibbs Jmy need her to brng trunks 4 RJ. Hotel gone let him swim in pool. Hurry!*

"Bad? What do you mean 'bad'? I got to hurry and get back. It's quarter past." She turned off the faucet and virtually ran throughout the house, picking up the slip, the soiled dress, and even managed to wash the used glass.

"You look very nice, Dr. G. Can I help with anything?" She had changed into a light blue cocktail dress by Zac Posen, sleeveless. This and the wine-stained one were the only real formal pieces she had in that closet of hers. Slipping into her silver heels, she grabbed a navy scarf to offset any possible cold temperatures in the hotel, along with her earrings. She hated when hotels turned their air on Alaska, thinking they were offsetting temperatures outside. She'd put the earrings on in the car.

"No, just grab the umbrella on the way out. Let's go." She grabbed her keys. "Close the door so I can set the alarm."

With the countdown in motion, he opened the door, and she scurried through the hall toward him, only a few feet behind. Grabbing the umbrella, he half-stepped outside but remembered. Turning back around, he stated, "Oh, Dr. G, I forgot. Jamay wants you to—"

Never in a million years would he ever forget the image that his eyes were trying to make him believe was real.

GABRIEL

TO CALL THE view from the Bellagio breathtaking revealed how limited one's range of vocabulary was; the word that described the majesty of the buildings and crisp skyline didn't seem to be invented yet. The spectacle of the dancing water fountain from the thirty-second floor was a sight to behold. The hotel did its part to contribute to Independence Day festivities by creatively adding red and blue lights to the conventional bright white ones to complete the patriotic vibe for the weekend.

Manuela leaned against the window sill, inhaling deeply and enjoying all that her eyes were privileged to witness. She had taken in the fountain show beneath and was anxiously anticipating the fourth-of-July fireworks show that would happen shortly. She absolutely adored the room and the sights that it offered, so she always requested this one in particular. A few times, some other party was occupying it, but she was very fortunate that it was available more times than not. Its whirlpool tub, the marble entry, eclectic wall patterns, and soothing comforters were just some of the amenities that made her feel like a queen whenever she stayed.

"Enjoyin' the view, baby?" whispered Kemal into her ear. A pair of hands caressed her hips, startling her. The hands moved slowly alongside her torso, landing on her breasts. She had on no bra. He kissed her neck as he pressed himself against her.

"I sure am. You scared me. I thought you were in the shower."

"I was. But you know how quiet that shower is. Crazy powerful and crazy quiet. And those massage settings are just what the doctor ordered for these stiff shoulders." He turned her around to face him. "But how about this view?" She didn't realize he was still a little damp and dressed in his birthday suit. He had freshly put on some dabs of his He Wood Rocky Mountain Wood cologne, so he had that subtle masculine and cedar smell. It always triggered that giddy and sexy part of Manuela, the part that made her melt and drop all inhibitions.

"Yes, this view is pretty good, too," she giggled. She noticed that his manhood was between soft and hard, curved to the left, and demonstrated its own heartbeat, slightly bouncing up and down on pace with the pumping of blood in his chest. The vein that shone through was repulsive and inviting like a moth to a flame. *How did it protrude through like that?* she wondered. She turned back around to stare out of the window and tease him just a little while longer.

"I see what you doin'," he joked.

"What?"

"What?" he mimicked her and gave a casual laugh. He rested his piece firmly between her butt cheeks and grabbed her breasts again, loving the semi-foreplay. "I can't believe it's been two years, baby. Time just seems to fly by." He had begun moving his hips in circles against her cushion, waking up his weapon even more.

"Yeah, it does."

"I don't see how those things get curves in it. It looks freakish."

"It takes more than just that to make somebody a freak. Gotta have skills to match."

"Oh, and you definitely got skills," she quickly cosigned.

He went ahead and removed her shirt, tossing it on the sofa. He planted his lips against the back of her neck as she swooned and put her head back, closing her eyes. Before she knew it, her pants were by her ankles. She had on no under-wear. She knew early where things would go. No need for any extra barriers. Kemal was a monster when he was aroused, and the monster was loose. He was 6′3″ and weighed in at 193. He was blue-black, possessing a dark, smooth, even skin tone. He was the poster boy for those who wanted to bring dark skin back in. Having only 4% body fat, he wore a size thirteen shoe. His other name was Manaconda.

After she stepped out of her pants, he turned her around again and lifted her as she wrapped her legs around his waist. As he steadied her to the bed with one arm, he threw her Puerto Rican hair behind her while she wrapped her arms around his neck. Both were the multitaskers par excellence. He fondled, carried, caressed, massaged, and French kissed her at the same time, all while walking. She was just as talented. She balanced herself, rubbed his head, kissed him back, moaned, and scratched his back gently with her newly mani-cured fingernails. The down-stuffed comforter served as just the right welcome mat they needed. The stresses of life had beat them almost to a pulp, and this was the moment they had been waiting for to recharge and let it all hang out.

Kemal had tried different foreplay techniques before: the chocolate-honey mixture, the dirty talk via text and sexting images, and the dressing up as Tarzan and Jane. The last time he did the dress-up thing, though, he accidentally knocked over a lamp when he cracked the whip, breaking it and leaving him with a $199 replacement charge at check-out. Second, they didn't make the male outfits for black people. A large wasn't a black man's large. It didn't account for a black man's behind. Kemal looked like he was wearing something from OshKosh B'Gosh. Last, when he looked at Manuela and said, "Me Tarzan, you Jane," she burst out laughing. She killed the mood and any prospects for anything hot and steamy that evening, other than the popcorn they ate. They turned it into a TV night, watching reruns of *Martin* and *I Love Lucy*, skipping sex altogether and laughing until the wee morning hours. But tonight was no laughing matter.

What seemed to be working recently was the figure-eight tongue technique down there, so that's where he started once they hit the bed. He'd always heard that women loved the stimulation below the belt and was skeptical to try it at first. After realizing it was indeed true, he decided that he had better not reinvent the wheel. He just wished the church would offer discussion on sex tips such as this one. He had to learn about most of these methods through trial and error, by Googling, or while reading through Song of Solomon in the Bible, surprisingly. He promised that he would have a talk with the pastor and ask to lead a class dedicated to spicing things up between the married couples at the church. He even knew the name of the class: Solomon's Sultry Secrets.

Each time Kemal's tongue performed an eight, Manuela's body made a jerking motion. On her back, her legs were spread widely apart, and she lay helpless, allowing him to continue showing his expertise. She had gone into another world as he had successfully got her hot and bothered. In this space, she had somehow found the terminology that turned him on even more. What started out as "daddy" quickly turned to "Papi" as her area had become self-lubricated, a sure sign that he had gotten through to her emotional zone and, hence, her erogenous one.

"You like that?" he rhetorically inquired.

"Yes, Papi." She turned her head left then right then left then right.

There was no more need for preliminaries, so he made his real move. He placed one leg on his shoulders and gained skin-to-skin entry. Her gateway seemed to be made specifically for his manhood. He had learned to turn slightly to the right before entering to account for the curve but, once in, had mastered the rhythm necessary to please. After about five minutes, he turned her on her stomach and managed to work out the right angle of entry. She couldn't believe that he was hers, she his. She lay with face turned to the side, resting on the pillow. She wasn't sure what to allow herself to feel the most. Each inch of his uniquely made rod? The stimulating effect of his low-hanging scrotum as it hit her clitoris with every back-and-forth thrust? The grimy language that he used to keep both of them in the moment's mood? Several times, she wanted to turn her head around and say, *"Wait, now. Who you callin' a bitch?"* That was a little outside of all things Christian, but she continued to play along. He was in his own world, and whatever made him put it down like a champ was ultimately fine with her.

After three more position changes and with his body glistening with sweat, an hour and a half had passed. Somehow, she had ended up on top of him, feeling the deep, tickling effect of the curve's path inside of her. Her hands rested on his abs while he bent his legs for better leverage. As her hair stuck to her own perspiration-soaked skin, she could tell he was close to climaxing. She was glad because so was she. It was magical if they both managed to reach that place at the same time.

As he closed his eyes and continued with the blissful gyrations, he felt her walls get looser and then tighter and then looser. She was almost there. He began what seemed like a marathon of an ejaculation process. It actually began on the inner part of his feet. He didn't know how or why the blood vessels started constricting there, but it seemed to turn him into a little boy, the way he started whimpering and all. He responded by flexing his toes, scrunching and then releasing them. The sensation made its way up both legs, climbing into his calves, up the back of his knee, swerving to his inner thighs, and moving like a snail toward his scrotum on both sides. It seemed to take an eternity for all of his liquid passion to congeal within his testicles, reducing him almost to a baby. This was the only thing Manuela hated about these moments. One time he actually put his thumb in his mouth during the build-up seconds. *Really?* she thought.

His scrotum stopped hanging low. The testicles began constricting, making his sac rise and become tighter. This rising and falling happened five times until the final time, in which he literally felt what seemed to be a centipede hurriedly crawling through his shaft, looking for a way out. He let out a deep, sustained grunt and then a series of loud grunts as his cannon shot upward. Returning the favor, her own cannon shot downward. To put the cherry on top, the fireworks outside started exploding at the same time. Three explosions at once. She felt his liquid warmth, and he hers. She was a quiet climaxer but just as intense as he. The neighbors next door could have thought they heard a noise through the wall but concluded it must have been the booms of the holiday sky show. She found her way off of him and collapsed beside him on the bed.

There was no need to wash immediately after, so they both just lay there, basking in their exploits. "Yo, it's getting better and better," Kemal broke the silence and broke wind rather loudly.

"Why you gotta do all that?" she asked as she turned away from him in order to avoid the skunky fumes. "Ugh!"

"All what, baby? That's just my body responding to a good workout. That was just like going to the weight room or doing about twenty laps in a pool. In fact, I need me something to drink." He walked naked to the refrigerator and brought the bottled water back to the bed. Fireworks were still cracking outside, so they both turned their attention toward the window. The spraying effect of the lighting almost gave off as if actual sparks would come through their room. His phone signified that he had a text message. He already knew who it was but observed it anyway and placed the phone back down. He wished she would stop already. Manuela acted as if she didn't see or hear it.

Instead, she agreed. "Yeah, it does make you weak. Lemme have some." He handed her the water, and she drank out of it just as he had. "Woo! Refreshing." She looked at the label and vowed to switch to it on the regular. "Anyway, lemme get in this shower. I got all you all over me."

As she laughed and rose to head toward the bathroom, Kemal stopped her. "No, baby, just lay here and enjoy it. We'll both shower together in the morning. Just enjoy the moment. Enjoy the view. Enjoy me." After these couple of years, he was still the sweet talker. He placed his arm around her, pulling her closer to him and rested his hand on her right butt cheek. She lay facing him, placing her right arm across his stomach. She looked down and noticed his attachment had retreated to its innocuous, non-menacing state. Even the curve had disappeared. That to her was a mystery. He stared out of the window at the remaining fireworks action. She stared at his chiseled, shaved face, and then down at his Adam's apple. She wondered why it did what it did when he swallowed. Another text came through but was ignored again. This was their moment. This was their time.

And Gabriel, witnessing all that had just transpired, stood at the foot of the bed, staring at them both.

The Evidence of
Things Not Seen

THEIR MEETING WAS to convene earlier, but Gabriel had been slightly detained. Some felt strong, others not so much. Regardless, they had to try and be about their business, as a great deal of people depended on their help. Their strength was directly tied to how fervently prayers rose from their jurisdiction. Gabriel had reported on the circumstances that he'd just witnessed at the hotel and was back to meet with the other two. All three were primarily responsible for this jurisdictional community.

"Sorry I'm late," said a forlorn Gabriel. "Was checking in on Kemal. Doesn't look like the situation's going too well."

"That's on him," Raphaela noted. "He knows what's expected by now. What else we got?" She was in charge of the meeting and had to report back to the Boss and provide updates on those assigned to them.

"I'm looking after Nieko," expressed Uriel. "He's at such

a vulnerable point. He's doing pretty well, but he's trying to maintain his victory in his own strength. I'm not gonna be able to intervene as much because a lot of his success will come from his choices and reliance on the Holy Spirit. It's gone be tough on him, though. It's definitely gonna be tough."

"Okay."

"And I'm trying to do my best to help the lawyer with his case involving the school," he continued. "But honestly, that one doesn't look promising. It's not a wash, but the way things are turning, it probably won't come out positive."

"What about Garnet?" she inquired. "I got my eye on the kid. Sad he has to deal with so much at a young age, but we all know the enemy doesn't play fair. If it was up to him, all children would be wiped out. We all remember Mr. Herod the so-called Great. Anyway, as long as prayers are going up, the little one should be fine."

"I got Garnet and the kid's father," said Gabriel. "She's a major target, so I have to put in overtime for her. The enemy's banking on destroying the kid's father because of distance. As long as she keeps praying, he'll be fine. But he can't rely on her prayers forever."

"Alright. And then Davida and Tario?" asked Raphaela.

The other two kept quiet and stared up into space.

"I see. So nobody wants to take responsibility for them, huh?"

"It's not so much Davida," confessed Uriel. "But that Tario is . . . I just don't know if we can help him. He's just . . . he play too much."

"Agreed," chimed in Gabriel. "Some people are special. But Tario is *special* special."

"I'll look after him, then," said Raphaela. "Thank goodness his grandfather laid a good foundation of prayer for him before he went to glory. From what I see, the prayers are still active. Rest his soul." She exhaled and confirmed again reluctantly. "I'll look after Tario and make sure he comes into the fold. Lord, help me."

The other two breathed a sigh of relief.

"Well, that does it. The Lord is expecting us to deliver, serve, and protect. Let's trust the prayer base is there for us to do the work effectively."

"When do we meet back?" asked Gabriel.

"In a minute," responded Raphaela. "Let's meet back here in one minute."

Before leaving for their assignments, they headed back to His throne declaring a continuous, "Holy, holy, holy, is the Lord God Almighty!"

Raphaela and Uriel finally left. As Gabriel prepped to fly away, he received an unanticipated and direct command from the Lord concerning Kemal. The directive was short but explicit. "Handle that."

Without hesitation and just as quickly as he received the instructions, he vanished.

Their meeting was supposed to convene earlier, too, but Mictian had been detained.

"Why are you late?" inquired Belial.

"I was involved with an accident on Interstate 15," replied the latecomer. "Poor motorcyclist." He laughed a dark laugh.

"Involved? Isn't that kind of misleading? Involved? Well, just make sure you're here on time the next time. Play your non-essential games on your own time. The group's business is more important than your individual pastimes. You should know that by now."

"Can you two knock it off?" asked Ashtoreth. "We all have jobs to do, and all this extra chatter is useless. I have a special assignment this evening, and I need to get the hell out of here. I have to go hang out with the two lovebirds tonight."

Everyone snickered.

"Yeah, we all know you got them under your little spell," they all affirmed in one form or another.

"Well, we'll hurry so you can go do your thang, Ms. Ash," said Belial. He was in charge of the meeting and had to be prepared to give a status update to the boss. To the group, he asked, "Who is having problems staying on task, other than Mr. Interstate?" He glanced at Mictian again to slightly reprove him one final time. "You all know our deadlines, and I will have to give an account of your progress. Or lack thereof. I would hate to have to give a bad report."

"We good. We all good," answered Mictian. "The boss will be proud. Actually, we *were* supposed to be further along, but some people out there keep praying and throwing our timeline off. Especially that bitch, Garnet, and people like her."

"You mean, Lite Brite?" joked Ashtoreth. Everybody erupted in hideous laughter. Ashtoreth continued, "She always pleading the . . . well, you know."

"Don't say that shit in here!" Mictian took umbrage at the unfinished phrase and what it insinuated. "Take that somewhere else."

"I'm just saying. That bitch gets on my nerves. Always on her knees or mumbling some words that I can't figure out."

"I can bring somebody into her world to make use of her being on her knees, if you know what I mean. Find a way to shut her up!" Belial was invisibly chafed. "Attack her family, her children, her grandchildren. Find a way!"

"Look, I'm monitoring the family," added Mictian. "I got

Garnet under my thumb as well as her daughter. I'm still playing on her low self-esteem from her situation. Her growth is
still stunted from some childhood stuff. And I got a master
plan to destroy that son-in-law of hers. He don't pray all like
that, so her prayer babblings won't carry him but so far."

"Good. I'll watch her grandson," offered Ashtoreth. "I'm
still watching him to see what I notice. I think I have a good
strategy of attack for his li'l nappy head. It has to do with his
father not being there, the usual reason with little boys. I just
love it! Gimme a sec. I'll follow up with him and let you know
how I plan on destroying him."

"Bet!" said Belial. "I been working on this project to
get this college closed. They think they can just ignore this
new policy from the feds. I'm sick of these private Christian
schools. Stuck in the past, holding on to these ancient rules.
I'm shuttin' it down. And Garnet keeps praying for this loser,
Tario. She really thinks he gone turn his life around and walk
the straight and narrow. That one will be easy, though. All I
got to do is keep appealing to his pride and that should take
care of that. He won't surrender his will to the Lord. I promise. And I got the ultimate strategy to kill him if it comes to it.
He don't got the balls to make a solid decision. All of you guys
already know that he just play too damn much."

"We glad you the one assigned to him," admitted Ashtoreth. "We don't feel like wasting our energies on that fool."
Mictian agreed.

"But I'm daa-finitely loving my other assignment," added
the female spirit. "Ms. Vogue-and-Slay boo think she gone
just walk away and start a new life. Talkin' 'bout she trying
to get her life together and leave the scene altogether. Chile,
please. This gone be easy. I got his ex waiting in the wings,
ready to make that move. He ain't finna pass up on all that,

though, not with all he packing. I'll keep reminding him of all the sex he used to have, and the rest will be history. Yas!"

"Nice!" voiced Belial.

"And I got one final ace in the hole that ain't got nothing to do with none of our current tasks, my friends. I been working on this one for a long time. It's just about ready to reveal. But it's gone go down soon in that church Garnet go to. Nobody is gone be ready for this one. I'm gone stir up a little racism that's been boiling for a minute in somebody I've been monitoring. Wait and see what I tell you. You'll thank me later."

No one responded but knew this girl didn't mince words. They'd have to wait and see what she referred to.

"But as for now," she stated, "you don't have to worry about me failing on my mission tonight. He all about his image. I can't remember the last time he prayed when he was by himself. He's so used to the limelight and being in front of people, and I love it. That's the only time he prays, when he has that mic in his hand. Gone be up there acting like he got power and ain't got nothing but a form of godliness and a loud mouth. I love my job! Turnin' preachers into sex freaks."

"Anyway, off I go. I'll keep you idiots posted. Meet me back here in another minute. 'Til then, see you next time, you spineless losers." And just like that, she was gone.

"Speaking of mouth, she sure got a lot of one," confessed Belial. "But she gets the job done. I *will* say that. From Samson to David, she's been doing her thing for some time now. And she gets results. At least I know I can count on her."

"I guess," Mictian jealously replied.

Mictian's mind was elsewhere, and now was the time to go revel in the aftermath of his handiwork on the highway. "Later, you insecure underachiever," were his departing words.

As they all disappeared into nothingness, the smell of sulfur lingered thickly in the atmosphere.

4

HALFWAY HOLY

IT WAS CARDIO Day at Alive, or at least that's what most members had jokingly dubbed it. They knew that by the end of worship, sixty-five percent of the congregation would be dripping with sweat, while the other thirty-five would be praising in its own way by raising hands or by sitting and crying. The latter group was generally those over a certain age. The church was mixed and changed worship-leader types every Sunday so those in attendance would experience the different ways that various cultures went about expressing their love for the Lord.

Today, it was back to the red-hot, fired-up group of young adults and millennials, who had a knack for leading members into a respectable frenzy of giving thanks, singing, and dancing. They took no prisoners and could have cared less if everyone knew what they were saying. Whether they possessed any power to back up what they were singing or to heal was irrelevant. What they were saying over the microphones *had* to be right. They were loud, and that was all that mattered. More often than not, the team was comprised of blacks, Hispanics, and maybe one white. And depending on whichever of them was in charge of the worship flow, the energy level of those in attendance would follow suit. To be honest, though, it really didn't matter which of the group did the leading. Either way, the energy level would definitely be somewhere in between crunk, lit, and off the chain.

This time, Jamay had the honor of leading the way. Along with her backup worship team, she coaxed and cajoled congregation participants into giving Him their all. "C'mon everybody, lift up His name!" Most of the crowd obeyed and erupted in praise. The backup singers did their best to keep up, but Jamay was an Energizer bunny. Kemal mixed in well with the other ministers on the platform and lifted his hands. He was a talented somebody and was scheduled to lead worship the following week. He loved to encourage the people and got even more antsy as the current group ushered the people into public intimacy with God. He desperately wanted to grab the mic and have at it. Worship leaders were actually singing a contemporary gospel song that played on the local FM dial throughout the city. It was well-known to those in and out of the church. It was the group's way of holding fast to their conviction of spirituality while wooing in the unchurched generation, those who had no knowledge of what being saved meant. It was a strategy that the group had long discussed as one of the best methods of reaching everyone for God's mission and purpose. Some of them came to the realization that, although the church would not adapt its message, it would alter its methodology to reach the many who wouldn't understand those old-school songs from way back when. Not all were on board concerning this approach but it was fine for today.

Jamay continued, "That's it! Celebrate the King of Kings

and the Lord of Lords! He's worthy to be praised!" Just then, the worship leaders, under her guidance, broke out in a choreographed routine that was sure to confuse most of the crowd. After completing the series of movements once, it was time for the congregants to join in. She urged everyone, "Alright, lean over to the left like this! Now hop back two steps. Reach up with your right hand to the heavens. Great! Now make a complete turn and show Him how much you love Him!"

The majority of the members hung tough. They tried their best to keep up with the hip-hop type moves. A few of the older folk had begun their retreat a while back, choosing to sit, fidget, and offer an occasional hallelujah. They didn't want to offend, but they were just tired. There was no sense in being phony. The Lord would understand. It was a domino effect. Several of the other aged members in the congregation put up a good fight and then scanned their area for those near their age. They all seemed to get winded around the same time, but no one wanted to be seated first. Neither wanted to be the first to give off as though this newfangled worship experience was wearing them out and making them feel their heartbeats in both feet. Once one of them succumbed, however, others followed. They started, one by one, dropping like flies into the welcoming cushions of their seats, rocking side to side and rubbing their knees. From there, they'd just watch the rest of the spectacle.

And what a spectacle it was. The younger people and the more adventurous middle-agers kept up pretty well. Once the planned singing and choreography came to an end, the Holy Spirit was now free to move. Today, He performed no major signs and wonders, like the time a few years ago when He healed a visitor from cancer right on the spot during worship. He'd just make Himself known by pouring out His spirit and causing a tumult through dancing and clapping. The live band, called Joshua's Horn, sat in their own special corner to the right of the singers. They were comprised of skilled musicians who played the trumpet, trombone, sax, flute, clarinet, and drums and cymbals, of course. They even had the nerve to have somebody playing the triangle. The excitement had finally risen to a height where the praises were now revealed as fancy footwork. As the instruments played and the drums offered a hypnotic beat, many had moved from their standing positions, entered the aisles and went forth, zoning out anyone else who may have been surrounding them. Eyes were closed as people almost magically avoided hitting anyone else or bumping into anything. Almost. One lady danced into a folded metal chair that sat on the end for the usher's use. She sat down, not wanting to admit she felt the effects of hitting her shin on the chair pretty hard.

The worship leaders somehow managed to pour fuel on the fire. Jamay barked, "Get your dance on! Get your dance on! He's been too good to you!" What did she say that for? Those who disobeyed just decided to stay where they were and praised by clapping. The blacks and Hispanics clapped on off-beats two and four. Everyone else clapped on one and three. The drum's tribal beats brought the dancer out of the non-dancer. They strongly resembled those perfected by the Senegambian Jolla tribe in western Africa; the Bukarabu-like drum call to war signified victory for the saints and defeat for any who opposed them. Fittingly, a few worshippers seemed to dance the Agbekor dance with its war-like and battle-ready overtones. Others who may have been less coordinated still honored the rhythmic pulse of the drums by praising Him with their warrior jump, their Adumu. No reason why they couldn't get in on the action as well. They jumped as high as they could with hands raised, hoping to touch some form of the heavens. The praise scene understandably scared some but energized others. Everyone sensed a feeling of war in the air but, more importantly, of victory. No sense fighting if you thought you were going to lose. It was victory in the air. Sweet victory. Indeed, most African villages would not have drumming without dancing. And neither would Alive.

It was exhilarating to watch, so Garnet did just that. She sat a couple of chairs from the rear.

Nieko sat two rows ahead of her. He'd just lowered his hands. Eyes closed, he thought on the Lord's goodness. Nobody would have believed what he endured this past week. Staying away from Maurice was proving to be tougher than he originally thought. He finally sat.

On these high-energy Sundays, Garnet didn't want to unduly influence the people around her as she sat, having them think she wasn't interested in the service. She vowed that she would start walking on the roads in her community as these Sundays approached to give herself a shot at keeping up with the calisthenics of it all. Life after fifty was no cakewalk, and she was ten years past this midpoint. She placed her arm across the seat to her right, tapped her left foot at the same tempo as the prevailing church beat, and turned to Dedra. "You think heaven still got space for us old fogeys?"

Dedra replied, "Speak for yourself, doctor. You may be getting older, but I'm getting better."

"You can tell yourself whatever you think you need to. This left hip and right knee don't care nothin' 'bout them little sayings o' yours. They tryin' to do their own thing, but I command them to get with the program in Jesus' name." She placed her left hand on her right knee and waited for His power to zap it.

"Hallelujah!" Dedra lifted both hands and waited for the surge, too. They laughed and realized it would probably happen later.

The praise was high but was mellowing out a bit. Everyone seemed to be readying for a breather. A worshipper half-trotted, half-skipped past where they sat. A row in front of them, an eighteen-month old stood on his pew chair, leaning against it for support. He stared at them like the toddlers who engage flight neighbors on planes, smiling and laughing and sucking on his fingers as saliva drooled onto the chair. His mother was somewhere in the sanctuary praising God, relying on the kindness of other members who sat nearby to babysit for a brief moment. It was Garnet who normally took up the task of watching when the parents sat near her. She didn't mind, though. She was thankful that the baby had gotten accustomed to what she looked like and didn't judge her, unlike when he first used to stare at her and unlike most people in general who ran into her these days. They could be so rude, staring at her like some freakish object. At least they could have the decency to glance, turn their eyes away, and then glance back again. Most people, however, just stared and stared until Garnet stared back, making them realize how rude they were. Over time, Garnet developed thick skin but wished people had more discretion with how they dealt with their curious itch.

Just then, the baby's mother returned and claimed her parental oversight. Garnet and Dedra continued to have idle chatter before Dedra left for good. This was the second service. Dedra arrived at the first service in time to hear the preaching and stayed for the second service to partake in worship. Interestingly, she timed it just right to miss the offering for either service. She claimed to give her tithes and offering online, but that was between her and her God. Jamay and the gang gathered themselves and prepared to relinquish themselves from this round of leading the people into touching His garment. She verbally gave thanks to the Lord one final time as sweat beads made their way down her smooth, caramel skin tone. As her backup posse wiped away its own sweat, she urged the people one final time.

"Saints, let's never forget where the Lord has brought us from. He's been too good to us for us not to remember his strong hand in our lives. If you're visiting, I know what you've just witnessed may seem a bit weird, but we don't apologize for expressing our gratitude to God, who keeps making our lives matter." She would have continued in her exhortation, but she saw Pastor Castillo in her periphery moving his way to the platform. The praise team had gone over the allotted time, and he was ready to take the mic to move the service forward. There was a message burning in his heart that he needed to share, and he inched closer and closer to the stage so as to suggest to Jamay to shut it down. She did, and he came forward. The Holy Spirit workout session for today had concluded.

Having grown up in Reno, the pastor was of Dominican and Haitian descent. Both of his parents had migrated to the States in the 1940s for the proverbial better life, his father's family from La Vega and his mother's from Jacmel. Primarily, he was raised as a traditional Roman Catholic, giving full attention to all the catechism and teachings attached thereto. He began breaking away from such an allegiance in his twenties, although he had thought, much earlier in his life, that drinking communion wine from the same cup as others was a questionable practice. In fact, he thought it was gross. Of more importance to him, however, was the notion of lionizing Mary and raising her to the level and status of God. Asking her to intercede for the saints went against Biblical teaching in his mind. He referenced 1 Timothy 2:5 and Hebrews 7:25 to a few of his Catholic peers to no avail. Tradition was not called tradition for no reason. They just agreed to disagree with the young upstart and figured he'd cool off soon and go with the religious flow. And now here he was at fifty-eight years old, Ato Castillo, shepherding a melting pot of ethnicities, cultures, and nationalities at The Alive Christ Church of Las Vegas, Nevada.

His chocolate skin tone made his Haitianness win out as it related to his physical appearance, but his Dominican heritage easily overpowered any other cultural sign of who he was when he spoke, especially when he became excited. English was his everyday language, but his father was adamant about speaking only Spanish at home, much to his mother's frustration. Nowadays, Spanish would roll off of Ato's tongue like a waterfall when he needed to get his point across or accentuate the point he was already making. No one expected that a dark-skinned man would be fluent in Spanish. At least there was no Haitian accent. Speaking Spanish with a Haitian overtone would have been brutal. For him, most of these Spanish-speaking times occurred during his preaching. He had gotten it somewhat under control, understanding that going in and out of two different languages during the service was rather confusing to the hearers and also to the deaf. Efforts at church were futile to have a ministry for the hearing impaired because those hired to do sign language didn't know both languages. Members had gotten used to it. Non-Spanish members knew how to block out words that were foreign to them. Visitors were mesmerized, not realizing this bandying was more unintentional than deliberate. He never considered what he did on Sunday mornings as giving a sermon or a speech. To him, what he offered his flock was a God-breathed, life-altering message of hope, of inspiration, and sometimes of reproof. Today, he taught with an urgency.

"You know, I turn on the TV and see people at sporting events, concerts, and other gatherings where the crowd is just going wild and ballistic. Screaming at the top of their lungs, high-fiving, and showing their support. And we serve a moving, breathing God Who is alive, and we think we are supposed to just be silent and reserved. Well, if they can get loud and show support for some game or parade that will be forgotten about in a few weeks, why can't we get loud and praise the God of the universe, the One Who walks and talks with us, Who intervenes in our very lives each day to protect us and shield us from the hand of the enemy? He loves us with a mighty love. I know this is the twenty-first century, but He's alive and well now as much as He was in the beginning of time. He's not some dead God, locked up inside of stone or any other material. He is the Holy Spirit, and He is concerned about every aspect of your life—your past, your present, and your future. ¡Gloria a su nombre!"

A few of the visitors tried to figure out the enemy to whom the pastor was referring. Amens permeated the airspace. Garnet sat back, nodded in agreement, and lifted her left hand. She rubbed the right knee with the right hand. She didn't shout amen as the rest of them did. Quiet was more her personality and style, but she focused on living the Word. She gave all she had during the praise service, as much as her bones would allow. One would have thought she was a mute during the preaching, however. She wanted to take it all in and not let a word fall to the ground unheeded. And the words kept flowing from Pastor Castillo's mouth.

"The Lord is coming back for a church without spot or wrinkle, according to Ephesians 5:27. I know we don't hear of Christ's return anymore. We're so busy accumulatin' things and gettin' stuff that we don't wanna hear nothin' 'bout Christ comin' back to get us. But how many of you know He's coming back for His church? He's constantly sanctifying us and making our character more like His. He's coming back for a holy church, a church with no stains or cracks. It doesn't mean you come to Him spotless or wrinkle-free, but His power helps you to maintain a certain level of living. You can't do it in your own strength. You pray and seek the help of the Holy Spirit. He helps your tongue when you feel like cursing somebody out. He gives you the strength not to put false times on your time card, stealing that job's money. He gives you power not to sleep with somebody who's not your wife. He gives you the power not to answer that text at two o'clock in the morning. You know they ain't callin' to ask you the words to 'Nearer, My God, to Thee.' ¡Aleluya!"

Manuela glanced toward Kemal's direction but glanced away when she noticed him look toward hers.

"And how does He get these spots and wrinkles out?

Well, how do *you* get the grass spots or grease spots or wine spots out of *your* clothes when you do the laundry? You put a little detergent directly on it and rub the material together to loosen up the stain. And how do you deal with wrinkles? I see some of you don't deal with them at all."

He peered at the crowd over the top of his glasses and paused for a second to entertain a few chuckles from those who caught the joke. He looked at some of their clothes, suggesting they had little experience in preparing their wardrobe for the day. More chuckles.

"You get your trusty iron and apply some heat and use some elbow grease. And when the Lord really starts working on His Bride, He puts you in situations that start rubbin' against you and applyin' some heat to you. He is determined that He will do what He has to do to get us in a state of readiness to go back with Him. He gives the church space and time to get her act together so those who are not in the body yet are not hindered by our hypocrisy. He gives us time, but He's not a fool. He warns us but will not warn us forever. He's sick of us livin' halfway holy lives and bein' stumbling blocks to those who are lookin' for a better way. Nobody will feel compelled to give their heart to the Lord if they see us stealing, molesting, cursing, and treating people like scum. And now we find the church having to deal with a hashtag named 'church hurt.' God is going to hold all of us churches responsible for injuring folk who came to get strength but got hurt instead. He's on a set time and wants us all to escape His wrath upon the earth. How do we do it? By letting Him help you be holy. By letting Him help us be holy. ¡Gloria a su nombre!"

He went on for about another ten minutes and called it a day. The amens had waned somewhat. It was a sure sign that people were processing what the shepherd said. He had a way of making the message sink home. Sure, he had a funny bone on occasion, but his attempts at humor didn't overshadow the message's meat. After admonishing the people again, he wrapped it up. A sense of solemnity pervaded, nothing like the commotion that went on during the praise and worship service. As the pastor left, the back of his blazer was drenched in sweat, and his team of helpers followed him back into his study. As members and visitors alike filed out, Garnet continued to sit tight, contemplating the message. No reason to fight all that traffic anyway. She kept whispering *"Thank you, Lord"* calmly and quietly. The single parent whose baby she had kept an eye on earlier toted the little one and touched Garnet's shoulder on the way out as a way of saying thanks again. She believed that she was ready to face another week and let her light shine amid a callous and everything-goes world.

5
SIZE MEDIUM

THINGS WERE IN the process of changing for him now, but he remembers the episode from a few years ago like it was yesterday. He had decided to make a stop before heading home. Grinning, Ashtoreth watched him as he had entered.

Once he got there, he noticed how beautiful it was inside with the different stations and all. It was his first time. He just needed to blend in, to act normally. Butterflies flew around in his stomach, softly marking their territory. He hoped other guys would be present to make him feel a little more comfortable. Thankfully, they were, sitting as bored as ever on the husband and boyfriend chairs. There they sat, texting, checking emails, and giving an occasional, "Oh, that's nice." He couldn't come across like those irksome tourists in a new city, looking gullible and appearing aimless. Though lost, he kept sauntering about until he ran across the ones he had seen online. There were so many colors, so many sizes. He was like a rat in a maze. He felt the fabric, took a few off the rack, and held them up to the light. He turned them around in the air to get a better sense for how they would look. Nieko was the most methodical shopper, sometimes taking as much as an hour to decide on the simplest purchase. His focus was so laser-sharp that he didn't even see the woman inch beside him.

"Welcome to Victoria's Secret. Did you need some help?"

He laughed. "Finally . . . yes. I'm not quite sure what size to get."

"Is she slim, big-boned, fat?"

"Kinda like, um." He eyed her body as she turned to the side a little while he assessed her situation. She was used to letting her body be a guidepost for men who had no clue what size their girlfriend or wife was. "Mm, she's about your shape."

"You need a medium, then."

"Nice. I wouldn't have known which one to get."

"That's why I'm here. Lemme know if you have any other questions. Let them know Pam helped you when you check out."

"No doubt. Thank you."

He shifted through the different colors on the rack. He settled on the calypso blue Dream Angels lace-trim hipster panty with the thong attached. He had to smile to himself at how sexy the see-through nature of it was. He grabbed a large.

Making his way to the front, he gave Pam's name and fielded two final inquiries at check out: whether he wanted to buy three and get three free and if he'd be using the Angel credit card account.

"No, ma'am. Just this one, and if you could see how much debt I'm already in, you'd understand why I don't need no new credit." They both laughed it up.

"It's just my job. Gotta ask."

Grabbing his receipt, he adjusted his cap to make it cock to the left and secured his Timberland laces once more before leaving. With pride, he held onto the pink mini bag with product inside, shielded by pink wrapping paper. Uriel eyed him as he exited.

As he rode the bus home, he could discern that women were looking at their men with envy as they noticed what he carried. Their love life was probably suffering and could use a bit of a boost from this mysterious Victoria, whoever and wherever she was. He sat back, enjoyed the ride, almost missing his stop.

Rushing inside, he hurried to the bathroom and took a leak. He didn't know why he felt such a strong urge to pee whenever he got home. It happened like clockwork and was probably psychological. After flipping through a few channels, he decided soup and popcorn for dinner were sufficient. He took a nap and decided he'd go ahead and give Giselle a buzz. She was so gorgeous to him. After insulting each other in jest for a few moments, he decided it was time to crash. Tomorrow would be another stressful and challenging day.

Showering was extra special these nights. He'd recently purchased a shower head from heaven, which allowed for five different settings. His ritual was down to a science. The shampooing, the facial scrub, the moisturizer, the brushing the teeth, the flossing, the mouthwash, the shaving, the astringent, the Murray's pomade. His waves were already spinning at 360 degrees, but he could never be too careful. The wave cap would still have to be placed on his head and tied. He dried off and stared at his naked self in the full-length mirror.

His new purchase lay across the sink, looking as tempting now as it did earlier. He balanced himself, stepping in first with his left leg and then with his right. He pulled them up to his waist and cringed a bit because of the thong's role. It felt a little constricting, but unique, different, lovely. As he turned to observe the rear, he observed that the panty rested a little more than halfway down his butt cheeks and stopped. He wished it halted sooner. The thong extension, nevertheless, took the baton and continued to the finish line. He turned around to the front and did what Giselle taught about tucking. It was too uncomfortable, so he untucked. He slipped on the red heels he'd bought the week before. Looking behind him in the mirror one final time, he stood seven inches taller but became mildly irritated, realizing the underwear didn't look how he had envisioned.

"That's what I get," he said out loud. Peering into the mirror and sucking his teeth, he made a final assessment. "She was right. I shoulda got a medium."

T AND T

THE SECURITY OFFICER at the front entrance of UNLV's campus was used to this time of the year. The summer term was basically reserved for two types of students: those who wanted to forge ahead and stay on top of their academic game and those who had slacked off during previous terms and needed to get back on solid scholastic footing. This was the first day of the third summer term, which started shortly after July's early holiday. Students, faculty, and administrators alike could start afresh after rebounding from fireworks hangovers. A frantic student arrived to ask of the officer directions to the Harter Classroom Building Complex for a class that started five minutes ago. The class was Recent America: Era of Franklin D. Roosevelt, 1920-1945 and was taught by a Dr. Garnet Gibbs.

"Oh yes, Dr. Gibbs. You'll love her class," said the officer. "You're a bit late, though. Don't make it a habit. She has a reputation for being strict with tardies. Maybe she won't be so hard on you since it's the first day."

"Okay."

"Here's a map. You'll have to walk north for about three minutes then bear left. You'll see the row of shrubs in front of the building."

"Thanks a bunch." After rushing ahead, the student made the journey in a minute and a half, climbed the stairs to the third floor, and entered the classroom with as little disturbance as possible. As he sat in his seat, he glanced at the professor's name on the board, along with the name of the course. He zoned out for about two minutes just staring at Garnet. He tried not to judge her physical appearance but couldn't help it. After a while, he thought he had better focus on why he was there and pay close attention to what was actually coming out of her mouth. A fellow student passed him a syllabus, which he glanced over. No late assignments accepted. Simultaneously, he listened to her instructions.

"And so, as you see, there will be a midterm and a final. In addition, each of you will have to give a ten-minute Prezi presentation in front of the class on an approved topic. The semester will go really quickly since it's the third summer phase, so you need to make sure you give it your best effort, which starts with being here on time for each class." She cut her eyes over at the student who had arrived late.

"Can we use PowerPoint instead of Prezi?" inquired Aadhya, an Indian student, who sat in the front row.

The professor replied, "Unfortunately, no. PowerPoint is becoming somewhat outdated. Prezi is not the wave of tomorrow. It's the wave of today. You'll need to be adept in using that platform when you make your presentations. You'll thank me later. It's free for you to use as long as you register with your E-D-U email. Just be sure to use the classic version."

After going through the remainder of the syllabus and

entertaining any lingering questions, Garnet decided that she'd stir the pot and see how current students were with the latest political happenings. A course focusing on a specific former president easily provided segue to discuss matters concerning the current one and any other modern-day political connections. "So, in this class, our focus will be on the era of F.D.R., his policies, his legacy, and his shortcomings. Of course, everyone knows about his hand in raising the country from the grips of the Great Depression. Some people think we're in our own great depression, not because stocks are going down but because of who's in office." She had to traverse lightly, for hers was a task of encouraging young folk to be politically informed and to become a part of the political process, not to sway. "Who do you think's going to win the election next year?" This was her testing ground to see what they knew or thought they knew.

Lindsay walked the plank first. "I like Kamala."

"Why?" They had to know this would be the natural follow-up question, given who stood in front of the class. She hoped they'd been privy to her teaching style via word of mouth or even on RateMyProfessors.

The student danced around and landed at some semblance of a response, but it lacked a real reason to persuade or, more importantly, defend.

"But are you aware of her policies on criminal justice reform? Did you know that, as a prosecutor, she was a champion of prosecuting parents and sending them to jail if their children cut school regularly?" asked the doctor.

It was clear Lindsay had done little probing into the candidate's background and record; she was so hyped that she was a minority candidate that all else seemed to pale in comparison to what was on the surface.

"She's done what others would say are good things, too," the professor balanced. "Her positions on climate change, education, and immigration, especially DACA, are rather progressive, according to some. All I'm saying is make sure you know where candidates stand and don't just justify your reason for liking her based on her being a person of color. And by the way, it's *Ka*mala." A wave of quiet laughter rumbled about. "Anybody else?"

Conrad, the latecomer, thought this to be a chance to redeem himself. "I'm hoping Joe Kennedy will throw his name into the race. He's made a few waves on the political scene, the most notable of which is his response to the president's SOTU address. Not too bad of a way to make an entrance on the national scene. He's pretty liberal on health care; he supports ending gun-show loopholes and is against privatization of social security. Sounds pretty solid to me."

"Only that he himself said out of his own mouth that he's not running in 2020," countered Felipe, catching his classmates off guard. "Maybe that's his strategy: to keep himself under the radar and enter at the last minute. He seems to be very calculating to me."

It was the interchange Garnet had hoped for – one in which students took the lead and had an intelligent conversation and without her prompting. "Well," she added, "at least he didn't justify the man's candidacy based on his family dynasty and red hair." She quietly thought of her grandson and smirked to herself. Others added their favorites to the discourse: Booker, Kasich, and Schultz, the Independent runner and Starbucks CEO.

"What about you, professor?" inquired Francois. "Who do you think's gonna pull it out?"

"Oh, you guys don't want to know my take."

A chorus of affirmations suggested otherwise. Over the years, she had learned how to keep students captivated and on the edge of their seats. A certain self-deprecation always won out with the eager beavers. "Well, I'd tell you to sit down, but you're already doing so. I think he'll get reelected." She couldn't even allow herself to say his name.

Her prediction was met with some hmpf-like glances, some affirming smiles, and some out-and-out guffaws. Some agreeing head nods, too. She assessed the political leanings of the students from her one response. She took mental notes of such. "Well, when you consider," she continued, "that he has a relatively strong base throughout the country, it's not such an outlandish idea. And did you guys notice his presence in the gubernatorial midterms over in Georgia and Florida? He had those people in a trance. One simple visit from him helped to turn the voter tide and keep those states from turning blue. It was quite interesting to watch." She had mastered choosing the right words as a professor, so as not to disclose her personal feelings. Her conversation at home was different. "Anyway, we're done. Good discussion. Hopefully, this gives you a peek into how this course will run. Come with your perspectives, but make sure they are based in facts."

Student rustlings began and continued through her final words. "This will be the only time we dismiss early this term. I don't want you to think this is normal. You could say I'm giving you a little more time to get yourself ready for a rigorous course of study. If you have any more questions, you can meet me in front of the class. If not, you still got time to go play some slots on the Strip. Remember me if you hit the jackpot." Everyone laughed. "Class dismissed."

No one met her after class, so she headed back to her office, spoke to Opal, the secretary, and collapsed in her swivel chair. Exhaling, she kicked off her heels, leaned back, closed her eyes, and sought the Father. Since she was in her own office, she had no qualms about quietly speaking into the air.

"Lord, thank You for getting me through today. I need Your help to make it through this summer because You know I'm not used to teaching during this time. I need your help not to get burned out. Show me how to pace myself and not overdo it. Give me Your wisdom, so I can be firm but fair with these students. Help them to pass the class. Anoint me to lecture well. Bring what I study back to my remembrance, so I can give them the best information. Help me be a light. Thank You so much. In the name of Jesus." She whispered a few more hallelujahs and just sat with her eyes closed. She was talking to Him just like He was in the room. To her, He was, without a doubt. She finally opened her eyes only to observe Celeste as she stood in the doorway.

"Girl, I didn't hear you come in."

"No, you were prayin'. You know I don't fools wit' nobody when they gettin' their prayer on. I'm tryin' to get to where you at. I ain't as saved as you."

"Stop. Ain't no levels in salvation, just sanctification. If you saved, you saved. Just like if you pregnant, you pregnant. Ain't no almost pregnant or halfway pregnant. Either you got a bun in the oven or you don't."

Garnet had somewhat assumed the role of being Celeste's mentor in Christ. Celeste, thirty-three, childless, and on a dating hiatus, wanted to do better, be better. She still had a few rough edges but was making strides toward developing the fruit of the Spirit. And Garnet welcomed the challenge.

They had met on campus during a lunch meeting some time ago and clicked when they both discovered they both were believers. As educated as Garnet was, she had let the loose nature of Celeste's speech rub off on her time to time. In the classroom, she was so erudite, but around Celeste, it was a completely different story. All the years of her formal education, which culminated in a PhD in American History, was no match for Celeste's upbringing in Tennessee as it related to speech and communication. She was not intimidated one bit by the letters behind Garnet's name. Her southern Memphis drawl and lazy way of finishing sentences made Garnet laugh on some occasions and want to cry on others. Celeste's ten years in Vegas had done little by way of changing how she spoke. Her familiar speaking roots dug deep. She was a Memphis girl through and through. In fact, that was the main reason the two of them hit it off. Garnet came to the States from Toronto to attend college at a southern HBCU. So there was this regional bond, this undeniable linkage of sisterhood that existed between them both.

"I just had to take a break and get out dat office. Gettin' too claws'taphobic in there. Plus, my doctor told me I need to make sure I stand and move 'round at least once an hour. Says sittin' too long without a break can increase my chance of gettin' the sugar or heart attack."

"Well, I'm glad I can give you the opportunity to avoid 'the sugar' and cardiac arrest." She teased Celeste by doing air quotes for the diabetes reference.

"You a mess," joked Celeste. "I ain't studdin' you. I just wanted to see if you wanted to grab a bite, so I thought I'd come by and offer to treat you to a sensible lunch, with it being the start of another term."

"Sensible?"

"Yeah, being just uh humble li'l secretary and all, 'sensible' means we ain't goin' out for no sushi or nothin'. Not in the budget. Maybe a number four from Wendy's or somethin' like dat. A small."

"Cheap ole' Lessie at it again. We are gonna pray that the Lord send you a better paying job on this here campus or somewhere else in the city so you can up your lunch-treating game. You know He's able."

"Mm hm. Dat's nice. But until He do, a number four it's gone be."

Garnet chuckled and said, "Thank you, girl, but I'll have to pass on the offer. I brought my own. Jamay put some of her leftover baked chicken and lime rice in a container for me. She had so much of it left that she didn't want to be eating on it four days in a row."

"Shoot, you coulda brought me some o' dat."

"I sure could've. I didn't even think about it. Next time."

"How Jamay doin' by the way?"

"Great. She led the praise team at the church Sunday. She's really growing up. I'm so proud of her. I can't believe she's twenty-eight. Where did the time go?"

"Girl, it be flyin'."

"She's still trying her best to deal with the whole Redd thing, though. I can tell she gets a little down sometimes, so I try to keep her spirits lifted, 'specially since she has R.J. to look after. I guess service to the good ole' US of A is what it's all about, huh?"

"I thought I heard you guys in here," said Marjorie, a fellow professor in the philosophy department, whose office was a few doors down from Garnet's. Marge was the name she preferred. Only her birth certificate dubbed her by her official identifier.

"Hi, Marge," answered Garnet.

Marjorie continued, sticking her head in even more, "If it isn't the T and T partners in crime. How's everything fairing over in chemistry, Celeste?"

"Things in chemistry are doin' fine, Dr. West. Of course, I'm doing all the grunt work. Now if I can only get the chemistry in my personal life to go better. Men are so complicated. Neal and I are taking a li'l break from each other right now. But that's a whole 'nother story."

"I see. Well, I hope you're able to work things out in that regard," Marjorie laughed. "Sorry I can't help you out with that."

Garnet looked down, entertaining a weird silence that lasted for about three seconds.

"Anyway, I just wanted to stop in since I heard Celeste in here. I'm not teaching this summer, but I'll be around working on a proposal to become a MacArthur Fellow. It's such an arduous process."

"Oh, that's great," interjected Garnet. "One of those 'genius' grants. I'll pray that you get it. That would be wonderful."

"Thanks, but you already know I'm not one really for prayer. It's all about focus and hard work. Putting in the time and being ready. That's what it boils down to, at least for me."

"But I'm still going to pray for you, and you can't stop me," Garnet jovially retorted. "Everybody who applies is equally as intelligent as the next person. It's good to have an extra edge that they may not have. Every little bit of support helps."

"I don't understand nothin' y'all talkin' 'bout," said Celeste. "I don't know nothin' 'bout no MacArthur nothin'. But y'all can drop the Mac and give me Arthur's phone number, wherever he at." All of them laughed. "But it's sholl working up an appetite in me."

"In me as well," Marjorie responded. "I'm heading out to grab something. I'll see you all later."

"See ya," said Garnet.

"Bye, Dr. West," added Celeste. After making sure

Marjorie was out of the office area, Celeste started in, partially knowing Garnet wouldn't go deep into the gossip thing.

"I think she the only one who call us the T and T duo. How in the world she even waste the brain space to come up wit' dat name?"

"Be nice. Makes sense to me," Garnet said. "Ain't you from Tennessee?"

"And so I guess that's supposed to be the first one."

"Hence, one of the T's."

"And I guess since you been to Toronto, dat 'posed to be the other T, huh?"

"Not just *been* there, Lessie. *Born* there, *raised* there. I think that makes it qualify as a T."

"And what she mean by, 'I can't help you out wit' dat'?" inquired Celeste.

Garnet smiled, not answering and grabbing a bottled water from the refrigerator under her desk.

Almost on cue, Opal announced from her desk back to Garnet's office, "Professor Gibbs, your daughter is on the line. Would you like to take it?"

Celeste stuck her head out of Garnet's office and into Opal's general area, shouting, "Hey, Jamay!"

Opal smiled and said, "She's giggling and said, 'That must be Celeste in mommy's office.'" Opal informed Celeste that Jamay returned the greeting.

"Thanks, Opal. Can you see what she wants right quick? I'm actually finished for the day and just need to tie up a few loose ends and grab a bite before too late. She probably wants to know if I'll go pick up R.J."

After a brief silence, Opal confirmed, "Yes, she's gonna be detained a while and hoped you could swing by and get him from camp."

"Let her know I will. Tell her I'll just see her at home."

"No problem."

"Bye, Jamay!" Celeste exclaimed.

"R.J. has been battling a summer cold," Garnet told Celeste. "I hate to see him suffer like he is. He's a trooper, though. I've been giving him chewable Vitamin C pills, but he just probably needs some rest. Ain't no cold like a summer cold. He came in my room last night and asked if I'd lay hands on his chest and pray for him."

"Aw, that's sweet. Girl, you the only one I know who will get your oil and lay hands on somebody in a minute. If you ain't got no holy oil around, I bet you use Crisco, don't you?"

She forced a fake laugh but refused the bait. "Now, if I can only heal my own problems when I lay hands on my own self."

"I just don't get why people think you gotta turn the air on Alaska just because it's super hot outside," Celeste responded. Just make sure it's comfortable inside, not bitter cold. I don't know when folk gone learn that. Makes people's body get outta whack and get colds and pneumonia and stuff."

"Anyway, lemme get outta here," said Garnet as she started placing papers in her attaché case. She put on flats and left her heels underneath her desk for the next day's outfit.

"Yeah, me, too. Them people upstairs probably wondering where I'm at. I'm headin' to go get somethin' to eat and get back to the office. I'll talk to you a little later. Maybe we can meet down at the track later this week before or after work. I'm tryin' to keep myself fit and may need a little inspiration."

"Sounds good to me."

"Bye, Dr. Gibbs," Celeste joked. As she exited Garnet's office, she lightly knocked on Opal's desk and uttered, "See ya later, girl. Keep handlin' stuff around here. Everybody know you the one who really run everything 'round here."

Opal smirked and said, "You a mess. Bye, girl."

Garnet sat back one final time and decided that she needed to amend the prayer she offered earlier.

"And Lord," she said, *"please cover and bless that nut case, Celeste."*

7
LIKE SON

FEES WOULD BEGIN accumulating in about five minutes. Garnet had broken out into a mild trot as she approached the Centennial Hills Y. Officials were strict about pickup times for summer campers and didn't hesitate to tack on the extra fifty bucks for every thirty-minute interval that parents arrived late. Or in this case, grandparents.

Garnet made her way down the hall and made a right into the holding area. She brushed past another parent-and-child pair, who had avoided the monetary penalty this time. They spoke but only briefly so as not to disrupt Garnet's mission. As she entered the room, Vesta, the camp leader, greeted her.

"Hi, Dr. Gibbs. It's so good to see you. Your daughter called and said you'd be picking up Redd."

"Hi, Vesta. Good to see you, too. Glad I made it just in the nick of time." She wanted to make sure it was known she was on time. Vesta wasn't as by-the-book as some of the other counselors, but Garnet never knew which one would be on duty whenever Jamay couldn't make it. "How's my little prince doing?"

"He's fine. He's over in the corner playing with his electronic device."

"I don't see why his mother spends all of that money on gadgets like those. They sure aren't cheap. They've turned into the modern-day babysitter. Anyway, how was he feeling today?"

"Not too well. Sort of quiet. He said you prayed for him to feel better. And on top of that, I think he still misses his father." Vesta knew of Garnet's faith and of the boy's father. She never thought twice about talking to her about faith and family matters.

Garnet turned toward the young one and got his attention. "Hey, R.J., I'm here. Let's go, baby." She turned her attention back to Vesta and continued, "Yeah, I know it's kind of hard on him. He loves his daddy so much. I never really understood the whole protecting and serving thing. It just seems to tear up so many families. But all we can do is pray about it, leave it in the Lord's hands, and trust that He'll raise these kids the best way possible."

R.J. walked over with his backpack secure over both shoulders. He was walking and had his head buried in his game, being instinctively careful to avoid bumping into anything on his way to Garnet. He got into her vicinity and kept playing.

"Well, hello to you, too," Garnet mildly chided. "It's so good to see how much you're excited to see me. Get over here and give grandma a hug."

"Hey, gramma." He gave her a hug while Vesta smiled.

"He hung in there today," interjected Vesta. "I could tell he was a little under the weather, but he participated in everything as much as he could today, so I'm proud of him."

Garnet kept her arm around him and looked toward his way and said, "Yeah, I guess we pretty proud of him. He's growing up so fast. He'll be eight next month. If he's good, we may have a party for him." She rubbed her hand through his copper-toned hair and noticed his slight approval concerning the possibility of a party. "And that ain't the only thing that's growing fast. This hair is getting to be too unmanageable. We gone see about getting him to a barber shop quick. Anyway, let us get outta here. We don't wanna see any surprises on our next bill saying we overstayed our welcome. That's fifty dollars I can keep."

"Yes, indeed," stated Vesta. "As long as I'm working, I won't do that to you."

"Thank you, dear. I appreciate it," responded Garnet. "You ready to get movin', R.J.?"

"Yes," he answered while still being e-distracted.

All three walked toward the door, and the obvious two continued their journey out of the building. "We'll have to stop by Health Hub to pick up some fresh tomatoes. I want to make some lasagna for dinner tonight," she said to her grandson. "Your mother will be home later this afternoon. She has to stay a little later at work."

They got in the Jaguar and made their way out of the parking lot. R.J. had resumed playing his game, uttering very little. Garnet knew her grandson and had learned well how to interpret his different silences. Whenever he tuned her out but kept his mind preoccupied with playing his gadgets, this was a sure sign that he was undergoing that battle in his young mind again. This wasn't like other silences, during which time he was quiet and melancholy. During those moments, he was either terribly sick or irritated and wanted none of the electronic world. Although he was feeling a little under the weather, the mild discomfort was passing and not affecting him as much as it was this morning. He may as well have been Garnet's own child because she could read him like a book, more than Jamay ever could. He'd never initiate conversation about his feelings when he felt this way but appeared relieved when his grandmother did. The Lord always gave her the wisdom that she needed to address this challenge with him, and this time was no different.

"So what did you guys do at camp today?" she asked.

"Nothin'."

"Nothing? Really? I better tell your mother to stop sending her money to the Y if you guys are spending all day doing nothing."

"Well, you know what I mean, gramma."

"What are some of the things you all did today? You don't have to list *all* of them. Just a few. I just wanna know if it's a good program you're going to." She turned on her signal as they got closer to the grocery store.

"A little painting. They gave us cocoa and we had to paint our own names. It was wack."

"Oh? You used to like those kinds of creative things when you were real small. You loved to try new and different things."

"It was boring," he grumbled as he kept shooting the enemies on his screen.

"That's all you guys did?"

"After lunch, we went swimming. Well, they did. I wasn't feeling good, so they lemme stay inside with the counselor."

Garnet sensed this was her moment. "Whoa, swimming? That sounds fun. I remember the first time you went swimming. You cried and cried and cried. The closer you got to that pool, the louder you boohooed. As soon as they put you in it, you went from cryin' to laughin'. After a while, we couldn't get you out that water. You just loved it so much." She reached the store, found a parking spot, rolled down the window, and turned the car off. "Your daddy is a great swimmer."

His thumbs stopped clicking buttons, and he started staring outside.

She continued, "Yes, Lord. He is a fish, shonuff. I recall one time when you were about as big as a minute and all of us went to one of those beaches in California. I forget which one. He got out in that water and went all the way out there. We were getting a little worried because we thought he shouldn't have gone so far out. Before we knew it, all we saw were arms splashing and feet kicking. He was swimming back to the shore where we were. Oh, my God, it was so beautiful. He was doing it so smooth and effortlessly. Your mother and I were so impressed. He kept swimming and getting closer and closer and closer. It was beautiful."

As she reminisced, she happened to glance over at him. He was staring directly into her eyes as she recounted the story, savoring every detail she spoke. He seemed to be in some type of a trance, visualizing each image of his father. He saw the arms flailing in the water, the feet smacking the water, his gait as he waded through the shallow waters onto the sandy shore.

"I didn't know daddy could swim like that. Mama never told me that. Maybe that's why I can swim so good. We both can swim." And he went on and on. Garnet always seemed to have a different story to tell the kid at the right moment. It would be information overload to tell him all the stories at once. Just a little at a time when the moment appeared right. R.J. hadn't heard this one before, so he was all ears. He had to learn how to hold on to the stories as they came. After all, it had been four years since seeing his father, and the memories of actual interaction with him were faint. He longed to be near and with him.

"Yep," she intermittently interjected. She knew she had gotten him out of his slump. Although she couldn't physically get them together, her grandson had a fresh boost in his spirit. And now she couldn't shut him up. She just let him talk because it was good therapy for him. She hated his daddy couldn't be with him, but the kid was a trooper. Whenever he got to the point where he was a talking machine, she knew he was doing considerably better. After about three minutes of entertaining her grandson's semi-monologue, she figured that they should finish their mission and head inside. "Just remember what grandma always says. Whenever you think about him, you can talk to the Lord and let him know how you feel. You can just talk to Him like a regular person. He understands what you mean and where you coming from. That's just how He is, okay?"

"Okay."

"Alright, R.J. Let's get in here and grab these tomatoes. It's gonna take me a while to make this pasta sauce, and we need to have everything ready by the time your mom gets home."

"Okay, gramma." He leaped out of the car and shut the door while Garnet grabbed her purse and followed suit. He left his game on the backseat floor. She locked the car doors with the keyless remote, taking note of the affirming horn sound. As the automatic door to the store opened, he continued talking her head off, but at least she had the assurance that he was fine, at least for now.

RAININ'

GARLIC, OREGANO, MUSHROOMS, basil, black pepper, and tomatoes provided the nose an intense workout in Garnet's kitchen. And a dash of salt. She had done it again. The portion of each ingredient that she placed in the concoction was deliberate and calculated. She had created a tomato sauce that could have appeared on any cooking show. *"Thank you, Lord,"* she said. *"Thank you for helping me make this sauce. It's terrific."* She stirred it again with the wooden spoon, lifting some of it from the pot and placing it against her lips. Perfection. She placed it on simmer and would prepare the pasta next. Right now, she could just lie down and relax a bit.

"R.J., I'm gonna relax for a bit until your mom comes home. She should be here in about thirty minutes. Don't touch anything in the kitchen, especially near the stove area, okay?"

R.J. was feeling tons better since the conversation in the car, so he was in his own happy place. "Okay."

He sat in the living room, watching the television and eating some grapes given to him to tide him over until dinner.

He didn't want to watch anything in particular since nothing that catered to him specifically was airing. It was the general time when the news came on, and he definitely didn't want to watch that. He started spanning channels and saw nothing that caught his attention. After a while, he landed on BET and decided to cease his channel surfing there, in part, because his little thumb started tiring from pressing the up arrow button.

Garnet herself made it into her bedroom and fell across her bed to get a little rejuvenation before dinner. Although she didn't watch it faithfully, she turned her TV to the local news station. She really didn't care which one she'd watch. She only watched to see what the trend in weather would be for the rest of the week. She didn't get into the habit of pondering the bad news that was reported from the time cameras started rolling. She would have about eleven minutes or so to endure all of the sky-is-falling perspective that embodied most of the leads.

The in-studio desk reporter prepped the story and cut to Ava, the reporter who was in the helicopter that hovered over the scene of the incident. Garnet watched and listened to the reporter describe what appeared to have happened. Out of habit, she started praying under her breath, as it didn't seem to be a positive story.

"Thanks, Spence. It's a pretty tragic scene out here. It appears that a guy on a motorcycle lost control on I-15. As you see from the images from Copter-7, motorists are at a standstill as the ambulance team is struggling to get through. His bike is on one side of the highway, and he's on the other side. It does appear that he has on a helmet, but from what we see, he looks pretty bad."

"Ava, any indication for what caused it?" asked the reporter in the studio.

"No. There appear to be no other cars or trucks involved. Maybe he just lost control of his bike. It's still too early to call. It looks like he's finally on the stretcher, and cars are still crawling. As you can imagine, there's rubbernecking out here like you wouldn't imagine. Everyone seems to want to know, 'What on earth is going on?'"

"Wrong question," mockingly giggled Mictian, who somehow magically heard her question. "It's not what's going on on earth, you stupid and clueless mortals." It had returned and sat on the bridge where the accident occurred with its hooves-for-feet dangling and swaying back and forth as he observed his latest exploit. From the bridge was a twenty-five foot drop. It glanced down with no fear and looked back again at the accident scene. "Aww, poor boy," it uttered in a fake voice of concern. "Did Mr. Motorcycle Man fall a sleepy poo?" It belted a hideous laugh. It got such a rush out of chaos. It was normally preoccupied with causing gang wars and upheavals in most Las Vegas neighborhoods, but this was the first time it used its powers to cause what it considered wars on the expressway. It had been toying with the idea of causing drivers to fall asleep to cause highway wars or crashes. Starting small with a motorcyclist was just a way to test the impact. Injure one for now. Assess the results. Injure more later, especially with those driving big rigs. These test results were promising. Only one injured and look at the domino effect. Backed-up traffic. Helicopters overhead. Other news crews on the way. Ah, it was a form of hell. Such a breath of sordid air.

So that it could see more of the fruit of its effort, it needed to view things from a different perspective, a bird's eye view. It pushed itself away from the bridge where it sat and began a free fall toward the distant street below, as though it would hit the pavement below. Soon, its hidden wings appeared from nowhere and started flapping, propelling it high into the sky. Its ascent stopped once it reached an altitude that matched that of the helicopter. It peered inside the flying bird and noticed the pilot and Ava inside.

As both helicopter and creature hovered some eighty feet in the air, Mictian looked into the distance and saw bumper-to bumper vehicles detained for miles. It scurried away from the helicopter and flew at breathtaking speed to see exactly how far back traffic was creeping. It was delighted. It flew the four point two miles in a jiffy, passing the fly zone of McCarran. It noticed where the clumping of the traffic began, and, in two blinks, was suspended beside the helicopter again. "Alright. Well, looks like my work here is done. Next time, the ante will be upped, and Mr. Lone Ranger in the ambulance won't be so alone." Feeling a jolt of satisfying wickedness, Mictian returned to his headquarters near the Strip, waiting on an opportunity to create more mayhem.

"Well, keep us posted Ava on any new developments that come out of this. We always have to let the viewers know to think 'safety' whenever they're on the highways of the city. Such dangerous places to fall asleep."

"You got it, Spence. Will do. We'll stay here for another moment and gather as many details as possible. But again, he looks in pretty grave shape but seems to be clinging to life. We'll keep you in the loop. Reporting to you live from I-95 in the Summerlin section of the city, this is Ava France, KABC-7 News."

"Lord, help that man," Garnet spoke into the air. All hopes of catching a nap were dashed by this breaking news. She knew now why it was called breaking because all it did was seem to break your spirit, break your hope, and break your sense of rest. She decided it was best to turn off the television and spend a little time communing with the Lord until Jamay got home.

"Hey, ma, I'm home," Jamay announced as she stepped onto the linoleum, parquet flooring in the doorway entrance. "Hey, knucklehead," she said to her son, who either didn't hear her or was used to letting his silence be what spoke back. He was distracted by what he was watching on the boob tube anyway.

So much for communing with the Lord, at least for now. "Hi, baby. I see you made it in. Work a little demanding, huh?"

"Yessiree." She walked over to her mother and gave her a peck on the cheek. "Look who I drug in. I saw her hitchhiking on the side of the road and decided to give her a ride."

A few paces behind Jamay was her close friend, Davida. "Girl, you better behave yourself," she joked. "How are you, Ms. Gibbs? Good to see you again."

"I'm fine," said Garnet as she hugged Davida. "Are we doing better?" she asked, having common knowledge of recent situations concerning Davida.

"Yes, I'm doing well now," answered Davida. "Just one day at a time."

"That's all any of us can do, doll. Leave it in the hands of the Lord. I pray for you often. The Lord gives you strength to continue making the right choice."

"Well, I'm glad He is. It gets a little hard sometimes with Tario and all, but it's fine."

Jamay jumped in. "I told her she needs to leave him alone, mama, but you can't say but so much. The Lord is calling her higher, but she don't wanna go."

"Be quiet, Jamay. It takes some people a little longer," Garnet said, coming to Davida's defense. "When the Lord is ready for her, He knows how to put a hook in her mouth and lead her into the fold."

"Um, hello, you two," interrupted Davida. "I'm standing right here if you haven't noticed." She hated when the mother-and-daughter combo spoke about her in the third person, as if she weren't there. Davida loved herself some Tario. She had gotten saved two years ago when she went with Jamay to Alive one Sunday. She was trying to live the saved life but didn't really tap into the power of the Holy Spirit to help her do so. As a result, she seesawed between doing what the scripture commanded and hanging out with Tario. Bluntly, he was her Achilles heel. All of her Christian leanings went out of the window when it came to his swagger and influence on her good intentions. Right when she was on a roll of living a committed life to the Lord, Tario would contact her out of blue and want to hang and "chill," which often ended up being more than she anticipated. And he succeeded more times than not.

"Anyway, that's enough double-teaming for now. We gone keep praying for Tario," laughed Garnet. "It's time to eat. I'm starving." As Jamay and Davida got comfortable and prepared themselves for some pasta and salad, Garnet started setting the table. She turned her attention to her grandson and requested that he prepare himself for dinner. He didn't hear her because he was transfixed on an R&B video he was watching on TV. When she noticed he hadn't moved, she called again but louder, "Redd Moultrie, Jr., come in here and wash your hands. It's time to eat." He knew what it meant when she called both of his names as well as his suffix.

He finally obeyed but not before taking one last glance at the video he was watching. The artist was mesmerizing him with her sexy moves she made in her bikini; she had sucked R.J. into her hypnotic vortex.

Everyone washed up and found a place at Garnet's table. The salad had already made its way there as had glasses with melting ice. R.J. grabbed his seat and lay claim on his own glass, turning it upward to drink the swig of cold water that barely awakened his taste buds.

"Well, somebody's thirsty," said Jamay to her son. "I'm sorry I couldn't pick you up on today. Mommy got a little busy at work. How's my baby?" She leaned over him and planted a kiss on his forehead.

"Good." He turned up his glass again and positioned his lips to catch the freshly made water from his ice cubes, creating that slurping noise.

Just that quick, she transitioned into mommy mode. "R.J., really? Can you please not do that? You're not *that* thirsty." He smiled as she finally sat down at the table in the chair diagonally across from him. She began helping her mother straighten out some of the place settings.

"Hey there, R.J." Davida was coming from the kitchen, wearing one of Garnet's aprons and toting a towel, a bowl of salad dressing, and a pitcher full of orange juice mixed with ginger ale. She placed the bowl and towel on the table and started pouring the concoction into the glasses on the table.

"No, not R.J.'s.," cautioned Jamay. "He'll drink every sip of it before he eats."

"Aww, mom," grumbled R.J.

"Aww, mom nothing."

Davida laughed and touched the kid's shoulder as she walked by him and his glass of ice. She placed the pitcher in the center of the table.

"Now, everybody just hush! Ain't nobody gone be drinking nothin' no time soon. Not before you eat this here." She slowly glided toward the table, steadily balancing a piping hot dish of her famous lasagna. The smoke emanating from the pan was almost blinding to her, so she had to take special care as she made her way to the table of predators.

"Gramma, that look good!" exclaimed R.J.

Garnet carefully placed the pan on the towel and encouraged her folks to dig in. "Now, be careful. You see how it's smoking. We don't need anybody getting hurt."

Jamay fixed R.J.'s plate and then her own. As Davida and the matriarch fixed their plates, R.J. grabbed his fork and began helping himself.

"Excuse me, sir?" upbraided Jamay in a disturbed Jamaican accent. It only surfaced in her speech when she somehow became worked up for whatever reason. She presented it as a question but meant it more as an exclamation. "Have you lost your Jamaican-American mind?" She corrected him not so much for not waiting on the rest of the gang but more so because of what she thought was a given in the Gibbs household.

"Oh, sorry," apologized R.J.

"Uh oh, R.J." joked Davida. "You got your mama seeing black, green, and yellow."

"He knows better," Jamay continued on.

Garnet finally sat and smiled at her grandson, understanding how hard it must be for him to please all parties and still have some semblance of a childhood. She calmed the mood, encouraging everyone to join hands while she blessed the meal.

"*Dear Lord, thank you for this time of fellowship. We*

appreciate this moment when we can relax and think on your goodness. Thanks for Jamay, Davida, and R.J. Thank you for this food, Father. Thank you for the strength to cook it, and thank you for giving us taste buds to taste it. Let us always remember that you are the Giver of all good things. Let this food strengthen and nourish our bodies. In Jesus' name. Amen."

Faint amens echoed around the table, including one from R.J.

As they satisfied their hunger pains, Garnet resumed with more small talk. "So you don't have to lead praise service this weekend, honey?"

"No, not this weekend," answered Jamay. Her Jamaican tone had subsided. "Elder Kemal's leading it. He's such a gifted singer. He can blow."

"Yeah, he can sing," Garnet offered.

"It's just so good to be able to enjoy praise service in the crowd as opposed to having to lead it," added Jamay.

Davida chimed in, "Yeah, I remember going with you to church the first time, Jamay, and hearing you sing. You didn't tell me you were going to be leading the devotional. I was just sitting there, and you walked up and started singing. You really shocked me. I had never experienced anything like that before."

"That *was* funny when you came up to me after the service with your mouth opened," Jamay chuckled.

Davida's phone rang. She saw that Tario was calling and pressed the button to send his call directly to voice mail.

Garnet interjected, "This lasagna is delectable, if I must say so myself."

"Delish, Ms. Gibbs," Davida cosigned.

"Mama, this *is* good, and the salad is so juicy and crisp," Jamay swirled her fork as she praised her mother's culinary prowess. The silence around the table confirmed everyone's words. As was customary around many a dinner table, the degree to which there was talking was a direct sign as to how good the food was. Much talking, horrible food. Little talking, so-so food. No talking, the food made you want to slap your mama. And around this particular table, Jamay would have slapped Garnet, if she thought she could get away with it. Not a word was uttered for about two minutes. And R.J., thinking he was contributing to the food discussion, did the equivalent of slapping his, piggybacking on the praise she had just given.

"Ma," said R.J., "I was watching on TV, and the lady was talking about eating too. She was singing, 'He toss my salad like his name Romaine.'" He sang it like the lady did in the video. He'd never sung any song like it, not even the ones in church.

Davida dropped her fork, which hit her plate and then ricocheted onto the floor. She began laughing, wondering how Jamay would handle this one.

Jamay turned to her son in disbelief with her mouth opened. "Davida, don't laugh at him." She turned toward her son and managed a "R.J., how dare you!" in her Jamaican accent. It had resurfaced just that quickly. "Where did you hear that?"

"How dare I what?" R.J. honestly responded. "I heard a lady singing it on TV. She was in a weight room and lifting some pretty pink weights."

Calmly, Garnet turned toward her daughter and gently scolded, "Now, Jamay, it's not like he's saying it out of spite. It's an honest statement. He thought he was adding to the conversation about dinner. And the only reason I know is because of those college students I interact with every day. But the child got a right not to know. I would rather he talk about it here than at summer camp."

Davida had made her way to the kitchen to retrieve another fork and had sat back down.

"But Mama, you know I don't like for him looking at those channels on TV like BET and MTV. You know the kind of stuff they show on there."

"I know. I'm sorry. I got so focused on cooking, and then I turned on the news for a little while. He must have been in there scanning the channels when I wasn't looking. But truth is, baby, you can't raise this child in no bubble. We live in a real world with real people. And you got to be able to teach him how to deal with real issues, and you gotta be willing to answer real questions."

Jamay had transfixed her eyes on R.J. again as if she were a superhero trying to shoot laser beams through a stone building. It was more so out of frustration than anger. She wondered how she would teach him how to hold on to Christian values amid such an anti-Christian and cynical world. At the moment, all she could do was shake her head and relinquish her death stare at her mini-man.

"What?" he purely and respectfully questioned to his mother.

With no accent, she answered, "R.J., you'll learn about things like that as you get older. Just know it's something you shouldn't say out loud in public. It has to do with sex. I guess it's good that you brought it up here and nowhere else. Mama was just shocked when you said that. But I don't want you watching those channels like BET and those other channels with big numbers. Okay?"

"Yes, ma'am," he replied, still confused and still with no

explanation to his earlier contribution. He had blown his chance at having a significant part of the dinnertime conversation. So, he would just remain quiet. His lasagna had disappeared, and he'd have to get through his salad. Jamay wouldn't let him escape without eating his greens. He'd temporarily get out of it by asking to be excused for a minute, to which his mother agreed.

"He'll be fine," reassured Garnet after making sure he was nowhere around them. "We just have to keep the prayer covering over him and all these young children. They have it a little tougher than we had. More distractions, more temptations, more everything. The enemy ain't pulling no punches with them, either. The younger he can woo and claim them, the better."

"I can imagine," chimed Davida. "The stuff kids say these days. I was over my cousin's house and just happened to walk by my niece's room. I heard her talking to one of her friends on the phone and every other phrase was, 'Girl, bye' and 'I can't.' And she is eleven, mind you. Just grown."

Said Jamay, "She can't what?"

"That's exactly it. She wasn't saying she can't do anything specific. Just something they say. It's almost like they're saying they've reached some breaking point. No more. Enough is enough. They just can't anymore."

"I guess. It's that devilish TV they learning that mess from," added Jamay.

"Now Jamay, the TV itself ain't devilish. Maybe some of the channels show some not-so-good content," added Garnet. "We just have to stay vigilant about what the children watch. I know I dropped the ball today, but I just didn't think he'd be flipping through the channels and land on BET. He's getting a little older and a little more curious about life, I imagine."

"It's got to be a reason they used to call it the one-eyed demon," said Jamay. It's always some truth to those little sayings. This is just one of those days I miss that father of his. That was definitely what I call a Redd, Sr. moment. I think he would have known exactly what to say." She looked up toward the ceiling and voiced, *"Lord, help me raise this boy."*

"He'll be okay," reassured Garnet. "Pastor Castillo and some of the other ministers are starting to take up more time to chip in and help many of the single mothers around the church. Bowling. Skating. We'll make sure R.J. gets in with them."

"I hope so, mama. It was easy when he was a little bitty thing that did whatever you told him. Now, he gettin' a mind of his own."

"He been had a mind of his own," Garnet responded. "He just gettin' more of it."

Sensing R.J. was planning on not returning to the table, Jamay yelled, "R.J., don't think you're getting out of eating this salad. When you get hungry tonight, no doughnuts or sweets. This salad will be waiting for you in the refrigerator."

She was right. He had made his way into his room and started playing Fortnite again. "Okay," he answered.

The women exchanged a few more words before Davida realized she had to get home. "That was great, Ms. Gibbs. Absolutely great. I'm set for the rest of the night." She noticed a noise from her phone, signaling an incoming text. It was Tario again, and she ignored it again. "I better get home and get some rest. I have to be at work before the sun comes up."

"Okay, let me drop you off," added Jamay.

"No need, girl. I'm just gonna walk up the street and catch the RTC. It should be coming soon."

"Alright. Well, stay saved," Garnet said as she continued

cleaning the table. "I keep you covered under the blood. You know that, right?"

"Of course, Ms. Gibbs. I know that. Thank you for praying for me."

"I *keeps* you covered," she joked and started doing her holy dance in the kitchen.

"Ms. Gibbs, you are too much. I thought you had a PhD. Up there talkin' 'bout 'keeps.'"

"I'm only a doctor by day, Ms. Davida. By night, ain't no tellin' what may come out this mouth o' mine. I ain't got nothin' to prove to none o' y'all."

"Let me get out of here before your uneducatedness rubs off on me," Davida said as she laughed and made her way to the door. She grabbed her stuff and headed toward the door. "Bye, you guys." She yelled to the rear of the house, "Bye, R.J."

"Bye," R.J. answered.

As she headed out of the door, the two in the kitchen continued laughing at everything that had transpired. Davida left Garnet's and briskly made her way to the bus stop. As she crossed the street, she heard her phone ring as she got halfway across. Once she noticed that she had cleared all oncoming cars, she saw the bus approaching in the direction she needed to go. She removed her bus card and waited for the bus to stop in front of her. Right as she stepped onto the lower step to enter her ride, she succumbed under the pressure and answered her phone on the last ring before it went to voice mail. "Tario, what do you want?"

THE ASSIGNMENT

BEDS AT TRUMP Hotel were king-sized and made for a king, especially the one in Vegas. Although it didn't overlook the Strip, it had its own advantage in providing breathtaking views of the mountains and the major expressway. Kemal and Manuela had stared out the window after having worked up another sweat. They had gone at it for a complete hour. It felt like lust, given how intense the session was. The sheets were drenched with both of their sweat. They had to admit, they were made for each other. He was the yin to her yang. They just lay there, enjoying the other's company after a fulfilling episode of deep, passionate sex. Again. This time, they had chosen to do a staycation at this downtown oasis. They had heard of how swanky this hotel was and thought to change it up and give it a try.

As she lay in his arms, he kissed her on the nape of her neck. She protruded her rear end against his manhood, awakening it again. But he was a little worn out and would need at least another thirty minutes to rebuild his stamina and his sperm count. As he whispered sweet somethings in her ear, she turned toward him and began caressing his buttocks and staring at his goatee. Point blank, Kemal was just fine. And he was all hers.

Leaning back against the ceiling and smiling at both of them was Ashtoreth. She hovered over both lovebirds, dwelling on the fruit of her work. She herself was somewhat tired in her own way, as she had been whispering her own recommendations in both of their ears during the hot and steamy episode. She told Manuela which angle to open her legs while Kemal did what men were skilled to do. She gave Kemal suggestions for making Manuela moan. She told him to keep saying that he loved her when he was deep inside of her. There was something about the emotional tie that came from his words in her ear while his body was inside hers. Ashtoreth kept alternating between giving instructions to them both, all spontaneous, all intentional. She just loved making two people act like stone-cold freaks.

"Do you *really* love me?" asked Manuela.

"Huh?" said Kemal.

"Do you really love me?"

"Now why would you ask me something like that? Of course, I do."

"Well, you never really say it until I tell you to say it in the heat of the moment."

Kemal's cell phone rang, but both of them acted like it didn't. The caller left a message. The Old Car Horn ringtone informed him.

"Lemme take a leak." He took his phone with him as he headed toward the bathroom. As he entered, he closed the door and listened to the message. It was Randi.

Returning to the bed, he placed the phone down. "You have to do the praise service tomorrow, don't you?" asked Manuela.

"Yeah," answered Kemal. "I'm not sure what we'll be singing yet, but we'll think of something."

"We have to get ready for the guest church that's coming. Their pastor is bringing the Word on tomorrow, and we're feeding the members of his congregation that are coming with him. You know, I handle things in the kitchen." Manuela was president of the hospitality committee and had to oversee food preparation during the service.

"Much like how you handle things in the bedroom, huh? With perfection."

"You so crazy, papi."

They found themselves back in the bed, cuddling together. His manhood had awakened again, and he was indeed ready for Round Two, as was she. Ashtoreth was tired of all this jibber jabber and lowered herself from the ceiling and grabbed Manuela's hand.

Manuela's hand grabbed his unprotected bulge. It was alive, very alive. They had begun pleasuring themselves again. As Ashtoreth worked her magic, Gabriel peeked his head through the wall. Ashtoreth noticed him and started hissing toward his direction, her beautiful visage transformed into that of a gargoyle with sharp and pointy fangs.

Gabriel retreated and disappeared, not because he was fearful. He just needed further confirmation.

On this lovely night, the two satisfied each other some more, knowing this was precious time that they rarely had. Work, church, and other distractions crowded out their ability to spend quality time like this.

About an hour and a half earlier, Garnet was on her knees by her bed. She had been heavily interceding for a few people. For Davida. Kemal. Tario. Somebody named Krunch or Krunchy, whom she didn't know. While praying, the Lord checked her spirit and instructed her not to pray anymore for Kemal.

Gabriel had arrived early. Now that he was there alone, he had time to take in the place and not be so driven by assignment, at least for now. The pews were nice, reddish, and had that velvety feeling. The balcony was a church's dream, spreading itself in a type of curve pattern so that those on either of the furthest ends could stare across at their fellow worshippers. Behind the pulpit rested a modern-day choir loft with the noteworthy baptismal pool stationed behind it. The loft seemed to be able to hold a hundred singers. Microphones swan-dived from the ceiling above and stopped magically right above the soprano, tenor, and alto sections so they could capture the harmonies just right. The baptismal pool was porcelain. The painting by the pool was a huge rendering of the baptism scene of Jesus. John the Baptist had locks and a six pack, and Jesus seemed to have a dark-skinned, Mediterranean look. The pulpit itself was a preacher's dream. The two shrubs that stood aside the glass podium on each side added a touch of class to what was already a gorgeous setup. Then there were the six mics for the praise team that stood about three feet apart from each other, spanning the length of the pulpit, while the five leather chairs on the stage assured those in attendance who were the key figures in the church. The largest of the five was Pastor Castillo's, of course, but he never let it go to his head. He was as humble as they came.

Although Gabriel shouldn't have been, he was startled by a noise in the bathroom area way on the other side of the church. In a half of a blink, he was at the east wing of the church to investigate. It was Jurnell, the church custodian. He always arrived at the church around 6 AM to make sure the bathrooms were clean, lobby floors mopped, and the pulpit area spruced up. He did so without fanfare but with the minimal chastising of his wife, Beatrice. "Why can't somebody help you out on some Sundays?" she would ask. "You mean you got to be there every Sunday? What if something happens to you? What if somebody sees your pattern and robs you?"

"Well," he'd answer, "if it's your time, it's your time. The good Lord and His angels got my back."

She hated when he responded this way. She knew he was right, but someone still needed to share the burden, according to her. As was his custom, he was caught up in his own quiet praise service as he cleaned. Today, his spirit man had been singing one of his favorites.

"Father, I stretch my hand to thee.
No other help I know;"

He sprinkled Ajax on the toilets and started scrubbing, using some of the water to mix with the powder to create a blue, disinfecting agent.

"If thou withdraw thyself from me,
Ah! Whither shall I go?"

Gabriel smiled and took it all in. These were the saints he loved. No frills. No put-ons. They just loved God and lived a holy life while they were by themselves. Jurnell kept singing and finished up with cleaning the sinks. He had to get to the other three bathrooms within the next hour and then get to mopping in the lobby, so he picked up his pace.

"Jamay, come on, baby. We don't wanna be too late. We got a

guest church coming in, and you know how seating can be," encouraged Garnet.

"I'm coming, mama. This slow poke in the form of R.J. has decided that he wants to go the pace of a snail on this morning." R.J. sat motionless on his mother's bed. Looking at him through her bedroom mirror, she grumbled, "R.J. come on. Don't just sit there, knowing we gotta leave in a few minutes. Put your shoes on. I told you about staying up so late playing that . . . whatever is the name of that silly electronic game you be playin'. Now, you gotta pay the price. You going to church, and I better not catch you in church sleeping either. You not gone be awake at home and then get all sleepy in church. The Lord has been too good to you for you do that." Some of her Jamaican accent was leaking through, although she wasn't upset.

Half-sleep, half-awake, he obliged.

"I'm in the car," announced Garnet as she headed toward the door. "Hurry up, now. We have to stop and pick up Celeste."

"Oh, she's going? That's great," said Jamay. "I haven't seen her in a while."

In about seven minutes, the other two were out the door as well.

"Lookin' good, baby," doted Kemal. "My wife is about to make me lose my religion." He slapped her on the rear end.

"Stop," she pretended not to like it. "The neighbors are watching. Plus, you got to stay focused for the praise team this morning. We don't need nothing hindering that."

He opened her door and let her sink into the seat. "So what?" he countered. "They lookin' because they jealous.

Besides, ain't nothing wrong with a man spanking his own wife." He closed the door, made his way to the other side of his Beamer, and got in. He started his iPod so he could listen and sing along to "Made a Way." He'd start off with this song first and would figure out the other songs as he proceeded.

Ato turned into the parking lot at 9:24 AM. He was finishing up with his conversation with his adjutant, Minister Carl on his hands-free phone. "So are you sure everything's fine with Pastor McElroy?" he asked Carl.

"Yes, I have him with me right now." Carl's job was always to pick up guest speakers and escort them to the church after having breakfast. "We just finished grabbing a bite at The Big Egg. He really seemed to enjoy it."

"Indeed I did," interjected Pastor McElroy playfully over the car's speaker phone. He and Castillo were close friends. McElroy insisted that his comrade not go through all of the formalities of sending his assistant to pick him up. He was content with riding with Castillo and going to Burger King to grab a quick breakfast sandwich. Castillo declined nowadays, however, because he was escorting his own troop comprised of his wife and little one.

He pulled into his reserved space and placed the car in park. Hadi, a second adjutant, stood by the Reserved-For-The-Pastor sign. He would swing into action once the car door opened. He knew not to open it immediately because Ato was often finishing up on a call and appreciated privacy when doing so. Said Ato to McElroy, "Hey there, doc. We're looking for a mighty move of God on today, so you better come correct. Don't come half-steppin' with no little piece of Word. We need our souls fed well on today."

"Hi, Uncle Lloyd!" blurted Ezra.

"Darling, let's just let dad just do the talking right now." Shanshan mildly corrected her son. "Remember what we talked about concerning when daddy is on a call on the speaker phone? No interruptions."

McElroy ignored her chastisement. "How's my little extra Ezra?"

Shanshan relented and stared at her husband to intervene. He just smiled.

"Fine," added the little one. "We're in summer camp this summer, and we're doing a lot of fun stuff."

"Well, that's good," the preacher added. "Keep being smart like your mom, and you're gonna go places." Shanshan grinned toward the window.

"Well, we're at the church now, about to head inside," said Ato. "We'll see you guys when you get here. Drive safely, Carl. No need in breaking any speed limits."

"Alright, sir. See you in a few."

"Bye!" yelled Ezra toward the invisible microphone.

The calls were disconnected.

"Okay, gang, out we go."

As they exited, Hadi reached for Ato's attaché case and greeted the family. "Hi, Pastor. Hello Sister Castillo. Hey, Ez."

They all responded pleasantly. Shanshan was the only immediate one who engaged him. "Good morning, Hadi. You look mighty sharp on today." She placed her hand on Ezra's shoulder and ambled toward the main entrance as her husband and Hadi prepared to go through a separate entrance.

"Well, thank you madam. I'm learning my sense of fashion from your husband," Hadi joked.

"Well then, that means you're learning it from Shanshan," confessed Ato. He grabbed his suit jacket from the back seat and prepared to carry it himself, but Hadi took it from him. "Now, you know I couldn't scratch my way out of anybody's fashion paper bag. Left up to me, I'd be wearing greens with oranges. Always make sure you listen to your wife when it comes to things like that."

"Point well taken," said Hadi. "Point well taken."

"I'll see you in a few, baby," said Shanshan. She'd have to sit on the pulpit with her husband but had to get Ezra situated first and remind him of his ensuing punishment if she found out he was misbehaving during the service. "See you inside, Hadi."

"Alright, Sis."

"Bye, daddy," said Ezra.

As his family moved in the opposite direction, he and Hadi started walking toward the secluded entrance door. Ato opened it and let himself in and held the door for Hadi, although Hadi wished he was allowed to do his job involving such trivial matters as opening doors and the like. At least he was carrying the briefcase and coat. Ato was not caught up in all of the you're-my-servant madness. If the door was there and it needed to be opened, he opened it and often let his assistant enter first.

"So how are we with our meeting on next week in Phoenix?" inquired the pastor.

"We're just about set, sir. The flight is done, but we're waiting to see if the hotel prices will come down a little more."

"Well, don't wait too long. Odds are prices won't come down too much more if it's just a week out. They could even start rising again. Let's go ahead and book."

"Sure thing."

They arrived at Ato's office. Hadi unlocked the door, and they entered. Gabriel was already inside, arms folded, sword on holster, wings giving the appearance that they were slowly bouncing in place. He was staring out of the window. Hadi hung up the suit jacket, placed the briefcase on the desk, and opened it so it faced the owner. Ato sunk in his chair and gathered himself. Hadi knew what was next, so he sat down to catch his breath.

He started, *"Thank you, Lord, for this day. We appreciate all you've done and all you're gonna do. Thanks for Hadi and the blessing he is. Gloria a su nombre. Lord, we appreciate your standard. Give us to please you on today. Give us an unusual service on today. Show yourself strong. Show us your strong right arm. Protect us, and we will be protected. Help us, and we will be helped. Gloria a su nombre. Thank you, Jesus. Thank you, Jesus. Give us strength on today."* He and Hadi sat in silence. Amen was implied.

Ato relaxed and started rummaging through his briefcase. He found his Listerine strips and popped a few in his mouth. "Yes, I'm believing for a great service on today. The Lord will do it."

"Amen, Pastor," said Hadi.

As they continued to chat, saints began filing into the sanctuary and deciding on their seats. Sunday School was still going on in classrooms outside of the main gathering place and would be over soon. Scarves and other items had already found themselves on a few seats as a mark of territory. Their owners would be back after class to claim their seating space. Pastor Castillo asked them not to do this. It looked tacky. Saints obeyed for a good two weeks but then resorted to their old habits. The balcony was filling nicely. It was something about the view from above that the saints loved. Plus, they would not be too much of a distraction if they had to step out early. Members from the home church welcomed those from the visiting one. It would be a packed house this morning with both congregations meshing. Expectations were indeed high, and a feeling of excitement was in the air. The Lord would have to show up and meet His people there.

"Come on, slow poke," said Jamay to R.J. They were walking, nearing the entrance of the church. R.J. was lagging behind and yawning.

Garnet and Celeste had already left them in the dust and made it inside. Whenever Celeste entered the church, she was enamored of its beauty. "Garnet, this is absolutely gorgeous."

"Celeste, you say that every time you come in here," Garnet joked.

"I'm serious. It's really nice."

They entered the main sanctuary and were able to get seats close to the front, but not too close. "I'll be back," said Garnet. "I need to go to the little girl's room."

"Okay," Celeste said as she crossed her feet. "I'll go when you get back."

Garnet walked toward the main doors. Right before she reached for them to push, they swung open from the opposite side. Davida was pulling the doors from her end.

"Davida! How are you? What a surprise," exclaimed Garnet.

"Doin' good, Ms. Gibbs. I decided last night that I would come by, so I hopped on the bus this morning and made my way here."

"It's so good to see you. Well, if you don't have anywhere to sit yet, we have a few seats up front. You better hurry, though, because we have a guest church visiting with us on this morning. As you can see, the seats are filling up quickly. My co-worker is sitting down front. She has on an orange and white summer dress. Just introduce yourself to her. I'm so glad to see you." It had been about two months since Davida had come to that church. She had visited elsewhere during that time but felt a special something whenever she visited Alive.

"Good to see you, too," responded Davida, and she continued to the front to get acquainted with Celeste.

As Garnet continued on, she stuck her head inside of children's church and saw Jamay hugging Shanshan. Both had just dropped off their little men and had just finished reminding both of the consequences if they clowned in their mothers' absence. R.J. and Ezra were the best of friends and could easily lose focus during their service, as they wanted to spend time telling the other how their summer was going.

"Hi, Garnet," Manuela said.

"Oh, hi Manuela. You startled me. How are you?"

"Doin' good. Getting things ready in the kitchen for the visiting church. Looks like we're going to have to feed an army. I hate not being in the service, but we have to make sure we're ready."

"I hear you. Don't be shocked if you see me in the line after the service. You guys really do it up in that there kitchen." She laughed and touched Manuela's arm. "Anyhow, let me get to the restroom. I gotta get situated since I'm seated close to the front. I'll see you after church."

"Okay. Talk to you later."

Both made their way to their respective destinations.

Minister Carl and Pastor McElroy made it to Pastor Castillo's office. The pastors embraced for a good ten seconds. One would have thought they hadn't seen each other in ages. They loved supporting each other's ministry and did well to avoid the stereotypes associated with being a leader in God's vineyard.

"Old buddy, old pal," joked McElroy to Ato, "you know I must love you since you got me here on a Sunday morning. You know I don't give up my Sunday mornings at my church. That's high holy day."

"Well, I thank you, my brother," answered Ato. "It's good that you thought it not robbery to sacrifice your Sunday morning and be here to share with us. Anything you can think of that you need? We'll have to go out to the pulpit pretty quickly. We're a little late. I like being out there during the praise service."

"Wow. You're definitely one of a kind. You know most of us like to be grand and make our entrance right after the praise service is over. We're too anointed to be seen praising God with the masses," laughed McElroy. "And you know people have to see how well our socks match our tie, so we can't stand too long."

Ato chuckled, "Okay, Saul." They gathered their materials. McElroy had his iPad and notes. He didn't flip through an actual Bible when he preached. He had learned how to find scripture references electronically. He forgot to ask if there was Wi-Fi in the sanctuary. He needed to be able to load his references online. He'd figure out a way to make do if not and didn't press the issue at the moment.

They were preparing to leave the office as Ato paused to remind either Carl or Hadi that they were ready. He always had to remind himself to beckon for one of them to accompany him to the pulpit. Both assistants had been relaxing and looking over Ato's schedule for the coming week. "Coming, Pastor," replied Hadi. Carl would hold down the office fort for a while and make his way to the pulpit later to make sure McElroy had water and a sweat towel available. The three headed out of Ato's office and decided to walk to the pulpit the long way, through the regular hallway and lobby as opposed to going through the shorter route. The church had recently done some upgrades, and Ato wanted to show them off to McElroy.

They walked down the long hallway as Ato told his friend of the budget it took to do upgrades at the church. A few members, slightly shocked, walked by and spoke to Ato. They weren't used to seeing him make his way to the sanctuary through the major hallway. He pointed at one of the nursery rooms. "And we knocked out one of the walls adjoining this nursery and made it twice as big. Our members keep on being fruitful and multiplying."

"Indeed," said McElroy. "Nothing like making way for quivers full o' youngins."

They walked toward the pastor and the guest speaker.

Kemal, some of the other praise-team members, and a few more people were running a little late after they took a little longer than expected to go over the itinerary of songs for the praise service. On her way to the kitchen, Manuela just happened to turn the corner at the same time the group was making its way to the main sanctuary doors to mount the pulpit. The group en masse walked toward the pastor and the guest speaker.

Ato was happy to bump into Kemal so he could meet McElroy. The praise team would be singing at the visiting pastor's church for a program later in the month. A face-to-face meeting between the two would be great, and the timing couldn't have been perfect.

As both groups got closer, Ato started the formal introductions. "Pastor Lloyd," Ato stated, "this is Kemal, one of our key praise-team members. He'll be in charge of the group who will be ministering in song at your church soon. I just wanted you to associate his name with his face." Turning toward Kemal's wife, Ato exclaimed, "And this is his beautiful wife." Pastor McElroy extended his hand.

Manuela looked at both pastors and kept walking toward the kitchen. She scooted by all parties without speaking and made a left into the kitchen to start the church dinner. She commenced small talk with her cooking pal, Jackie.

Randi accepted McElroy's handshake, providing a firm, sure grip and added an extra feminine curtsy. "Nice to meet you, Pastor. I'm Randi. I'm sure my husband and all those on the praise team will represent our ministry and the Lord very well. I know you'll be pleased and the Spirit of the Lord will be glorified."

"Thank you, sister," exclaimed McElroy. "I'm excited whenever I can find good, solid praise teams that know how to usher in the Lord's Spirit. Too many people don't realize how serious that responsibility is. So I'm gonna hold you to your promise." They all laughed.

"Nice meeting you, Pastor McElroy," said Kemal. "Can't wait to minister in your service. Just like I can't wait to get inside this sanctuary and get this praise service started. I'm running a tad late."

"Well, at least you got feet to run with," joked Pastor McElroy. "Let the Lord use you." To Randi, he said, "Nice meeting you as well, Randi. Thanks for all you guys do to support Pastor Castillo."

"Likewise," voiced Randi. "Our pleasure."

They all made their way inside the main sanctuary door. Kemal trotted a bit to join the other praise members who were already in the pulpit area. The pastors lagged slightly behind as those in the congregation started gravitating toward and speaking to one of the two pastors, whichever pastor was theirs. And Hadi followed. Kemal and the praise gang continued to set the atmosphere for worship. Unbeknown to everyone, Gabriel was slowly making his way from the rear of the church to the front. Although he had feet, he didn't need them. He simply floated toward the pulpit steps. He would have gone quicker, but he was waiting to hear if there was one final command to stop, perhaps some prayer of repentance, some request for mercy. Nada. He reached the bottom of the pulpit steps and rode the air until he stood atop the pulpit, hovering, still invisible. He inched closer to Kemal.

"The Lord has done marvelous things," exclaimed Kemal, making final adjustments to the microphone stand. The pastor and guest speaker were ready for a fiery service. They stood clapping.

Soon, Gabriel stood in front of Kemal. The difference in stature was mesmerizing. Kemal was stunning. But he was no match for Gabriel's physicality. His height alone made Kemal look puny, whose face stood directly at Gabriel's torso level.

"Everybody, clap your hands and give God a praise of thanksgiving," said Kemal. And the people obeyed. Kemal lifted his own hands, which stopped right at Gabriel's chin.

Gabriel drew his sword from its sheath and held it by his side, gripping the handle tight. His eyes were closed.

Kemal kept exhorting. "Let Him know just how much you love Him, how much you appreciate Him. He's God all by Himself. He rules the earth. He rules the heavens. He rules the stars, the sea, the mountains, the–"

In a moment, Kemal dropped to the floor and lay flat on the pulpit, motionless. Carrina, the singer closest to him, placed her hand over her chest, and stepped to the side a little, staring down at him. She, like some others, thought it was a joke. Still, others believed he was lying prostrate before the Lord. All were wrong. In a flash, Gabriel darted out to complete his final mission.

The congregation finally came to itself and realized something wasn't right. Pastors Castillo and McElroy stared, wondering if what had happened really happened. Praise leaders began gasping and saying, *"Jesus!"* It was sinking in that this was reality. The Spirit clued Garnet in as well as Pastor Castillo. She grabbed Celeste's and Davida's hand and started tearing up. The congregation had gotten restless. The music continued but only because the organist didn't know what to do. Mostly everyone began crying and becoming frantic. Jamay wondered what was going on. She hadn't entered the sanctuary yet, but several members came storming out into the lobby area where she was, proclaiming, "Oh, my God! Oh, my God!"

As Pastor Castillo sorrowfully made his way to the podium, he heard a scream. No, it was a shriek. Within a matter of seconds, someone brushed past Jamay and the others in the lobby, burst through the sanctuary doors, and commanded, "Help! Call 911! Somebody, anybody, call 911!! I think Manuela's dead!"

10

WAR'S ART

AFTER THE AFTERNOON'S mayhem died down, Nieko took his usual path out of the church toward the bus stop, swerving past those who still couldn't believe what had just happened. He just wanted to let the authorities do their investigations, get home, watch TV, and get to the foolishness on the Gram. He noticed a couple of text messages after turning his phone back on, both from Maurice. Only the phone number appeared with the message. Nieko had long since deleted the number but knew it when he saw it. After changing his own number three times, he decided it wasn't really worth doing anymore. Maurice was persistent and always figured out a way of tracking down his ex. *"Miss you!"* and *"Wus good?"* were the normal texts he sent. And they mostly seemed to come on Sundays, when Nieko had received another jolt of spiritual strength from the services.

Right as he deleted the second of Maurice's messages, the phone rang. Often, Maurice was bold enough to place a real call, hoping Nieko would give in.

"Answer it," whispered Ashtoreth. She often followed Nieko out of services and provided temptation in one form or another. True to form, this time was no different. *"Answer it. A brief conversation won't hurt. Besides, he's where he's at, and you're here. Stop being overly dramatic."* She kept pressing Maurice to call, and he finally did.

Nieko normally rebuked the enemy and didn't entertain these suggestions. Today, he was a bit off of his game. "Mo, what do you want?" he said into his Samsung Galaxy in a nonmistakably curt tone.

"Well, at least I know you alive," responded Maurice. "You don't respond to my texts or nothing, Neek. Shit, son. How you been?" If he reminded him how much he genuinely cared about him, perhaps it would lead to Nieko's agreeing to have coffee or dinner. Then maybe it would lead to something else. A rekindling of sorts.

"I been good. Just tripping a little bit. Somebody at church up and died today. Crazy."

"Damn! What happened?"

"I don't even know. It happened so quick. The cops showed up. They still there dealing with it. I had to get out of there."

"Oh, aight. I miss you, yo." He wasted little time and started in. "It gets lonely here without you being around. Your smile. Your intellect. Your corny ass jokes." He was lying. He was a hottie and knew it. There was no shortage of options for him when it came to partaking of the man-buffet. And he had eaten from many of Vegas' choices since breaking up with Nieko.

Nieko was starting to beat himself up for answering. Maurice knew just what to say to make him think and reminisce. "I guess, Mo."

"Let's just meet up at the coffee shop tonight. I respect

your choices. I don't understand them, but I respect all this Jesus stuff you trying to live by."

"No, don't do it," interjected the Holy Spirit to Nieko.

"Jesus stuff? What you mean by that?" Nieko hated when somebody tried to categorize his change of lifestyle that way or as a temporary change.

"Nothing. I just don't get how you can be in a relationship one minute and then cast everybody off the next. I don't think you realize how much I cared about you. And still care about you. You just don't know how much I love you, man."

It was hard for him to stay angry with Maurice. He always had a way of sneaking in an insult and ending it with a love compliment. How could he fight that? "I just don't trust myself around you and your game-spittin' self, that's all."

Maurice laughed. "See, you wrong. It's all good, though. You know I ain't got nothing but love for you, nigga."

"Hang up," encouraged the Holy Spirit to Nieko.

Maurice continued, "You're a special man, and I just want you to know that. I was your first, so I know I still hold a special place in your heart, right?"

Infatuated for a brief moment, Nieko finally came to himself. "Thanks, Mo, but I need to get home. Maybe we'll do coffee some other time. Not right now. It's just not good for me to do that right now. I'm gonna talk to you later, man. You know I'm praying for you." He felt that he had better bring the conversation to an end. His manhood was coming alive. *"Jesus,"* he whispered to himself, *"touch my body."* He didn't realize he himself was the culprit behind what was happening. Nobody forced him to answer the phone. Yet, the Lord was faithful.

"I love you, Neek," added the ex.

Chuckling, Nieko answered, "Talk to you later, Mo. Bye."

"Shoot!" exclaimed Nieko. His phone fell from his hands. He picked it up and noticed a hairline crack on the screen. *"Lord,"* he said, *"you know that man make me weak. If you don't help me, it's not gone be good. In fact, it's gone get real bad."*

Ashtoreth was noticeably upset. She hoped a face-to-face meeting would come out of it. The rest would have been history. In frustration, she had hit Nieko's wrist, causing the phone's fall. She'd heard the prayer, though, so she'd just try again another, better time. All she needed was one good opportunity.

Uriel observed from a short distance. He knew Nieko would have to develop his own sense of resistance and pray daily for strength to the Holy Spirit. Intervention would have to be kept to a minimum. But he watched, knowing he'd step in if a real need arose.

On the bed, Chaz lay back with his legs crossed, watching the television. He had trained himself to follow the storyline minus the sound. His headphones took care of providing the noise. He was listening to Chopin on full blast.

Redd shifted restlessly in his own bed, a lazy stone's toss away. He could hear Chaz's classical music just like it was playing in his own ear. And he didn't know why Chaz had to be entertained by both, with the volumes reaching toward the heavens. After tiring of shifting, he grabbed the remote and turned the volume down on the boob tube.

"Hey, Amigo, I'm watching that," Chaz said as he turned his head toward Redd.

"Then watch it, then. That don't mean the volume got to be up. You over there listening to your Mozart or whoever, and believe it or not, I am too. You got it up way too high."

"It's Chopin."

"Whoever. I just know I can hear it just like your headphones sticking in my ears. Turn it down, please. I'm trying to sleep. Since when do folks from Miami like listening to classical music anyway?"

"Nothing to do with folks from Miami, amigo. Has to do with me. I just happen to be from Miami, and I like classical music. Case closed. But since you bring it up, since when do people from Vegas . . ." He paused. "Shh! You hear that?" Both of them recognized the sound that trumped all sounds, at least where they were. Who cared what was on TV? And Chopin would have to wait. Piercing through the arid Afghan air was none other than the welcomed arrival of the jingle truck.

Hopping from their beds and running to the outpost door, the two of them may as well have been six-year-olds spellbound by the Orpheus-like tunes oozing from the neighborhood ice cream truck in the States. The brightly colored U-Haul-looking truck, mostly pink, was quite successful in its secondary duty, to be a catalyst at engendering quite the laugh. It was too pretty to be ugly, but too ugly to be pretty: prugly. And everyone knew not to be embarrassed by it, not with all the comic relief it provided. The sound accompanying the prugliness was unique, amicable, pacifying. The bells bedecking the bottom panels of the truck alarmed all of the troops that refreshments were on their way. The water, the vittles, and all the other goodies. But what the approaching truck and bells really symbolized was the weightiness of the primary mission, the arrival of much-needed comfort and camaraderie. The kind needed in the midst of what some of the troops considered to be hell. The trucks were driven by friendly locals, whose mission was to see to it that these troops' feet were planted in something that felt like home. These deliverymen took pride in their hospitality to visitors of the land, especially U.S. troops, who were there fighting on their behalf against Taliban rule. All of the troops were there for this last leg of Obama's troop-withdrawal phase; the rest of their compatriots had returned to the States to experience their inevitable plight of harsh reentry into civilian life, with all of its PTSD-related unfairness. These, this last remnant, were Marines holding it down for America, often feeling the pressure that came with such a tall task. And it seemed as though the truck driver had keen insight on when spirits needed lifting.

As the truck inched closer, the other troops spilled out of their own bunkers, awaiting the day's surprise drop-off, for the jingle truck always came without warning.

"Now everyone just wait," Kabir, the driver, said jovially from his window. As the truck came to a halt, the bells continued singing for a while and then ceased. "We have plenty to go around for all of you." He hopped out of his driver's seat and approached the American gang. Baktash, his assistant and helper, climbed out of the passenger's seat and extended the same greetings as did Kabir.

"Kabir! Baktash!" exclaimed Jerome. "How the hell are ya?" Jerome was from northern Cali and had been serving his country for six years, ever since he had finished high school. He was known to be a prankster and was the closest friend Redd had overseas. "I'm still waiting for you guys to teach me how to say *jackass* in Dari."

Both Afghans laughed and opened the door on the side of the truck. "Okay, Jerome. We'll teach you one day," said Baktash. "When we do, we'll be sure to attach your picture above the definition so everyone will have a visual to go along with it, my friend." He said "friend" with a hard roll of the "r." Everyone exploded in laughter.

"Okay," Jerome said in his you-got-me-this-time tone. "Someone is learning how to joke the American way."

"Alright, fellows. Gather around," said Kabir. "We got some goodies for you." Right then, he and his delivery buddy started grabbing bottles of water and distributing them to the troops. Then came the stuff to satisfy their sweet teeth: baklava, gosh feel, firnee, kolcha. Endless were the treats. The troops literally felt like they had hit some kind of jackpot on these days. These were the small things that made their stay overseas more bearable. They then passed around some unwrapped games for the soldiers to pass the time away: parchesi, chess, caroms, and the ever-popular standard deck of cards. Cards had been delivered before, but several of them always ended up missing, making the deck useless after a while. Surely, nothing could or would beat a historic game of bridge or spades. The troops would retreat into their common area like kids on Christmas morning. There were only ear-to-ear smiles.

As the troops sat, ate, burped, farted, and played, the two Afghans continued to bring the rest of the drop-off inside, placing cases of bottled water and the rest of the truck contents in the general area. The troops continued joking with each other. A few women were a part of the camp and withstood their fair share of taunts from the boys.

"Ey, Jones," said Redd. "Do your womanly duty and bring me another bottle of water. I'm thirsty."

Jones, who had no problems standing her ground replied, "Sure." She twisted off the bottle cap first and then tossed to him the full, uncovered plastic bottle.

"Damn you!" uttered Redd as he caught the bottle but suffered the natural consequences.

"Well, you didn't say how you wanted me to bring it. I'm just a woman. You have to tell me exactly what you want me to do." Water was all around him and had splashed onto some of the other fellows too. They all tried to clean the water from them without having to get up to get a towel.

"I tell you, man. I'm not sure how much more I can take being over here," said Patterson, shifting from the Christmas-like feel in the room. The Oklahoma native popped a butter cookie in his mouth and placed his right leg over the arm of the leather chair. "It just seems like the date to go home keeps getting pushed back further and further. Just when it seems like we getting outta here, we gotta stay another month. And then another month."

Chaz added, "I feel you Pat. I try not to think about it too much. I don't really know what to say to my wife when she asks me when I'm coming home. I just say whatever I think she needs to hear so she can stay sane and happy. You know what I mean?"

"You guys are real brave," added Kabir. "We don't know exactly how you feel, but we try to make it better for you. You have pressure on you to try to make a home in a place that's not your home."

Baktash kept helping Kabir deliver the goods. He seemed shy and like he didn't really know what to say. So he said nothing more, just assisted.

No one could see the invisible guest hanging out in the common area. Gabriel had made a special trip overseas in response to Garnet's prayers to see about her son-in-law.

"Thanks, Kabi." Redd had given Kabir a nickname, despite how short his name was already. He stood and saluted the American flag by the door. "Operation Resolute Support, I'm at your service!" announced Redd. "Here to serve and pro-tect!" The other guys chuckled a bit. That was just Redd, the clown of the group. He became more serious as he sat down and continued. "I tell you, man. They got us over hear train-ing these Afghan armies over here and don't realize we still in harm's way. Maybe more now than before. Not that many of us over here in the 'bad' lands." He was making fun of the name of the city in which they were stationed. "And they act like these extremists over here are scared. They not scared, man. They just waiting for us to leave, so they can get back to doing what they do."

Jerome grabbed a deck of cards, opened them, and started shuffling. "I don't think Jalalabad's all *that* bad, homie. I can live without the heat, though. Straight up. And then gotta wear all these clothes and go out in it and try to run. That's crazy."

Merrick, a white, blond-haired god of a man chimed in, "Yeah, I know. Heat's terrible. But were any of you ready last January when it started snowing? It looked like a scene from Star Wars when you looked out at the mountains in a distance."

Redd livened up, "Yo, that took me for a loop. I just thought it was hot year-round up here. Them winter months be freezin'. I took a picture of the snow and sent it back home to my folks. My boy couldn't believe it."

"Oh yeah, how *is* little Redd?" inquired Jerome. "That kid gotta be going through some hell. A black kid with red hair."

"R.J. doing good, last I heard. And his hair ain't red. It's more brown, copper-like."

"Red. Copper. All the same to me. It ain't black."

"Yeah, he managing. Last I heard from his mama and grandma in a letter, they were saying he have good days and bad days. They say he stay quiet about it most of the time. Hard explaining to him why I'm here and not at home, but it's just one of those things, you know."

"Yep," said Chaz as he bounced a tennis ball on the floor, which ricocheted off the wall and came back to him.

"Alright, ladies and gentlemen. I think that's it for our deliveries this time," voiced Kabir. Baktash followed behind him and made his way to his side of the truck. "We better get back. We got a good hour-and-a-half drive back to Kabul." As they headed to the door, the troops casually walked them to the door back to the truck.

"Thanks again, fellows, for the stuff. We love when you guys come by and leave a little love," joked Jerome.

"Oh, by the way," remembered Kabir, "if you guys get too tired and bored of sitting around here as they say, 'playing with yourself,' you should see about coming to Kabul to relax a little. Once a year, they have poetry day in our village. I know you all are macho and everything, but it might be good just to have a change of pace and listen to some of the art that our people make. And if you have your own poems, I'm sure they won't mind you giving a taste of some of your poetry."

"Poetry?" Jerome interjected. "Troops going to a poetry party? Um, I'll have to think about that."

"Just a suggestion, my friend," said Kabir as he entered the driver's side. "Just a suggestion."

"That actually might not be a bad idea," said Jones.

"Says the sensitive woman," joked Redd.

She threw water on him again, this time from her own bottle.

"Stop, now," Redd said. "You gone get enough of that."

"And you gone get enough of insulting me, dipshit."

"Well, thanks for letting us know," Redd told Kabir. "That actually may *not* be a bad idea. Anything to get us away from here might be a good thing. We train the Afghan soldiers during the day, so we can probably step out and let our hair down. We'll see about checking out the one this year."

"Well, take it easy, my family," encouraged Kabir. "Thank

you very much for being here helping our country. We appreciate all of it, my friends." He started the truck and started inching off.

Baktash said his goodbyes through his window, waving.

The spectacle of a truck gave the troops one final reason to laugh heartily. They couldn't get over how primitive and ass-backward the truck looked. And the cacophonous jingling didn't help matters either. It jingled out of sight as it had jingled on arrival. More and more laughter permeated the slightly humid air. The troops had received their share of entertainment for the afternoon.

All were laughing except for Gabriel. He remained vigilant and watchful. Garnet's prayers had him there for a reason. He didn't just show up anywhere just to show up. Soon, he witnessed why. As he glanced toward the direction of the departing truck, he observed that atop it sat the evil Mictian, who had made his way to Afghanistan for his own intents, schemes, and purposes.

WHOOOO'S THAT
KNOCKIN' AT MY DOOR?

"¡GLORIA A SU nombre!" shouted Pastor Castillo. He was at it again, delivering his message of hope and relief. Regaining some sense of normalcy in services was his mission since Kemal's passing. His message came from Acts 27:22-41, Proverbs 4:23, and Isaiah 29:13; the message title was "A Heart Attack."

> "No one knows the day or the hour when our wonderful Savior will appear. We all know earthquakes are common in Japan, China, and even out here on the west coast. But who would have ever imagined that earthquakes would happen out east, over in Virginia and New York? I think those would qualify as 'divers places.' This stuff is not just happening by mistake. ¡Gloria a su nombre!"

"Amen," everybody agreed.

"The enemy knows his time is short, so he's trying his best to pull you away from the Lord. I know it was your marriage that may have failed, but he's not after your marriage. I know your money may be funny, but he ain't after your coins either. You thought you were gonna get that degree, but it didn't work out. But the enemy is as intelligent as intelligent can get. He don't need no degree. That's not what he's after. And like Paul, your ship might crash and sink, but he's not after your ship. What he's pursuing, what he's going hard after, what he's trying to steal . . . is your heart. He knows if he takes something you love, you'll probably get upset with the Lord and put a pause on your commitment. You'll relinquish your stand and take down on your profession of faith, getting an attitude with God. You'll start listening to the voices of Job's friends, who tell you to curse God and die. But don't you fret, and don't you fear, my friend. You're just having a heart attack. The enemy's is trying to stop you by attacking stuff close to your heart.

"So, if the marriage fails, let it fail. If your money never gets right, so be it. If you never get that degree, you make sure you stay committed to the Lord. If the ship starts sinking, that doesn't mean you have to sink with it. Wave bye-bye to it as it's going under water. Tell your sinking ship to tell the Titanic you said hello because it's not over until God says it's over. You have to stick with the Lord, so He can show you that you didn't need the ship after all to fulfill His purpose in your life. Just be sure to guard your heart, beloved.

Guard your heart. Guard your heart. Don't let the attack against your heart cause you to walk away from Him and His mission for your life. The Lord is coming back for a church whose hearts have stayed guarded against every attack waged by the enemy."

As the live service came through across the television screen, Rusty sat back on his black wool sofa, chewing on his peppermint-tasting snuff. Beside him was his spit cup, filled with his brownish saliva. His wife, Martha Jo, brought him a slice of crumb cake and a napkin.

"I don't see why you sit there boilin' while you listen to that preacher," she said. "He ain't doing nothing but good for this Vegas community."

"He just makes me sick," responded Rusty. "Leadin' all them gullible people to nowhere. All he do is talk about, 'The Lord coming back' this and 'The Lord coming back' that. And all them folk just stupid enough to believe him while he take they money."

"You ever been to the man church?"

"Naw. And I ain't goin' neither. You bet not go neither."

"Don't tell me what I bet and bet not do. And if you ain't never been there, then how you know what he do with they money?"

"He on TV, ain't he? And I heard he drive a Mercedes." He spit out the rest of his stuff and took a bite of cake.

"It ain't got nothing to do with what you heard. That man could be doing the right thang with the money. You can't believe everything you hear."

"Why you defending that man, Martha Jo? Something 'bout him ain't right." His redneckness would become more evident. "That damn spic just rub me the wrong way. He need to go back to his own country. Comin' over here, takin' up all our jobs. Just listen to him. He ain't even really speaking English right. He sound too spicish. Here we are over here struggling and he got a job leading all these people and promising they gone get to heaven." He started shaking from anger and thought he'd put the cake down.

"Well, you can run your blood pressure up 'bout it all you won't. Ain't gone solve nothing. If it worry you that much, you need to do something 'bout it." She meant for him to get involved in providing more opportunities for those in the community who needed work. Rusty worked construction and had some say in the hiring of those who needed temporary part-time work.

But he didn't take her statement that way. She straightened up some of the furniture, wiped up some of the saliva that didn't make it inside the cup, and headed back to the kitchen, leaving her disgruntled husband on the couch. He stared at the TV in utter disgust. He grabbed his Confederate flag, which rested atop the sofa, which accented its color scheme.

"Maybe you will," said Ashtoreth as she rested her invisible arm across Rusty's shoulders, whispering in his ear.

"Maybe I will," responded Rusty aloud to himself.

The gang made it back from church and was preparing to eat. Garnet was old-school and tried her best to cook the entire Sunday dinner before leaving for church. Although she wasn't able to do it on a consistent basis, this Sunday was a success. The thought of having to start from scratch after possibly being worn out in the worship service was often too much to want to process. After all, nobody knew how the Spirit would move in the service.

Davida had ridden home to the Gibbs' at Garnet's prodding. There would be more than enough food. Jamay was arguing in the back room with R.J. about something unimportant. Again. And part of her Jamaican accent was coming through. Again. That boy knew he could push her buttons in his own way. Davida had been rather quiet on the ride to Garnet's. Jamay had been attempting small talk with her, but she seemed preoccupied with texting on her phone. It kept making the periodic dings, informing of incoming texts. Jamay had even turned her head from the front seat to see if she was still breathing. When she did, she caught her smiling at one of the text responses and thought she'd ask about it later.

They finally got home, and started in. "I saw you grinning ear to ear in the back of the car. Who were you texting, girl?"

"Nobody."

"Well, if nobody was making you do all of that, I'd hate to see what somebody could do. That's what I was fussing at R.J. about in the back. I asked him, 'Who put these dirty underwear in this chair?' 'Nobody,' he would say. 'And who left these plates beside the bed for insects to be able to crawl on?' 'Nobody.' I told him that I was going to have to find this 'Nobody' and start charging him rent since he causing so much turmoil in this house."

"Girl, you and that R.J. always at it. But no seriously, it was just Tario being Tario."

"You light up every time you mention his name. We gone have to hurry up and get him saved, so you guys can walk down that aisle."

"He saved . . . I think."

"If you got to say, 'I think,' then he not saved, my love," asserted Jamay.

"Amen," interjected Garnet. "It's one thing to be saved. It's another thing to be good 'n saved. We need for him to be good 'n saved. When that devil get hot on his track, he got to be able to have some power to come against him. Ain't no good looks gone be able to help him when that time come. Can't be lukewarm and beat the enemy. You gotta be on fire."

"Jamay," said Davida, "don't get your mama started."

"You know it doesn't take much for her to get started, so . . . there you have it."

"Anyway, that's why I was texting Tario. He's actually on his way over here to pick me up. We just have a few things we need to talk about as it relates to us."

"Good," Garnet said. "He can come here as much as he wants, but he knows he gone get a good dose of Holy Spirit fire during his visit. He bold enough to come over here, he bold enough to keep hearing about Jesus. You heard Pastor Castillo this morning. No man knows the day. No man knows the hour. You just got to be ready."

"So, you really think Jesus is going to physically come back?" Davida asked honestly. "It just seems so out there, so farfetched."

"I know. But that's what we believe, that He's gonna come back and get his saints before the complete drama on earth starts. Once he comes back to get us, there won't be any more prayers to hinder the enemy from doing what he really wants to do in deceiving people and wreaking havoc. That's what some people say second Thessalonians, two and seven is referring to. The devil can't really do what he wants to do because the church is stopping him with its prayers and all. But once the church leaves, it's going to be a free-for-all."

Just then, the doorbell rang. R.J. ran from the back and straight to the door.

"Are you crazy?" Jamay stated. "Don't you go running to

that door and acting like you gonna open it. You have no clue who that is."

"Well, I heard Ms. Davida say Tario was coming over," R.J. snapped back.

"I don't care if you heard her say Hilary Clinton was coming over. You don't go opening doors in this house like you own it."

The doorbell rang again, accompanied by a rap on the door. Whoever it was was impatient. Just then, Jamay opened the door. As she said it, she said, "Who is this ringing the doorbell and knocking at my door at the same time?" She opened the door, only to be met by the lunatic Tario and his shenanigans. Belial tried to get him to go out with his boys since he knew how Garnet could be. She spoke of the Lord mildly when she was out and about, but she could be a beast in her own home. His efforts failed.

He started stepping and chanting at the same time. Only he and his group of special brothers knew something about it:

"I said whoooooo's that knockin' at my door?"
    Two foot stomps.
"Well it's the Quuues tryna break it on down!"
"I said who's that knockin' at my door? Well it's the Quuues tryna break it on down!"

He continued, stomping on Garnet's floor, making the armoire in the hallway shake and making R.J. give a hearty giggle. In fact, R.J. started mocking him, doing the stepping moves as best he could. Jamay could do nothing but shake her head and smile, while Davida looked at him like the was the best thing since free gubment cheese.

"Well you can break down my door if you want to. Just

make sure you have enough insurance money to pay for it," Garnet interjected as she put on her apron. "And if this armoire falls, it's gone be hell to pay. One can assume that you just love your Omega Psi Phi, huh?"

"Them my brothers, Dr. G. We done been through a lot together." He had pledged while at UC Davis and finally became a member after a grueling initiating process. "Ain't that right, R.J.?"

"Yeah."

"Oh, R.J. don't know nothing about that. Up there talking about 'Yeah,'" added Jamay.

Garnet resumed, "Well, I know a little something about fraternities and sororities. They mean well. Some people just go overboard with them. They can get to a point where they become a little too gung ho for me. I was a Delta at Tennessee State. We were oo-ooping all over the place. Lord, have mercy. I can't even fix my face to tell you all the stuff they did to us to see if we really wanted to be a part of that sisterhood."

"Trust me, I know, Dr. G," responded Tario.

"I remember vividly. I was finally crossing over, and it was the day of our inauguration service. They called each of us to the center, handed us a personalized plaque and said something to each girl once they reached the platform. We patiently waited for our turn in line backstage and couldn't hear any of the stuff being said over the microphone. It was supposed to be a surprise to us. I was wondering what in God's name they were saying. Individual, one by one, there was at least a one-minute call and response between the leader and new member. I would find out soon enough. Like it was yesterday. My sorors tease me to this day about it. My turn came, and I made my way to the center. The upperclassman gave me my plaque, and it all started from there."

"Soror Garnet Gibbs aka Li'l Chisholm, congratulations on being a part of the best sisterhood family on earth, that of Delta Sigma Theta, Incorporated. We pride ourselves in choosing the best of the best. So, you should count it an honor to join the ranks of Ruby Dee, Dorothy Height, Nikki Giovanni, and Mary McLeod Bethune. There is nothing greater than the distinguished Crimson and Cream. You should be proud to be a member for life. Please repeat after me. 'I pledge to serve while upholding the sisterhood of Delta Sigma Theta.'"

"I pledge to serve while upholding the sisterhood of Delta Sigma Theta."

"I vow to represent well the organization's Five Point Programmatic Thrust."

"I vow to represent well the organization's Five Point Programmatic Thrust."

"And I finally promise to dedicate myself wholeheartedly to the principles and mission espoused by Delta Sigma Theta Sorority, Incorporated."

"And I finally promise to dedicate myself wholeheartedly to the principles and mission espoused by my Lord and Savior, Jesus Christ."

"Dr. G, no you didn't say that. Not in the middle of the ceremony," said Tario. He had gone over and sat beside Davida.

"Hmpf. Yes, I did, too. The Lord don't play that. Even back then, I didn't play with the Lord. He said he was a jealous God. She was fine up until she said 'wholeheartedly.' When it comes to matters of the heart, you gotta be careful. The enemy's desire is to turn your heart away from the Lord, and he doesn't rest until he succeeds."

"So what did the poor sister say in the middle of the stage with everybody looking?"

"And listening, too," Garnet added. "My soror didn't know what hit her. She started stuttering through the rest of the pledge. She started shaking, too. Like she couldn't control herself. Clearly, she's never been put in that situation before. I didn't mean to cause a scene, but I had to stay true to my God. He said if you deny Him in public, then He'd deny you before His Father on that Great Day. I ain't trying to end up in that position. Li'l Chisholm had to stand up for right on that there day." She started chuckling as she set R.J.'s plate on the table.

Raphaela lay on Garnet's roof laughing an inaudible laugh as she listened to the recounting of the inauguration. She distinctly recalled the ceremony. She was the one who'd made the lady start shaking. While Garnet spoke during the ceremony, she had whispered, *"Lord and Savior, Jesus Christ"* in her ear right before she was to utter the sorority's name. It was one of the most hysterical comedic acts she had performed in centuries.

"Did they get your sorority name from Shirley Chisholm?" asked Jamay.

"Yeah. They said I was a firecracker like she was. She was a Delta, too. I guess they all found out that day just how much of a firecracker I really was. You just have to be careful with these allegiances you develop, especially with these types of groups. Just like my Uncle Sylvester was such a diehard member of the masons, that other fraternal organization."

"Oh, I think I know what you're talking about. My cousin is a member of the Eastern Star. Sometimes, they call them Shriners. Aren't they like a similar type group? He was always wearing that weird-looking hat that looks like a cylinder," added Davida.

"Yeah, almost one in the same. They do a great job when it comes to doing charitable work, feeding the hungry, and the whole nine. But when it comes to scriptural foundation, they encourage members to believe in a 'Supreme Being' instead of Jesus. And you get to have a relationship with that 'Being' through good works and community service. But when you get a chance, read what it says in Acts four and twelve. It's quite clear how we make good on our relationship with God."

"That's kind of deep, mama," Jamay interjected.

"I know. I stand by it, though. Most people join the fraternities and sororities and groups like the masons because of strong tradition and emphasis on goodwill and family values. Slowly but surely, though, you start drifting away from the Lord. As opposed to seeking the Lord for strength, help, and direction, you start trusting your networks and connections through those organizations. When you are a part of those groups, you may or may not pray to ask the Lord to be your daily guidance and seek his face about certain decisions in life. It's a tough way to view things, but when he said, 'no other gods before Me,' I take it to heart. Period. And sometimes, people join just simply to fulfill a need to belong. Humans just have an inherent need to feel accepted and be a part of something greater than themselves, not realizing they are already accepted in God's beloved. So, they keep seekin', searchin', lookin', hopin', and wishin'."

Jamay was waiting for her mother to say her usual Ephesians scripture about being accepted already in the Beloved, but it didn't happen.

"I'm finished," R.J. said, leaving some peas on his plate.

"No, you're not. Eat all of those," Jamay retorted.

"Dr. G, you just a maverick, just causing all of that commotion at your inauguration," Tario laughed. This was getting too heavy for him. He figured he'd get back to her original Delta incident.

"Yeah, I guess I am in my own way. I don't go on like this outside of this house, but you all are family. So I'm passionate about making sure the people who come into my world are right with the Lord." She started in more on Tario, "And since you came in here doing all that stomping and question-asking about knocking, I can tell you the main person who's doing the knocking. The one knocking on *your* door is named Jesus." She stomped twice, mimicking his earlier antics. Everyone fell out laughing, even R.J. Ordinarily, she was a shy lady. But around her kinfolk and friends, she sometimes was in rare form. "I'm sure you read Revelation, where it talks about him knocking. He said, 'I stand at the door, and knock.' He wants to prove to you how God He can be in your life. Now, don't keep acting like you don't hear Him knockin' and keep Him outside waiting. Just like we opened the door for you to come in and stomp your way into our house, you gotta open your door for Him. But He ain't gone stomp His way into yours. You gotta invite Him in willingly."

Tario continued, "I hear you, Dr. G, but I just don't know about getting with no white man's religion. How they stole people from other places and forced them into all that hard labor. It just ain't right. All them people packed on slave ships, stuck together like sardines. I know you seen them pictures before."

"Yes, baby, I have. And I'm not saying it was right. But if you're gonna use that as a reason not to follow Him, then don't think about selling no bean pies or Final Calls no time soon."

"Huh?"

"Well, Islam has its own checkered past related to imperialism. Its rise is very much connected with military and spiritual conquests. Much of west Africa was raped by so-called Christians, and much of north Africa was demolished by so-called Islamic conquerors, especially Egypt. They did numbers on Morocco, too, and on up into Spain and Portugal. Mohamed himself was a religious, political, and military leader. In other words, you don't think 9/11 just up and happened out of nowhere, do you? There is a lot of military background that's deep-seated in that community. And I know you've heard of the term *jihad* haven't you?" This was the stuff her graduate thesis was made of, and she shared it whenever she felt like it.

"Really?"

"And later for kneeling to some bald, fat guy sitting cross-legged."

"Man, what you talkin' 'bout Dr. G?"

"Buddhism ain't no better, considering what some of its leaders did in the name of so-called spiritual expansion."

"Say it ain't so, Dr. G? Not Buddhism. Hell, I just bought a picture with that Buddhist man on it and put it in my guest room. I got a nice rug and some candles and everything. I'm trying to get my *feng shui* on."

"Well, you better blow them candles out and roll that rug back up, not if you gone base your decision to follow its principles on its so-called aggressive past. Different forms of Buddhism have been instruments of war and violence. During the Meiji Restoration, Japan became a huge powerhouse of a nation in East Asia because of a few wars it instigated in the late nineteenth century. And it annexed Korea and captured Manchuria in the early 1900s. Several Buddhist nationalist movements justified Japan's military expansion as it related to the spread of Buddhist teachings."

"What 'annexed' mean, gramma?" asked R.J.

"It means 'added to itself' or 'took for itself.'"

"Y'all done got mama shonuff started," admitted Jamay. "She getting in UNLV mode, like we sitting in one of her history classes."

"All I'm saying is be fair. If that's the standard you're going to go by, do it across the board. Almost every religion has to some extent authorized some form of religious warfare. But it's probably not the true essence of the religion. Just because it's been misused doesn't mean it's not real at its core. You don't hear people say, 'This company is corrupt with all of its embezzlement, unfair treatment of Hispanics, and pay discrimination. I'm not gone work on no job nowhere. I'm done with the whole institution of work everywhere, period.' No, they just leave that corrupt company and find work somewhere else. Otherwise, they'll just end up jobless, homeless, hungry, and begging."

"Ms. Gibbs, you a mess," joked Davida.

"And I got one final shocker for you," the matriarch confessed. "Make sure you're sitting down."

All ears, they waited.

"What if I told you Christianity existed in Africa way before any European folk got there to spread their false version of it? Research it. Do your own study on it independently. Don't go by what anybody says, not even me." She sat on the couch and removed her academic hat. She placed her right foot on top of her left knee and started rubbing it. "Woo, what else is spreading is this pain going through this foot. It's barking like nobody's business."

"I hear you, Dr. G. I'm getting there," said Tario. "I'm gone do my own research. We'll see what happens."

Davida lit up. She was hoping he'd get his life together. The thought of spending the rest of her life with a blood-washed man was encouraging. Garnet was saying all the things Davida wanted to say, even though Davida was not in as strong a place in the Lord as she wanted to be. But at least she had reached first base and had given her heart to the Lord.

"Well, okay," Garnet said. "I'm gonna keep praying. My job is to plant and water. But the only one who can reach you ultimately is the Lord Himself. I just don't want you to get left behind, baby, when He returns."

"Returns? From where? Dr. G, you be weirding me out with your phrases."

"I'm just trying to talk what I believe is Bible. Pastor Castillo was talking about it a little today in service. The Lord is set to come back to get those who are in relationship with Him. On that day, people will actually rise to meet Him in the heavens. They'll defy gravity and be elevated to spend eternity with Him. It'll be the end of the dispensation of the Holy Spirit and will set the stage for 'The Great Tribulation.' And you don't want to be here for that. There won't be any restraining force to stop Satan from doing as he pleases on earth. You can still be saved during this time, but it will be much more difficult. Many more will lose their lives for failing to conform to the order of the day. It will be horrible. That's when the anti-Christ in the form of a person will be revealed and will mesmerize the masses because he will have observable powers. Or she. Literal powers. So everyone will believe that it *must* be God."

Tario and Davida started gathering their things to leave. "That's some scary stuff," declared Davida. "I'm think I'm just gonna take one step at a time and follow Him one day at a time. God knows, it's a challenge just doing that. I'll let God be God and handle stuff like that."

"I agree," said Garnet. "All we can do is do our part and stay ready."

"I got you, Dr. G. I got you."

"Well, you two be safe. Don't do anything I wouldn't do."

"That's a lot, Dr. G," joked Tario.

"Precisely my point. But you both grown, so I commit you into the Lord's hands. Just know He's watching you and watching over you every step of the way." She knew how to sick the Lord on them by making them know He was always watching. Davida was growing in Him, but that ole' Tario was cut from a different cloth. Garnet never played God in either of their lives, however. She lived and let live but only after giving her impromptu sermons.

"Bye, Doc." Toward R.J., he said, "Bye, big man."

"See you later, Tario. Bye, Davida," answered Garnet.

"Okay. Bye bye. I'll see you later, Jamay. We'll talk more about Jamaica later." They had talked last week about Jamay's going back to visit, not realizing that mother and daughter hadn't discussed it yet. It made Garnet perk up. She wondered why Jamay was contemplating a trip back there without talking to her about it. She'd ask about it later.

"Alright, girl. We'll talk," said Jamay, consciously avoiding Garnet's stare. Purposefully, she turned toward R.J. "Okay, little one, time for a nap."

R.J. got up and began stomping like Tario as he made his way to the back room. "Stop all that stomping," his mother said. "You're not Tario." To herself, she uttered, "I'll be so glad when your father comes back so he can teach you how to be a man. Good Lord. Everybody seems to be rubbing off on him." To the Lord, she said, *"Jesus, I need you to do more than take the wheel. I need you to take control of the whole car."*

12

YEAH, I KNEW

GARNET ARRIVED AT the track at Centennial High and started some pre-workout stretching. She tried walking in her neighborhood but often found herself distracted, finding a reason to reenter her home to retrieve the silliest thing, thus shortening her workout. Driving the thirty minutes to the track helped her stay focused. No clothes to put in the washer, no chicken to thaw out, no nothing. Plus, she could clear her mind spiritually. Listening to some good gospel music kept her mind calm, especially since the incident at church had transpired. She had seen a lot of stuff, but nothing where somebody straight out fell dead in church. Dead.

She got out of her Jag and moved toward the track. She didn't know where Celeste was. She was her typical late self. No matter what time was scheduled, Celeste always arrived on C.P. time. Garnet promised that she would start subtracting forty-five minutes from the actual scheduled time of their meetings, but she also hoped Celeste would grow up and start being punctual.

A car pulled up, but it wasn't Celeste. It was Randi. Garnet wanted to be a good shoulder to lean on and thought doing a little exercise would be good for Randi, with everything that must be going on in her husband-empty world now. She stepped out and saw Garnet.

"Hey, Nette."

"Hi, Randi. How's it going? How you holding up?"

"Pretty well, considering."

Just then, Celeste came driving around the corner and parked. She had on her fashionable tights, just in case. Who knew who would be at the track? She couldn't pass up on any possible suitors, and her Hello Kitty athletic gear was just the eye candy he would need. Unfortunately for her, only an eighty-year-old woman was the only other one on the track, creeping along.

"Well, I see somebody's ready to get sweaty," said Garnet.

"You just never know," replied Celeste.

"Celeste, you remember Randi from church," Garnet reacquainted them both with each other.

"Yeah, I've seen you around the church time to time," Celeste said toward Randi. "Glad to meet you formally."

"Nice to meet you, too."

"Okay, let's go. Let's get walkin'," said Garnet.

The three of them started walking at a semi-brisk pace. Water bottles and towels in hand, they each hoped to cover three miles, twelve laps. Really eleven in a half because they would walk in the outer lanes. Garnet was a little uncomfortable because of what happened at the church. She wanted to keep Randi encouraged but didn't want to come across too nosy or overbearing.

The gentle breeze was just what they needed to kickstart their motivation for the walking assignment for this day. Garnet lifted a hand, thanking the Lord for it. It was the only words any of them spoke for a whole lap. Just occasional grunts and "woo, chiles" that signaled how much of a task this was going to be. Garnet found a way to strike up small talk.

"You know, I used to walk alone in my neighborhood consistently," said Garnet. "But I started to lose focus. Every time I used to walk a lap, I always had to go back into the house to fetch something. Or pee. Or whatever. I had to get disciplined and drive here to work out. That way, I have no excuse not to get it done."

"I know what you mean," Celeste confessed. "It's hard to go at it alone. Seemed like my mind kept playing tricks on me, telling me I wasn't making no progress, that it wasn't worth it. But it's been better coming here and having a partner to work with. Makes it a whole lot better. At least for me, it does."

"I can't lose my momentum, especially with my health history. My doctor has stayed on me these last five years. I have to stay on top of things. The iron deficiency. The fibroids that came and went and came and went. I didn't know how many more surgeries I was going to have to deal with for those pests. They took 'em away and they came back. Such a mystery to me. I never *was* able to have children. Just had to make the best out of the situation. Staying active on a regular basis seems to be the best way to deal with this crazy body, which seemed like it grew a mind of its own the second I turned forty." They giggled.

"Yeah," agreed Celeste. "I'm not quite there yet, but that's what I keep hearing. That's why I'm gone start busting my tail out here. People ain't finna start callin' *me* R. Belly."

Randi exploded in laughter, throwing her head back, while Garnet shook hers. After a few moments of entertaining the hilarity of it all, they became more sober regarding the joke's reference.

"It's really sad when you think about it," admitted Randi. "I saw that documentary earlier this year and just felt so numb when I watched it. I was like, 'I can't believe this is happening now, as in today.'"

"I wanted to watch it with Jamay and my grandbaby," chimed Garnet. "I just haven't gotten up the nerve to do it yet."

"You wanted R.J. to see it?" Celeste asked, surprised. "It's some deep stuff going on in there. R.J. is so young."

"Yeah, I know. That's what has been causing me to hesitate. But on the other hand, the devil don't care nothing 'bout no age. The earlier he can get you, the better."

"That's true, Garnet," chimed in Randi. "If you look at it, that poor man was abused when he himself was R.J.'s age. Somebody said it was by his older sister. I'm no psychologist, but it seems like all the destruction he caused to all those girls and women was his way of getting revenge on her indirectly. Also, the girls he dealt with were pretty much spring chickens. So, when you look at it from those perspectives, the younger you can expose R.J. to the realities of this sick world, the better."

"You can call that man 'poor' all you want to. He just sick," Celeste barked. "It's plenty of men who have experienced that, and they don't go to those extremes to deal with it. The same thing happened to his younger brother; he was violated by the same person. He ain't resort to doing all that foolishness, though. Truth is, that man just sick and need some serious counseling. He used his position of power to dominate, manipulate, and get his own rocks off. He was a pimp, and he had a client of one: himself. Then, he got to where he was so busy paying people off and settling out of court that he ain't take the time to deal with himself to get the help he needs."

"Mm hm," added Garnet. "I hear you. People deal with abuse in different ways. Some people get caught up in it and perpetuate the same abusive cycle. Others become sensitive and overprotective of others, keeping a sharp eye out for it and making sure it doesn't happen on their watch. It's just strange how people can react differently to the same stimuli. But I will say that the only way this redemption thing works is that it has to be something in you that *wants* to change. If not, it's no use just going through the motions."

"It's just sad all the way around," Celeste said, as she gulped a bit of Gatorade. "And all those people in his camp just as guilty, knowing everything that happened and wouldn't do nothing about it. Got their eyes wide shut. All of 'em are complicit – body guards, assistants booking flights and hotel rooms, drivers. I don't see how any of 'em can sleep at night. They gone have to face the music eventually, no pun intended. He really could have helped those girls. And if they didn't have what it took to make it in the industry, he should have been honest enough to tell 'em. I ain't got to tell you what woulda happened if any of them girls were white. They woulda hung that man up by his nuts."

"Celeste!"

"Y'all know I'm right. And that's only if they didn't castrate him first. Then had a nerve to have one of the main girls do a so-called interview on TMZ. If you looked into her eyes, all you could see was confusion, sadness, and depression. You could tell she was trying to force herself to smile, but she just couldn't. It was like she was hoping somebody would be able to see she needed help. You could see hand gestures in the shadows of her shirt, so you knew he was in the background, telling her what and what not to say. Trying to cover up for that sicko. Her parents been ride or die throughout the whole process, but I'm sure they're heart-broken."

"Sounds to me like she has Stockholm syndrome," suggested Garnet.

"That's exactly what it is," Randi agreed.

"I guess another sad part about it is that he was raised in the church, too. Most Black singers that have become famous were. They just go on their own way and forget about their little humble beginnings and go on to make that paper. I wish more of them would come back to their local churches and the projects or communities they grew up in and at least give a speech, just so the kids can know they can make something out of themselves. You don't have to give a whole lot of money or any money at all. Just let 'em see you human. I could be wrong, but to me, it sounds like he has a God complex. And history has shown what happens to people who are plagued with *that* problem – Saul, Nebuchadnezzar, Belteshazzar, Satan."

"Ike." Celeste added her own villain. "And had the audacity to come to Whitney's funeral that time and fix his mouth to sing "I Look to You." Them dumb preachers sittin' up there eggin' him on with all their heads buried in the sand, just like they didn't know nothin' 'bout the stuff he been doing. I wouldn't've been surprised if he started gyrating and singing like this." She stopped right in the middle of the track and started mimicking the artist's suggestive concert behavior, "'I look to you . . . with a little bit of bump and grind.' Wouldn't've have been shocked at all. Right up in that pulpit. How 'bout he need to look to Him to free them girls so they can go on and have a regular life."

"See, Celeste, now there you go. You going overboard

now," inserted Garnet, half-jokingly. "We have to be careful not to judge. The Lord will have the final say concerning him. He takes into account the whole picture."

"Well, if holding him accountable for his actions is judging and if speaking up for his victims so he can't do it to nobody else is judging and if muting his concert venues as a way for him to get the point is judging, then yeah, I guess I'm judging . . . because all I see right now is a trail of tears." She remembered something else, "Oh and wait . . . you know he just recently turned himself in . . . for the exact same thing. Years later, they 'found' another video with another young girl. People were saying one of his disgruntled employees got upset with him for not paying them for overtime hours and leaked the tape. Better learn how to treat people right, 'specially if they got dirt on you."

"Are you serious? Arrested again? Lord, help the man," offered Randi.

"Let him himself help the man," Celeste retorted with frustration. "Lord, help the victims."

There was a moment of pause, of silent reflection. Physically, they all had found their sweet spot in the workout and almost seemed to be walking in lockstep. "You still over in the Summerlin area?" Randi finally broke the silence again.

"Yeah. I'm off of Tropicana," answered Garnet. "It's a small garden style. Big enough just for me. I had a two bedroom with a basement, but I had to move. I wasn't up for no massive upkeep. Seems like dusting didn't do anything but move the dust to a new place on whatever I was dusting. And the vacuuming, the mopping, the stair climbing, the everything. It was wearing me out."

They approached the elderly woman on the track again, who was walking in the opposite direction. As they passed each other each time, the woman gave a casual side-eye glance at Garnet. She saw Garnet often on the track but still remained intrigued at her odd appearance.

"Well, it's better than where I lived when I first moved here from Tennessee," said Celeste. "Ain't no place worse than that. I don't even know how I survived, living over there."

"Where was that?" asked Randi.

"Please don't get her started with that story," Garnet interrupted.

Ignoring Garnet, she continued, "Off of South M.L.K. Not far from the outlet mall. I didn't visit before moving here, and I didn't know anyone here either. I just looked at the website of the place, sent the deposit, and stepped out on faith."

"Or foolishness," joked Garnet.

"The apartment looked great, but the area not too far from it was horrible. I can't believe I fell for it. Every time I walked on that M.L.K., I kept looking over my shoulder. Didn't matter if it was day or night. Girl, you woulda thought I was an owl, the way I was walking and turning my head, making sure it was safe. People asking you for a quarter. Or a cigarette. Others sitting on benches, stoned. And once I finally made it home, it always seemed like anytime you turned on the news, M.L.K. was always the place of random gunshots. Or some woman getting hit by her husband or boyfriend. I had to get away from there. I think I stayed over there about three months, which was still too long in my book. It's a shame 'cause you would think it would make people live better knowing it was named after a man who fought to make things better for black folk, for all folk, really."

"My cousin lives in Atlanta," said Randi. "And she says they have an M.L.K. Drive there, too. Same basic story with all the craziness going on where that street is. Prostitution, drug pushing, the whole nine."

Garnet's scholarly side awoke. "Just about every city has one. Chicago, Baltimore, Cleveland, Houston, New York. Of course, Atlanta and Memphis. Even got some of his streets overseas, too. Germany, South Africa, Brazil, India."

"And I wouldn't doubt that ain't none of them in no nice neighborhood. Y'all remember when Chris Rock told those jokes about streets named after Dr. King? It was too funny. Y'all should pull it up on YouTube and watch it," said Celeste. "Poor man. If he could wake up now and see how much we haven't overcome, he would turn in his grave 180 degrees and lay upside down."

Garnet added, "Yeah, well while he at it, he might as well keep turning *another* 180 degrees and be right side up again, the way his children been actin'. Fussin' and fightin' with each other over stupid stuff like their daddy's Bible, who gone keep the Nobel Peace Prize. Every time you look up, they're in court fighting again over one more thing. That's some drama to make him do some more turnin', shonuff. That can't be the way he thought all this would turn out. Done unified the world, but his own kids at each other's throat. I guess his dream done turned into a nightmare." They all agreed, laughed, and drank a little water. Time flew by as they made their way around the track. Lap after lap, they engaged in small, unimportant talk, just enjoying each other's company.

Since the mood was lightened and the ice broken, Garnet thought this was a good moment to walk softly and zero in on the inevitable. After about another minute, she started in. "So, you say you doing okay?" she directed toward Randi.

"Yes, the Lord is giving grace. It's somewhat of a whirl-wind, but I'm okay."

"Well, just know I'm here if you need me."

"Thank you. I appreciate it. At this point, I'm not even taking one day at a time. I'm just living moment by moment."

"That's got to be a hard pill to swallow," interjected Celeste.

"Yeah, it is," answered Randi. "I can't say that what Kemal was doing took me by surprise, though."

"Really?" said Celeste.

"Yeah, I knew. The Lord gave me heads up about eight months ago. I didn't know He was going to handle it the way He did, but He's God. But, yeah, I was aware."

Said Garnet, "I have to admit that I was praying recently and was interceding for a number of people. I started praying strongly for Kemal, and the Lord told me to stop praying for him. That was actually the first time the Lord has ever told me to stop praying for anything or anybody. It was so weird. He didn't tell me why. Just told me not to talk to Him about Kemal anymore."

"I still don't get what you all mean when you said the Lord told you whatever," said Celeste. "I don't know if you mean He talks to you like a live human being or what. You all are scaring me."

"I hear you," Randi laughed. "He mostly speaks out of His Word, but if he needs to, He'll speak to you directly, most of the time through dropping His intentions or directions into your spirit. You just end up knowing what He wants you to know. Some people call it the Word of Knowledge, but He'll get you a message if He needs to. He knows you and your makeup. He made you and knows how you think, so He can get through to you if He needs to. But you aren't supposed to be listening for no voices, per se. If you hear a voice that tells you to walk off a building, that ain't God. I don't care how angelic it sounds."

"Speaking of makeup, I need to freshen up a little bit," said Celeste. She unzipped her jacket pocket and pulled out her compact, revealing reddish powder and an attached mirror. The brush followed next. While walking, she gave herself a basic touch-up, looking back and forth at her face and the track. "As I said, you just never know."

Garnet simply shook her head, knowing that no comment would do any good at this point. Celeste was Celeste, and that was that.

"It was sad," admitted Randi. "You would think your husband would have more sense than that. Everything started out so nicely. Our honeymoon pictures could have been on anybody's brochure. Then he started volunteering at the church more and more. I guess that's where he met the other young lady. She was a sweet woman from what I saw. I didn't interact with her that much. But apparently, he did. I'm not really sure what happened. Maybe it was because I was the quiet type and acted like I didn't know. He would come home and act so sweet. He would cook, clean, do everything."

"Maybe that was a guilty conscience," said Celeste. "I knew a few men who did that with me. Granted, I wasn't married to them. But when they started doing things without me asking, I knew something had to be wrong. And many times, it was. Low-down dogs."

"Be nice, Lessie," Garnet said.

Randi continued, "But more than being my husband, you would think he would do the right thing just being the Lord's child. When he didn't hold any positions in the church, he was just fine. As soon as he started getting elevated, he started to lose his mind. Started acting like he wasn't accountable to anybody. 'Mr. Untouchable' is what I started calling him. I guess he was feeling like him and God were buddy-buddy.

People don't realize that the more you go up, the more you better go down on your knees and stay humble. Or the Lord got a way to humble you Hisself. He's gonna hold the church to His standard more and more. People must think the Lord is playing when it comes to first peter, four and seventeen. But He's not gonna let the church just get away with stuff anymore. Too many sinners watching. They don't have any reason to feel like they have to come clean if we so busy hypocritin'."

"Amen, Randi, amen." Garnet knew it was good that Randi was able to get her feelings out. She was so meek and quiet and was known for holding a lot of her thoughts to herself. "So when's the funeral?"

"I don't know. His family members are still trying to wrap their minds around it. Most of them are in Selma, so they won't be able to get here. They're thinking of shipping his body and having the services there, especially his sister."

"But what do *you* want? You *are* the wife and should have some say."

"I wish I knew what I want? I just don't. What I do know what I want is peace at this point. So I may just honor their request, make a trip there, and call it a day. I'm still getting his things together. I've been looking at old pictures, wondering where things went wrong and what I could have maybe done differently."

"Don't start with that, Randi. You know this has nothing to do with you. People make their own choices in life and have to deal with the consequences of their own actions."

"What did the authorities say the cause of death was?" Celeste asked.

"Heart attack," answered Randi.

"Strange. It's the same title as Pastor Castillo's last message," noted Garnet.

"But I know better. I told them to write down D.B.G., but they thought I was playing. But I was as serious as the words 'heart attack' themselves."

"D.B.G.?" questioned Garnet.

"Death by God."

"Randi, stop!"

"You know it's true, and I know it's true. Too bad there's no box you can check off on the form that takes into account the hand of God."

"Well, we all know the Lord is going to have his way, box or no box."

"Let's hope he has His way with this last lap," said Celeste. "'Cause it don't feel like I'm gone make it."

"Almost there," encouraged Garnet.

Before they knew it, they were finishing up the last one hundred meters. Randi even had the audacity and nerve to start jogging.

"Go 'head, champion!" exclaimed Garnet.

"I'm a new me!" shouted Randi as she crossed the finish line. "The Lord is still worthy and still able to perform wonders!" She jumped around like she had just won a heavy-weight fight.

"I guess," said Celeste as she flopped to the ground, land-ing on her back. "Those three miles hurt."

"It's good pain," maintained Garnet. "No pain, no–"

"Yeah, yeah. We get it," interrupted Celeste. "We get it."

In fact, all three of them lay next to one another on the grass, reveling in their three-mile accomplishment. They agreed that death had struck, but it was strangely creating new life and a renewed sense of strength and hope.

13

YOU ARE OUR TARGETS

HARDWOOD FLOORS WERE a beast to keep clean. That was really the only aspect of Garnet's house that she disliked. It wasn't the best surface to protect her knees either, so her morning prayer experience included reaching for her flip flops and placing them comfortably underneath her as she entered into prayer. They weren't overly soft, providing sturdy and firm resistance against her frame. Placing one under each knee was the best remedy she had come up with over the years. Once they were in place, she was able to focus on weightier matters.

"Thank you, Lord. Thank you, Jesus." She whispered this for several minutes in His ear. *"Thank you, Lord. I thank you, Lord. You've been good to me. You've been kind. Hallelujah."* And then she would venture off in an unknown tongue. His presence would be physically apparent to her, rocking her to the left and right a little. *"Hallelujah. Thank you, Lord."* She spent five minutes with her elbows resting on the bed while both of her hands were stretched upward. Tears were beginning to form

in her eyes, and one managed to force its way out of her right eye, streaming down her cheek.

She prayed for blood covering for the usual cohort of friends and family. Jamay, R.J., Redd, Celeste, Davida, Randi, Opal, Nieko, Tario. Especially Nieko. Especially Tario. They were the normal names that rolled off of her tongue like clockwork. And whoever Krunchy was, she kept praying for him. Sometimes, she would change up the ordering to make sure the Lord knew she wasn't just saying names without thinking. She prayed for her family back in Toronto and anyone with whom she would come in contact today. She spent a good ten minutes interceding for church leadership, including Pastor Castillo and all other clergy in the Vegas area.

After a while, she started pacing the floor and continuing to bombard heaven with praises, thanks, and requests. It was often at this point when she would begin praying for people and situations that she didn't know anything about. Sometimes, she would turn and point to some invisible being or entity. Or she would draw closer to the window and start pointing in certain directions, binding the hand of the enemy. Gabriel loved when she prayed. He often walked around her apartment with her as she strolled and pleaded the blood. She prayed against terrorist attacks, ISIS-inspired meetings that plotted innocent peoples' demise. This prayer had been more intense over the past month. There was no news of such in any reports on news stations. But maybe it was because people like her took the time to pray and prevent it from happening.

"And Lord, bless this neighborhood. Cover us on the highways, trains, airplanes. Cover these houses in this area. I thank you because this area is blessed because I'm here. I'm your ambassador and know you'll protect these houses because I'm here. Don't *let any fires break out or any robbers break in. The blood be a shield. Be a shield. The blood. The blood."*

She focused more on her son-in-law. *"Lord, send angels now to cover Redd. Protect and cover him by your anointing. Lord, you know no distance. Protect and cover. Protect and cover."* Just then, Gabriel darted out of the room and was in Afghanistan within two seconds. He took a peek at Redd, saw that he was okay, and made it back to Garnet's room within two more seconds. He paused again, wondering if he saw more than he witnessed at first and decided to dart back across the oceans to see once again. Meanwhile, Garnet didn't miss a beat. She began clapping and lifting her hands. All while walking from room to room. *"Cover Marge. Cover everybody on campus. My students, Lord. Help them stay focused and pass my class. Cover the administration at the school. Help me be a light."*

She peaked in Jamay's room. She was sound asleep. So was R.J. Garnet had mastered the art of praying fervently and effectively yet quietly. She didn't have to pray like she was trying to wake up Lazarus. She was simply intense, quiet, and persistent. *"Bind up the hand of the enemy, Father. Every senator. Every congressman. Let your people in government speak up and speak out. Give them boldness and a backbone to stand for right. Shut the mouth of the enemy speaking in their ear. Touch Governor Sandoval. Mayor Goodman. The president. God, help them today. And Krunchy."* She still didn't know who this was, but she learned how to just flow with what was flowing. This would normally go on for about an hour, sometimes longer. It ended up as it normally did, with her back on her knees, atop the flip flops, allowing Him to speak to her heart and mind. She leaned against the bed and looked up to heaven with her eyes closed and hands raised. Several hallelujahs would escape her mouth until there was just silence, at which point she would read a few scriptures.

Gabriel had returned to Afghanistan and continued to mill about.

While the rest of the platoon dillydallied outside, Redd and Jerome engaged in small talk inside their quarters. Lounging was the best remedy for this limbo time. No more hardcore war. All they needed was the word from Washington and they'd be home in no time.

"I guess it's not too bad up here, huh?" asked Redd.

"That's how I know it's getting to you, my man," responded Jerome. "Whenever you have to find a reason why it's not as bad as you think it is, that's just your mind trying to cope with the conditions. Survival mode."

"Thank you, Dr. Jaxon. Where do I send the payment?"

"No payment. I'll just add it to your tab."

On cue, Redd replied, "Okay. While you're at it, add this, too." He let out the loudest prolonged fart. His position in the bed provided the best platform for the release. On his back, one leg extended and one leg bent, foot on bed.

"Damn, man! You rotten!" Jerome turned toward the wall on his own bed, as if that would stop the smell from traveling to his nostrils. "Nigga, you smell like five boiled eggs. You need to get your insides checked out. That don't make no damn sense." He flailed his sheets to push the smell somewhere else, anywhere else.

"My insides are just fine. It's the Afghan food here."

"Nigga, you been here how long? Your insides should have been done adjusted by now."

"It's my son. I think my insides are just nervous about not seeing R.J."

"Yo, whatever!" Jerome joked. "Get on with that bogus ass

excuse. Your insides just nervous about not seeing water. You need to start drinking more water. Damn!" Redd couldn't help but laugh. Soon, Jerome couldn't either. "Since I'm in counseling mode, here's some more advice. You thought about using Google Hangouts to talk with your boy? It's not the same as seeing him in person, but it's better than nothing."

"I'm not really up with all of that technology, man. I wouldn't know where to start with all that."

"That's why you learn, imbecile. It's a whole lot of stuff you didn't know before you learned how to do it. With everybody else here on base, hell, just ask. Jones uses it all the time to talk to her son back home. Must do it like three times a week."

"Sounds good. I knew you were good for something. But how will they know I'm calling? Don't we have to organize it?"

"Well, yeah. You have to set up when you want to call so everybody can be by the computer at the same time. Just account for the twelve-and-a-half time difference when you call."

"What? Yo, I forgot about that."

Just then, Chaz and Jones entered the common area, arguing about the mild competition they just had outside.

"That's why I don't like playing with you," grumbled Jones. "You always find a way to cheat."

"Why is it that when *you* win, all is fair in love and war? But when *I* win, it's a different story?" answered Chaz.

"We gone give you two some wedding rings and a certificate," yelled Redd from the bunk area. "What were you all playing?"

"Don't worry about it. All you need to know is that Chaz is a cheater," said Jones. "I see now how his parents got his name. They knew he was gone be full o' shit. That's exactly why they named him what they did. They started with cheatin' and ended with ass. Then, they put it all together and got his name."

"How long did it take you to think about that one, Jones?"

questioned Chaz. He had to admit to himself that that was a good one but would never give Jones the satisfaction of knowing how on point the joke was. But he didn't have to. The others acknowledged its strike value and wrote the invisible chalk mark in their heads. Jones, one. Cheatin' ass, zero.

Shifting subjects, Jones inquired, "You losers still going to Kabul to the poetry reading on this Thursday?"

"Oh yeah, I forgot about that," said Redd. "That may be a good change of pace for me. Ain't nothing happening 'round here. I need to brush up on my poetry anyway." He grabbed a towel, placed it on his head like a bonnet and stood with one hand on chest and another raised. He performed in front of an imaginary audience, "Ahem . . . Romeo, Romeo. Wherefore art thou, Romeo?"

Staring blankly at him, Jones instructed him on what he didn't know. "That's a play, fool!"

"It's all the same to me. Plays are full of poetry."

"Not that one. By the way, did you know that 'wherefore' doesn't mean 'where'? It means 'why.' She wasn't asking, 'Romeo, where you at? How come you runnin' late? We gots to go.' She was asking, 'Romeo, why do you got to be who you are? Why you got to have the last name that you have, knowing our families hate each other's guts? You wrong for that, Romeo.'"

Redd paused and shifted his eyes to the right, then to the left, the back to the right again. "And this lesson on Shakespeare, ladies and gentlemen, has been brought to you today by the letter 'S' as in 'So, the hell what!'" he retaliated.

"See, that's what's wrong with you all. You don't appreciate culture," Jones responded. "Anyway, Kabir called this morning and wanted us to confirm that we still wanted to come. Said he'd arrange for transportation to pick us up and even bring us back the next morning."

"As long as he doesn't pick us up in one of those jingle trucks, I'm good," said Jerome.

"We'll just have to see when they get here," said Jones. "It's about a two-hour ride, so he said they'd have to be here by late afternoon, early evening."

"What's the worst that can happen?" asked Redd. "Us gettin' caught behind a camel traffic jam?" No one but him laughed.

"Um," said Jones. "I don't know where you'll be riding. But where I'm riding, we're gonna be on roads, as in streets. We're not traveling two hours by desert, Einstein."

"Yeah, I knew that." Redd grabbed some water out the frig. "Oh yeah, Jerome said maybe you could show me how to do this Google Hangouts thing. I don't know nothing 'bout no part of technology that let you do that. We trying to set something up, so I can talk to my boy back in Vegas."

"Okay," answered Jones.

"What? No smart aleck remark about me knowing nothing about technology? That all I know about technology, I learned in kindergarten? Or when people ask me where I was born, I tell them, 'On Facebook'? Nothing?"

"See. I've programmed you well. I don't have to. You do a good job at it all by yourself. We can set it up for Thursday, before we leave for Kabul. Just email your people at home and let them know what time to be ready. It's probably better for us if we do it shortly before we head out to Kabul."

"Thanks." He turned up the TV volume, plopped on the couch, pulled out R.J.'s picture from his wallet, and stared at it. Aside from the red hair, the kid was Jamay's spitting image.

The ten were one. The script had been rehearsed several times before so that no nerves had to be dealt with. They sat perched in a semi-circle, cross-legged, backs straight with rifles in hand standing at attention, the butts of which rested on the dirty floor. Black was the obvious color choice for the uniforms. They were almost heroic. Almost. Completely covering their heads could have been interpreted as cowardice. The other ones who had done this had shown face and did it with pride. But these justified their visage shrouding by agreeing that it would make them more effective, strategic, deadly. As the others sat stoically, staring at the virtual audience, the spokesperson stood, cleared his throat, peered at the camera, and began. The blinking of the red light confirmed the camera was recording. In Arabic, he calmly spoke.

"To America and its allies. You will not defeat us. We stand unified, united, ready to defend Allah's will and Allah's way. You think you scare us with your threats and your bullying. But we will strike back. We will strike the soldiers, strike your police, strike your security, and your intelligence members."

As he spoke, Mictian paced the room, circling all ten, walking between the speaker and the audience, undetected by either. He was quite the proud one and couldn't wait to report back to the others.

"We will target your major cities in America, France, Australia, and Canada. This next wave of attack will make 9/11 look like a picnic. You are our targets, especially your Christians. We will wipe them out and make their blood nourish our Afghan soil. You cannot escape us. We are where you are. We blend in well. We're your teachers, your neighbors, your co-workers.

Don't be cowards and attack us with drones. Instead, send your soldiers, the ones we humiliated in Iraq. We will humiliate them everywhere."

After finishing two more fiery pages of wrath, the leader was finished. He slowly walked toward the camera, reached out his finger, and turned it off. The red light disappeared, reassuring everyone that all was clear. They began ripping off their headgear to get some fresh air. Many of them were still getting used to just how uncomfortable those contraptions were. Breathing in and out of the mouth during these recordings was just par for the course. They could endure a little discomfort for the greater good. As they placed their guns on the ground beside them, they relaxed a little, proud of their stand in solidarity. The spokesman eased away from the camera, double-checking to make sure it was really off, and finally took a seat on the floor among the rest. Grabbing the mask with both hands, he wrestled a bit to get it from underneath his chin and then from around his nose and then from over his eyes and finally from over his head. Using his right hand to stroke through his brunette hair, he was back to being his normal self, back to being Baktash.

Everyone dispersed, blending in with the normal Afghan evening crowd. People were merely focused on getting home to just live and be. Feed the kids, unwind, watch a little Tolo TV. Only a few had become activists, dedicating themselves to making their country better by opposing the American agenda within the borders of their nation. It didn't matter to them whether there were only a handful of themselves; strength to them wasn't measured in numbers. One could get the point across very well if calculated correctly. Devout husband reformers had a way of convincing the wives that the cause was not just worthwhile but necessary. Her role in it would be crucial to the furtherance of Allah's law and will. Fathers trained their sons to be warriors of the movement, both intellectual and physical, if need be. They trained their daughters to be sympathizers. That way, they could grow up to be supporting activist wives. And the cycle perpetuated itself. Well, almost. Baktash's son was only three months old, so he'd have to wait to teach him the sharia law of the land. And his wife was no shrinking violet.

"How was the meeting?" asked Najiba.

"Fine," answered Baktash. He was far from the jovial persona he exuded when around others. That was his real costume. At home and at the meetings, he was direct, calculating, mission-oriented. He and Najiba had been married for five years; they'd witnessed how things developed in the country they loved over the years. "Just fine."

"That's good." She smiled a bit after he pecked her on the cheek. Although rather focused on the overall goal, he was still romantic. "Zahoor has a slight fever. He's not doing so well. He's not really eating anything."

"Poor kid." Baktash went over to the baby's crib and planted one on his cheek, too. He lifted him, sat down, and let him rest his head over his shoulder. Indeed, the youngin' was a bit warm. He was the only thing that made Baktash's heart melt. Yet, his birth was planned, scripted. The father only wanted a son to move the mission forward. It was crystal clear. He'd have someone to continue the fight. "Where's his bottle?"

"In there." She pointed at the stroller.

Securing the bottle, he tried to get Zahoor to drink. The kid was having none of it. Not a bunch of crying and fussing. Just rejection. He kept moving his little mouth from the tip.

"Well, little buddy, if you're not hungry, you're not hungry. I won't force you."

"So were many there?" asked the wife. She'd hope he would feed her details, but he never did. Goings-on at the gatherings were held close to the vest. Wives knew of the seriousness of the matter but not how far their own husbands would go sometimes to make their points. She was well aware that Baktash had assumed the role of leader of the devoutly rarefied band.

"About the same, nothing major. The same faithful few." He normally resisted the urge to provide specifics to her but had recently been feeling inclined to share more and more. "You know, Allah is depending on us to keep his torch of hope and freedom lit. No outsiders are going to come in here and impose upon Allah's will." He started walking around, eventually getting to the crib. He placed Zahoor, who had fallen sound asleep, back inside and continued on. "Nothing will hinder Allah's will and our future."

"God be praised," Najiba agreed.

"What do we stand for? It's no time to be silent. They come from the outside and try to change us. And we should stay silent? Silent is death. We have to stand up and uphold his will." He went on and on, pacing about the house. During his rant, he mentioned those ungodly American soldiers that he and Kabir visited regularly in the jingle truck. He had to smile whenever he was around the troop so as not to blow his cover, but he would behead each and every one of them, if he had his way. He casually disclosed that Kabir had invited the troops to his side of town to the poetry reading.

"He did what?" she questioned, not believing her ears.

"Yeah, you know Kabir. He loves the new direction the

country is going. He told them he thought it would be a good idea if they came here to Kabul for the poetry meeting."

"The one creative thing we have on our own, and now they have to trespass there too. It's not just enough to come to our country. Now, they have to invade our artistic space, too?" She was noticeably livid. Baktash seemed somewhat pleased. He hadn't really seen her that worked up over news such as this. He had underestimated her. She was ready to help, which was a shock to him. Women weren't really allowed in the fore of the movement because of their perceived fragility. Not even the teachings of the land allowed for the extremist of females. But they could help in other, more substantive ways.

All three sat at the dinner table, mulling over their thoughts. Two of them couldn't wait for this drama to subside so that things could get back to normal. Didn't the American government know things would regress back to the way they were before the cavalry rode in? Troops couldn't stay there forever, so it would just turn into a waiting game. Until then, the goal would be to make the troops' lives as much of a living nightmare as possible. But how? Baktash placed his elbow on the table and fit his chin into his palm, allowing his fingers to cover his mouth. He stared at the portrait of Hamid Karzi, which hung next to the refrigerator. Slowly leaning over to Baktash, Mictian began whispering a string of suggestions into his ear. Almost dumbfounded, Baktash wondered why he hadn't thought of something like this earlier. *How stupid of me*, he thought. Mictian pulled away, wearing a grin for the ages. Baktash kept his body, face, and elbow right where they were. Only his eyes moved, from the portrait to the wife. He moved his fingers away from his mouth and made the most satisfying statement as his eyes radiated.

"I have an idea."

TO GO OR NOT TO GO

14

"SO YOU'RE THINKING of going to Jamaica?"

She was hoping that her mother had forgotten about it, but Garnet was an elephant. "Yes, mama. It's just been something I've been thinking about here recently."

"Well, it's not like I didn't imagine this day was coming."

"I don't know. I guess it's just something I've always thought about, especially the older I get. I don't want to come across like I'm ungrateful. You know I appreciate all the love you gave to me then and now."

"No need to explain, baby. I guess it's only natural that children grow up and want to know the truth. Everybody wants to know where they came from. I think it's a gnawing that God puts in people so they have a sense of belonging."

"I feel like I belong, mama. You're my family. R.J. is my family. And Redd. And Davida."

"You know what I mean. It has much to do with your heritage, too. Your Jamaican roots. I just wish you would have spoken to me about it first. It hurt a little when I heard

Davida mention it. I figured you would eventually get to this point, but a part of me was hoping you would discuss it with me first."

"I know. We were just casually talking and it came up. I didn't plan to tell her. She was talking about going there on vacation. Before I knew it, I told her I'd love to go back one day to do some investigating on my own. It wasn't like I set out to put her in my business. I'm sorry, mama."

"Don't worry. No need to apologize. Just know that you are loved." She thought now was a good time for a joke. "At least after I finally got you, nobody looked at me anymore like I was a freak. You had a way of stealing the show."

They laughed a bit. "Aww, ma. You're not a freak. You're beautiful just the way you are. The Lord said we're fearfully and wonderfully made."

"Emphasis on the 'fearfully' part with me. Maybe I'd be a little terrified if I saw me and didn't know me either."

"Ma, stop it." They were comfortable talking about Garnet's appearance this cavalierly at this point. No stress.

"I couldn't pass you up. I must have visited that foster home at least four times, before you were born and then after. It was a really nice lady who helped me through the process. I never wanted you to feel as though you weren't loved, but I didn't want to spoil you either. That's such a challenge, trying to find that balance."

"You did a wonderful job. I can't really explain why I wanna find what I'm looking for. It's just a curiosity I have inside."

"It makes sense to me. Biological parents are important. It's a part of your life's puzzle that can add a little clarity to who you are. Let me know when you're going. I'll give you the contact information of the agency there, but be prepared for whatever happens, though. No telling if things will line up the way you may be expecting. There may be some laws in place that might hinder what you're trying to do. I know that in the States, you just can't go barging back into people's lives. They're real strict about that. You can get sued if you contact them if they signed certain legal documents."

"Do you know their names?"

"No, the agency wouldn't give me that information. Granted, I didn't put up a big fuss about it. I was just happy to know I was finally going to be able to give some love away. Only thing I heard was that you were placed in the system because your mother was so young, around fourteen or fifteen. Not sure about the father."

"I'll go online and find out more about the place, just as a starting point. I know nothing may happen, but at least I want to try."

"Good for you, Jamay." She thought that now was a good time to lighten the conversation a bit. "List one person in the Old Testament and one person in the New Testament who were adopted and went on to do great things."

"Mama, it's too early."

"Oh, c'mon. Let's see what you learned in Bible school."

"Mama, you know they don't talk about stuff like that in Bible school."

"Well they need to. They can't assume the Lord only blesses those who come from regular, traditional homes. He uses all types of people. Name one."

Jamay thought and thought and thought but couldn't place anyone. She knew she should have known and would be able to find it through careful study, but her mother had caught her unawares. "Let's see." Finishing up the tea, she pensively looked upward. "I don't know, mama."

"Remember Esther? Smart and drop-dead gorgeous. They

don't teach in Sunday School that she won a beauty pageant back in her day."

"Oh, my God. Yes, she sure was."

Garnet continued with the antics, imagining herself the pageant host. Grabbing the spoon that she used to stir her coffee, she made it her microphone. "And the winner of Miss Persia 478 BC is . . . Esther from Shushan! Come hither, Esther, and taketh thine crown. Take a seat beside your new husband and partner for life, King Xerxes."

"Must have been nice to have all of that fame and clout."

"Perhaps. But remember she won so that the Lord's purpose would be fulfilled. She didn't simply win so that she could sit on top of a camel and wave while riding through her own parade, celebrating her own self. The Lord put her in place to spoil the plot to kill His people. He gave her favor to win so she could be in position to help His children. When the Lord gives you favor, He has more than you in mind. That should be a good way to help us stay level-headed. We realize we aren't all that. Such an inspirational woman. Some sources say that her daddy died while her mom was pregnant, and her mother died during childbirth. Her uncle decided to adopt and raise her, and the rest is history."

"Herstory. Her story."

"His story."

"Cute."

"We don't talk about stuff like that in the church. But like Esther, we're supposed to have purpose outside of the four walls and make an impact in the world for His kingdom. Most of us are too interested in impressing people in the church but never become a witness in our own spheres of influence, major or minor. And when the Lord finally does give some of us a platform, we squander it and forget Him. That thing called fame can be a beast. Anyway, how about the New Testament? Name someone else who was adopted who went on to do great things."

"You got me gain on this one, mama. It doesn't say anything about anybody being adopted in the New Testament."

"Yes, it does. It's so obvious that it's right under your nose. You remember the saying, 'If it were a snake, it would bite you'? Consider yourself about to be bitten."

Jamay pondered and pondered to no avail. "Mama, see. You always do this."

"Give up?"

After thinking for another minute, she admitted defeat. "Who, mama?"

"Your Lord and Savior."

Jamay laughed but not too loud so as not to awaken R.J. "How you figure that?"

"He was, baby. He didn't come from Joseph's loins. He came from God's throne itself. Remember how Joseph was skeptical and was going to leave Mary? He probably thought she had cheated on him. The Lord Himself had to step in and let Joseph know this was all in the Plan."

"You a mess."

"And Joseph had to make a decision to obey the Lord. He chose to adopt Jesus and be his surrogate father. Now that's a strong man, having to raise somebody else's child when you still able to make your own baby. Anyway, it's just one school of thought, one perspective. It may be a little farfetched, but I get it."

"Well, maybe you're kinda right. I don't think brothers in the twenty-first century would be able to do anything like that. Even with God Himself sending them a dream, brothers nowadays would just take a loss on that one and be out."

"Perhaps. The Lord would have to know whom to trust when it comes to weighty matters like that. But that's so amazing. He was adopted and did his Father's will to turn this world right side up." She tried to regain focus regarding the original topic at hand and tried to reassure her daughter of all possibilities. "Anyway, whatever happens, be at peace with it. And as I always told you, the Lord doesn't love you any less. In fact, he has a special place in his heart for those of you who have gone that route. You're one of His special ones."

To prepare herself for the day's running and rippings, Jamay placed her forehead on the table while gathering her mind. She'd have to pick up some shoes for R.J., secure a few groceries for dinner, and fill in Davida on this conversation. So much to do, so little time. "We're all special in His eyes, mama. We're all special."

15

WERK AND SERVE AND SLAY

"YAAS, YOU BITCH!"

"She is killin' it!"

"Werrrrrrrrrrk, Nieko!"

"Serve, Neek!"

"The slayage is real! You better slay, girl!"

The peanut gallery was giving Nieko his props as he performed during the summer ball. Between the flinging hands, the air kicks, the duck walks, the dips, and the drops, Nieko's voguing skills were not to be played with. When he was really feeling it, he would constantly flip his head back and forth as if it were full of hair, right before he dropped himself to the floor in dramatic fashion. Onlookers lifted their right hands and repeatedly snapped their fingers, their version of clapping. A few drag queen judges sat on the stage with legs crossed, fierce. It was their decision to determine whether Nieko would be chopped or not. There would be no chopping today, though. He had learned how to coordinate his routine with the announcer's chants, which added to the overall theatrical effect. By the time the chant crescendoed and climaxed, Nieko ended up on his back, wowing the crowd and securing the accolades of all. He had finished his routine. All that could be heard were choruses of "Yas," "Eat it!," and "Yes ma'am!" Another performance made it through the judges' keen sense of evaluation. The announcer yelled his form of congratulations, "Tens across the board! Stand to the side."

After all preliminary rounds were done and the final battle was done, Nieko emerged as the overall runner-up and would receive a cash prize. When the competition finally ended, the DJ needed a well-deserved break. So before the butch realness phase would begin, he would let the crowd go wild and feed their frenzy. He turned on the track for "The Ha," which eventually led into Basement Jaxx's "Fly Life." These were two of the anthems the crowd so desperately loved. When the music started, members of the different houses hopped onto the stage one by one and began their Naomi walks and Tyra struts. They got to the end, posed, and turned back around to return to their starting point. Attitudes for days. There must have been about twenty or more men stallion-walking, half of them in heels, as if Christian Dior himself were in the audience conducting a runway search for an upcoming Paris show. Among them was Nieko, moving, gliding. His feet were wheels. He felt so at home.

But that was then, two summers ago at the Latex Ball in New York City. He traversed his way to the east coast to go after the prize, the clout, the love. He decided to walk away from it all, the glamor, the glitz, the everything. No more ballroom scenes. No more Labor Days in Atlanta or Memorial Days in D.C. And frankly, Miami Sizzle for him had sizzled out. Managing to kick all of his past life to the curb, he lived a pretty uneventful life. His new friends were those around his catering job at the university and at the church and some even from his former lifestyle, the ones who didn't try to make him explain himself into oblivion. Many of his old friends called him a hypocrite, claiming he was trying to be better than them. One of them promised to save a seat beside the catwalk for him because he would be back on the scene soon. Shady. He didn't lie and claim that he didn't have some of the same feelings. He just made a weird decision to steer clear of following them. He'd joked to himself often that maybe becoming a monk would be the right choice for him then quickly tossed the thought, realizing that route would be rather futile.

He was no Superman, though. If he resembled the superhero at all, it was the kryptonite version. He had learned how to steer clear of temptation, except for those rare moments. There was just something about his ex that wreaked havoc in his mind and especially his body. As long as Nieko could avoid him, he was fine. The bubble of his condo was just the shield he needed. As he watched the finale of *The Voice*, he found himself rooting for the contestant who was a country singer. His rendition of "The Old Rugged Cross" was unexpected and on point. All of America was getting a dose of Christ on live television. He was digging Pharrell's style and watched to see the rags he'd be wearing this go-round. As the winner was about to be announced, he received a text, which he ignored. He turned the volume up a couple of notches so he could experience the moment like he was in the audience. Carson Daly had prepped viewers and had paused as long as he could before declaring the winner to be the selfsame country singer. He gave Blake, his coach and mentor, a hug and enjoyed the confetti that rained down. By this time, he heard a knock at the door, actually a banging at the door, a fist pounding.

"Yo, open up, Neek."

Nieko looked through the peep hole. Kryptonite was knocking.

"Mo, what you want? What are you doing here?" yelled Nieko through the door.

"I gotta piss, Neek. I sent you about five texts. I was in the neighborhood and saw the light on through your window, so I knew you were home. I'm 'bout to piss on myself, Neek. Open the door."

"Don't open the door," warned the Holy Spirit.

"Pee outside," said Nieko, hoping that would solve the dilemma.

"I ain't pissing outside, yo. You trying to get me arrested? Damn, man, come on! I ain't trying to do nothing to you. I'ma piss and leave." Against better judgment and advice, Nieko agreed to let him in. He unlocked the door and cracked it open. Maurice pushed through, exclaiming, "Why you playin'?!" He rushed to the john, unzipping his pants in the process. An ungainly spectacle it was, almost funny.

Nieko sat on the couch, listening to the urine flow hitting the water, which had that deep, full sound. It was one of Nieko's strangest weaknesses with Maurice. That sound. It reminded him of what it implied, what he knew. That sound meant one thing and one thing only. Small peters only made the water sing alto or soprano.

"You were about to make me piss on myself, Neek."

"I didn't make you do nothing. You shoulda peed before you got in your car, Mr. 'Just in the Neighborhood.'"

"Anyway, 'preciate that playa. A nigga had to drain the vein. What you in here watching? You ain't gone offer a brother no wine."

"I was watching *The Voice*. It done went off. You know I

don't drink no more, Mo. And you said you were going to run in and run out. So bye."

"I don't know why you trippin', son."

"I ain't trippin'. I just know my limits. I ain't tryin' to go there no more."

"Limits? Go where? Your mind be playin' tricks on you, Neek."

"Nah. No it don't. Just trying to stick with my commitment. I know you might not understand, but it's all good." He was putting up a strong face, but he hoped Maurice wouldn't try anything. He wasn't sure if his actions would match his confession.

"It's hot as shit out there. I'll just chill just for a minute, and I'll be out of your hair. So, tell me about your church. Are they the ones putting you up to this?"

"Putting me up to what? This is my choice, my decision. Why it can't be that I can have my own mind concerning this?"

"Tell him to leave, son," said the Holy Spirit. *"You're not strong enough yet to entertain him for this long by yourself."*

"I'm just saying. I just don't understand this new you." He took the liberty to grab the remote and turn to the rerun of the summer's NBA finals game. "The Warriors shattered all LeBron's hopes for another title. This probably gone be the last season he stay with them Cavaliers. I know I wouldn't stay no longer. He can't carry that city forever."

Nieko pretended to be interested in the basketball game but couldn't focus. His body began responding to what he remembered about being intimate with his visitor. He moved from the couch to his blue accent chair for one.

"Yo, come on now. You ain't got to move. I'm just watching the game."

"If your goal is what you say it is, tell him to leave. Or you

leave and tell him to close the door when he decides to go home.
How serious are you about the change you say you want?" The
Holy Spirit was gentle but persistent in offering his sugges-
tion again.

Nieko figured he'd better take heed this time; he got up
and headed for the door. "I'll have to do my best to explain it
to you later. No matter what I say, you'll never really understand it. I know you, though. All you got is one thing on your
mind right now." He reached the door, unlocked it, and began
to turn around.

Maurice was indeed the sly one. By the time Nieko turned
from facing the door, Maurice was up close on him with both
hands on Nieko's waist. "Just relax, Neek. It's all good. It's me.
I ain't no stranger. We got history. Just relax." He pressed himself against Nieko, hoping they'd make it to the bedroom or
kitchen table or wherever.

"Nah stop, Mo. I'm good. For real. I ain't trying to do
that no more." He was handling the kryptonite rather well,
although he realized he shouldn't even have had to. He just
wanted Maurice out. Admittedly, he had gotten weak. He
had been celibate for quite a while but clearly remembered
the sex. He had since learned how to cast down imaginations
when they came. Sometimes it worked. Other times, it didn't.
They engaged in back-and-forth banter for about two minutes. Maurice wouldn't let go, hoping his ex would break. He
hoped Maurice didn't persist; he was quite the charmer and
knew how to get what he wanted. He kept giving responses
along the lines of, "I'm good, Mo" and "Nah stop, Mo."

"Come on, Neek. Why you doin' this? Just do it and
ask for forgiveness? It's just one time. Nobody gone know. I
thought you liked the pipe."

Realizing he should have taken the Holy Spirit's advice

earlier, he tried to stand his ground after praying in his mind. "I'm good, Mo." He removed the hands resting on his waist and just held them. "I can't, man. It don't have nothing to do with you. Trust me. If I didn't believe it's sin, I'd probably go through with it, yo."

"I'm sayin' though, baby. What if you wrong? You puttin' all this pressure on yourself. What if you wrong? You only live once."

"Yeah, I know. But what if I'm right? You may only live once, but you also only live forever. I ain't trying to make the wrong choice and have to pay the consequences."

"Consequences? What consequences? Come on, now, Neek. You buggin'. You just human, yo." His member hadn't gone down yet. He really was pressed to get Nieko to indulge one more time.

"Nah, man. I'm good. You know I love you, Mo. But I think I love Him more."

Noticeably erect, Maurice respected him too much to force it. He laughed it off and tried to save face. "Aight, Neek. I hear you, son. You know I could get it if I *really* wanted it, though, right?" He acquiesced, refusing to press the issue. He'd just call Tameesha, his baby's mother, later tonight and satisfy his desires with her.

"Yeah, okay. I'm sure you could." He unlocked the door and opened it. "I'm glad I could be of service to you tonight, Mr. Maurice."

"Well, it wasn't really the kind of service I was looking for, but I guess I better take what I can get. But a brother can't even get no water?"

"To fill up your bladder again and for you to be running back in here talking about how bad you got to drain the vein, or however you call it? I think not."

"Smart ass. You and your smart mouth. That's why I love you, boy. You the only one that can go toe-to-toe with me intellectually."

"Mo, this is not hardly an intellectual conversation."

"See, told you. Let me get my ass outta here. Some of us gots to go to work tomorrow."

"Yes, some of us do. Take it easy, and I hope you washed your hands."

"Nah, but you can wash 'em for me." Maurice made his way outside. He wasn't completely soft yet, but thank goodness it was nighttime. So nobody would see it. "I'll holla at you later, playboy." He unlocked the door with his remote and slid inside.

"Aight, Mo. Be safe, man."

"Call me if you get lonely."

Nieko shut the door and leaned his head back against it. He couldn't believe how fast all of this unfolded. He had just finished watching a finale and within seven minutes, he was staving off sex. He turned the TV off and just decided to go and lie on his bed. The memories had been stirred, and he was feeling some type of way. He really did want to be with his ex, but he wanted to stick to his guns more. The mental struggle he felt was torturous—as if he were trapped between two worlds. All the previous experiences with Maurice had become awakened, even though this time nothing happening. He pondered a bathroom visit to grab the Vaseline and towel. His laptop, he thought, could come in quite handy right about now. Those porn sites would provide some brief relief without the actual sex. Or maybe he would just call the phone chat line to talk to anonymous people in heat and get his rocks off that way. He could change back to his softer voice and catfish unsuspecting victims, convincing them to send their pictures and nude images. At least he could look and wouldn't have to deal with face-to-face encounters, just an imagined one, which often led to nowhere fast. After the tug of war continued in his mind, he decided to roll onto his knees by the bed and just kept whispering, *"Jesus."*

"I got you," said the Lord. *"I got you, and I love you. But this could have been avoided, my son. This could have been avoided."*

16

GOING UP!

ORDINARY IS HOW you could say Garnet's day began. After her normal communion with the Lord, she headed out to her classroom. Today, she was fortunate that she'd be giving final exams for the summer, so that would allow her a bit of rest, although she always managed to find something important to catch up with during exam time so that the two hours would be used constructively. Most of the time, she found herself interceding for the students taking the exam. She hated failing students but often did. Maybe her prayers would get them over the hump, but she knew it was no hope for her prayers if they hadn't studied.

Between the losers who slowed to a snail's pace after cutting in front of her and a certain security guard who refused to let her onto campus without seeing her faculty ID, she made it to the office about forty minutes early to gather her mind and decompress. At least the Vegas heat, normally unforgiving and unapologetic, was on the mild side. It was actually rather cool, unseasonably so.

"Good morning, Opal."

"Hi, Dr. Gibbs. How are you?"

"I'm here," laughed Garnet.

"Well, so is that plant?" joked Opal. She pulled on her iced tea lemonade from Dunkin Donuts. "That's what you say to people who give that kind of response to you."

"You're right!" laughed Garnet. "You got me. It's just these drivers in the city are pathetic. And I don't know why Walt has daily amnesia when it comes to whether I work here or not." She quit the complaining. "But you are definitely right. If I could sing, I guess I'd sing 'I Won't Complain.'" She pushed past to get to her office and just sat.

"Ohh! Not that one," said Opal through the air. "Any one but that one. By the time he get to the end, I don't know if he singing or getting his tooth pulled, with that scratchy voice."

"He does seem to be struggling a little, doesn't he?"

"By the way, looks like you have a dinner appointment with Attorney Zimmerman this evening."

"Goodness. I forgot about that. I wonder why my phone didn't remind me about that. I thought I set it to remind me. I would have left him high and dry. Where is it?"

"The Eiffel Tower Restaurant. Starts at 7:30."

"I sure would have missed it. Looks like I'll have to bring R.J. with me. Jamay will be pulling another late one tonight. What would the world do without grandmothers, Opal? I tell you."

"I'm sure that's a rhetorical question, right doctor?"

Before she got too comfortable, she remembered that she had to remind Marjorie that the diversity meeting had been pushed back a week. Garnet was sure Marjorie would get the message, but she was worst at e-anything. She checked her email so infrequently that she would often be guilty of finally responding to messages that were two months old. As a courtesy, Garnet kept her abreast of anything that both of them were a part of.

"I'll be right back. I've got to go down the hall to Marge's one second." As she left the office, she realized she very well could have picked up the phone and gotten the same results, but a little more exercise wouldn't hurt.

One of her students passed her in the corridor as she made her way. "See you in a few, Dr. Gibbs."

She spoke and acknowledged the student and made the right turn into the office area. Renee, the administrative assistant, would probably be back soon. Garnet decided just to head into Marjorie's office, whose door was opened. Entering the doorway, she took to it.

"Can't stay long, Marge, but I just wanted to remind . . ." Nobody was there. She'd just take a seat in what she assumed was the student's chair beside the professor's desk. In all of the hustle and bustle, she had never really been inside of Marjorie's office. It was always in passing, sticking the head in and rushing out. There was a nice vintage clock that hung from the wall. It had an actual mini-pendulum that made that tick-tock sound. And a small cactus plant that graced the desk. Surprisingly, it added to the sense of class in the office. It was both retro and modern in its own strange way. And the mahogany shelves were replete with all kinds of history books. A copy of the grant that was written earlier in the summer was neatly placed in the to-do tray, although it was done. And this. And that.

And the picture. The framed wallet-sized picture. One of those open-and-close frames. The kind you could set on the desk like it was an opened book standing on its base. A picture on both sides. Both pictures of two people, the same two people. They could have been mistaken for the same photo, but a closer look revealed one of their hands in a pocket that was showcased in the other. Marjorie and another. They were cheesing away, these two. Opposite arms of each resting on the other's shoulder furthest away. Both donning DKNY tuxes. *"Spiffy,"* Garnet breathed to herself. *"Mighty spiffy."* Garnet had never seen Marjorie's hair in person as lengthy as it was in the picture. It touched her shoulders in the still shot. Nowadays, it was quite short, more manageable. Right before Garnet decided to write a note on the white board, Marjorie entered. "Garnet, you startled me. You trying to give me a heart attack."

"No, indeed. I want you blessed and prosperous. No time for such attacks."

Not really comprehending those terms in the context in which Garnet meant them, Marjorie ignored them and came around, making her way to her desk. "You wish you were a student again, Gibbs, don't you?"

"Not in the least. Those days were tough. I'm only trying to return the favor of torturing this next generation like we were. Sitting in this here chair feels weird, though. Almost like I'm in time-out or the principal's office. I'll have to maybe think about redoing meetings for my office hours. Just feels crazy sitting here. I can see why students don't come to office hours."

"So what do I owe this pleasure?"

"Oh. Yeah, right. I just stopped by to make sure you knew the summer diversity meeting has been pushed back a week. You know you and email have a love-hate relationship."

"More hate than love. But I did actually get a phone call last week from Paolo. She wanted to make sure she called everyone. Said something about a special guest speaker coming in and how she wanted as many faculty there as possible."

"Well, I don't know if most people will be there since it's a summer meeting. Most of these people don't teach during the summer. Anyway, let me get out of here. I have to go give this final. I'm sure these students are ready to salvage some sort of break before the fall starts up." She approached the door as Marjorie sat.

"Thanks for stopping by. We need to visit each other more often and not just run in and out. If I don't see you before the meeting, take it easy and get some rest."

"Sure thing." She was about to tell her that she was praying for her, but that would have been old news. Marjorie could have predicted it and mouthed it with her. It was always Garnet's departing words. "Catch you later."

Making her way back to her office, she noticed Leigh walking toward her and wondered if it was possible to get to her office a different way in spite of the fact that it was only steps away. "Hi, Leigh."

"Hi, Garnet. Are you still highly favored? This is definitely the day that the Lord has made. We shall rejoice and be glad in it. How many people have you won to the Lord this week?"

"None yet. But it's only Monday." This was the best way she could answer right now. Her focus was on getting to class. Leigh was just being typical Leigh.

"No excuses, Garnet." Never mind she hadn't won any souls either. "The Lord didn't make excuses when it came down to saving His people from demise. He didn't do it at a time that was convenient. He paid the price and paid it well."

Garnet had no time to correct or argue over pettiness at the moment. But oh, did Leigh know how to twist and misconstrue. Garnet made a mental note to have a conversation with her later. As for now, she only had eight minutes to get to class and get set up. All she could manage was, "Yes, He did."

Further along in the corridor, Leigh turned around but continued walking backward to her room, reminding Garnet, "Don't forget the diversity meeting soon. I think the date has been changed."

"Yes, thanks. I remembered." Deep down, however, she was wishing that the closer the date came, Leigh wouldn't.

Moving this and that around the house for Martha Jo was taking its toll. She never could make up her mind about where she wanted things, so Rusty was always having to move things here, not there. A nice soak with rubbing alcohol and Epsom salt would do the trick tonight. A quick stop by Walmart would do the job.

In the checkout aisle, Patsy smiled at him as he walked slowly to her register. "Hi, Mr. Umstead."

"Hi, Patsy." Good to see you again.

"Patsy, we need you in the pharmacy ASAP," said a mystery voice on the intercom.

"Oh dear, Mr. Umstead, I gotta run to the back right quick. T'Shay is coming to check you out right quick. Give your wife my regards."

"Aw, so soon?" joked Rusty. "I don't see you that much, and here you go running off on me."

"You know I loooove you," Patsy reassured. They both laughed as she kissed him on the cheek and scurried away. He looked down to reach for his wallet so he could pay for the items.

Just then, a tar-colored, glasses-wearing happy camper approached the register, grabbed his items, and scanned them through. "Hello, sir," she bubbly chirped in her jovial, welcoming voice. "That'll be five, sixty-six."

As Rusty looked up, his visage changed from lighthearted-ness to disdain. All in a record-breaking moment, he changed his mind about the purchase. He placed his wallet back in his pocket and slowly headed toward the automatic exit door, mumbling something under his breath. He wasn't about to touch nothing that someone like her had touched.

Half-confounded, half-pissed, T'Shay watched Rusty limp toward the door, saying to herself but out loud, "I know this old man did *not* just call me a four-eyed, shiftless nigger."

Five thirty had come sooner than Garnet had expected. She had left the office right after giving the exam and picked up R.J. from summer camp with the hopes of avoiding traffic. She did so, except for the last stretch on I-15. Someone's blown tire had created a lengthy backup and hindered those who hoped to avoid the normal 5:00 rush.

R.J. was taking a quick nap. The day at camp had worn him out. Between the tug-of-wars, arts and crafts, and every-thing in between, nothing else would recharge his batteries other than a power nap. Even at his young age, he learned the value of such and didn't contest when his grandmother made the suggestion.

Garnet turned on the TV and let it watch her while she tidied up and prepared for her meeting with Cason in about an hour. He had been a member where Garnet attended but left on a job-related mission for an extended time. Garnet and he had developed an interesting friendship. Different sexes, different races, just different. Their love for Christ and pen-chant for academic excellence were the ties that bound them together. He'd been back in the Vegas area for another assign-ment linked to his job but only for a month. He had been working remotely, but now it was time for a site visit. He had always vowed to use his law training to fight or advocate on behalf of the little guy. As a believer, he felt a special calling to help those institutions or people he felt were being mistreated. He spared Garnet details, only telling her he needed her prayers for this current fight he was in. A dinner meeting would allow them to catch up and make it easy for him to reveal to her all the details related to this current dilemma.

At present, she was trying to make sense out the dialogue coming from the TV. Somehow, it was on the Adult Swim channel. The show that was playing featured a black man dressed like Jesus: the long hair, the brown robe, a supposed thorny headband of sorts. He first argued with a homeless man. The back-and-forth banter ended with the Jesus character insulting the disheveled man: *"Yeah, fuck you too, homeboy. I still love yo' bitch ass . . . by default, fool!"*

Next, there was a scene in which Jesus was in the process of receiving a ticket from a cop for having his van illegally parked. Attempting to receive a low-five and sweet-talk his way out of his punishment, Jesus held his hand out. The cop placed the parking ticket in his hand instead, leaving Jesus owing $79. As the copy walked off, black Jesus decided to give him some last-minute health advice through word of knowledge: *"Ey, Eugene . . . go get yo' colon checked, pimpin'."*

She couldn't figure what kind of show this was that seemed to be mocking Jesus. It was supposed to be funny but was more blasphemous than amusing, in her mind. She wasn't sure what was the purpose of this savior-in-the-hood show. It probably would get funnier and more focused, but she wouldn't watch any more to find out.

There were a few more minutes to spare before she had to wake R.J. up, so she switched to a more predictable channel, one with Jack van Impe and his wife, Rexella. She was always intrigued by how well they fed off of each other. And how they managed to weave in contemporary happenings with Biblical prophecies was beyond her. Quiet as it was kept, she loved how Rexella's hair remained flawless. Jack was becoming physically and noticeably worn, unlike the youthful appearance he was known for. But his fire and passion was just as evident. He was responding to an interview Obama gave to the *Chicago Sun Times*, during which the president claimed that there are many ways to heaven. Van Impe was clear about his convictions.

> "That proves your ignorance, Mr. President. There aren't many ways. Twenty-six books of the New Testament of the twenty-seven says Jesus is the only way. And I don't know where you got your stuff, probably from your pastor, Jeremiah Wright, who I call Jeremiah Wrong because he didn't have it right either. The Bible says, Jesus speaking, John fourteen and six, 'I am the way, the truth, and life. No man, no woman, can come to the Father but by me.' Many ways? Acts four and twelve. 'Neither is there salvation in any other. There is no other name but Jesus under Heaven whereby men must be saved.' Think it over, Mr. President. I want to see you in Heaven."

"Whoa, Dr. Jack," Garnet said to the TV. "You going after the president now, huh? You haven't minced your words before and you not mincing them now. I guess the Word is the Word is the Word, no matter who says differently." She listened a little while longer at the old man's raspy voice, which had a way of mesmerizing her to no end.

"There's something, though, that has thrown every Christian off. They say, 'Oh, we've always had wars, rumors of wars, and famine.' But those are not that important. Why? Because they are tied in with two things that had to happen and they never happened until our generation."

He went on to explain the first point.

"And you know what? That is Matthew twenty-four and thirty-two. 'Learn a parable of the fig tree. When its branches are tender and bringeth forth leaves, you know that summer is nigh. So likewise, when you see all these signs in connection with the fig tree, that's when I'm coming back.' The fig tree is Israel. That is Joel one and seven, Hosea nine and ten. No doubt about it. What has to happen? They have to become a nation, and they have to control Jerusalem. It only happened in your lifetime."

Garnet was enamored of his ability to weave in current events with scripture that was written centuries prior. As the camera panned to a nodding Rexella, he continued.

"In 63 B.C., Pompeius, the Roman general, went down to Jerusalem and took the Jews away and for the next 2011 years, they were controlled by all the other empires. But on May 14, 1948, they raised the six-pointed Star of David and called themselves Israel. And then nineteen years later, they captured Jerusalem. Why is that important? Because when Russia and the nations of the world fight the battle of Armageddon, they come against Israel. There was no Israel to come against in 1818 or 1914, not until 1948. And they had to be in control of Jerusalem because they fight World War Three, Armageddon, over Jerusalem. You couldn't do it until 1967. He says, 'When you see all the signs in connection to the fig tree, that's it!' All the signs then become meaningful. We are the generation! That's why in Luke twenty-one, verses thirty-two and thirty-three, He says, 'The generation that lives to see what I just described, what I just told you, shall not pass from the earth.' We're going up!"

"Gramma, I'm thirsty."

She hadn't noticed R.J. when he entered. She had been leaning on the kitchen counter, watching the television as the show progressed.

"Oh, hey baby. I didn't hear you come in. Did you enjoy your nap?"

"Yes, ma'am."

After getting him some water, she encouraged him to put his clothes back on. "We going to meet somebody for dinner, so I want you on your best behavior, okay?"

"Yes," he responded although he wasn't sure why she felt the need to prep him for it. He was always a relative gentle soul. He was still doing quite well, considering the situation with his father. Managing quite well.

After another twenty minutes, they were both dressed and headed to meet Cason. Both had grown rather hungry. On purpose, the station was left on Dr. Jack, who had begun expounding upon his second point, admonishing, encouraging, warning.

11:59

17

RE-UPPING

ASHTORETH CAME IN loud and boisterous. "Hey, y'all!" she belted. "Time for us to check in. What it do, bitches?!"

"Things are good, Ash," answered Belial. He was a bit more reserved than normal and seemed quite pensive, less upbeat. Whenever he was his less playful self, it was because certain destruction was on his mind.

"Uh oh," observed Ashtoreth. "Something's eating Belial. What is it, B?"

"Time is short," he responded. "We need to make sure we raise the level of our game. We can joke around and laugh, but at the end of the day, what results are we getting?"

Serious, Mictian validated Belial's concern. "Yes, he's right. I don't care how much prayer is out there, we can get results if we really want. What's everybody's status? Where are we with our tasks?"

Ashtoreth started in. Her visage had become more grave, dour even. "I have a plan for Nieko. He'll be rethinking his plans of changing by the time I'm finished with him. I'll keep using Mo to get at him. If that don't work, I got the porn lined up and that other solo thing. He won't be able to shake loose. Everything is also set to get rid of that little brat."

"You mean R.J.? You really gone hurt a helpless, fatherless kid?" Mictian feigned concern. He then allowed himself to grin a sinister grin.

"And you know this," answered the villainess. "You already know I don't give a shit 'bout no age. As far as I'm concerned, he's dead and gone."

"Who you got in mind, the twins?"

"Nah."

"Ms. Violet?"

"Nah. I thought about using her, but that would be too much planning."

"Well, it ain't nothing but two more left that you normally destroy kids with. Is it Jessie?"

"You gettin' warmer."

The other two started beaming from pointed ear to pointed ear. All three locked talons and started dancing, swirling around in a circle. They knew who the last solution was. They sang in a chorus as they celebrated. "Em-i-ly! Em-i-ly! Em-i-ly! Em-i-ly!"

Belial interjected, "That's my little bitch right there, sweet little Emily! I don't know how you didn't start guessing right with that one, Mick."

"Hell, Ash ain't called on her in a minute. I thought she forgot about her."

"You have to pull the right card at the right time," reassured the female imp. "And now is the right time." She began disclosing the lurid details of what was going to happen, much to the other two's wicked approval. She stood straight, head up, tail to the sky, and released a loud shriek, "NOW

CALLING FOR EMILYYYYYY!!!!" Thunder and lightning, only visible and audible to the trio, appeared. Wind stirred, causing the wings of the three to flail vigorously. The climax of all the pomp and circumstance was no climax at all. An unassuming silhouette of a tiny girl – about four feet tall – stood before them. Her ponytail was, in fact, a real tail, almost low-fiving the ground. She looked away from her conjurer into celestial space. Though petite in stature and donning an innocent smile, her eyes were two abysses that led to inexplicable depths. She uttered nothing, simply waiting for the command.

"Go and do what you do!" instructed Ashtoreth.

The youngster smiled more broadly, parting her scaly lips, which revealed no teeth. It was just a dark, empty hole for a mouth, from which screams and cries of children emanated. She was almost always called upon when another child was to become a victim, and she had an undefeated record worldwide at 79,956-0, and she wasn't about to start losing now. She twirled in place slowly, laughing. Her onlookers laughed, too. They knew what this meant. She kept spinning, twirling, and giggling. Without any notice, she shot downward to earth, leaving behind a sulfuric trail. The children's cries tapered off, and she eventually appeared on scene, blending into the Vegas night and relishing that this was her first assignment there.

The three snickered. "Yesss," said Belial. "That's a *bad* little bitch. I love me some her." There was more ominous laughter.

"Anyway, I think I got Rusty right where I want him. I've been showing him some upsetting stuff about him and where he fits in society. I've gotten him pissed at how everybody seems to be getting attention except for him and his kind. If everything works out, you'll be proud of what I convince him to do."

"That's what I'm talking about," stated Belial. "We gotta go hard!"

"What about you?" she asked Belial. "Is everything set up for Tario in Huntridge, like the master requested?"

"Trust and believe. Tario will be dead within a week. Period. Point blank, no pun intended." He smirked. "Let's just say it's going down at the frat party." They celebrated quietly. "Where is he anyway?" Belial asked.

"Who, Tario? You're supposed to have your own three eyes on him. How would *we* know?"

"No, you imbecile . . . the master?"

"Still roaming, seeking the next one to eat up, to devour. What else would he be doing.

Just make sure you're doing your part. I have to answer to him before too long." She continued. "And I can honestly say we can put one in the win column for closing down another Christian college. It's just a matter of time with that one. The lawyer's hands are basically tied, so we good there."

"Nice," added Mictian.

"And I'll be attending the diversity meeting at Garnet's campus. She act like she so holy and righteous. We'll see what happens when she gets put on the spot concerning her beliefs. By the time that meeting's over, she'll be compromising what she thinks she believes. Or she gone end up looking like a fool. I can't *stand* that holy hoe."

That was a natural transition for Mictian. "Speaking of which, we'll destroy her by destroying what's close to her. She herself is covered, but we're affecting what's around her. I'll see to it that her daughter doesn't recover from being adopted. She's going to Jamaica to find her so-called roots, and I'll be over there. I been waiting for her to see this day. She gone find out some news that's gone make her feel even more insecure than she already is. Can't wait. She'll never rebound from this."

"And the son-in-law?" inquired Ashtoreth.

"Oh, he'll be dead as a doorknob," responded Mictian. "I dropped an idea in Baktash's mind. He got his wife on board to do some shonuff damage. Let's just say, 'Dead Tario is to Huntridge as Dead Redd is to Kabul.'"

"That has a nice ring to it," admitted Belial. "Dead Redd."

"Anyway, I gots to get to Jamaica," Mictian stated. "Time to get things on and poppin'. Yeah mon!" He'd thought about adding extra turbulence to Jamay's flight but knew Gabriel would probably be assigned to making sure she got there fine. And just like that, he was chillin' in Kingston.

"Bye to you, too," said Ashtoreth. She and Belial discussed the next meeting time, promising to fill Mictian in on when later.

Uriel sat in the room around the corner from the throne, awaiting the arrival of the other two. He wanted in on more of the action. Nieko's plight was more or less dependent on his own daily choices. He'd get help with specifics as he prayed and asked for help. And nothing really seemed to be developing with Cason. He'd let his feelings be known.

Gabriel and Raphaela zoomed in together, chatting it up. "Hi, Uriel. The Lord bless."

"He is worthy! Blessed be the name of the Lord!" he responded.

"So how are things going?" inquired Raphaela.

"Managing. I just need to be more involved. You guys are getting all of the action."

"How's Nieko and Cason?" asked Gabriel.

"They're hanging strong. Cason's fighting a losing battle, but I'll hang in there with him. Those policies are forming rather strongly, and the school isn't proactive. Probably won't work out for them."

"Okay. We'll get you in on some more stuff. We have our hands full, no doubt. Jamay will be taking a trip that will hopefully boost her self-esteem. She's been hanging on to some feelings for a while. And it looks like her husband may be facing some challenges overseas. I'll have to keep my eye on him. Something doesn't feel quite right concerning him. I know Mictian and how he works. He's been rather silent, which is unusual for him."

"I am ready and available to help," interjected Uriel. "We've got to represent the Most High well and cover all bases."

"Indeed. There may be another plot developing regarding Pastor Castillo. I'm not sure yet. But with him preaching the Word the way he does, he's sure to be a target at some point. I'll keep you posted."

"¡Gloria a su nombre!" joked Uriel. "I love it!"

Raphaela joined in. "I've got my eye on Tario. He's still in his own zone. I have a feeling the enemy has a plan for his demise that may be revealed soon. We need to bring him into the fold so others will follow him. I have to watch him closely. My eyes are on the kid, too. The enemy's not gone just let him go. Garnet's praying, but we can never be too careful."

"This is true," agreed Gabriel. "We can *never* get too comfortable, even if the saints are praying. The enemy's people are praying as well. The best defense is a great offense. We don't always want to be reactive. Stay ahead of the game and a step ahead of the drama. This is chess, not checkers."

"Just be sure to keep me in the mix," reminded Uriel. "I want to please the Most High in the best way possible. He is depending on us to work as a team to accomplish His mission and purpose."

"I gotchu," reaffirmed Gabriel. "I gotchu."

"I have a feeling the opposition is gonna try to up the ante," added Raphaela. "They know time is running out, and they gone do whatever they have to do to stop His will. Keep focused."

"Anyway, compatriots, I gotta be out. Jamay's about to board the plane," Gabriel announced. Gotta make sure she gets there okay."

Before she asked what time they would meet again to provide updates, Gabriel disappeared, headed toward McCarran.

Uriel and she decided to meet again soon and would contact Gabriel later to inform him. Before dropping back down to earth, they headed back to His throne declaring a continuous, "Holy, holy, holy, is the Lord God Almighty!"

YU HAFFI SATISFY WID JANCRO

SCURRYING VISITORS TRAIPSED through Norman Manley International, finally able to exhale. The next few days would promise bliss and an escape from the normal humdrum existence that life had beaten most of them into. Gleams twinkling inside of foreign eyes seemed to corroborate the veracity of the brochures, at least for now. Whether white-sand beaches, crystal-clear water, and to-die-for plantains existed remained to be seen. But Kingston's first impressions didn't disappoint.

Gabriel rode underneath the plane to ensure a safe landing. It was no secret that Jamay probably desired that the circumstances leading up to this, her first visit, were different. She had at least made it to first base, however; she was home. Although there was zero recollection of ever being here, a part of her heart skipped a minor beat. Then, she waited for some specific magic, some feeling that was supposed to let her know this trip was the right choice. Nothing. She had previously talked it over with Garnet and agreed that it may be better for her mother to stay in Vegas. She had debriefed Jamay and had given her necessary contact information for the agency. She asked Davida to accompany her, though, for moral support. Both barely spoke during the flight. Davida feigned sleep because she honestly didn't know what to say about the visit's purpose.

"You hungry?" Davida asked. "Maybe we should grab a bite since we're finally here. Those peanuts did nothing for me."

Focused, Jamay demurred. "Nah, I'm good for now. Let's go 'head and get to the CDA. I told them I would stop by after I landed. They aren't open the weekend, so I wanna make sure we catch 'em."

"You alright?"

"Yeah, I'm fine. Just a little nervous, a little excited, a little everything."

"Well, just know I'm here with you, girl. I haven't really said it, but I admire you for doing this. It takes a strong person to go through with this because you might not find what you necessarily lookin' for."

"I know. I've taken all of that into consideration. But I know if I don't do it, I'll always be curious about it. Can't no singin', shoutin', preachin' or nothing else silence that curiosity. If I don't find out what I need to find out, that's fine. At least I tried."

"I hear you. So how we getting there? We catching a cab? Uber?"

"No, they have something here called Get There, similar to Uber. I downloaded the app before I left the States." Looking at her phone, she woke the app and requested the driver. "There we go. She should be here in five minutes."

"She?"

"Yep, she. It's a female's picture that popped up when I confirmed the transaction."

"You trust a total stranger in Jamaica, just like that?"

"Well, it ain't no different than what we do back home. All drivers are total strangers. As long as they turn in their documents to prove that they're real and accountable, that's all that matters to me."

"I guess you're right."

They eventually hopped in and, as the business name suggested, they got there in about thirty minutes.

"Hi, I'm looking for Linda," Jamay stated. Davida and she approached the front counter as they lugged their bags.

"I'm Linda, 'ow can 'elp?"

"I have an appointment with Eralia, a Miss Eralia."

"Are you Jamay?"

"Yes."

"Great. Yeah, she expectin' you, yeah. So 'ow was your treep?"

"It was good." She realized they had been discussing her arrival or, worse, discussing her.

"Okay, just one second. I tell hah yuh 'ere."

The two visitors leaned against the pink counter, believing it wouldn't take long for the worker in the back to welcome them. They were right. Within a minute or so, an elderly lady, who had to be pushing ninety, came from the back set of offices. With no cane, no walker, or anything else to assist her mobility, she made spriteful steps toward the lobby. She even wore a pair of Skechers Flex Appeals. In obvious good health, she didn't look a day over eighty.

"Waa gwaan?" She gave the two ladies a big hug. Jamay

got an extra second's worth of a hug. To her, the lady voiced, "My, 'ave yuh grown. Good ta see yuh again, mah dear. Come on in."

Again?, Jamay thought to herself. *How does she even know this is me? How she know Davida ain't the one trying to find her folks?* She'd hope the meeting would clarify these and similar questions. They left their bags with the receptionist and followed the leader to her office.

After grabbing a seat, Miss Eralia wasted no time. "My God, yuh lookin' just like yuh mudda."

Taken aback, Jamay could say nothing but, "Oh."

"Yeah, if you can't tell, Miss Eralia been around for ah long time. Not just 'ere as in life but 'ere as in workin' 'ere. I done seen a lahta stuff through the years. It's just funny when things come full circle. Mi seen a lot o' full circles, mah dear. Lahts."

"Well, thank you for seeing me, us. This is Davida, my close friend from back home."

"Hi," said Davida.

"I guess I just always had questions concerning my real family here. I always think about what life woulda been like if . . . well, you know."

"Yes, I know. Cahn't say it, cahn you? Feel like a curse word, huh? Well, it ain't no curse word, mah dear. For some people, it's the best word thata ever ever exist, yuh know. Adahption. Say it."

"Adoption," Jamay repeated.

"You say it, too."

"Adoption," Davida mimicked, although she didn't know why she was saying it.

"It ain't no curse word, chil'ren. Just a word. Mi not no couns'lah, but at least mi try ta get people at least ta say what done happened to 'em." She placed her right leg on her desk and started stretching. She was so in tune with her health and staying flexible.

"So, I guess I was just wondering if you can give me any leads concerning where I came from or if you know where my mother or father is. Or their family . . . my family. Or something, anything."

She could tell Jamay was semi-frustrated. All who sought to complete the circle were. "Well, to be honest, our 'ands are tied by the Jamaican law if the 'riginal parents sign off on the form, sayin' they don' wahnt to be foun'. It's d'ere right, yuh know. Good fuh you, though, that they didn' sign off on no such form in yuh case. She no wanna be no ghost to yuh. Us 'ere never know what 'appen to 'em after yuh get adopted, but most times, they can be foun' and wanna be foun' if they no sign."

"Well, that's good news. Thank you, Jesus."

"I give you the info in a minute. But why I say yuh look like yuh mudder when yuh first walk in is 'cause I knew she didn' sign. To be honest, mi rememba the day dat poor chile and huh parents contacted this office about givin' up hah baby. Ha was so sad but so brave, yuh know. Met wit' ha in this same buildin', yuh know. Down tha hall. Like it was yesterday. A lot ah stuff yuh don' know. But just know she lovejah. Gracious, she lovejah. Das all I can say, mah dear. Yuh 'ave to contact the family on yuh own. Here is where they at." She gave Jamay an address. "'Dis is down in the Broadgate area, 'bout 'alf an 'our from 'ere. You will do good 'cause you no let nothin' distrac' yuh, mah dear."

They didn't know what to expect, but at least they had a better sense of where to go, where things started. "Thank you so much for all of your help, Miss Eralia. You don't know how much this helps me."

"Thank you," repeated Davida. Noticeably silent during the meeting, she kept hearing Garnet's voice telling her not to say too much and just be there to lend an ear and provide support simply by her mere presence.

"Ah, yuh welcome, mah dear. No madda what yuh learn, jus' know that yuh loved. Dat's what everybody dat come back 'ere wonder. Deep down, dat's what they travel all dem miles fuh. Just to see if they loved. Well, even if yuh didn' or don' find out nothin' spectacula', yuh livin' and got a chance to make someting out yuhself. Out of everyting that 'appened, yuh got a life to be able to do someting wit'. You got a mudda who picked you out an' loved yuh like yuh hah own. Hah came in and went through the long process. Got ta admit, hah looked a little weird hahself, but as long as hah had love in hah, dat's all maddered to us. Hah was so happy, and yuh look so scurred. But we knew yuh wood be fine. Jus' know yuh loved, mah dear. Yuh loved."

Jamay felt like she was getting closer but just didn't know to what. The main part of her made a decision to take the old lady's advice, just so she wouldn't set herself up for major disappointment. This probably wouldn't be a happily-ever-after ending. Having low expectations guaranteed that let-downs would offer less of a sting. There were so many emotions going through her mind, almost causing the makings of a headache. Some food and a good night's sleep would calm and refocus her.

After they retrieved their luggage, Miss Eralia walked them out, partly to comfort Jamay one final time and partly to get ready for her daily two-mile walk. As she headed for the walking trail, the other two knew they would have to use the Get There app one final time.

Mictian followed along, hoping the information she would shortly receive would damage her spirit and arrest her development even more than it currently was.

In fact, they had kept the driver's contact information just in case. Jamay didn't want to start from scratch, so she just trusted the same driver's ability to negotiate her way through Jamaican traffic. Plus, she was a woman, so it was a girl power kind of thing. They'd already worked out a deal where she'd hang out with them today while they were on this journey of discovery. Otherwise, they wouldn't have had a way back to Kingston. All of this driving on the wrong side of the road, though, was working her and Davida's nerves. She knew they did in London but had no idea that a place like Jamaica had them driving on the other side, too. She'd explained to the driver the purpose of their trip, and she was tremendously helpful and sympathetic to their cause. She agreed to be their Jamaican host as it related to driving, of course with pay.

By the time they got to the more rural parts of the journey, it made little difference anyway as roads turned into one-way passageways. Huge green shrubbery on both sides and then an occasional driveway leading up to a house or two. Then repeat.

"Says here," the driver said, "that we're roughly point one miles away."

"Really? I was born in *these* parts?"

"Kinda secluded," added Davida.

"In all my years, I never been ta dis area. Heard of it, just never been 'ere." They pulled up to a rocky driveway. "Says this is it." Pulling in the driveway, they saw a little girl observe them while playing in the yard. She disappeared into the home.

After going about twenty feet, she came to a halt. "I'll wait in the cah. You be fine." Get There drivers were so much more personable than Ubers or Lyfts.

"You're more than welcome to come in," invited Jamay.

"No. You go 'head. I wait 'ere. No rush. Take as much time as yuh need. No cost fuh mi waitin' fuh yuh. Only drivin'."

"Well, here goes nothin'. You ready?" She looked toward Davida.

"I'm here for you, sis."

"We'll be back."

The thud from the closing of the door seemed to serve as indication that there was no turning back. All had led to this moment: the wondering, the doubt, the questions, the second-guesses. Whatever misgivings she had up to this point made no difference now. Every step toward the door was a step toward identity. As soon as the door got within arm's length, she knocked on it, surprising even herself.

"You didn't pause or nothing, huh?" joked Davida.

"I didn't want to give myself a chance to back out."

Five seconds went by. Then ten. Jamay felt the butterflies twirling in her stomach. This is why she had hurried and rapped on the door. Because of *this* feeling. The delay in answering only added to the doubt she was already wrestling with. As she poised herself to knock again, someone on the other side began fiddling with the knob. In what seemed to be an eternity, the crack in the door appeared and widened. The two found themselves staring at a young gentleman, perhaps in his mid-thirties. He was on the lighter side, not the typical dark Jamaican. He spoke a thick patois, but Jamay's ears had become quickly accustomed to translating what he spoke into her English.

"Hello." Jamay broke the silence.

"If you're looking for Kingston, it's the other way, about thirty minutes from here. Up on that way." He pointed.

"No . . . um actually, I think this is the address I'm supposed to be. My name is Jamay and this is my friend, Davida. I think I have reason to believe that my real birth mother . . ." She looked down to check the name. ". . . Um, an Addie Frazier lives here."

Without any pause and with no dramatics, he stated, "She died. About three years back. AIDS. Died of AIDS." So anticlimactic. He clearly hadn't seen American movies, where the punch line was to be revealed after a brief build up.

Not knowing how to follow up, it only made sense for her to ask the most natural next question. "So, you knew her?" *What a dumb question!* she thought, as she stood there for the obvious answer. Thankfully, it didn't prove too dumb.

"She was my sister."

Standing in awe, all parties were at a loss for words. The awkwardness was too thick in the air to act like it wasn't. They just looked at each other, shifted uncomfortably, and processed.

"Come on in." Finally, he broke the silence in the strangest of ways.

Although disappointed, they had come too far not to accept an invitation inside her relatives' home. They obliged. The driver soon stared at an empty porch.

"Have a seat. Let me get you some water."

"Thank you," they both said. He made his way to the kitchen.

"Well," whispered Jamay. "I guess I found my answer. It

was kinda weird how he just came right out and told us she passed, but–"

"At least you know. We said all along to expect whatever, especially the unexpected. So just stay positive. You'll get through this."

"Here you are," he voiced. "Water should be good and fresh. Thank goodness because we went through a time where our water had turned brown from all of the nasty pipes in the area. A lot of people take it for granted."

"Sounds like Flint," Davida mentioned.

He didn't catch the reference but guessed it had to do with water situations. "You'll have to forgive my rudeness. It's not every day that people come by here out of the blue asking about my sister, saying she their mother. I'm Brantly."

"Nice to meet you. I guess we didn't really know what to expect by coming." She brought him up to speed with what happened since landing and how this was somewhat of a long-shot visit. "I don't know. A part of me wanted to leave it alone, but another part of me just wanted to see who I really am."

"I don't really remember a lot," confessed Brantly. "Addie was almost ten years older than I was. I vaguely remember her even being pregnant when I was small. Even if I saw her during that time, I had no idea what it meant by her stomach being so big. I think I remember her doing a lot of crying, but only God knows why. It's hard to distinguish different cries from the same person."

That's when it clicked with Jamay that Brantly wasn't that much older than she. He was probably only about seven years older. "So, do you remember anything about what she was like?"

"Of course, it's just that when it comes to details of the pregnancy, I myself don't really know. And whenever I would ask questions, they would just tell me not to mind grown people's business. It was just a strange time. I can remember my mom and dad in the room with her. There was a bunch of yelling and crying. From what I'm told, the yelling had to do with asking her to get an abortion. And the crying had to do with Addie saying no. She was a stubborn girl, that Addie. Even as we got older, she was stubborn and never let people tell her what to do. Anyway, afterward a while, people just stopped talking about whatever had to do with any kind of pregnancy. A lady from the CDA started coming by regularly and then after she gave birth, she stopped. I never saw no baby. I just remember her stomach wasn't big anymore."

"Sounds like a special lady, your sister," concluded Davida.

"And what about my father?"

Brantly became a bit sullen and looked down. "I didn't know him, but I heard my parents didn't take to him too well. Him and Addie knew each other from high school. After he got her pregnant, he got in trouble with the law. Started going on the wrong path, hanging out with the wrong group of people. Robbed somebody, and then they got scared when the person fought back. One of them in the group had a gun and shot the man, who died a few days later. They found all of the kids who were there that night and all of them went to prison for a long time. Split 'em up. I think he ended up at St. Catherine's, over in Spanish Town. Still there from what I hear. My folks didn't talk about it that much then and don't now. It was just sad all the way around. I'm sort of glad I was too young to understand."

Brantly allowed himself to smile in reminiscence. "She was a good sister, though. We teased each other a lot. She got on my nerves. I got on hers. Since I was so much younger than she was, she bossed me around a lot with that bossy attitude and personality. She shouldn't have been taken out like she did. Some guy she was dating gave her the disease. Said he loved her, but apparently he was saying it to a whole bunch more women. Found out he had seven girlfriends at one time. Running around having unprotected sex with everybody. Finally caught up with him. And her. He passed and that's when we found out about him. And then Addie got tested, but it was too late. No amount of drugs would help. I visited her every other day. She lived in Kingston, so it was nothing for me to drive the short distance to check on her. Then, she just kept getting worse and worse. Died at home at our parents' house. It was tough on her son, who also lived with our parents. He had just started high school in Kingston and was going through his own challenges related to that. He hung in there, and now he graduating. Says he might go to America for college."

He shut down any emotions. In Jamaica, it just wasn't the masculine thing to do. He almost forgot, "Oh! Let me show you this." He stepped away to fetch something and returned. "I've been holding on to this. We didn't take that many pictures when we were growing up. She the only one who I know in this picture. But I figured it was pretty important since she kept it. I only took it after she passed. Ran across it while we were cleaning out some of her things at my parents' house. It was in one of her desks. I don't recognize nobody in the picture but her." He handed it to her.

Worn and discolored because of time, the picture featured three people. There was Addie as a teen, who held on to relative newborn. Jamay's vision became a bit cloudy from tears but not because of either of the first two images. What tugged at her heart strings was the third person who stood behind the first two. It was Miss Eralia, a younger version, appearing in her late fifties, early sixties. As the mother and child sat, she stood behind them, both hands on Addie in a type of comforting manner. All smiling except for the crying baby, whose face contorted the way babies' faces do.

A tear dropped onto the picture.

"Aw, Jamay." Davida scooted closer to her, placing her arm around her shoulder. She began to tear up as well. Brantly clearly now realized why she did. He almost felt embarrassed that he had caused such a scene.

"Would anybody like any more water?" was all he could muster.

Ignoring his question, they both continued to stare at the picture, seeing what else they could see. It must have been taken at the CDA. That was the only logical place it could have been. Jamay kept looking at the baby, trying to decipher clearly if it was her.

"Well, I'm guessing this is me," she surmised.

"She just had you and Jevaun. So that's got to be you there, yes."

This was a good enough answer for her. Although she couldn't tell the sex of the baby, a boy currently in high school didn't fit the visual narrative that the picture presented. Boy *or* girl, for that matter.

"She's so beautiful," Jamay kept repeating. "Addie is so beautiful."

Not knowing quite how to respond, he was finally rescued from an unlikely source.

"Daddy, I'm hungry," stated a voice by the living room entrance.

"Daddy gone give you some food in a minute, baby. We gone have some nice plantains and red beans and rice. You like that."

"Yes."

"Come on in here first. Let me show you these nice people."

She came closer. "Why are they crying?" asked the little one. "Are they lost?"

Laughing, Jamay said, "No, darling. We're not lost anymore." The kid didn't catch the double meaning, nor should she have. "My name is Jamay. This is Davida. It's nice to meet you." She extended her hand. "What's your name?"

"Raeni."

"How beautiful."

"Can you tell them what it means?" prodded Brantly.

Almost automatically, she responded, "Queen."

"Well, you definitely look like a queen," complimented Jamay. "How old are you?"

"Nine. Why are you crying?"

"It's a long story, Raeni. But just know they are happy tears. I'm not sad."

"You don't talk like a Jamaican."

"All people don't sound alike," her father intercepted. "She lives in a different part of the world. So, they may not sound like we sound. But they are just as smart and just as kind."

"We better be going," suggested Jamay. "We've overstayed our welcome. Us coming barging in like this." She took one final glance at the picture and laid it on the coffee table.

"No, it's yours. I think you will get better use out of it than I will. It's the least I can do."

"Oh, my God. Thank you! You don't know what this means to me. I will cherish this forever."

"You can actually get it restored and blow it up," Davida added. Technology can work wonders on it."

"Oh, my God. Thank you again."

"You're more than welcome to stay. We have enough food."

"No, no. We better go. I'm so glad we came. I didn't know what to expect, but this has been good. A bit bittersweet but still good."

"Well, I told you everything I know." They switched contact information and email addresses. She would have given him contact for social media, but he didn't have any. "You can visit any time. My parents gave us this house, me and my wife when they moved to Kingston. She'll be back after work. We don't plan on moving or going anywhere, so feel free to keep in touch. Just do us a favor in the future."

"What's that?" Jamay inquired.

"Just call us next time before you come."

Bursts of laughter followed.

"We will. I promise." She placed the picture inside of her purse. "Thank you so much for opening your doors to total strangers. It was so kind of you."

"Mi, no problem, guhl. Ahfter mi discover yuh mean no 'arm, everyt'ing work out."

They headed toward the door. They'd totally forgotten about the driver, who was still waiting. She was a trooper. They could see she had reclined all the way back and was probably sleep.

In a final gesture, everyone hugged it out, even Raeni, despite her still not knowing who they were or their reason for being there.

"Do you mind if I take a selfie?"

"Not at ahl."

Everyone pulled in tight. They had to squat a little bit to get the little one in. Light and shadows played in their favor, as they were able to get the perfect shot.

"I'll send you a copy of it," promised Jamay.

They opened the car door to a now-awakened driver. They

got in and powered the window down. Raeni had resumed entertaining herself outside with what she had been doing before the strange car pulled into the driveway.

"Good bye, Raeni!" Jamay yelled out of the window. They backed out, headed toward the road.

"Bye," she responded and waved.

"Be sure to hahv a safe trip bahk. Keep yuh head up. Mi proud of yuh. As we say 'round these pahts, 'If yu cyaan get turkey, yu haffi satisfy wid Jancro.'"

She had no idea what he said, but she waved and acted as if she did. As the driver shifted gears into forward driving mode, Davida yelled, "Bye, Brantly."

Much to Mictian's chagrin, she seemed to be on a sure path of healing. No generational curse of low self-esteem appeared to be festering. She was dealing with it and seemed to be coming out on top.

A thought popped into Jamay's head on the spot as she was leaving. Before she knew it, she waved and yelled as loud as she could as the car sped forward, "Take it easy, Uncle B."

19

Q PHI-EEE!

WALKING TRAFFIC DURING business hours on The Strip sounded as if horses galloped on open ranges. High heels and Cole Haans clunked their way asynchronously past each other into work areas to make their six figures, or five, or seven. Irritated by an overwhelming tourist presence, this traffic did its best to arrive at its destination to attend board meetings, show slides, hire, fire, double-check budgets, and take extended lunch breaks. It was the kind of traffic that allowed execs and other go-getters to reside in abodes of luxury and taste the finer things of life.

By the time night fell, horses still galloped, but they were of a different breed; new high heels emerged, the owners of which leaned into windows of Benzes and Beemers to woo these new and old Cole Haans owners. Business was still had. It only tended to reach into three figures and, if lucky, four. Tastings of the finer life things were yet happening but of a more scintillating, titillating sort, resulting in at least three climaxes per half hour.

Garnet rarely ever walked the Strip but had to park a ways away because of construction near the restaurant. If she would have thought more carefully, she would have told Cason to meet somewhere other than here. Lunch would have been a better meeting situation, but it was what it was. She just hated to be dragging R.J. along. His little eyes weren't ready for the Strip show.

"Come on, R.J. Stick by me. Walk up," she encouraged. Giggles from giddy visitors who would have otherwise been cautious in their own cities seemed to win out, prodding Garnet to take special care in assuring her grandson's safety.

R.J. was distracted in his own right as he made his way up the boulevard. He only came through this mayhem in a car. This was the first time that he traveled by foot. It was exciting and captivating. The man who played the violin with the case full of dollar bills. The lady singing opera, hoping for some of the same kindness. The lights shooting through from every direction. The ticket booths selling Broadway-type tickets. The skywalk that hovered above cars below.

Because the density of the crowd thickened, Garnet resorted to her protective, mother mode. Grabbing R.J.'s hand was second nature. She saw the restaurant about two hundred yards ahead, which looked to be miles away, given her impatience and others' aimlessness. She started praying in tongues under her breath. The kid was walking straight but looking to the left and right, mesmerized by the scenes of people that kept shifting.

"Aww, he's so cute," said a scantily dressed, handcuffed prostitute, who was telling her cigarette-pulling partner-in-crime about R.J. as he walked by.

The policemen detaining them helped them regain their focus. "Alright, Trixie and Sapphire, in you go." Both made sure the women's heads didn't bump the car as they entered the backseat. "We're gonna take you down to the station and process ya . . . again."

As Garnet moved with laser-like focus, another voice came from the left. "Hi. Ma'am, can you come over here one second? I'd like to give you a free psychic reading. I see some great stuff in your future. Ma'am? You're a very lucky woman. Can I tell you more?"

"Gramma," said R.J. "Did you hear that lady? She's trying to get your attention. She wants to tell you stuff like Pastor Castillo does in church."

Without showing her anger and frustration, she continued forward, correcting him as much as she could, given the circumstances. "No, baby. It's not the same. It's not quite the same." Making her way through all the revelry, she finally saw the base of the French-inspired building. The mice had found their way through the maze.

She finally felt comfortable enough to release the child from her grip of life. As she prepared to call Cason, her phone indicated via text that he was already inside, waiting for her. This was her second time dining here. Last time was five years ago at a wedding proposal. This space was known for those type of carrying-ons. She remembered she had to catch the elevator but couldn't recall which floor. Thankfully, the attendant assisted her. "Good evening, madam," he said to her. "And you, sir," addressing her sidekick.

"Hello, sir. God bless you," responded Garnet. Nada from R.J.

As they entered, the attendant pressed the only button that would send them upward to the eleventh floor.

"Whoa!" exhaled R.J. "Look outside, gramma!" She hadn't realized that he hadn't ever been inside this fancy-shmancy edifice. To the adults, it was a palace. To kids, it rivaled Disneyland. "Whoa!"

"I know, baby. Isn't it gorgeous?" Both observed how the Bellagio was shrinking through the glass elevator. They were so high up that R.J. was able to cover up the dwarfed hotel across the street with his right hand.

After the elevator bell dinged, they exited to find Cason staring out the glass as R.J. had been, fascinated in his own right. She'd sneak up on him and hopefully would elicit quite a laugh. "You know, they say the food here's great. But if you can't pay your bill, they make you wash these windows, inside and outside."

Turning, he erupted, "Nette!" He laughed hysterically and hugged her. "And how exactly are you supposed to reach the windows on the other side without a crane?"

"Management folk say that's not their problem. They say you should have thought about that before you ordered your food." Both guffawed. They even made R.J. chuckle, even though he was rather clueless about the joke itself.

"Is this little Redd?" asked Cason.

"Indeed. He's not really little anymore, though."

"Hi, Redd."

"Hello."

"R.J., this is Mr. Cason. He used to go to our church. He's a big shot now, though. He's too big for us little people." She directed the statements more to Cason than to her grandson.

"Shall we grab a seat?" asked Cason. "I'm famished."

"Okay."

Those weird stares from other customers went unnoticed by the three. Together, they could easily have been a husband, wife, and child. So, really, they were only staring at Garnet because of the other reason. As usual, she had gotten used to paying the glances no mind. They walked to the front to be seated and were eventually led to their table. "Your server will be by shortly," said the maître d'. "Please relax and enjoy your stay." He placed three warm bath cloths on the table and a couple of menus.

They all grabbed a cloth. "I can't believe I'm sitting next to the one and only, the famous Attorney C. Z. Zimmerman."

"Oh stop," Cason uttered. "You and I both know I'm just Cason."

"No, sir. When I walked in, I was looking for the man with the black cape attached to his ensemble and the black mask. You're a superhero to those whom you represent."

"That cape sure would have come in handy on today. Temperature seems cooler than it normally does around this time of the year. I got off the plane and wondered if I was in the right city. But the Lord has blessed me so I can bless other people. I'm not the richest, but I'm not the poorest either. Hence, we're able to dine here." He spread his arms out in grand fashion. "How's Alive?"

"It's doing fine. Pastor Castillo is just as fired up for the Lord as one can be in these times. He preaches with conviction, no matter what laws pass or what the Supreme Court says. He always says he's accountable to *the* Judge and *the* Court of courts. He's no wuss."

"A man of conviction. Wish there were more of them around. Women too."

"No, R.J.," said Garnet to the younger one. "You don't wipe your face with that, just your hands."

"But it smells so good. And it's warm."

"I know, but you don't take a shower with it."

"So, how's school, little Redd?" the attorney interjected. "What grade are you going to?"

"Third," he answered.

"That's fantastic. You're going to do really well if you keep listening to this lady right here. She's a smart cookie, your grandma."

The waiter arrived. "Bonsoir Monsieur et Mademoiselle."

"We don't speak French, sir," Cason clarified.

"I don't either," confessed the waiter. "We're just required to say it during our opening greeting."

The group laughed. After the waiter informed them of the special of the day, he promised to return to take their orders.

"My goodness," sighed Garnet as she looked over the menu. "When you said you're not the richest, you could have fooled me. These prices are through the roof. This caviar costs just as much as a Cancun vacation for five days and four nights, seriously."

"Never mind it. Just order whatever you want for you and R.J. I'll write it off as a business expense."

"Must be nice."

"Gramma, is mom coming?" asked the youngster as he played with centerpiece of pink roses and white hydrangeas.

"No, baby. We'll see her when we get back home. Be careful with those."

Orders taken and water, bread, and butter delivered, the conversation took a more serious turn. Especially of interest to R.J. was the delectable garlic, balsamic vinegar, Parmesan cheese, oregano, and pepper mixture woven together with the olive oil. It with the bread could have been his entire meal.

"So, to what do I owe the pleasure of this meeting?"

"This is a tough one, Garnet. I'm serving as counsel for LCU."

"Lincoln? The Christian school over on South Eastern?"

"Yeah. They're looking at losing their federal funding

because of their perceived lack of compliance with Title Nine. Basically, it's a private school with Christian values but receives public funding from the government."

Uriel listened intently as he hung out inconspicuously by the piano, a few feet away. He'd seen this play out before, and it didn't look good for this college based on what he'd observed with others. The government seemed to be felling any institution that remained myopic concerning its mission and twenty-first century changing norms.

"Uh oh. I can see the handwriting on the wall."

"I think I can, too, but they at least deserve a fair listening to. It all started when some people started complaining about the school's diversity statement. Said it's so yesterday and that it should change to reflect the changing world we live in to accommodate and welcome all students." He pulled a crumpled sheet of paper from his pocket and unraveled it. "See, here it is. Listen to this." He began reading, "Blah, blah, blah . . . okay, here we go . . . We want a learning environment that engages men and women of various ages, cultures, nationalities, races, abilities, exceptionalities, and socio-economic backgrounds who support our mission and core values for Christian unity and Biblical authority in carrying out God's global mission." He stared at Garnet and smiled.

"That's funny. The infamous sins of omission. I'm just not sure what people expect for a Christian school's diversity statement should say. It makes sense to me. We actually have a diversity meeting coming up at UNLV soon. I don't want to think about what's going to happen. That diversity word is definitely the buzzword for today."

"And, of course, the university is digging its heels in the ground so that it can hold on to its founding beliefs. How long have they been around?"

"It's been around since 2007, but the main one out in Illinois was founded in the 1940s. So, it's the main one out there that's feeling the brunt of opposition. Whatever happens there will trickle down and affect the other campuses. I'm part of the legal team defending the university system as a whole. Since I lived here for a while, I volunteered to do a site visit and meet with leadership at the campus here."

"Sitting back, I guess I can see the other side's point. Main thing is that they are receiving federal funds, public money. So it seems like they would eventually have to follow public rules."

"Yes and no. Precedence has been set with a few other schools across the country, out in Oregon and pockets in Cali. Down in South Carolina. Mostly out West and down South."

"Where?" The ambiance music was a little loud, and some crowd was noisy because of a marriage proposal not too far from where they were seated.

"In the West and South."

"Figures."

"Many of those schools applied for a Title Nine waiver. Congress gave colleges a way out as long as they could prove they were controlled by a religious organization. But the applications didn't start pouring in until a couple of years ago when Obama said your funding would be jeopardized if your campus discriminated against any group. This had implications for a lot of the students on campus like students who may have had abortions, or those who had babies out of wedlock, also those who said they didn't identify with their natural birth bodies. Waiver applications started being filed like the plague. They couldn't see themselves having to accommodate any of the students in these categories, especially with their moral stance."

"I bet. They aren't going to just lie down and take it. They've been around too long. I just don't see it lasting, though—the fight the schools are putting up. It can't. By all means, do your lawyerly job and do it well. People can even pray about it. You know me. I believe in prayer. But the fact remains is that it's federal money. Whether it takes five years or ten years or however many, pressure will eventually force them to change or lose their funding. That means no Pell Grants or work-study programs or federal loans for students."

"That's why I wanted to speak with you Garnet. You have a way of helping me see the big picture."

"Gramma, when the food coming?" R.J. inquired.

"It's coming in a minute, baby. Gramma knows you're hungry. They have to cook things to order here. It's not like a fast food restaurant."

She continued with the attorney. "I don't mean to be a killjoy, Cason. I really don't. You're a great lawyer, and I know you'll find a way to make it work. I'm just saying, and I always have said, it's always better when you're in a place of self-sufficiency. You don't really have that much say or sway with those who are keeping you afloat financially. You may think you do but you don't.

"If they really want to survive and stay true to their fundamental beliefs, you and the rest of the lawyers are going to have to guide them in the way of producing their own revenue to sustain their own operations. I don't have the solutions in that regard, but they'll have to do their due diligence and start appealing to their alumni base or finding some other creative way of generating funds. It depends on how important it is to them to keep the university open. I think it's admirable that they have convictions they are standing for, but they also have to have a plan and put themselves in a position where they aren't begging from the government and can thrive off of their own financial strategies that they implement. They could learn a thing or three from Jews in that regard. They've learned to stick together and pool their resources to a point where they function as a tight-knit community and make themselves independent financially. They're their own community within the community. And they're running things."

"Yeah, that's true."

"It's just a matter of time. If they keep receiving federal funds, they're going to have to comply with what the federal government mandates. Now or later."

Belial didn't waste any time on attending such a pointless meeting. While the two met inside, shot the breeze with a few of his impish friends along the Strip, wooing, harassing, and threatening. He knew the problem could be solved through institutions' becoming more self-supporting but was further aware of their indolence in doing so. As long as the government freebies streamed in, they had no need to shore up their financially independent strength. This pulling of the carpet from under their financial feet should have been a wake-up call for them, but Belial had witnessed, time and time again, these schools' whining and state of fiscal impotence. Their lot was either to get disciplined and self-sustain or to stay dependent and conform. Or to be shut down. The final two options were often the verdict, and he reveled in their ultimate demise.

The waiter arrived with their entrees. "Here we go, Sir and Madam." He placed each dish in front of the appropriate owner.

"So how did you go from 'Monsieur et Mademoiselle' to 'Sir and Madam'?" joked Garnet.

"The closer the time comes for me to get off," the waiter jested, "the less French I remember." He could do nothing but laugh, clear their bread plates, and refill their water glasses.

Conversation continued about the case. It was going to be a doozy. Cason loved his gifted and beloved church buddy because she shot straight, and he believed her gift was indeed working tonight. He promised to keep her posted on any new developments but mostly asked her to pray for the best outcome. As for R.J., he was simply learning to like his first taste of hand-harvested sea scallops.

Parks were never really her fascination. They seemed to represent a fake world within a world of reality. Trees blew in unorganized organization. Skateboarders never fell. No matter how hot it was, a puddle that was just the right size for birds to play and wash in always appeared out of nowhere. Families walked through the grassy fields, feigning happiness. Davida laughed at the notion of how couples could walk across the park's heavenly terrain hand in hand with baby in carriage and dog in tow but return home and fight tooth and nail about frivolities. She played out how he probably called her fat when they made it back home. She wasn't cynical, just realistic. It was in part the struggle she was having with following the Lord wholeheartedly. All this nature stuff came across too neat, too phony, overrated. If this was supposed to be a reflection of God, there was no way He'd be able to relate to her and her flawed, imperfect self.

But she couldn't pass up Tario's invitation to pass some time away at Lorenzi Park. Two sparrows, both on the lookout for threatening prey, anxiously jostled each other over a piece of cone that fell from Davida's ice cream treat. One grabbed it and started hopping away, only to be bumped by the other one until the prize was released. And then roles reversed, ending with the same result.

"Don't they know that they can both be happy if they learn to share?" stated Tario.

"Let's see if we can get humans to learn that lesson first. Then we can worry about teaching it to birds."

"They turnin' what's supposed to be a peaceful moment into fightin' and bickerin'."

"Listen at you. Sounding all sensitive."

"Nah, just sayin'."

"Anyway, thank you for the ice cream. You can't beat the thirty-one flavors of Baskin Robins."

"And you damn near got all thirty-one of 'em. Greedy ass."

"I knew I wasn't paying. And don't curse at me."

"I didn't cuss at you. I cussed about you."

"Don't do that either. Or I'm gonna have to pray that the Lord get you, right after I ask Dr. Gibbs how she does it," she announced.

"You and that Dr. Gibbs. She know she is some kind of funny. She learning you well, ain't she?"

"What you mean by that?"

"She helpin' you get your life together. That's what you want, ain't it? That's what made you kick me to the curb."

"Tario, stop. I'm just taking some time to get myself together. You should, too. I'm not perfect, and I have a long way to go. But I'm learning how to get closer to Him every day. I don't know how to pray no long, drawn-out prayers. Jamay says to just talk to Him just like I'm talking to you."

"Um, if that's the case, you in trouble. Have you heard how you been talkin' to me lately?"

"You know what? I can't with you."

"I'm just sayin'. And It sounds like you giving me the typical it's-not-you-it's-me talk."

"Well, it's *not* you. It *is* me."

"And you gone pass up on all this?" He lifted up his shirt, revealing his defined six pack. She couldn't resist the urge to look and laugh.

"See. You need to quit. I don't need to be lookin' at all that. I'm trying to stay on the straight and narrow."

"I got something for you that's straight and narrow."

"Excuse me, either of you got a quarter?" They were interrupted by a homeless man.

"No, sir."

"No," echoed Tario.

"Thanks, anyway. God bless." He continued on his way, looking to find others to ask.

"At least he said, 'Thanks' and 'God bless,'" said Tario.

"That was reverse psychology. He was hoping you would see how great of a personality he has so you would change your mind on the spot and give him some change. He don't know that I know reverse reverse psychology. I can beat him at his own game."

"Stop judging that man. You don't know that. I thought you were supposed to be so saved. Now there you go, sizing that man up. He just asked for a quarter, not your life savings."

"Call it what you want to. I guess that's where the Lord gotta help me big time. I lived in New York for a good minute. I've seen it all. If I told you all the stuff I saw when I was there, we'll be here for another two days."

"I forgot you lived in New York. My cousin just moved over there about two months ago. Over by some street called Green-wich."

Davida laughed and corrected him. "Grennich. It's pronounced Grennich."

"Well, that ain't how it's spelled."

"I'm just telling you. Just like another street is pronounced

How-ston, but it's spelled like the major city in Texas. Just one of those things you learn when you move there."

"And what braniacs made the decision to pronounce the words different than how they spelled? Somebody musta said, 'We wanna confuse the hell outta people, so let's spell it one way and pronounce it another.'"

"You so dumb."

"Now how 'bout you go home and make me a sannich."

"You got jokes."

"According to you, that's how you 'posed to say it."

"It's not no 'according to me' nothing."

Tario received a text, showing a link to a Facebook page with wacky jokes. "Look at this stupidity on display." He handed her his Galaxy S7. It was the soft-drink station inside a fast-food restaurant. The carbon in the Coca-Cola fountain had run out, so the worker had taped a sign on it that read, *"Sorry, out of Cock."*

"Some people! We gone get them some help."

While showing her several more absurdities, another text came through, asking if he was going to the Greek party tonight.

"Somebody wanna know if you going to the Greek party tonight."

"Oh, snap. Give it here." He grabbed his phone. "No doubt. I'm definitely gone have this fine face in the place."

"I guess. Where is it?"

"Over by Huntridge. One of my frat brothers rented out the rec center in his complex."

"Huntridge? Isn't that area sort of uppity?"

"Don't know. Never been there. His parents footin' the bill while he in school. They say they don't want him bein' distracted, so they found a real nice area for him to stay in. Spoiled ass."

"Oh, well I think it is. Y'all better be careful over there. That's not the hood. Those people over there are on the snooty side."

"They better be happy we gone be there. We gone bring character to the place," he promised. "They gone know that Omega Psi Phi was in the place." He stood up, patted his overlapping Omega brands on his right deltoid, and shouted in his manly voice, "Q PHI-EEE!"

Those in the park within earshot of his rant looked toward their way and began smiling, while the two blue jays surprisingly were still trying to solve their cone dilemma.

In the tree next to the couple, Belial watched them, knowing this assignment wouldn't be as smooth-sailing as that concerning the college. Although Tario was obnoxious, he was a potential danger to the kingdom of darkness because he had such a following, not just on social media, but he was a natural-born leader; what he did, people seemed to do or want to do. If he came to the Lord, others would surely follow. So he'd have to hatch a plan to have the man destroyed. In fact, Belial was the one who prodded his Greek brother to send him the text about the frat party. Tario wouldn't pass up this chance to be the life of the party. This is where it would go down.

Smiling, Belial looked down and gazed at Tario. And smiling, Raphaela, perched away at a distance, looked down and gazed at Belial.

MEETING PREPARATIONS

AN HOUR HAD gone by, and it seemed as if she had only just begun. A tear made its way down her left cheek. By this time, she sensed it wasn't her praying. She was just the vessel, the conduit. She heard herself but knew she couldn't possibly know to pray for or against all the stuff that came out of her mouth. Some of it made sense to her: Cason and LCU, Jamay, the two Redds, Mayor Goodman, Tario. Other things confused her to no end: UNLV's assistant basketball coach, something called Tornado Alley, and still she prayed for whoever Krunchy was. Out of those, she kept praying intensely for three of them.

"Father, protect Tario. Protect my son-in-law. Cover Krunchy. Help them, Lord. Don't let the enemy have his way with them. Bind up every force of hell that comes to wipe them out. Tario, Redd, Krunchy. Tario, Redd, Krunchy. Tario, Redd, Krunchy." She lifted from knees and began her usual ritual of pacing the floor. *"Tario, Redd, Krunchy."* She began walking through the house, not caring specifically if she awakened anyone. *"Bless*

them, Lord. Keep them out of harm's way. We need You. They need You. If you don't help them, Lord, they aren't going to make it." She walked and lifted both hands and continued for another fifteen minutes or maybe longer. She didn't know.

"Mama, you okay?" asked Jamay. She knew her mother was fine but just asked anyway. She knew that once her mother got in this vein, there was no stopping. Sleep could be recovered, but lives couldn't.

"Yes, baby. I'm fine. I need you to help me call out to Him. Something's wrong." As Garnet repeated the three names, Jamay joined in. R.J. was awake by now, too, and stood by his door quietly. "Come on R.J. I need you to pray with grandma. Just say what I say. You don't have to say it loud. Just repeat it."

Garnet walked. Jamay walked behind her, and R.J. followed. He only repeated Tario's name and replaced Redd with "daddy." He knew of no Krunchy. They all carried on until Garnet felt the intensity subside. She was used to not questioning these moments. Praying like this didn't happen too frequently, so she just yielded and grabbed those in the home into her vortex whenever it occurred.

Gabriel perked up at the family's intercession. Prayers this intense suggested something dire in the making and would go south if help was not released. He'd have to spend most of his time in the near future in Afghanistan. He sensed some strategy of the enemy that would affect Redd. He knew these strategies were well-planned and methodical. He put nothing past the enemy, who was wise and shrewd in his own right. Belial was often involved in the execution of such plans of destruction, but he wouldn't be surprised if Mictian's assistance would be enlisted to fight this one. He had recently been promoted to being chiefly responsible for wreaking havoc on families in this district.

While R.J. made his way back to bed, the mother and daughter decompressed in the kitchen, relaxing at the kitchen table. Garnet had brewed a single cup of Sanka. Jamay grabbed her Kamboucha black tea from the frig.

"The Lord is wonderful," breathed the matriarch.

"Yes, mama, he is."

"His wisdom is far above any education, any degrees, my PhD, or any letters you can put behind your name. I wish more people would realize that. Paul said that everything that had to do with his earthly smarts or pedigree was but dung when compared to God's excellence. Once we get to a point where we think we're more intelligent than the Creator, we end up in a place of disaster."

"He's worthy." After a moment or two of silence, Jamay felt comfortable enough to change the subject. "Redd emailed me and said it would be a good idea if he and R.J. meet."

"Meet? And how are they exactly supposed to do that? That child can't go to Afghanistan any time soon."

"No, not like that. But they can meet on the computer using Google Hangouts."

Garnet was no Luddite, but she wasn't exactly sure how a meeting on the computer would take place logistically. She had barely become at ease with Facebook. In fact, that was all she knew. Nothing more made sense to her. No Instagram, No Twitter. No nothing. She got nervous when one of her students in class said something about the message from Snapchat self-destructing. She thought it was a real bomb that would blow up in class and sharply warned students not to use any of that foolishness while she was teaching. No bomb would go off on her watch. "How are they supposed to do that?"

"They would just call each other on the computer and

start talking when they got connected. But they wouldn't just be able to hear each other. They could see each other too."

"Get outta here. Really?"

"We've come a long way with technology, mama."

"Well, however it works, I know the child will appreciate it. He doesn't talk much about his daddy, but I know he misses him. I can just see it in his face. It's a shame he still has to serve in that military. Why can't they just send them soldiers home. Seems to me like since it's only a few of them over there, they're in more danger. It's not like it's a bunch of them over there."

"Yeah, I know. They're the last group over there. Redd said they're just training the soldiers who live there to know how to defend their own country against ISIS."

"So they're basically teaching them how to fight, huh? The real way to fight is by dropping to your knees and dealing with the problem from the *real* source. These other problems are just symptoms."

"Other problems?"

"You know what I mean, Jamay. We're focusing on things that are not getting at the root of the situation. It's like putting makeup on your face to cover up acne. You know you had acne real bad. It wasn't until you started drinking more water that your face started clearing up. You have to get to the core of the problem, which is always a spiritual core. Only fervent prayer makes the difference."

Jamay consumed her health drink in silent agreement.

Nieko got to the gym around 6 in the morning. Lately, he'd started swinging by City Athletic Club before heading into work. With his twenty-sixth birthday approaching, he'd promised this new membership would help to slim him back down an extra five pounds or so to 190. Not bad on a six-foot frame. He initially pointed the finger at his daily three cups of coffee, but that finger-pointing was getting old, too. Laziness was the real problem as was his slipshod diet. Going to the gym was helping to keep him focused and healthily distracted.

Usual members filed in and did what needed to be done to make the visible baggage whittle away. Dedication was key, but some managed to overdo it, showing up every day, including Sundays. Nieko conquered machines like nobody's business. Granted, not much weight was on them, but a trainer had clued him in to the secret of doing more reps with less weight as opposed to doing less of them with more. He was advised to be more consistent with taking multivitamins and extra doses of vitamins C and D. But now, he just sat and rested between sets. Frequently catching himself looking at guys through the huge workout mirror, he'd get a few glances back but opted not to pursue what he thought was there. *"Lord, help. Keep my mind. Stay focused,"* he said to himself. He'd give himself these pep talks whenever he felt like he needed an extra push to keep on path.

He had gotten into his workout rhythm, deciding to end with the decline bench press. Burn from going through the upper-body circuit was setting in. The lactic acid had begun flaring. It made sense to stop, but he was in the groove. No backing down now. One set down, two to go. Second set . . . five, six, seven, eight. The bar started upward but succumbed to gravity, resting on a war-torn chest. He struggled to push it up, blowing hard and hissing.

"I got it, yo." A pair of light-skinned hands grabbed the bar and steadied it upward. "Push, man. Come on, push." It reached the top.

"Nine. One more," signaled Nieko. The bar lowered one final time as it reached his chest.

"You got this," said the guy. Gripping the metal opponent, the four hands pushed and pulled, depending on who they belonged to. "Push . . . push . . . push!" The final slam onto the rack signified victory. "Told you, man. That was all you. I was just guiding."

"Yo, man, that hurt." Nieko rubbed his pecan arms and his chest. "Relief!"

"Good job, yo. That's that good pain. People don't realize how important doing declines is. It beefs up underneath the pecs. You see those people that just do regular bench press and inclines. They ain't got no definition underneath to balance it out. Look like they got straight up titties hanging down." He demonstrated on Nieko's chest, touching the area underneath his pecs to drive home the point.

Nieko laughed. "Yo, you wild. I'm Neek, man."

"I'm dead ass. You gotta balance it out. Jacques." They shook hands. Nieko noticed the one-piece Jacques wore that stopped at his knees, similar to professional weightlifters. It suggested that whoever wore it was comfortable in his skin. Nobody just up and wore one-pieces to the gym unless they knew who they were. "Let me get one in while you wait." Although there were 145 pounds to be lifted, Jacques breezed through ten reps like he was lifting only the bar.

"I could do that, too, if I just walked in," joked Nieko.

"Yo, I been here two hours. I done did uppers and lowers. I was on my way out."

"Oh, aight. You got me," confessed Nieko. "Thanks for help. Ya boy was about exhausted. I don't know if I should even do this last set."

"You good, man. I got you."

Two minutes crept by. Nieko stared at Jacques through mirror. He glanced a moment, stared away the next. He was trying to determine if there was any vibe his spotter was giving off. The spirit was willing, but the flesh was weak, especially in this place. None. Jacques paid him no mind, simply tinkering with his phone and presumably checking email or Instagram. He actually thought it refreshing not to have to deal with the stares, the secret looks, the maybe situations. Jacques just appeared to be a normal fellow.

But that didn't mean this last set wouldn't still be a challenge. Nieko set himself to give it a final go. He lay back on the bench. He had no choice but to extend all the way back and downward. If he stayed in the position too long, the blood would rush to his head. But that also meant Jacques had to assume the spotting position. There was no other way. He stood above Nieko, his crotch in eye view. The one-piece was body tight. He provided more spotting support with each rep for this set since the muscles were shot to hell.

"Let's go, Neek. You got it." With every rep came the assistance, the squatting, the view.

"Stay focused," Nieko encouraged himself. He meant this on more than one level. *"Keep my mind."* After much struggling, hard breathing, and grunting, he finally reached ten. "Whew. Thanks, man. I might have to take a whole week off after this. Ain't no way I can do no sit-ups after this."

"Ha. That's why I get mine out the way, first thing. I know I ain't gone have no energy at the end."

"Hey, baby, you ready?" a woman asked.

"Yeah, no doubt. Just helping my man get these last ones in. Neek, this my girl, Tessa."

"Nice to meet you, Neek. Gettin' it in, huh?"

"Indeed. I'm hoping I can start seeing more results soon."

"Results?" she interjected. "You look pretty good already."

"Just some things I wanna tighten up on."

"Yo, anyway, we out, big man," said Jacques. "Got some running around to do. We'll be seeing you around. Work smarter, not harder." He gave him dap one final time.

"Nice meeting you," Tessa said.

"See you guys."

As the couple left, Nieko stared at them through the mirror as they simply engaged in small talk. He wasn't sure why he felt confused. He was realizing that it wasn't always about *that*, trying to see if anything was there or not. These were just people, just regular people. He was convinced that he'd have to keep retraining, reprogramming, renewing his mind. Amused, Ashtoreth stood on the side, grinning at his sense of internal doubt. But Uriel was noting it as progress, slow but sure progress.

By the time Nieko arrived at work, Raechell and Ajoy were already there getting ready for the day's task. "Hey, Neek." Ajoy was first. He had just finished washing the decaf coffee carafe.

"Lookin' good." Raechell followed. She placed the container of sugar packets and Sweet'N Lows on her cart and whisked right by Nieko on the way to the sink.

"Hello, good folks. How are my favorite two people doin' today?" They didn't respond. They were too busy collecting and gathering. Nieko himself even knew the question was rhetorical. Not expecting or waiting for an answer, he went to the rear of the kitchen to check the corkboard for the assignments and was none too pleased. "I swear, Raechell, they always givin' you President Chu's function."

He took his index finger and scrolled down the sheet and

saw his name and related information. He repeated it quietly to himself. "Nieko. The Diversity Meeting. Greenspun Hall 513. 11:45 p.m. Oh, well this should be fun. Lemme go get myself ready." He took all his belongings and made his way out to get ready for the day. It was only 10:30, so he wouldn't have to race the clock, unlike Ajoy. He was already five minutes late and stormed out of the kitchen as the commotion from the swinging door announced his departure. "Later, 'gators." He had to truck it to Lied Athletic Complex for a luncheon there and would have to run across campus. He'd been written up once for being late. And this would probably be strike two.

Nieko entered the changing room and looked at the divo staring back at him through the mirror. He opened his locker, and gently placed his expensive shoes inside on the rust-worn surface. He hung the gym bag on the chrome hook and then placed the rest of his stuff inside. He stared at his uniform that was already hanging inside the locker: the tuxedo, the white shirt, the cute black bowtie, the black comfortable shoes. He'd complete the look with his rugby black socks.

He was born and raised in Vegas over by North 28th. After graduation, he managed to move east to attend the Texas Culinary Academy in Austin but only stayed for four and a half months because he couldn't keep up with the costs. No real financial support from parents existed because they didn't have it. Members of the middle class, they barely had enough to stay above board. Nothing extra was set aside for their son's college years. But they were his moral support, encouraging him as best they could with what they emotionally had. After moving back home to Vegas, he never really got up enough momentum to get back to pursuing his culinary dreams. At least he lived in a better neighborhood, over by his job and not too far from the Strip. The views from his apartment were of the Mandalay Bay and the Aria and gave him just the right motivation needed to stay focused. He frequently dreamed about weekend staycations in those swanky hotels. City visitors weren't the only ones who had a right to enjoy those downtown oases.

He was still around food but just from a different angle: catering at the university. It helped him keep his mind in the game locally while still hoping globally. Who knew what would come out of this if he stayed the culinary course? He'd just set up lunch for this afternoon's diversity meeting and dwell in the background, making sure the self-service meal, along with its teas, coffees, waters, and sodas, was all ready to go. These meetings were only an hour, and faculty and staff would have to go back to their classes and desk jobs at a precise time. Nieko had it down to a science. The lunch table would already be dressed, and he'd wheel in whatever had been ordered to make lunchtime go smoothly.

Raechell yelled from the kitchen, "Bye, Nieko. I'm headed to President Chu's office. I hear they got some heavy hitters meeting with her." She ate one of the pastries off her own cart to make sure it would pass everyone's palate test.

After putting on his garb, Nieko took one last look at his reflection. That mirror needed to be cleaned and needed it fast. Not thinking, he took one of his nails and started scraping through some gunk that had become lodged there. He regretted it and made a nasty face after the dirt came off the mirror. *Alright, Nieko, here we go.* It was his daily mantra. This was him. His nine-to-five him. God knows he couldn't wait to get back to his five-to-nine him. He breathed in and out and adjusted his clothes. The muscle burn was still thumping, so he just needed to make it through this meeting.

21

ROOM 513

CELESTE HAD TEXTED Garnet earlier asking if she'd be in attendance at the meeting at noon: *"u gone be at greensnug today for mtg?"* All lowercase letters in her texts were standard for her friends and less so for more professional communiqués. She had been waiting for a response for at least ten minutes. That meant Garnet was probably still in class, finishing her lecture. Soon, the new Android phone Celeste recently got made the familiar canary tone, buzzing at the same time. Garnet was responding, replying only with the question mark sign.

Celeste reread her initial text and blew out a whiff of air, clearly fed up with this new technology. She used her right index finger to text Garnet another message: *"darn autocorrect. sick of this fone. meant greenspun."* The speed at which she was able to text was insane.

Already alert to the mistake, Garnet just called Celeste on her office phone to save some typing time. Celeste picked up on the first ring, noticing her buddy's name and made her exclamation, "I am getting ready to throw this phone out the window!"

Garnet cackled her favorite laugh. "You and that phone. I remember the text that time that was supposed to say '*pedis and coffee?*' that you sent me. I ain't even gone remind you what your so-called autocorrect turned 'pedis' into. I was through. Too through."

"Don't remind me. That was so embarrassing. And you with your Christian self. I felt more stupid for that reason alone."

"Well, I've had sex before. Mind you, I been married before. So I know what one of those looks like. Admittedly, those two things together would have made a good duo to my former self," Garnet calmly whispered. She was still in the office, sitting at her desk with her right hand covered in chalk. "Anyway, yeah I think I'll be at the meeting even though I really don't wanna go. That Diversity Committee is something else. So many people on it. So many ways people think. So many points of view. We've had some heated discussions before, and I'm sure we'll have one today. That whole diversity thing on universities been causing up a stir, girl. But this my last year on the committee so I better go and show my face. I'll just sit back and observe like I normally do."

"You ain't got to tell me. I be sittin' right up in there, too, right along with you. That Leigh know she something else. Ready to argue with anything that come up against her Christianity. She be on a mission. She coulda been one of the twelve disciples."

"Perhaps. But it be the loud ones that wind up being a coward and denying Christ like Peter. So loud except for when it count. And by the way, it was more than twelve."

"And both of y'all are Christians and so different. You barely say a word about what you believe out in public, but you can't shut her up." Celeste logged out of her desktop and put her shoes back on.

"Lessie, I don't know. I just sort of let her be her. I think she means well. I pray for her a lot. Just like I pray for you a lot. We just different. I never really had an extended conversation with her. We just stay on our own path, I guess."

"Well, lemme get outta here. The meeting starts in ten minutes," Celeste said. "I think they gone have lunch for us."

"Yeah, I think so. If nothing else, girl, they know they be servin' some good vittles. I be's hungry," said the professor. "I'll be there in a minute. I need to wash this chalk off my hands." She had squirted some hand sanitizer on them during the phone chat, but chalk remained inside the M on both palms.

"See you in a minute. Hope it won't be no dramatics," she gave a final laugh.

"Keep hopin'. Save me a seat."

Room 513 in Greenspun had been host to many circus acts called meetings at the university. Planners booked it because it was extra commodious, had huge windows, and had those adjustable ergonomic chairs that had the erect spine built into them. The building was the first on campus strictly dedicated to passing green standards, with its stellar environmentally sustainable designs, including solar panels that harnessed energy from the sun. What was of greater importance to those attending meetings there was that the Wi-Fi was terribly strong, a plus for them who would use the meeting time to update statuses and peer into people's fake happy lives. Even in the basement, modems provided a connection of incomparable strength. Once, one employee who worked daily in the building even tried to get her doctor to diagnose her dizzy spells and nausea as being tied to her exposure to invisible radiation there. She thought it was just basically functioning as a big microwave oven and hoped to start drawing disability and unemployment checks. Her efforts failed.

But flies on the wall during meetings in 513 had taken many a juicy story back to their grist. The room seemed to have its own set of omens hanging over it. There was the time when the dean of Academic Affairs met with his staff and inadvertently snapped, calling his secretary a nigger. Then, there was the occasion where Coach Peters met with the assistant coaches in preparation for the upcoming homecoming festivities; while he was motivating them to stay on top of plans for this year, he suffered a stroke and passed away on the spot, right by the smart podium. And no one would ever forget when chief security personnel met there to conclude training for its newest staff. Everybody wanted to be the one in charge, and egos went a-flyin'. What had started as a decent, celebratory gathering ended with blows, fist-to-the-face blows. But these were all just coincidences. A room surely didn't have a heartbeat, a mind, a will, a personality.

Everyone started filing in around five of. Since the group met so infrequently, greetings and hugs were the order of the hour. Some placed their personals by their seat to mark their territory while they ran out for a quick bathroom visit. The conference table was a long table that took up almost the entire space of the room. In case more space was needed, other comfy chairs lined the walls of the room. Celeste was seated at the conference table and placed her dark yellow, button-down sweater across the back of the chair beside hers. "Yes, someone is sitting here," she told Nabuka from African Studies. "That Garnet's seat."

At the head of the table sat a guest, who mingled with no one. She just wrote on a notepad and calmly waited for the meeting. Celeste glanced at her and thought nothing of it. As of now, she was starving, and the announcement from Paola, the director of the committee, came right on time. "Everyone, we'll get started in just a minute. In the meantime, go ahead and grab lunch. We wanna start on time because we have a lot to discuss."

Nieko had arrived forty-five minutes earlier to set up. Plates first. Then food. Then utensils at the very end of the table. A separate cold drink and coffee station. He had experienced situations where people tried to carry and balance all of their stuff, often ending with a brooming or mopping. As faculty and staff made their way through the line, Nieko smiled and floated across the room, offering assistance where needed. There had to be at least three Niekos in the room, the way he was here and there at the same time. All treated him as part of the family, too, inquiring about his desire to get back to his culinary passions. He would go back to school soon was what he told them.

All finally settled themselves and grabbed their seats. Garnet had sneaked in and took her place beside Celeste. The conference table was full of participants, including the mystery woman who still sat silently, enjoying no food. She told Paola she'd eat after the meeting. Those less fortunate sat alongside the wall and used their knees to balance lunch. It was five after, so Paola decided to forge ahead with the day's flow. She began, "Hi again, everybody. I'm glad we could all make it today. You know, we don't get to see each other that often, so it's always good to catch up and handle business of the Diversity Committee." Paola knew she was being ignored. She was no match up against Nieko's spread. Mouths were busy chewing. Dalvin's from Physical Education was doing so obnoxiously. Chewing with his mouth open and didn't care. To say these folks were pigging out was an understatement. Except Garnet. Paola, while watching everybody eat, noticed Garnet with elbows on table, hands clasped together with fingers interlocked, and head resting on hands while her food patiently waited. She assumed Garnet was praying but never wanted to offend and ask. Maybe she was resting and trying to gather herself from a stressful job.

Indeed, Garnet was praying over her food. She didn't make a big deal out of it. Neither did she try to hide it like many, who rested their heads on their hand and acted like they were wiping their forehead with eyes closed.

Paola continued, "You all have had an opportunity to look over minutes from the last meeting. We sent them electronically. Were there any questions or corrections?" Silence followed. Nobody had read them but wouldn't admit that he or she hadn't. "If not, can we get a motion to approve and accept them?"

"I move that we accept the minutes," said Johnny from Physics. God forbid his being challenged on the details therein.

"So moved," Paola followed up. "All in favor of accepting the minutes as sent, let it be known by raising your right hand." All right hands were lifted. "Alright. We have accepted and approved minutes from our last meeting." She transitioned into the business at hand. "On to the new business. We're so happy to have a visitor today to join us for today's diversity meeting." The mystery guest looked up from her notepad and glanced at Paola. "I'd like for everyone to help me welcome Becca Dobson from The Los Angeles Pride Center. We've been planning her visit for quite a while and are happy to finally welcome her to our campus to talk about how we can make

our community a more welcoming place for the LBGT community." Everyone except Garnet stopped eating and drinking
and glanced up. They had discussed matters pertaining to tol-
erance among themselves, but this was the first time they had
discussed these issues with an outsider. Everyone figured the
conversation would be civilized and not over-the-top, especially since Leigh wasn't present. Most of the attendees were
silently relieved.

Paola finished her introduction, "Becca has extensive
training with helping university committees such as ours foster
healthy growth for all and reduce situations where people feel
marginalized and shunned. We're looking forward to a great
experience on today and would like to welcome her. So, without further ado, I'd like to turn the floor over to our speaker.
Becca?" She looked at the guest and started clapping.

Becca decided to remain seated. At Paola's request, Nieko
had fixed Becca a modest lunch plate and delivered it to her
right as she began speaking. Becca placed a grape in her mouth
and commenced, "Thank you so much Paola for that introduction." She looked around the table and continued, "And
thank you all for having me lead your discussion today. We're
always looking to help institutions increase their sensitivity
to making sure we treat all people equally. The idea is that we
want everybody to feel like they can come to the table and be
accepted as their whole self. Not just be tolerated at the table
but to change the table itself."

Her metaphor threw people off. Dalvin squinted, trying
to figure it out. Celeste nudged Garnet with her leg, but
Garnet ignored it. Celeste thought Becca was trying too hard.
Garnet continued sipping coffee and looking at Becca, who
indeed was an interesting spectacle to behold. On the left side
of her head, her hair was shaved. It slightly gained volume as

it maneuvered to the right side, covering her right eye and stretching to her right shoulder. She was attempting to give off a punkish vibe, but the wrinkles on her neck gave away her age. She tried to temper her style by donning a purple scarf. Everyone silently agreed that it was a fashion faux pas. It just didn't work.

The guest speaker kept going, "Specifically, we're looking to see if there's anything more we can be doing to be more welcoming to the LGBTQQIP2SAA community." Some around the table started shifting uncomfortably.

"Wait. It's two Q's and two A's? What do those stand for?" whispered Ming Lee, who taught in Asian Studies, to Marjorie.

"Questioning, queer, androgynous, and asexual." Marjorie quickly clarified. She wore her normal jeans, collared shirt, and skinny necktie, her signature look.

Celeste whispered to Garnet, "Girl, that's just too many letters for me. By the time they finish figurin' out who they is, ween gone have no letters left in the alphabet. Dis too much." Garnet tried not to laugh and said *"Jesus"* to herself. She was trying to ignore Celeste, but that was a tall task, given Celeste's stabs at comedy at meetings like these.

Becca took the reins again, "And with all of the hate crimes that have happened in the surrounding Vegas community, we just want to make sure that students and staff here who fall in that category are respected and protected. In fact, has everyone here gone through the Safe Zone training?"

"Yes," replied Paola. She was half-right, half-wrong. Not everyone on the committee had.

"Great. That's a start. And what about the bathroom situation? Do you have separate bathrooms for those who identify themselves as 'not male' or 'not women'? Are they easily accessible?"

Paola gloated, "Yes. We sure do. We have two."

"We do? Where?" Nabuka was taken aback. This was her fourth year on faculty and had no idea there were separate bathrooms on campus for such students.

Paolo answered, "One's in the Student Union and the other's in the Student Services Complex."

Dalvin chimed in, "Well, it'll be nice to have one built by the gym. As gym teacher, I had a kid ask if there was a special bathroom for him. I didn't know what the hell he was talking about. 'Til he told me to refer to him as 'she' instead of 'he' now. It's a whole 'nother ball o' wax 'cause now they gotta change clothes in front of everybody. You think you're saying the right terms, and then they get offended and think you're trying to disrespect them." Dalvin was an older guy, sixty-six to be exact. He was still an old-school fellow, not taking well to the new changes on the campus as it related to this thing called diversity. He tried to remain open-minded regarding change but reverted to his comfortable, conservative ways.

"I understand your concerns," Becca said. "We really do have to be aware of the soft spots as they relate to the community. Like the term 'queer' isn't really kosher nowadays. Back in the '50s and '60s, gay people wore that term like a badge of honor. They were here, queer, and told everybody to get used to it. Now, it's taken on more of a pejorative connotation. As has the term 'transvestite' or 'tranny.' It's not really used anymore. It's kind of offensive. The main thing is to use committees and forums like this to research and discuss the terms more socially acceptable to use at any given time."

Becca was warmed up now and was ready to get major discussions going, and she had the perfect exercise for the group. "So what we're gonna do now is an exercise I call 'Standing Up for What's Right.' I'm gonna read a few statements one by one. If you agree with the statements, I'd like for you to literally stand up from where you're seated. Since we've all pretty much finished with lunch, this will be a great time we can work off the wonderful food we just ate." As she offered the compliment, she looked over at Nieko, who was picking up plates from those who had finished and placing them on his cart. He also refreshed the coffee station. He had been eavesdropping, thinking how much of a coincidence this discussion was in light of his own journey. He thought participants might need a little extra caffeine, given the direction the conversation appeared to be going.

"Alright. Here we go." All seemed to be a bit nervous. Never had they had to stand for or against a statement individually and publicly. Their jitters wouldn't stop Becca, however. She stood up and would remain standing throughout the exercise. "Number One. No person should be discriminated against or disrespected."

Everyone stood and looked around. "Okay," voiced Becca. "It's good to know that we all believe that." She took a sip of Sprite. Buttocks found themselves back to their seats, and all awaited the next question. "Number two. If a student comes out to me as gay, I will be affirming and encourage him or her to live according to how they feel is right." Chairs scuffed the hardwood floor and bent knees became straightened—all except Celeste's, Garnet's, and Dalvin's. Standing members eyed seated members with half-surprise, half-confusion. At least for Garnet. They seemed to understand Dalvin's reason. He was old. And Celeste was just Garnet's shadow, or so they thought. But Garnet was always so nice, cordial, and seemingly liberal. "Okay, any discussion from those seated? No pressure," prodded Becca.

"No, not particularly," inserted Celeste.

Garnet added, "I would definitely thank the student for

feeling comfortable enough to approach me and tell me. After that, I'd refer them to counseling for more assistance. My own personal beliefs would hinder me from affirming them in that lifestyle, though." She said all of this with a gentle smile.

Smile or no smile, standing members thought she was narrow-minded and held a viewpoint that was a bit outdated. They reasoned in themselves why anybody who felt that way would be on the committee. They bit their tongue and sat down, but not before Ming Lee stepped out to use the restroom.

"Alright. Here's the third one," Becca proceeded, "All students should be encouraged to support gay rights and its political agenda."

"Yes, that's great," voiced Marjorie as she hurried and stood. Her standing wasn't enough, however. "Indeed. We've got to teach this next generation how to be tolerant and point them toward being a more enlightened generation than we were." Mostly all agreed and stood except for the obvious ones. Nieko had stopped cleaning and tidying, as he had become engrossed in these questions and responses. He sipped some coffee as things seemed to be getting heated.

As Garnet sat and grinned, she prepared her mouth to rebut but was forestalled by another sharper, louder voice. "That's absolutely ridiculous! There is no way you all can sit here, well . . . stand here and think that statement makes any sense!" It was a voice that belonged to none other than Leigh. A student who needed to meet with her about a missed exam had detained her in her office. She had quietly entered the meeting room and had gone by the lunch area to choose from what remained. She held her plate of a half-a-tuna sandwich and some fruit and made her way over to an empty chair by the wall. Nobody would have to guess what her vote was on the matter as she sat down deliberately while she had the floor and everybody's attention. Directing her attention to Becca, she dug in, "I know this is the Diversity Committee, but I have a serious concern about saying all students should have to do anything. Our role is not to make anybody feel the same way about anything."

She continued, "I remember I had a student last semester who shared with me that she was a Christian and didn't feel like being gay was right." There was no such student, but nobody could prove Leigh wrong. She could safely hide behind this imaginary student to channel her own views. "She told me she always felt like her feelings and perspective were pushed to the side just because she lived according to a very conservative, Christian worldview. She has a right to feel the way she does without having us try to change her belief core. She has a right to agree to disagree."

"Well, I'm a Christian, too," said Peggy from the registrar's office. She was standing and turned toward Leigh. "I can recommend to the student a nice reference book about how to be a Christian and embrace those in that community."

Leigh barked back, "No! I'm not giving my student any reference book to try to persuade her to stop believing what she believes. I thought that's what diversity was supposed to be. To appreciate all perspectives, not just one. Diversity means understanding that there are differences at the table and to appreciate all of them. All of them! As long as she doesn't use her beliefs to inflict harm on somebody else, she can believe what she wants. It's her God-given right. Actually, I wonder how many of us would still be standing if the statement was, 'All students should be encouraged to support Christian's rights, the Christian community, and its agenda.'" She paused and rattled her ice cubes in her plastic cup. No one responded. "My point exactly. If it's good for the goose, it's good for the gander." She looked at the discussion leader square in her face as though she had gained a small victory.

"I can sort of see what Leigh is saying," added Seyto, who was the rep from Faculty Services. "Some of these students have been raised with deep religious convictions. So it doesn't really seem fair to force them to have to support a cause or agenda that goes directly against what they believe."

"Well, a lot of times, they don't support that community because of fear," Marjorie countered.

"Fear? Of what? Why does it have to be about fear?" responded Leigh indignantly. "Just because I don't agree with an idea or cause doesn't mean I'm afraid of it. That's a very narrow-minded statement, Marjorie." Out of all the faculty, she was the only one who called Marjorie by her real name, probably out of spite. And she failed to catch herself in time. She meant to reference the student.

"I honestly believe that most people who can't understand the plight and struggle of the community are just trapped in fear. I'm sorry. It's similar to how whites didn't respect the rights of the black community in the Jim Crow south in the early–"

"Oh, Lord! I knew it would just be a matter of time before someone would go there and bring that up. That's what's called a fallacy of false equivalence. Marjorie, please don't allow me to go into why those two scenarios are not and will never be the same. The gay struggle is *not* the same as the black struggle. I get so sick of people trying to equate that struggle with racism. It's *not* the same."

"Well enlighten us, Leigh, since you feel so strongly about it," said Marjorie. She pounded the table with her fist, more out of frustration than antagonism. The pounding was somewhat awkward since she did it from a standing position.

"First, you can choose to hide your orientation if you wish." She outed Marjorie on the spot, but it really wasn't an outing. Everybody knew. "But I can't hide my brown skin if I wanted to."

"That still doesn't mean that both groups still can't be discriminated against. I didn't choose to be this way. It's genetic, a part of my biological code. Why would anybody voluntarily choose a lifestyle that puts them in danger every single day to be jumped, beat up, or tortured?"

"The all-to-infamous 'gay gene,' huh?" murmured Leigh. "I personally don't believe you were born that way. But that's just me. If it's so biological, then why would it only happen to only one twin in a family as opposed to both of them? It's more nurture than nature. Much of the literature out there supports that. You should take a look at the article by R.C. Kirkpatrick. And in the twenty-first century, most of these students seem to be doing it as a fad. You know, it's the cool thing to do nowadays, to experiment with their sexuality and all. And I didn't say both groups weren't discriminated against. I'm just telling you why it's not the same as racism."

"Yes, I've read Kirkpatrick's article. But *you* need to read the one by the other R.C. as in R.C. Pillard, which tells why it supports my position to the letter."

Becca wanted to regain some semblance of control and remind all that she was the expert with respect to the literature. "Actually, Jannini's article suggests that it's more of a combination of the two. Neither nature nor nurture is the sole deciding factor. But let us stay focused. Our goal is not to argue about what causes it. We're talking about making sure all people on campus are not discriminated against."

"So, then, we need to start talking more about *others* who are discriminated against. Disabled people, Asians, other minorities. We haven't talked about any of these yet, and I been on this committee for two years. This diversity discussion is never balanced. Why everything gotta go back to this same topic. But anyway," Leigh started again, "back to the issue of comparing both struggles. I believe that gay folk generally live their lives in peace. Nobody is turning water hoses on them. Police dogs aren't attacking them. No Ku Klux Klan after them. They're not being lynched en masse, taking drinks at separate fountains, or asked to sit in the back of the bus. Any hardships they face can't compare to what black folk faced a hundred and fifty years ago or even fifty years ago."

"Oh, my God! Are you serious, Leigh? Do you even hear yourself right now? I guess you haven't heard what happened during the Stonewall riots of the '60s. Or I guess the name Matthew Shepard doesn't ring a bell for you, huh?"

"Yes, we all know how the few mild indignities in your community are to be equated to the systematic exploitation and institutional degradation that blacks had to endure. They are *not* equivalent struggles, Marjorie." Leigh smirked and chomped on a juicy piece of pineapple. She could be so sardonic, and it was getting under Marjorie's skin. Although Garnet's views were loosely more in line with Leigh's, she became visibly upset with how Leigh was handling the situation. After all, every situation was an opportunity to witness and draw people closer to Christ. Arguing with people didn't seem to be the right way, Garnet thought. Where was the love? Why would anyone want to live the saved life you professed to live if they couldn't sense the love behind your words. You didn't have to relinquish your views, but you didn't have to taunt others' views either. Stand your ground, and challenge what needed to be challenged. But do so with dignity and in love, she thought.

"Just turn on the TV, and open your eyes," Marjorie clapped back. "You'll see the discrimination and violence we have to endure. We're still struggling to get health benefits and the like in the event our spouses die. We have no protection."

"Marjorie, I see plenty of stuff on the TV and social media. Like how you're able to swim comfortably in the pool in your own neighborhood. Like how you can study and sleep unmolested in the lounge of the university where you're duly enrolled. Like how you can peacefully barbecue outside. Like how you can sit in Starbucks for hours and not get kicked out, even if you don't order nothing. Like how you can rent a house on Airbnb and not be bothered." Sarcasm was Leigh's middle name.

"Either way, it's a civil rights battle one in the same. You can't be mad about injustice for one thing and not be just as outraged at injustice for another. Right is right."

"So, then, talk about all injustices equally. Let's have discussion about *all* injustices, not the same thing all the time. I just hate when you all play the victim as if you're making no progress, while we're over here suffering to no end. And then you try to bully everybody to make them do what you want. That's why I'm glad the Supreme Court ruled the way it did and supported that man who refused to make the cake for that couple. Enough bullying is enough! Bake your own cake!"

"Ladies!" interjected Becca. "This is not a session to see which group has been treated the worse. This isn't my intention."

"She brought it up," quipped Leigh. "Just know that there will be some people who will agree and those who disagree when you talk about sensitive subjects like this. And no party should be made to feel ashamed at whatever their position is. So asking people to stand or not stand is the definite match that will start that fire."

Room 513 was living up to its reputation. The discussion was becoming more heated than Paola had bargained for. She thought she'd better jump in and try to smooth things over, "As you see, this topic is quite hot. We won't completely solve it here. I just thought we'd address this particular topic today and address others in the future."

Everyone sat down instinctively. Becca would forego reading any more scenarios for this exercise, although she was prepared to ask three more; time had escaped, and the meeting needed to be adjourned. Marjorie's restless shifting was a telltale sign that she was still upset with Leigh. Both glanced at each other to gauge the other's disposition. Marjorie drank a final sip of water out of nervousness. Leigh did so out of mere thirst.

Paola made closing remarks as members gathered their belongings. "Let's thank Becca for coming out and leading our discussion on today. It's always good to be able to discuss matters of diversity to make everyone's lives on campus better." Hands clapped throughout the room, and Becca smiled, adjusted her scarf, and nodded in appreciation. Paola kept at attempting to placate heated tempers. "And even if we don't agree on all things diverse, at least we can keep the conversation going and grow as leaders on campus. It's all about our students. Thanks for coming. Feel free to take any of the food with you as you leave."

Her attempts at calming the crowd were somewhat futile. Marjorie pushed her chair back and walked briskly toward the door, hurrying to get to her class since she was giving an exam, or so she said. She gave Leigh one final glance, to which Leigh was oblivious. Few others straggled to the food and coffee tables. Nieko, who had been all ears, was ecstatic to have been privy to the drama that unfolded. He helped everyone gather their scraps. There was no Saran wrap, so everyone mostly put sandwiches and bland broccoli on small clear plates, covering it with a flimsy napkin.

As bodies filed out, Paola stayed back, poured a cup of coffee, and chatted with Nieko. "Thanks, Nieko. You always do such a great job for us."

"No problem. My pleasure. Quite a lively discussion today."

Paola ripped open two Splenda and poured the contents into her cup. "Yeah, that's putting it mildly."

"I didn't mean to be nosy or nothing. I was trying to do my job but just couldn't help but overhearing." He was lying.

"You don't have to apologize. How could you not pay attention? We have some animated members, as you saw."

"Yeah," Nieko chuckled. "That was some controversial stuff you guys were talking about."

"Indeed. We just wanna—"

"Boss lady, your one o'clock is here." She was interrupted by her secretary.

"Okay. I'll be there in a minute. Alright, Mr. Nieko, take it easy. It's meeting after meeting after meeting. I tell you. I'll see you the next time." She grabbed her coffee and headed out.

Belial had been utterly entertained by the meeting's discord. He knew the different personalities present would create enough drama to last for ages. He'd have to move on to more serious business in Huntridge. Planning a death took notable skill, wit, and calculation. So off he went.

Nieko said goodbye and trashed all the food that was left. After he wincingly folded the linen, he shook his head, merely shook his head.

22
HUNTRIDGE

ALVIS DARTED IN front of the car behind him just before both had gotten off the exit. "That's right!" shouted Tario. "That's how you cut that fool off," he said to Alvis. They all decided to park at Alvis's and carpool to Huntridge. After twisting and turning throughout the complex, Alvis found the clubhouse and secured a park. They would have been four deep, but Kory had opted out. They sat because they just wanted to chill a moment before going in.

The owners of the car that had been cut off essentially followed the frat guys, except for the turn into the clubhouse. "Why do they have to come *here* and act like hoodlums?" the driver grumbled, as she ran her hands through her blond, flowy hair. Her husband was away on business in San Diego.

"It's no act," responded the manstress. "That's just how they are." He put his hand on her leg, laughing a hearty laugh.

"Just give it a little time. Our leader has been in office going on four years now," she reminded. "Just a matter of time before American is made great again." She adjusted his red MAGA hat on his head and chuckled again.

"And we all know what 'great' is code word for," he chuckled. "And I love it!"

"Let 'em run down their own neighborhoods and leave us be! They not satisfied until they find a decent area and monkey it up." She circled back to catch a final glimpse of the setting. She saw several cars at the clubhouse and saw the trio heading inside to meet the others. She became incensed all over again. "I think I may have a solution." Belial sat on top of the car and whispered something in her ear as she drove off.

The three Ques walked in and joined the celebration. It must have been about thirty of them there, or round about. To the unlearned, it could have been mistaken for a dog kennel. The chorus of barks was deafening. And it went on and on and on, mostly deep barks, not high- or middle-pitched ones. Never that.

"If it ain't the three a-negroes!" Phil said. "Get y'all asses in here. We 'bout to get it poppin' in here, my niggas!" Daps and man-hugs pervaded. Smells of weed, Henny breath, Ck One, and Bvlgari permeated the air. The dog-catcher anthem played in the background. It was berserk, a circus.

"Yo, Rio. Show us how it's done," Max said.

"Oh, you don't want none of this."

"Show me how it's done, my nigga."

Tario ripped off his shirt and went for broke. If the floor wasn't secure and sturdy, he would have stomped right through it. Between the claps over and under the leg, he did his thing. He opened his mouth and made his tongue protrude as far as it could go while killing his impromptu routine. Well, sort of impromptu. He rehearsed on occasion to make sure he would be well prepared for circumstances like this.

"Get it, Casper," chimed in Ed. He always referred to Tario

by his line name. Line brothers had received code names upon crossing into the fraternity. If possible, names either reflected certain characteristics or poked fun at skin color. Tario's name was apropos since he was on the darker side.

Everyone else joined in and started spinning, sliding, hopping, leaping, grinding the ground, and dry humping the couch. It was controlled pandemonium. What started halfway harmoniously always ended turnt up to the umpteenth degree.

Topless and sweating, Tario hit up the open bar. "What it do, gorgeous?" he said to the bartender.

"Hi there," responded a high-yellow stunner.

"What yo' name is?"

Laughing, she responded, "I'm Therese. What can I get you?"

"A salty dog." He leaned in. "And your number."

She would have been flattered, but she was used to staving off such advances, especially from frat guys with their alter egos. As was her custom, she smiled. "Listen at you," she said with a high-pitched squeak. "A salty dog. You gotta keep the theme going of ordering anything that fits in the canine family, huh? You Ques are something else." She strategically avoided any conversation about the phone number. She was the master at declining such asinine offers while preserving what shred of dignity guys like this had left. "We're out of gin. Vodka okay?"

"That's fine, gorgeous. You got Ciroc?"

"Yes, sir. I do. Want that?"

"Yes, ma'am. Ciroc will be perfect . . . witcho fine ass."

Grinning, she kept deflecting. "P. Diddy would be proud."

"I ain't thinkin' 'bout no damn Diddy. He ain't puttin' no money in my pocket. In fact, I'm puttin' my coins in his." She turned the highball glass upside down into the mound of salt and turned it clockwise and then filled with ice. "Whoa, baby. Let's just go with half of that ice. I need to make sure I can feel it."

She was getting ready to remind him that it was an open bar anyway, so there was no need to get bent out of shape over ice. Just order another free one. Not to mention the futility of the glass tip jar. It only contained three dollars, two of which were placed inside by the bartender herself. But she relented and poured some of it out.

"I'm Rio, by the way. They call me Tario for short. Maybe I can grab your number?"

She reached for the grapefruit juice to finish out the cocktail, propping a grapefruit wedge on the edge of the glass. "Here you go, sir. Especially made for you." She was used to dodging the requests for phone numbers.

To her surprise, he dropped five dollars in the tip jar. "And this is especially made for you."

"Thank you very much. That's so kind of you, Rio."

"No problem. I gotchu."

"Yo, Rio! You ain't the only one who want a drink, my nigga," said Keith. "You need to get her number player and move on."

"Man, just wait, nigga. I'm trying to, but she ain't taking the ba–"

Out of nowhere, the doorbell rang.

Glenn, thinking more of his brothers were at the door, gladly made his way to let them in. With drink in hand, he grooved his way to let them in. When the door swung open, he was shocked to see four cops at the door, two whites, one African-America, and one Latina. Flabbergasted, he was stuck in his tracks, not knowing what to say.

"Excuse me, sir. Are you the one in charge here?" said the Latina.

"Um, yes ma'am. Is there a problem?"

Ignoring his question, one of the others butted in. "Did you properly reserve this space for your function?"

"Yes, we went through the proper channels. What seems to be the pr–"

"Do you know why we're here?" interrupted one of the white cops, abruptly cutting Glenn off.

By this time, Alvis noticed his buddy was still at the door but couldn't make out what was transpiring. So he decided to go see for himself. When he reached the front, he seemed a little nervous and wanted to keep the conversation as civil as possible. "Hello, officers. Did we do anything wrong? We're just trying to have a good time. If we're too loud, we can quiet down some."

"No, we just need both of you to stand right there and don't move," said the other white cop. Two of the cops stayed put while the other two approached the two frats. They circled them, casually brushing against them periodically.

Glenn was trembling slightly and wondered if his glass would fall out of his hands. "Exactly what did we do wrong, officer?" he asked.

"Sir, please be quiet."

"Okay. I'm just a little uncomfortable. I just don't know what's going on."

"Yo, be quiet, G-man. These officers don't play in this area," reaffirmed Alvis.

"So you're uncomfortable, huh?" inquired the Latina.

"Yes, ma'am."

"Well, be uncomfortable with deez," she joked as she grabbed his crotch. She started unbuttoning her fake cop uniform and proceeding with what she was really there for.

The other three, all women, started joining in with the fun and started removing their trousers. "I wondered how long you were gonna take," said Shayna. "These costumes itchy as hell."

Glenn looked in amazement at Alvis, who was in on it. "Man, no you didn't. You done brought strippers to this joint? You my nigga. Das wassup."

"If you coulda seen your face," Alvis kidded. "Looked like you just shat your pants—twice." He amused himself to no end.

Making its way to the general population, the hired quartet left all outfits in a clump by the doorway entrance, along with fake badges, belts, and play-play, retractable billy clubs. Clad only in sets of thongs, matching pasties, and high heels, all purple, of course, they spread out and entertained the thirsty group of ogling onlookers. They captivated, intrigued, enthralled, those four officers did. Splits, dips, twirls, and twerks were orders of the night. They were no novices, by any means. Sitting dogs were favored with lap dances and gropes. The gropes were welcomed, gratis, dangerous. To prevent the wasting of good alcohol, recipients of the favored dances spread both arms like an eagle's wings with drink in one hand, basking in the joy of having his privates bounced on. Hard-ons were inevitable.

"Damn!" exclaimed Tario. "Can I take you home, girl? I'm backed up for about a good month."

Therese looked on and shook her head in amusement, glad she had stuck to her guns earlier not to give that Rio character her number. She kept doling out the complimentary, tip-free drinks; the dogs kept spilling, swilling, sillying around.

"Get it frat!" egged on Zack to Tario. "Don't just sit there, fool. Let her know she been bit by the dog!"

By this time, barking had commenced again. Tario stood up and handed his drink to Alvis. To everybody's shock, he picked up the dancer, who wrapped her legs around his waist and her arms around his neck to maintain equilibrium. To the chants of his boys, he spun her around, making sex-thrusting motions. She could do nothing but go along for the ride as she screamed with excitement. The jolting, untamed, wild movement of her hair summed up the action going on below her midriff. He was the bull, she the rider.

The reactions from his boys, the dancers, and even Therese were electric. It had turned into a circus in a good way. In some form or fashion, "Get it, Rio," was heard throughout the room.

Dancers encouraged their girl, too. "C'mon, hoe, ride that bull."

It was a tug-of-war between the girls and the boys, a battle of the sexes for bragging rights. There was no winner in immediate sight. So they both continued. The bull bucked, and the rider held on. The rider dug her heels in, and the bull jerked from left to right, up and down, round and round.

The shouts and screams and barks were unintentionally deafening. No one anticipated that the level of insanity would wax so great. It elevated to the degree that no one, not even the ordinarily reserved Therese, noticed three more male officers standing by the front door by the mound of tossed clothes. They had let themselves in through the unlocked door. Belial had let himself in through the brick wall and hovered above all three. He had become particularly adept at causing death related to racism and violence, especially within the African-American community. He could turn the most innocuous of situations into a blood bath. Tonight, he was on a mission.

Noticing the officers, Zack nudged Alvis, pointed toward the entrance, and yelled, "Yo, dog, what the hell freakiness you trying to start. You know we don't roll like that."

Alvis got a little concerned because he hadn't put in an order for these three as he did for the others.

None the wiser and a bit tipsy, Tario played along with the obvious second set up by Alvis. He had won the previous competition, as his rider relinquished her grip and wound up on the floor. "Three more male officers show up to get it on and poppin' with the other three hoe cops. This 'bout to get freaky as hell." Making his way toward the front, he carried on even more. "Come on in, sirs. The night is still young. We got plenty of partyin', drinkin', and hoin' to do." The officers looked at each other and continued eyeing the joint, ignoring his statement for a moment.

As music blasted and revelers reveled, Tario extended his hospitality, even though he wasn't the official host. "Just get freaky with the *hoes*, though. Ain't gone be no sword fightin' up in here. It's an open bar, though. So you can get yo' drank on right now, fam."

One of the cops grabbed his radio and spoke, "Looks like we got a 9.08.050 violation."

"Yo," said Tario, "you really playin' this role like it's real. Speakin' into the walkie and everything. Just relax, my man. We all good. What you want to drink. I gotchu." Still, neither of the three responded.

Alvis cautiously started making his way to the front to see what was going on. He placed his rum and Coke on one of the speakers. The walk felt like an eternity. This surely was not in his plans, and he hoped Tario would do nothing that would get them kicked out or have to shut down the party. A different cop reached for his pad to begin writing a ticket. This was noise violation at its finest, and the ticket would surely teach these hoodlums a lesson.

"Gramma, mama said I'm gonna talk with daddy on the computer tomorrow," said R.J. He sat in the living room as she swept in the adjacent hallway.

"I know. I don't know exactly how they do that, but that should be pretty exciting." He had to be because he never really mentioned his father. His talking about it was a sign to her that his father still held a special place in his heart. He was still the child's hero.

"I don't really know what to say."

"Just be yourself. You don't have to say an–"

She felt the presence of the Lord overshadow her. The Holy Spirit gave her quick and succinct instructions. *"Pray now!"*

Within a flash, she knew why. Taken off guard, R.J. heard two sounds: the thud from her falling to her knees and a "Tario!" in a scary, shrieking voice.

As the cop began writing the ticket, Alvis approached to get clarity on what was happening. Maybe one of his frats ordered these cops as a joke, to add to the lightheartedness. Before he could inquire, Tario unfortunately upstaged him once more.

"Aight, man," voiced Tario, "enough with the act. You can remove all these props, yo." Figuring he'd help them and attempting to elicit a laugh, he reached out to unholster the gun of one of the other officers, a sandy-haired, no-nonsense egoist.

Out of the three officers, the egoist, Officer Schmidt, was the first to utter any words. Like an alligator surprising an unsuspecting boar, the officer forced Tario to the floor and placed a pair of plasticuffs on him. His drink fell to the ground.

Glass shattered everywhere, and the contents spilled in various directions. "Stay your ass on the ground," said the perturbed officer. The bull that had tossed the rider earlier was now being tossed. "You've lost your damn mind. Do you know the consequence for trying to discharge an officer's gun?"

By this time, all parties were observing the commotion. Decreasing in intensity and bass, the music volume had quieted to a whisper and then went silent. Alvis, feeling responsible, tried to clarify any confusion, which sat very thick in the air. "Officer, please, he meant no harm. He thought you were here to—"

"I don't give a flying fuck what he thought. All I know is he reached for my gun and planned on shootin' me with it."

"Yo, my wrists, man," Tario yelled in anguish. "This shit hurt. Ow!"

"What's the actual problem, officer? What did we even do in the first place?" asked Alvis.

"Noise complaint, sir," replied the second officer.

"Hey, wait. We went through the proper channels. We weren't *that* loud, Mr. Tillman." Alvis had noticed his badge. Unlike the egoist, this one seemed slightly more rational but was still rather testy. The Que also thought calling him Mister would lighten the overall mood, implying a certain deference.

Belial whispered in the egoist's ear, twisting the purposed intention so that it would be taken the wrong way. "And he trying to patronize us, too," said Schmidt as he held Tario to the ground. "Trying to be smart, calling you 'Mr.' He 'posed to be calling you 'Officer.' Disrespectful bastard." He seemed to overlook the other two times Alvis used the correct title.

"Yo, man. Come on. Loosen this shit up!"

Everyone else had noticed the stir. Music ceased, and antennae were raised. This didn't seem to be a part of the paid act. Tario seemed to be in too much pain. "Let him go," one of the hired dancers screamed. She began walking toward the officers in her half-naked state.

"Stand back, ma'am," said the aggressive officer. "This has nothing to do with you."

"The hell it don't," said Dray, a fellow fraternity brother.

"Oww!" screamed Tario. "It's too tight! My man," he said to the third officer, "you just gone let him do this shit?" No response.

"That complicit bastard!" said one of the frats to another.

"Sorry, sir, we're gonna have to take you down to the station and process you," said the ringleader.

"Process him? For what?" asked another frat. "This ain't right, and y'all officers know it ain't right. This that Freddie Gray and Alton Sterling shit."

The officer roughly handled Tario. The pain from the roughhousing made him stand to his feet to reduce the wrist pain. "Get your ass back down!" He was thrown back down to the ground. "You get up when I tell you to get up!"

The third cop appeared disturbed that his colleagues were acting in this manner. He had never seen them act this carelessly before. It was as if something was controlling the two, providing instructions for them to follow. He never really wanted to be assigned with this duo anyway and generally went silently along with their antics. But this was over the top, given this crowd. No gang bangers, just typical college kids having fun. This was highly unusual.

Tillman crouched and placed his hand on the side of Tario's head, pinning him in place and pleasantly surprising the belligerent comrade. In fact, Schmidt smiled and decided to escalate the drama. He obeyed the next command and, in an instant, reached for his Glock 22. He rested it on the back of Tario's head and screamed, "Is this what you were reaching for? Is this what you want? You wanna hold this? Is this what you wanted? Answer me! You wanted to get your hands on this? Damn prick!"

Without warning, Raphaela, who had been detained, darted through the roof and stopped directly in front of Belial, startling him and staring down upon him.

She towered over Belial and uttered, in a calm but firm tone, *"Enough!"*

The third, non-participating cop stood over his fellow teammates. "Enough!"

Belial, caught off guard, relented and backed away. He was no match for a prayer-backed Raphaela and knew it.

Schmidt looked at the ordinarily quiet cop and mean-mugged him, staring him up and down but secured his gun again. He couldn't believe that piece-o'-shit officer confronted them in front of everybody. Where was the solidarity? A unified front had been sacrificed, so this would definitely have to be dealt with later.

"Get up!" he said to Tario, who continued writhing in pain. "I'm still taking you down to the station to process you." He seemed to be directing the statement more toward the third officer than toward Tario. There was to be no mistaking who was in charge.

"Officer, can I just get my phone?"

"Fuck your phone, boy! Get your ass over here!"

The room gasped.

He carelessly steered the bound man to the door. Tario shuffled along in an understandably ungainly manner, still a little tipsy and in shock. Never had he imagined when he woke up this morning that things would progress to this. But that was Belial's modus operandi, to surprise and attack.

The officers and suspect approached the car. The rear door

was swung open, and Tario's head was shoved downward so he could enter.

"Officer, can you please take these cuffs off? They hurt, yo."

Officer Obnoxious slammed the door with no response. The officers entered the car, having their own issues that obviously needed to be worked out.

As the car inched away from the premises, partygoers approached the police car and made note of the license plate, not fully processing the turn of the night's events. "Don't worry, Rio. We gotchu. Stay up!" Alvis shouted. "We coming down to the precinct."

Belial, clearly frustrated, had wished tonight for a death in the form of an accidental gun misfire. It was thwarted by that meddling-ass Raphaela. He wished that the angelic bitch had minded her nosy business. But it wasn't entirely him. He knew Raphaela or someone like her only showed up to interrupt his plans when a certain criterion was met.

Onlookers wished they would have been a little more proactive. They had been carousing and partying one moment and in a sense of utter confusion the next. And it happened so quickly that they had little time to respond in a way that would be effective and lasting. All except Therese. She had been live-streaming the incident on Facebook from the time she turned off the music.

But for now, the cops had vanished into the night with an innocent victim in the back seat, handcuffed and surely terrified.

23

SOPHOCLEAN DRAMA

R.J. WOKE UP laughing. His dream seemed so real that he actually thought it was happening in real time. In it, Dr. Seuss had been traveling place to place by doing cartwheels, even when he had to go up a set of stairs. That just tickled R.J. to no end. It was probably a subconscious happiness that shone through because of what was to occur soon. Today was indeed the big day. The early hour didn't dampen his spirits at all. In fact, it made him more eager.

"Boy, what is wrong with you?" asked Jamay. She was straightening up his unkempt living quarters and decided to let him wake up on his own today.

"Nothing. It was just a dream. I saw Dr. Seuss playing. It was funny."

"It must have been. I never heard you laugh yourself awake." She continued tidying and got back into mother mode. "Now this *room*, on the other hand, is no laughing matter. It's more like a nightmare. I don't see how one person can keep this room like it's a pigsty."

"What's a pigsty?"

"Never mind, R.J. Just go ahead and get yourself ready for today. You remember what today is?"

"Yes."

How could he have forgotten? His mother had been counting down for a whole week, as if she was the one whose father it was. But maybe for her, this was second best. After all, she had knocked boots with him, changing his title from sexy, red nigga to first-time father. So she was just as excited for both. Coaches, teachers, and clergymen had all stepped in and made it a little more bearable for R.J. to have as normal a life as possible, but nobody would truly be a replacement for his real daddy. It had been years since hearing his father's voice or seeing him in person. Letters and cards had come in the mail regularly, but nothing would or could replace actual contact and interaction. This would be the best substitute. He didn't know how this computer thing was supposed to work, but apparently it was supposed to make it so he could see and hear whomever was on the other side.

"How does Google Hangouts work?" He sat upright in his bed and grabbed his controls to start up another round of Fortnite.

"I don't know exactly how, baby. It's sort of like a TV except you can really interact with the person on the other side. You can see them, too."

"But how do they come through the air?"

"It's just technology. Somebody discovered a way how to do it."

"Whoa! That's kinda neat." He was getting ready to compare it to how it seemed to be with Emily, the girl he met two months ago through the text chat feature while playing the online game. Except Jamay chimed in before he could do so.

"So let's go ahead and get moving. We have to be by the computer to talk to daddy in about an hour. He said he's calling early this morning around 7:30 our time. You need to wash up. Grandma's in the kitchen fixing something to eat, so she's gonna be expecting us soon."

"Okay." He hopped out of bed and felt the excitement brewing. Just an hour and he'd really be talking to his dad. He put down the console, not realizing Emily had noticed he was gaming and had typed a morning greeting message.

"Listen to this one, guys," said Chaz. "I'm practicing for tonight." He assumed the typical thespian posture, hand over chest, head and chest up.

> "Before I sleep, I think and pray
> About the way time flies
> Day in, day out, and then repeat
> Under these foreign skies"

> "Can't wait 'til skies above transform
> Although I love my clan
> The soldier's plight, a different norm
> From my American"

"Bravo, damnit!" joked Redd. "This nigga here is a poet, shonuff!"

"Did you make that up?" asked Jones.

"Nah," replied Chaz. "It's called 'Foreign Skies' by the one-named poet LaWyann. It's a lot of poems online by soldiers who served in the forces. They said writing poetry was one of the ways to help them deal with everything they had to put up with when they were serving. Said it was their out when things got rough."

"Deep! He's the Latino Langston Hughes. I'ma start calling you Luciano Hughes," kidded Redd. "Let me find out you got a hidden talent."

"Well, I didn't write it, amigo. Like I said, I'm just thinking about readin' it at the poet thing tonight. You got yours ready?"

"I might have a little somethin' somethin'," admitted Redd. "You just gotta wait and see what I got up my sleeve. But that poem you spittin' true as hell. The skies over here a bitch. Lookin' up and wonderin' when you gone stop lookin' at the skies here and get a chance again to look up at an American sky. A nigga here ready to get back home."

"Now, if I said that, y'all will be ready to crucify somebody," said Merrick out of the blue.

"Said what? You know I'm right. You get tired of the same ole same ole day in and day out."

"I'm not talking about that part. It's what you called yourself."

"Oh!" laughed Redd. "You right. I better not hear your Nordic ass say 'nigga.' Say it and you ain't gone be lookin' up at an Afghan sky or an American sky neither. You gone be *in* the sky."

They laughed. The sense of duty and sacrifice created a bond between all of them, male and female alike, so they could easily joke about what would have otherwise been overly sensitive topics.

"What time are we supposed to head out?" inquired Jones. "Kabir said he'd come and pick us up and drive us there. Says it's about an hour ride."

"He said he would be here around 7:45. The poetry program starts at 9:00," Chaz remembered.

They finished up with an early dinner as Redd reminded Jones about needing her assistance. "Don't forget now, mama. I'm gonna need your help with–"

"I know. I know. You been telling me every day for the last three days, twice a day. I need to set up the Hangouts meeting so you can see your boy before we head out. It's already set up. You just need to start it up and call. The contact number is already programmed, so it's ready when you are."

"They just under twelve hours behind us, so it'll be morning there and night here. When we finish meeting, it'll be 'bout time for us to head to Kabul. We 'spose to start in about thirty minutes. I'm gone need y'all to hang around so I can introduce you to the fam."

The plan was to talk to R.J. from 7 to 7:30, Afghan time, and then be on his way. It was 6:37, and he didn't realize why he was getting nervous all of a sudden. He missed his boy something terrible but felt like he was about to go on a surreptitious mission to capture some war thug. Just butterflies, he guessed.

Garnet was just as excited as Jamay and R.J. She had never witnessed any meeting of these kinds. A part of her also wondered how Redd had changed. Was he fatter, darker? Everyone had eaten the planned early breakfast. Jamay stared at the 7:19 on the digital clock. Only eleven more minutes to go. She checked all connections so there would be no last-minute snafus. The computer was ready. R.J. just sat in front of it, wondering how he would know when the call was coming through. All he could see was himself on the screen, so his entertainment was to make faces into the embedded camera.

"R.J., let me brush your hair," prodded Garnet. "You gotta look presentable when you talk to your daddy." She came to where he was and tidied up his naps.

"Ouch, gramma. That hurt."

"Just keep looking into that computer. It won't hurt as much."

By the time he figured out there was no linkage between his pain and whether he looked into the screen, she was finished.

"So I guess we'll just wait until the call comes through," offered Jamay. "It's ready to receive calls."

One minute.

Jones began dialing the number. She would have been confused, but she made these types of vision-calls all the time with her relatives back home, mostly while her comrades slept. Redd watched in a kid-like fashion. Patterson and Chaz were nearby, sensing his nervousness. Serving their country together had knit them together in a way that they knew when their partners were facing mental troubles. They told him not to worry and just take it easy. Redd hadn't quite come to terms with how magical this experience would be. He didn't know why he was so awe-stricken. If phones made it possible to hear someone from afar, why did he think this would be so difficult? Maybe he was just as thrilled the first time he used a basic phone. He couldn't remember.

"It's going through," affirmed Jones.

"So where am I supposed to talk?"

"Right where you are. The mic is built into the laptop. Just talk regular. It might be a little delayed when you talk so it might be some weird pauses during the conversation. But you'll get the hang of it." The first call had fallen into a state of buffering. "I don't know why it's giving me problems now. I never have had issues with this laptop before." She started doctoring with some of the settings and trying several options to diagnose the problem. Out of nowhere, the image of a kid with crimson-colored hair suddenly appeared on his screen. It caught her and Redd by surprise. "There we go. All set."

Redd simply sat there staring. He felt tears slowly forming.

"Don't just sit there doofus," joked Jones. "Say something. He can see and hear you."

"Daddy?"

Redd couldn't be shaken from his inquisitive stupor. *Who did the child look more like at this point? He looked like his mother the last I saw him, but now he's starting to look like me. Wow!*

After a casual swat on the shoulder, Redd pushed out, "Hey there, R.J. How's my man doin'? You look so great."

"I'm fine, daddy." He was just as semi-speechless. To no avail, he tried touching the screen to see if he'd be able to touch flesh.

"Hi, baby," interjected Jamay. Smiling, she had been off-screen but maneuvered her head into the sight frame, which displayed at the bottom right.

His face lit up. "My Jammy Jam Jam!" Time and distance hadn't change his corniness. His pen name for her still existed. "Look at you, baby! You look so pretty."

She had done herself up but swore to him that she looked like that all the time. "Oh, these old rags?"

"Just stop it," injected Garnet. "You don't just walk around like that, Jamay. She got spruced up just for you, son."

"Hey, mom!" He greeted his mother-in-law with an

unmatched perkiness. He was getting the hang of this thing. All he literally had to do was talk and stay in sight. "So good to see you guys. These fellows here are my partners in crime."

Chaz and the others casually moved into the vision area and gave a tepid wave and greeting.

"Well, I'm not one of the fellows, but I guess I still count as a partner," voiced Jones, distinguishing herself from the others. "Glad to meet you. Redd talks about all of you all the time and keeps pictures of him and his son over his bed, so you all are lucky to have a great guy like this knucklehead."

Jamay felt a certain comfort and ease with Jones. She didn't seem like *that* kind of woman based on her first impression. Besides, the other guys were there if it came down to *that*.

"I just basically wanted to make sure I set up the call and see that Redd got through. Now that I see you all are fine, I'ma leave you to yourself. Nice meetin' you again."

He turned his attention to his boy. "So, R.J., tell me what's going on with you. I can't get over how big you gettin'."

"I'm doing fine."

Jamay and Garnet sensed the alone time that was needed between the two and migrated to the living room. "We going in the other room, baby," interrupted Jamay. "Don't hang up after you talk with him. I wanna chat a little, too."

"You got it, baby." He saw them disappear into the background and focused back on R.J. "So you got a girlfriend yet?" The typical go-to line. Hadn't heard his son in ages and started in with the man questions already.

"No, not really. The girls that are in the summer program are okay. Just boring. I talk to a girl named Emily sometimes when I play my games on the computer, but that's all. You can chat with her while you playing the game. Like how we doing now, sort of."

"Look at you. Mr. Swagger with a girlfriend on the computer. Well, let me know when you need some advice on that. I can always help you out in that department."

"Okay."

"What else is going on with you?" He was looking closer at R.J.'s hair. Or was trying to. The pixels on the screen were not as clear as they could have been.

"Nothing much. I watch a lot of shows on TV and I like going to church sometimes."

"Sometimes? Why not all the time?" Redd himself wasn't a big church buff himself but continued on with the small talk.

"I don't know. It's fun sometimes and not so fun sometimes. It's fun when I can play with my friends in Sunday School before church. But the big service be too loud sometimes. And they be doing all this dancing and stuff."

"You better not let granny hear you talking like that," he whispered into the computer, even though he didn't really know where the mic was. "You gone get your head whacked. You know she love that type of carrying on." Redd laughed.

So did R.J. "I just watch them and try to figure out what they be doing. Mama can sing real good. She lead the singing and stuff sometimes."

"Yeah, your mama got the voice of an angel. She used to sing all the time when she was around me. I loved it."

There was a bit of a silence that was eventually broken by R.J. "So where are you at, and why you have to be over there so much? Like what kind of work do you do? Mama always say you at work but just in a place real far away."

Redd was glad he took Jones' advice to get a world map or something similar and have it nearby in case he was asked that question. She also gave him advice on how to approach answering since she had to give an explanation to her nephew about a month prior. "See this here globe, this is where you are." He spun it to his left until Africa went by. "This is where I am right here in a place called Afghanistan. We're over here fighting to help these people who can't really fight that well for themselves. But we're helping them learn how to fight back and stay safe. It's like, do you have any friends who get bullied?"

"Yeah, sometimes at school I used to see people in my class get bullied by other people."

"Well, it's sort of like you seeing the kid after school who gets bullied crying and you go over to him and say you'll teach him how to fight and stand up to the bully. But you keep staying there until he gets stronger and will be able to fight the bully his own self. That's what it's like here. And we at the point now where the ones who used to get bullied, they getting stronger and learning how to fight for themselves. As soon as they get real strong, that's when I'll be able to come back to Vegas and see you, big man. Do that many any sense?"

"Yeah I guess, sorta kinda. I guess it's good you helping people not be bullied."

"But I miss you so much, R.J. I miss all of you guys. I think about you all the time. Just because I'm a long ways away don't mean you ain't on my mind. I can't wait to see you again."

"I miss you, too. Mama gave me your picture, and I keep it on top of my dresser." He placed his hand on the screen once more just to make sure he couldn't touch his dad's face.

His dad saw his movement and placed his hand on the screen where his son's was. Both hands virtually touched. That would have to suffice for now. The elder noticed his hands naturally outsized the younger's, but not by much. A sign, front and center, which confirmed time was slipping away.

Before he'd be able to blink, both hands would be of equal height and width.

After about ten more minutes of chatter, Chaz reminded his partner about the poetry competition. Kabir would be showing up soon to scoop them up. "Alright, little man. You know we could go on and on. Now that I know we can meet like this, we gotta talk to each other at least once a month, okay?"

"Or maybe even more." The more they spoke, the more the kid was opening up. He was never this garrulous but perhaps because there was no reason to be.

"That's right, man. We can talk more often. Tell your mama and granny to come back in the room so I can say goodbye to them. We going to a place over here where they having a poetry party. But always remember to try to be the one who helps other people stand up to bullies."

"Okay."

"R.J., I love you."

"Love you, too." He turned his head, "Mama. Gramma. Daddy want to talk to you." That struck a nerve. He hadn't heard his son say "daddy" in years.

Garnet and a teary-eyed Jamay entered. She'd overheard the last few moments of the conversation and had become mushy. The two of them spoke with him for another five minutes. It was a bunch of reminiscing, laughing, promising, hoping.

Jones came back over to make sure the connection ended properly. "It was nice meeting all of you. Have a good night." They voiced their final goodbyes and kept staring into that magic screen until the call finally ended.

Excited, R.J. had run back to his room, started up his war game, and began to contact Emily, so he could tell her all about the exchange with his father. But he was too late. She had already noticed his avatar pop up when he first logged on to play, beating him to the punch. He accepted her request and did his usual bi-tasking thing: shooting down planes and chatting with her. As they chatted back and forth, Ashtoreth sat beside Emily, offered her a few typing suggestions, and smirked.

They were quiet, the scary type of quiet. The type of quiet that almost screamed. Baktash paced around his living room, while Najiba sat, holding the agitated little one. He knew that tonight would have to be the night. Mictian paced with him. Well, it glided; narry a hoof touched the ground. It was mandatory that it would happen tonight. Najiba's silence was all the confirmation he needed. Unlike the other wives, she was down for it, always had been. Even before the nuptials, causes like this had an advocate in her, an Afghan Angela Davis of sorts. She had protested right along the brethren, her male counterparts, even before meeting her man. It was what attracted him to her. The street marching, the Molotov cocktails, the animosity toward America. They were tired of them being on their turf, meddling. It was their country, their land, their issue. And she had been used to voicing her disgust about it. No one could shut her up about her disdain. Group leaders found themselves having to ask her to tone it down a bit. On occasion, she was *too* radical, which made her silence now deafening. After a few more minutes, she broke it.

"Did you find the blue one?"

"Yeah," the husband answered. "I put it in Zahoor's crib." His voice was shaking, exposing his nervousness.

"How about the red one?"

"It's in my back pocket."

She continued feeding the baby and said something in Arabic, to which Baktash nodded in agreement.

All was set. He'd told Kabir he would just meet him at the poetry gathering since the soldiers would have to be picked up much earlier tonight. Neither he nor Najiba were big fans of poetry, but both would be tonight.

"We'll just have to make the drop-off at Tafani's before we go. You told her we're coming, yes? She's prepared?" asked Baktash.

"Yes, she's aware. She's ready." They had to stop at Najiba's sister's place and make an unfortunate delivery. "She's made necessary plans," said Najiba, consoling her husband. It was the only sense of softness and vulnerability she had shown in a while. But it was short-lived. Stoically, she proceeded, "Just be sure everything else is in line and ready to go."

They gathered the rest of their belongings and the baby's necessities. Baktash pushed the stroller while Najiba texted her sister that they would be there in an hour or so. As they left, they pledged their allegiance to Allah again, murmuring something again in Arabic that was undecipherable. Mictian already sat atop the car, anxiously awaiting tonight's festivities.

Surprising to her husband, Najiba managed a lighthearted jab, "In my whole life, I never thought I'd fall in love with a poet."

"Alright, buddy. I need your undivided attention. Are you ready?" Gabriel burst into Uriel's space with some news that would hopefully be exciting.

Puzzled, Uriel responded, "What do you mean? I stay ready. Nieko is good, and I'm handling the college situation the best that I can."

"Well, hold on to your wings, yo. You said you wanted in on some action? Well, I got some action for you. The Most High has given me some inside info related to Redd and his friends. It's related to a function they will be attending, and they will need assistance big time, for real for real." He filled Uriel in on the details for a good while.

"Yo, are you serious?" Uriel asked.

"Yes. You've got to make sure things go according to His will."

"But I can make it so that—"

"No," Gabriel interrupted. "It's not about working things out according to how you feel. You have to stick to what the Most High requests. Will you be able to do it? If not, I will keep the assignment."

"I have it covered, my friend. I won't fail. Praise Jehovah!" In a moment, he landed in Kabul.

Everyone except Kabir joked on the way to Kabul. Kabir knew better. The glorious, mountainous views along the Kabul-Jalalabad Highway were deceptive. Those who didn't respect the ominous, winding roads found themselves dead, resting on the valley floor. The vertical rock cliffs dropped about 2000 feet above the Kabul River. With its twists and turns, this section of the A01 claimed the lives of many on buses that failed to slow down one time too many and reaped the rewards of their carelessness.

"Man, why you ain't talkin', Kabir?" inquired Redd.

But Kabir was a robot. He had traveled this stretch before and saw firsthand the devastation that often resulted. Never would he forget five years ago how his buddy's tractor-trailer, on its way to Pakistan, couldn't make it up the thousand-foot hill. It got stuck, fell backward, and almost tumbled over the cliff's edge before he was rescued by a good Samaritan. "No, my friend, I'll joke with you once we arrive in Kabul. Very dangerous road."

The rest of the riders remained oblivious to the dangers of the winding roads, trusting Kabir to navigate safely and arrive without incident. Thankfully, they arrived in Kabul at sundown. "We're here, my friends. We're here." Other than Kabir, no one really understood the gravity of such a statement of relief. They made it ahead of schedule.

The reading would be later in the evening, so there was time to slouch around and do nothing for a little while. As they entered the grounds, they were thrown aback at how inviting the compounds were. Light-years of difference with what was the norm back at the Jalalabad base.

"A garden?" marveled Chaz. "A freakin' garden."

"Yeah, who would imagine anybody would have enough time to maintain it," cosigned Jones.

As they continued onto the premises, Redd burst into excitement. "A gym! A real gym." This was no makeshift, second-rate workout area, where cinder blocks served as weights. The equipment was Nautilus-caliber. "How in the hell did they even get this stuff out here?"

"They got assistance from a special NATO-supported grant, my friend," chimed in Kabir. "Supporters wanted them to know how much they appreciate their sacrifice to help out the country. Most of the troops here are from those other NATO countries that sympathize with our plight, like Germany, Canada, Italy."

"Yeah, well most of the troops come from the U.S.," interjected Jerome. "Where the hell is *our* gym? What are we, chopped liver?"

Once they arrived at the poetry room, they were elated. A little tired but elated. Greeting them was a svelte, gorgeous blond from Poland, who was cofounder of the poetry event and a fellow soldier. Donned in her soldier's fatigues and pinned-up beehive for hair, she broke ice. "So nice to meet you. I'm Agata. I hope the trip from Jalalabad was not too rough. We're glad you could join us for this celebration. We're looking forward to an inspiring time. Good to see you again, Kabir."

"Feeling's mutual," responded Redd. He felt like he had to be the spokesman of the group.

"We'll be ready to start soon. Make yourself at home, relax, and feel free to check out our makeshift theater space where the event will be."

Redd laughed to himself. *Theater space! Who the hell would think a base for troops would have theater space?* "Thank you. Will do."

After walking inside and decompressing from the journey, Kabir turned toward Redd. "Just relax, my friend. It's not a real theater. They just set up a tent outside and decorated the area."

"You knew what I was thinking, huh?" joked Redd. "I was getting ready to put in my request to be transferred to Kabul for the rest of my time here."

Time flew. Before anyone knew it, it was time to put their poetic chops to the test.

"Enjoy these." Kabir brought the table a round of feel-good. "They're on the house."

"Now see, that's it. You mean to tell me they got a bar in here?" asked Patterson.

"Just a little something to get everybody in the mood for poetry."

Soon, the room grew darker, and the spotlight was directed to the stage microphone. Bugs of the night convened and began playing tag with each other around the newly dimmed lights. A pair of heels clicked-clacked on the dirt floor and made the way up the stairs, resting in front of the mic. She stood clad in her trendy kaftan with matching hijab. If she hadn't spoken, the Americans wouldn't have realized that it was the same plain-Jane, now-reinvented Agata, who'd greeted them earlier.

"Welcome to the third annual Poems for Peace gathering. It is my pleasure to be your host for this wonderful event. Sometimes, it is easy to get consumed with the day-to-day functions of helping the people of Afghanistan. But sometimes, we need to stop, make the best of where we are, and take time to enjoy the journey. Today, we are pleased to welcome the American troops from Jalalabad." Applauses followed. "They made the trek to join us here today, so please make them feel at home. We are all one in strength and one in solidarity. In fact, without further ado, we would like to invite our first speaker of the evening from that very troop. Let's put our hands together and welcome them to the stage."

Caught off guard, the American troops sat at the round table and stared at each other, wondering which one of them would walk the plank first. They hadn't discussed, but the choice was obvious. Redd grabbed his poetic pad and made his way to the stage. As he sauntered toward the stage, Uriel glided with him. Gabriel had received another, unrelated emergency from the Most High and made sure Uriel was ready to step in. Things were progressing slowly with Nieko, so he had some time to spare regarding this. He explained what needed to be done and required an update after the mission was accomplished. *"You got it, my heavenly brother,"* assured Uriel to Gabriel. *"You and He will be pleased."*

"Evening, everyone. Thanks for having us. It's a major pleasure to be able to join you all today." This was Redd's feeble attempt at public small talk. Realizing he was no good at it, he angled himself toward what was more comfortable. "Today I'll be presenting a poem called 'She Tears' by LaWyann. I'm not a pro at this, so please bear with me." Because of the blinding spotlight, he didn't see Baktash and Najiba sneak in, pushing their baby in the stroller. Neither did anyone else. And Mictian, dressed in all of his ominousness, entered with them, hovering, suggesting. He was invisible to everyone except Uriel, of course.

"Eyes have dried from crying loud
For this prized troop who stood up proud
The casket holds the body bruised
While family, friends all stand bemused"

Uriel began circling slowly around Redd. He was half-walking, half-floating. Mictian began grinning as he stared at Uriel. Neither had seen the other in a while, and both were set on being the victor. Mictian's plan wouldn't be aborted. It was a battle of the invisibles. He whispered in Baktash's ear, prompting him to reach into his knapsack and hand something over to his wife.

"Just one more year, then two, then four
A timeline fraught with 'but' and 'or'
Now still, now calm, now hushed, now free
In loyal garb is this dead she"

No nerves. No butterflies. Redd was a pro. Najiba grabbed her phone and nodded at her husband; he nodded back. They looked deeply into each other's eyes, knowing that the mission was set. She leaned over and kissed him. That wasn't in the plan. No time for mushiness. Uriel had begun encircling Redd faster. Several sheets on his pad blew in the wind, but he secured them and continued reading. Uriel's revolutions strangely included the troops' table. Around Redd and then the table. Around Redd and then the table. Mictian was unnerved, for he hadn't foreseen this. He scoffed at Uriel, who paid him no attention. Uriel's directives from Gabriel were set.

"Mother, daughter, sister, niece
In these dear roles, she held a lease"

Najiba nodded to her husband again, arose, and pushed the baby to the restroom, presumably to change her. Surprisingly, the little one hadn't uttered a peep since entering. Mictian urged Baktash to move along with the plan. It was now or never. Najiba gave him the sign by leaving. His message to Baktash was stoic. In his ear, he prodded, *"Don't you back out now, you coward. Do it. Do it."*

"But pangs of grief from her great life"

"Do it."

"Were chiefly felt from title wife"

Uriel kept circling at lightning speed. Mictian tried to stop him but was no match for the velocity Uriel had built up. Mictian verbally observed, *"This weakling has gotten stronger."*

He decided to press his talons into Baktash's skull. The coward was taking too long. In a final effort to get it done, he silently shouted into his ear one final time.

"DO IT!"

As Redd started with, "A shero's badge of honor high," Baktash stood up and began chanting something undecipherable in Arabic as loud as he could. "Allahu Akbar! Allahu Akbar! Allahu Akbar!" Mostly everyone thought it was planned drama, almost Sophoclean. The voice bellowed so deeply that Baktash even shocked himself. Redd had stopped in his tracks, becoming a spectator like the others. Najiba listened from the restroom. No turning back now. She heard her husband continue with his rant-chant. Uriel ignored the humans and kept with his circuitous spinning path, going even faster.

The time was now. Mictian appeared next to Najiba in a flash. *"Now, bitch!"* She reached under the baby's cushy blanket and grabbed it. Mictian smiled and encouraged her again. *"Now, bitch!"* Kabir knew what the Arabic words literally meant and also what they meant figuratively, but they couldn't be coming from Baktash. It was in Najiba's hands, and she started praying in Arabic under her breath. The bitch did it.

Two hundred yards away, a platoon couple sat in the quiet of the night, enjoying each other's nuisance-like ways and thankful that they didn't attend the God-awful poetry slam. The sky was normal, which was why they both reveled in it. No planes, no helicopters, no nothing. The sky was finally normal. Until it wasn't. They jolted up. The sky above the poetry gathering was abnormal again, hosting a myriad of specific colors: yellows, reds, oranges, subtle blues.

24

SWEET LITTLE EMILY

"REMEMBER WHEN WE were walking through The Strip, and I was saying to stay away from that lady who wanted to read your palm?" asked Garnet to R.J.

"Yeah."

"Why do you think I said that?"

"I don't know." At this point, he had forgotten and really didn't care. He and Emily were chatting and making their avatars try out the dances that were recently added to the repertoire after the new version of Fortnite was upgraded. They typed their LOLs, SMHs, and OMGs at each other as their characters maneuvered, bowed, kicked, and otherwise showed their virtual versatility. Emily even squeezed in an LMAO every now and then, even though R.J. didn't know what that one meant.

She didn't notice his nonchalance and continued. "Well, I know you're a little young, but you have to be very careful about letting people do that. It's more than meets the eye. When you do that, you can open yourself up to spiritual forces that you don't realize. You must be very careful to keep your spirit protected from other outside spiritual influences. Only the Lord should have access to your spirit and nobody else. See right here what it says in Isaiah eight and nineteen?" She showed him her phone with the scripture.

"Yes, ma'am. Okay." He was too young to understand all of this stuff. She may as well had been talking Greek.

"It's the same thing with horoscopes in the newspaper. Have you ever seen those?"

"No, but sometimes I hear Ms. Davida reading them when she with mommy. She always talk about her sign being a bull."

"Oh, really? Well, sometimes people try to use those to live by. If anybody ask you what your sign is, tell them 'the Cross' and 'the Blood.' The only thing you should be living by is this right here." She held up her phone, her modern-day Bible. She wanted him to see the reference; as she started typing a search for Deuteronomy 4, her phone screen shifted to ringing mode. "And we'll talk later about tattoos, but grandma gotta get this call." The phone was placed on speaker. "Hi, Cason. How's it going? What's the latest on the case?"

R.J. heard Cason's voice grow fainter as his grandmother left the kitchen, leaving him alone to have some peace and quiet. He was able to play and chat with Emily, uninterrupted. "She's finally gone," typed R.J.

"Yay!" exclaimed Emily. "Parents can be so pushy. I know mine can."

"Well, that's actually my gramma, but she's cool. She's into a lot of Jesus stuff."

"Parents and grandparents can be so overprotective." It was quite a huge word for a preteen. "They should just relax and let us be kids. Don't you kinda wish you could just get away from them for a second and have a little more freedom?"

"I don't know. Never thought about it. It's not really bad around here. I just miss my dad sometimes."

That was the hook. How could Emily have not recognized it sooner? "He sounds like a great person. Where is he?"

"Somewhere in another country. He's fighting for America."

"Wow. How long has he been over there?"

"A long time."

"That's so sad. Maybe we should try to meet so we can talk about him some more. He seems very cool. I've never met anybody in person from here before. I think it would be neat."

"I don't know."

"Aw, come on. It'll be fun. I've always wanted to see what it's like to sneak out, and plus you and me have been talking for a long time. I think we can trust each other and have a good time."

R.J. thought about the possible adventure. This *would* be a chance to make Fortnite come alive. No longer would he be constrained to the adventure online. He could have his own adventure and meet somebody in real life who loved the ins and outs of the virtual experience. "Um, okay. Maybe."

While Emily was typing, the home office door to where she was sitting cracked open and a voice made an announcement, "Jim, dinner's gonna be ready in five."

"Thanks, baby. I'll be there in a minute. Finishing up with some of this office stuff. Big presentation tomorrow. Love you, baby. Keep the vittles hot, just like you." He blew her a kiss and turned back to chatting with R.J. Emily sat on Jim's lap, while Ashtoreth rested her talon on his shoulder. "Well, I have to go now. My mom is calling me for dinner. Wanna try to meet this weekend? My parents are going to Meadows Mall Saturday at one o'clock. See if you can have your parents go at the same time. We can meet by the fountain at the bottom level of the mall. It'll be fun. We'll finally get a chance to meet each other."

"Okay, I'll see. I want to meet new people, too."

"Well, I gotta go eat. I hope I see you by the fountain. I'll know what you look like because you said your picture on the screen is really you, right?"

"Yeah."

"Okay, well I can't wait to finally see you. I feel like we are really good friends. You'll know it's me because I'll surprise you and call your name, but you have to come alone. We have to be there alone. Can't wait to finally meet you. Bye." Emily's teeny avatar evaporated.

"I'll take it from here, my little Emily," gurgled Ashtoreth. "You've done another great job." The little one performed her twirl-and-dance routine, giggled, and headed back northward.

After R.J. typed "Bye" back, he logged off, causing his own picture to disappear from the screen. He thought about what Emily said and was not against having a little more freedom. Garnet made her way back into the kitchen, a bit perturbed by the news Cason had shared and equally thrown off by what her grandson asked out of left field.

"Gramma, can we go to Meadows Mall on Saturday?"

25

ALL BLACK LIVES MATTER

THERESE'S FEED HAD gone viral and had been shared nearly 10,000 times. News stations caught wind of it and began airing.

"What we're seeing here is apparently a case of good cops gone bad. The students seemed to have been having a good time at a party when cops entered and harassed at least one of them, according to the video. Many are saying it went too far. One of their actions is raising eyebrows across the country. A simple confrontation escalated to an almost deadly experience. We'll have to see what becomes of it, as we have not heard anything from officers or their bosses. A lot of people are wondering what would have happened if one of the other cops hadn't intervened and contested the actions of his partners. Everybody's buzzing. There's much more to find out about this story. This is Joyce Ludlow live in front of the Huntridge Police

Department, where the young man is being held. KRB-9 News."

As she reported, the video footage kept repeating on the country's television screens. First, the initial takedown was shown. Following that, the gun-to-the-head moment was presented. Although both incidents hadn't occurred directly in succession in the actual clip, editing made it suggest such.

"My Lord! That is terrible." Martha Jo placed Rusty's glass of lemonade beside his dinner plate. As was their normal routine, they made sure they watched the evening news while eating dinner. "It's just so sad. I don't know what's going on in this world. They didn't have no right to mess with them people at that party. They couldn't have been *that* loud. And to think, that cop went all the way to pointing a gun at his head. That is absolutely unacceptable. You would think this was still the '60s in the South. Seem like we goin' backward instead of forward. Them men is just racist. That's all to it."

Not to her surprise, Rusty never chimed in during her news rants. Silence was his normal lot as he devoured her edible preparations, no matter how insipid they were. But especially not this one. His silence today was other-inspired. His vittles remained untouched, as did his drink. With the wife walking about and chuntering on and on, he delightfully gazed at the story unfolding and simply smiled.

"Sitcho ass down, nigger!"

"Yo, I get a phone call, officer. I would like to talk to my lawyer."

"Yo ass don't got no lawyer. You probably don't e'en know how to spell it."

Schmidt was responsible for watching Tario. Tillman and the other officer had retired home after bringing Tario back to the precinct. There he was behind bars with this ignoramus as his overseer. Only God knows what would have happened if the cameras weren't there. Even with their presence, he was a contemptible idiot. Since there were no cameras inside, he still felt like he could get away with or say whatever he wished.

He walked up to Tario's cell and grumbled through the bars. "Just a big ole coon! It's not enough for you to stay your ass in your own community and run it down. You have to come to the decent area of Huntridge and dirty it up. Shoulda stayed yo ass in your own hood. Well, since you here, you gone get treated like the gorilla you is. By the time me and my partner get finished with you, you gone wish you woulda kicked yo' own ass . . . just like that jigaboo actor on that coon show you like where they be singing all that coon music. What's the show called, nigger? You know that show with that fine hoe on it named Cookie. I wish I could take a bite o' that damn Cookie. That's all you coons good for, giving us some good women that we can put a baby in. Coons and Cookie." He pounded the bars with both fists, hoping to intimidate the suspect. It didn't work.

"Well, why don't you tell me how you really feel?" He heard the commotion outside and knew their presence would promise some sense of exposure and protection. Raphaela was hanging out in Tario's jail for added protection. She knew the prisoner would not be in harm's way, but her mission was still to monitor and guard. "You all shouldn't treat people like you do. Slavery is over, but people like you don't want to let it go. Face it. We didn't ask to be here anyway. Not just not here in Huntridge but here in America. But you all think that the more diverse we become, the more of a threat we are to the establishment. I don't want to be here any more than you want me here. I didn't ask anybody to bring me over here on a ship. We were stolen and used to help your little cotton businesses."

Schmidt knew Tario was making sense but didn't need a history lesson at this point. "Nigger, shutcho ass up! Fake ass Nat Turner! If those cameras weren't out there right now, I'd Bland your ass. Sat down." It was a chilling in-house reference that cops had begun making ever since that horrific July 13. Corrupt cops often used it among themselves as a comedic interjection whether those in holding got it or not. Today, he didn't care that he used the phrase with no other colleagues around. He figured Tario was smart enough to understand it and would stop being difficult. "Ain't nobody here to help you today." Clearly, he didn't see Raphaela.

"Man, this some bull. I get a phone call. I know my rights."

"Rights these, boy." He grabbed his crotch. "I guess you don't know."

"Know what, yo."

"Time them cameras off and them people leave, it's gone be back to business as usual. I don't care how much money you make or how important you supposed to be or how many three-pointers your kind makes, it ain't gone make no never mind. Don't matter how much education you get neither. Ain't you heard what we call a Black person with a PhD?"

"Man, chill with all that." He knew the answer but didn't say.

"We 'round here call 'em a nigger with a PhD." He amused himself as he offered thunderous laughter.

They started hearing a rustling outside the walls of the precinct. A chorus of sorts. Tario couldn't see because there was no window on his side, but the ogre glanced outside and was taken aback by the site.

"FREE TARIO! FREE TARIO! FREE TARIO!"

In the quiet suburb of Huntridge, a crowd of what looked to be about 110 people or so had gathered outside the precinct. Mostly Instagrammers, Twitter-goers, and Facebookers, these supporters were just a few who had caught wind of Therese's stream and decided on a whim to head to the posh community to demand Tario's release.

"FREE TARIO! FREE TARIO! FREE TARIO!"

Tario took a seat on the hard bench next to his toilet, grinning ear to ear. "Well, go ahead, Mr. Officer. Start Blanding me away. You gone have some serious 'splainin' to do to all those people outside, though. This not gone be no 'nother Sanford or Ferguson or Baltimore situation, man. Y'all shouldn't be able to call yourselves cops. Y'all just need to learn how to chill. Ain't no justice for black folk out here. Black Lives Matter, yo. Think you can just do what you want and not be held accountable. Then we get locked up for something we ain't even do, just like the Central Park Five. In jail all that time and didn't even rape that woman. You don't even realize it, sir, but you helping to perpetuate the Prison Industrial Complex mindset. And can't nobody change that but Jesus."

Honestly, Tario didn't know where that came from. He was no preacher, but at the time it just felt right. Raphaela backed away from whispering *Jesus* in Tario's ear, giggling to herself somewhat.

The chants outside continued. Schmidt took a glance out the narrow window to see the placards. How could they have made them so fast? They probably had them on reserve and ready to use at what they deemed was the most opportune time. "Hell, Black Lives ain't the only lives that matter, dumbass," he grumbled to the detainee. "I'm so sick of all this rhetoric. ALL lives matter. That's all you all do, start division by thinking you the only race that has it so-called bad." He repeated it again, shouting toward Tario's direction, "ALL lives matter!"

Tario had heard this retort before and resorted to a comeback he had heard recently. He thought it most apropos. "Yeah, well all *houses* matter, too, but fire trucks only go to houses that are on fire at the time."

The officer couldn't think quick enough to respond so he continued staring outside, acting as if he didn't hear the logic in the statement.

Joyce was still on scene, so her crew filmed as she interacted with some of those who were in attendance.

"WE WILL STAY OUT HERE UNTIL TARIO IS RELEASED!" shouted one.

"NO JUSTICE, NO PEACE!" barked another.

"RELEASE HIM NOW!" ordered a white sympathizer.

Joyce approached one of the protestors. "Ma'am, can you express to us what you're feeling right now?"

An Asian woman with a placard spoke.

"It's like, why choose a job that you don't know how to do or you're afraid to do? But then we're always the liability, you know? Why do we get killed for no reason? Then the verdict always comes back the same. I mean, really?! They have no interest in protecting people of color. The only thing they are concerned about is the blue code. They no longer serve and protect. They are out here murdering black people on the streets. There is like *no* accountability! Shit is only gone change when we *make* shit change! And it's only gone change when people other than black people start standing up and speaking out!"

She walked away shouting the no-justice, no-peace chant. Back inside, things had grown strangely silent. Schmidt grabbed a seat in one of those worn green rocking chairs and just waited. And rocked and thought. Tario kept pressing his ear to the wall to try to hear some of the commotion outside. Although he couldn't make out details, the rustling gave him renewed hope. If no one would have shown up, anything could have and probably would have happened. He just listened and thought. Even Raphaela had become a bit pensive. Taking some time to pause as she stood on guard, she almost wept as her Boss did. She waited for her next directive and thought. But what she pondered was detailed and specific. *How had humanity*, she thought, *gotten to this point?* But she already knew the answer.

"I don't know. It just seemed wrong to me. I knew Schmidt wasn't all there sometimes, but I never thought it would come to this."

"Well, honey, I'm glad you spoke up. That wasn't right." She adjusted her nightgown and took one last look at the bathroom mirror before turning in. "You did the right thing."

George was hesitant to accept her praise. "I hope so. It just didn't feel like me. It was like I wasn't myself. It's hard to explain. At the moment, I just felt like I had to step in and say something. Honestly, Schmidt didn't seem like *himself*. Something had to be controlling him. If I hadn't said anything, I really think he woulda shot the kid."

"Things were going that bad?"

"Only because Schmidt kept pushing the issue. And the way he looked at me when I told him that was enough. He just had a different face." He spooned her and placed his arm around her stomach. His breath was a little tart, but she had gotten used to it.

"Imagine if you hadn't spoken up and said anything. It might be a different story on the television. It may have been one of *those* stories again. Another one shot dead where the cop claims that he felt threatened."

"It's just not right, baby. I've seen all kinds of stuff on the beat. I feel sort of in a bubble because I know the violence will never probably happen to me and probably not you either since we're both lily white."

She laughed.

He continued. "It just bothers me that things are the way they are now. White cops can pretty much get away with whatever they want. You should hear some of the conversations in the precinct, how the guys talk among themselves about minorities. I've even seen Schmidt put up a poster that had a black face with a target on it and a picture of the white cop using it as target practice. Sick."

"Wow."

"My gut feeling is that things aren't gone change until white people start speaking up against it. Sad to say, but seems like it's true. Seems like the more they protest in the streets, the less stuff gets resolved. I'm not saying we gotta be the 'Great White Hopes,' but we gotta make sure our voices are heard right along with theirs."

"I'd say you made your voice heard loud and clear last night. I'm proud of you, dear."

"Well, at least that makes one who is. But I'm definitely on the Schmidt Shit List. I really caught him off guard. He chewed me out when we got back to the precinct, asking me whose side I was on. 'Right. The side of right,' was what I told him. He didn't like that and told me I'd learn soon enough but to never challenge him like that ever again."

Out of the blue, Nan asked, "So where do Asians and Hispanics fall in this drama?"

"Dunno. There don't seem to be huge numbers of killings involving Asians or Hispanics. Just seems to be a thing with African-Americans. Just seem to be a lot of tension between whites and Blacks. I'm sure it still has something to do with slavery. I'm sure America is still rather proud of that."

"Oh, George. Everybody knows slavery was bad."

"Yeah, but when it's time to talk about some of the kickback and consequences from slavery, not everyone is willing to talk about. White people seem the most uncomfortable when race matters are addressed. Like people are blaming and accusing *them* today of it. No one is accusing us of anything, but it would be nice if we could understand our part in helping black people get their footing, economically or otherwise. Nobody's talkin' about giving them forty acres and a mule, but we can start with basic treatment with human dignity. There's a good starting point."

"So what advice would you give a mother who has to raise a black son in these turbulent times?" She could tell he was getting sleepy, even though he was talking logically.

"Yeah, I'd tell her to make her son pull his pants up and stop wearing hoodies. They need to put on a suit and tie every day and wear glasses, I guess. Walking through these streets in America looking like a bookworm may do the trick and make them look less of a threat. I really think that would work. A suit and glasses."

Nan chuckled a bit and turned to him face to face and dropped a bombshell on him. "So I guess you've never heard of anyone named Malcolm X, huh?"

"Oh yeah, that's right."

It was too complicated to solve tonight. All they could do was simply revel in the small victory that had been attained last night. Maybe preventing a possible homicide of another black guy with promise at the hand of an overzealous cop was all that was needed for the moment, for the present, for the here and now.

RIGHT VS. RIGHT

LEIGH WAS A piece of work. And it was Dr. Leigh Lundt to you. She hailed from Seattle and had a life that followed the typical rags-to-riches script, culminating with a PhD in Women's Studies. In particular, she loved finding women used by God in scriptures so she could argue about how God was no respect of persons, especially as it related to gender. A national search was launched for a tenure-track position at the university in Vegas, and Leigh became one of the three finalists. The other two candidates had been offered the position first, both of whom accepted jobs elsewhere. Leigh, next in line, agreed to come on board. Oblivious to the fact that she was the third choice, she half-arrogantly went through life thinking she had been chosen first. God had worked it out for her but in a way differently than she was privy to. Oh, how God wished the doctor knew that she was lower on the totem pole. It would have knocked her pride down a notch or two.

She gave her heart to the Lord when she was in graduate school at UW in response to a saint who preached daily along the Burke-Gilman Trail as runners and bikers scurried by. Leigh, jogging on one occasion, became particularly convicted by the hell-fire-and-brimstone message that she actually stopped one day and got saved right there on the spot. That may have been the seed that led to her brashness and uncompromising disposition. It was how she got saved and how she helped others get saved. There was no sugar-coating or glossing over. With her, a spade was a spade. She had toned down a bit concerning her delivery, but there was no mistaking her position regarding the state of the world and how it was going to hell, not even in a hand basket. Just going. It was a mystery how she ended up on the Diversity Committee, given her staunch stance on sin. Deep down, she resolved that her appointment to that committee was a sign that she was supposed to be the so-called voice of reason in the midst of views tainted by the world's downward spiral.

"Hi, Garnet." Leigh had bumped into her colleague in the parking lot as they headed to their cars.

Responded Garnet, "Hello, Leigh. How are you?"

"Blessed and highly favored of the Lord."

"That's great. I'm kinda tired, but I am, too." She smiled and kept shuffling along, with Celeste by her side.

"Yes, we all are," chipped in Celeste. This was as much substance as she'd be able to contribute to the conversation that was about to ensue.

"What an interesting meeting, huh, that diversity meeting?" started Leigh. "I can't believe how much they were trying to make people feel like they had to go along with saying sin was fine. The devil *is* a liar."

"Oh," responded Garnet. She knew Leigh and how she could get when she felt strongly about her faith. It wasn't worth an argument.

"It's time for people who name the name of Christ to stop allowing this foolishness to go on. The Lord has a standard, and we just sit there and let the world trample over us with its ungodly agenda."

"I see." Garnet was no pushover by any means. She just went about addressing situations differently as a born-again believer. She would only get most passionate when she was among her own, her family, her unsaved inner circle. As tired as she was, she had no energy to argue with Leigh about what a *true* Christian would have done during the meeting. Besides, she hadn't accused Garnet of anything directly, so everyone was entitled to her own opinion about the matter. *Just let it fly*, thought Garnet. She was almost at her car.

"And honestly, Garnet, I don't see how you could just sit there and say nothing about all that stuff they were saying. It was like you were agreeing with everything they were saying. I was really surprised."

So much for not accusing her of anything directly. Garnet made herself get another burst of energy. "Why do you think I was agreeing with everything?"

"*Oh Lord,*" said Celeste under her breath. "*Please don't get Garnet started.*"

"You were too silent. The Lord needs bold soldiers who ain't scared to speak up."

They reached Celeste's car. This was an opportune time for her to make her getaway. She'd have no more parts of this conversation. "Alright, doctors. I'll be seeing you later." She gave Garnet one final look as if to say, "*Behave.*"

"Bye, darling," responded Leigh.

"Okay. I'll talk to you later, Lessie." But Garnet's mind had been aroused. She got back to the conversation at hand after both grabbed a seat at a nearby bench. Garnet started in,

"So how exactly do you define boldness? More importantly, how does the Lord define boldness?"

Ignoring the questions, Leigh answered, "We're living in the last days, Garnet. The enemy is getting more and more brave nowadays. He's not retreating. He's moving full speed ahead and doing his best to advance his kingdom in the earth. But we have to say more and speak up more. The scripture says, 'For the mystery of iniquity doth already work: only he who now letteth will let.'"

"Yes, Leigh, but you have to use wisdom. Not all the time do you have to be so vocal about everything at that moment. People have to see your lifestyle and see that you care before they start hearing anything about the Lord and His standards. You can't just beat people over the head with scriptures and expect them to change and follow the Lord. I want to see people come to the Lord, too, but you have to use tact when doing it. The scripture says, 'Behold, I send you forth as sheep in the midst of wolves: be ye therefore wise as serpents, and harmless as doves.'"

"But time is winding down. He's trying to reach as many people as possible. We don't have as much time left before He comes back to get His bride. There's no time to be politically correct and be so concerned about people's feelings. I may make them upset now, but they'll thank me later when they get to heaven and realize they missed spending an eternity in hell. Remember, He said, 'And others save with fear, pulling them out of the fire; hating even the garment spotted by the flesh.'"

"Yes, I get it. Indeed, time is short. But in general, people don't take too kindly to what you have to say unless they feel it's shrouded in love. That means you have to take time to get to know people and invest in who they are as individuals. That means you can't judge them for being sinners. For the most part, people know the wrong they're doing. We have to make sure they see the light in us that outshines whatever darkness they're in. I don't have to tell you. You already know Matthew five and sixteen. The end result is that people end up glorifying God. They change when they can see *your* light, not listen to your empty words."

Leigh raised a brow at the "empty" comment. She popped a honey lemon lozenge in her mouth and offered Garnet one, who declined.

"Or not," said Leigh. "Some people see the light and get blinded. They run the other way. They get mad at you and get mad at God. He has a way of getting their attention, and it's not always pretty. People don't change until they see themselves in the mirror of the Word, and it's our job to hold that mirror up boldly to make them see His will for their lives. You have to keep planting the seed and plant some more and plant some more. It's a nonstop calling. The world is set up in a way to make people ignore God and pay him no mind. Remember, He said, 'Knowing this first, that there shall come in the last days scoffers, walking after their own lusts.' And you can't say these scoffers don't exist."

"They do. I know they do. But even they have to be dealt with in love. You can't scoff back at them. Jesus didn't scoff at His scoffers. It's about winning them over through time. Leigh, you can't possibly save everyone you meet. You do your part, and maybe your part is to break up the fallow ground and hardness in people's heart toward God. But after that, you have to let the Lord work on their heart from that point. You can't beat 'em up and then console 'em at the same time. Regardless of when He's coming back, He knows where everybody is on the journey and is responsible for bringing in His

own bride. We all have different roles. I'll stay away from criti-
cizing your methods, and maybe you can do the same with
mine. From what I've witnessed, I've always noticed that the
Lord uses different people at different times for different purposes. Paul summed it up best, saying, 'I have planted, Apollos
has watered, but God gave the increase. So then neither is he
that planteth any thing, neither he that watereth; but God
that giveth the increase.'"

"Yeah, but Jesus was no pushover. He was radical. He
walked into the temple and turned that place right side up
when he found out his people had turned His house into a business. He threw those tables around like they were toothpicks."

"Yes, He did. But he showed that side to people who were
supposed to be His people because they should have known
better. In fact, the only time he really spoke harsh to people
was when he was talking to those who were supposed to
be so holy and righteous but were hypocritin', never to the
hard-core sinner. Now, take this same Jesus, who was spotted sitting with tax collectors, publicans, and other sinners at
Levi's house. These people were known for doing some of the
same things they were doing when he turned them tables over,
being sheisty in business. But that's what they were supposed
to be doing because they were . . . um . . . sinners. So he deals
with people differently, depending on where they are."

"Well, people have got to know that they were born sinners, and there is only one remedy. Romans five and nineteen
says that. You can't deny the obvious."

Tit for tat. They continued. Both were well-versed and
sounded right during the moment they spoke. At least the
conversation was civil. They both were passionate, knowledge-
able, and had one mission. They wanted the soul to be saved.
Different tactics, worlds apart. Night and day. Between Leigh's

hate-the-sin message and Garnet's love-the-sinner perspective, they seemingly were oil and water. They must have figured they weren't going to persuade the other, and maybe it wasn't necessarily a bad thing.

"Well, I guess I better be getting out of here, girl," hinted Garnet. She grabbed her purse and stood, leaning backward a bit to stretch her lower back muscles.

"Me, too. I have to get to revival tonight and get some more strength for the journey. Plenty more people to bring into the fold, and they ain't gone come by themselves." It was a final, subtle jab.

"Yes, you're right." It wasn't a concession, just a tepid acknowledgement. She had her own summary statement tinged with a bit of its own wit, although she didn't anticipate for it to have some muted intention. "I definitely think Paul was on to something when he said, 'Only that in every way, whether in pretense or in truth, Christ is preached; and in this I rejoice.'" She only meant that the Lord would use any type of witnessing for His glory and to attain His ultimate purpose.

Leigh resisted the urge to internalize the insinuation, that her preaching was the one done in pretense. She let it fly. She grabbed her belongings and inched toward her car. There was really nothing left to say. Each had gotten off whatever was on her chest. They were good to go. After a little more irrelevant chatter, they ended with a humorous yet mutual sign of respect as they parted ways.

"Stay blessed, Dr. Gibbs."

"Have a good one, Dr. Lundt."

27
KRUNCHY

WITH ITS 400-BED capacity, Sardar Daud Khan Hospital was the premiere medical facility in Kabul, which primarily serviced those stationed there at military bases. Situated in the most affluent area of the town, it was a virtual stone's throw from the U.S. Embassy. It was the Mayo Clinic of the Eastern world, easily distancing itself from any of its closest medical competitors, like Afshar or Shar-Ara. The movement inside the hospital was no different than was normal. Needles pricked; bladders failed; visitors yawned; nurses congratulated, consoled. Nothing atypical.

To the two lying beside each other on the sixth floor, however, the last seventy-two hours had been anything but usual. They were nearing the end of the phase where they had been seeing walking chicken wings and floating bonnets. The wings turned out to be doctors who simply took their vitals and monitored their reentry into a physical, tangible milieu. The bonnets, hanging TVs. Before now, the only thing Redd could make out was the wing asking him some silly question about if he was okay. Now, he saw clearly the foreign-looking guy who seemed rather interested in his well-being.

"Are we feeling a bit better, Mr. Moultrie?" asked the doctor. "I'm Dr. Pirzada."

"I guess asking where I am wouldn't be a good sign, would it?" answered Redd with his own question.

"At least it means you're aware that you're somewhere. That's a start."

"Wanna be a little clearer, doc?"

"The easy answer is that you're in a hospital room. It's the 'why' that you may be more interested in. My friend, you just survived what is known around these parts as an SBM. Happened three days ago, and we've been nursing you back to health."

"SBM?"

"Suicide bombing mission."

"Damn." Most of the lower part of his body was wrapped in bandages to stave off any infections resulting from the blast. He was progressing fairly well, but total healing would take some time, of course.

"Yes, we have several around these parts per month. Turns out everybody at your poetry gathering wasn't concerned about poetry. Quite a few casualties. A handful of survivors. They brought you and your buddy here to Sardar and took the others to other places. Let me see your arm, please. Need to get a few vitals."

Redd obliged. "My buddy?" He hadn't even realized someone was lying in another bed a few feet away from him, separated by the typical white sheet that was supposed to guarantee privacy. This one was either beige or just dirty.

"Yeah, your comrade over there sustained a pretty major injury." The doctor didn't want to startle him, so he mentioned nothing of the injuries that Redd himself was pulling through.

He'd find out soon enough. He placed the stethoscope on Redd's chest and asked him to breathe normally.

Redd was hesitant to ask who his roommate was since it would have shed light on those who possibly didn't make it. A simple "Oh" would have to suffice for now.

"Alright, sir. Looks like things are slowly but surely getting back to normal. Heart rate's at 87 bpm's. That's still a little high but not too bad, considering. Respiratory's at 21 breaths." He'd just had him breathe for ten seconds and just guesstimated the overall result. "Blood pressure's 125 over 95 mm Hg's. Just a fancy way of saying you got a little hypertension going on. Again, that's pretty normal given what your body's been through over the last three days of recalibrating itself. Temp's holding steady at 99."

"Maybe it's these drugs I'm on, but I still don't feel right. I guess I better thank the Lord that I'm still here." Never had he thanked the Lord before in such an open fashion. It made sense at this point, though. Gabriel stood in the corner by the curtains with arms folded, quiet, preparing for what was next. It had to progress this way. There was something more important at stake.

"Now, all we need to do is get a reading on your weight, and we'll have all the stats we need. We don't have the weight beds, so you'll have to ease from under the covers and step on the scale over here." The nurse entered as if on cue. "Nurse Khan will assist you to see how much strength you have in your legs. She'll help you. Just take your time."

Gabriel turned himself and stared through the wall outside. He knew his kind was not supposed to show emotion, but he could barely help it. It was what his Boss ordained, so he had to believe it was right. As the nurse gently grabbed Redd's arm, the patient threw the flimsy sheet off of him over to the left. As he motioned to get himself out of the bed, he stared at what had to be a nightmare. Simply stared.

"You okay?" inquired the doctor empathetically.

Deflated, Redd tried not to seem too devastated. "Yo, I don't know man. Why didn't you tell me?"

"It's our policy here to let patients make their own discoveries like this. It's part of the training we've received from military psychologists."

Listening to what the doctor said but not hearing it, he offered his own remarks. "Wow, doc. What the hell am I supposed to do with one foot, man? Come on, doc. This can't be happening."

"Yes, my friend. It happened," the doctor succinctly replied.

All the earlier talk of thanking the Lord that he was still alive seemed to fade. How quickly his perspective shifted to a less appreciative, more accusatory one. And he had gotten noticeably louder, trying his best to process what he was witnessing. "How could this happen? What the f–"

"Yes, Mr. Moultrie," interrupted the nurse. "It's a hard pill to swallow, but we're here to help you get through it."

Dr. Pirzada remained quiet. He had been through this before and had concluded that initial silence was always best.

Redd sat still as the nurse held his arm, still hoping he'd make the effort to stand on the scale; however, the most he'd moved was his right leg, foot intact, so that it hung off the bed. He tried wiggling his toes on the imaginary left foot to see what it felt like in reality. It felt the same.

Since his emotions were being bandied back and forth, it only made sense that they became even more frazzled with the next discovery. All the commotion had awakened his roommate, who had grabbed the sectional divider and pulled it to the side to peep the drama. Groggily, Jerome asked, "Yo, what the hell's going on in here?" He already knew Redd was sharing the room but was not aware that he had gained consciousness yet. He was among those hoping that he'd snap out of it soon. Apparently, he had.

Noticing Jerome, Redd wasn't sure how to process this maelstrom of feelings. Anger. Perplexity. Elation. Relief. Woe. At present, elation won out. "Jay!" If he could have made his way over to hug him, he would have. Thankfully, he didn't have to because his compadre approached his bed and put a normal bear hug to shame. He managed to maintain his monstrous grip, even without his left forearm. From three inches below his elbow, it was gone. Gone.

A couple of days ahead of Redd he was with respect to the knowledge of his new normal. But don't get him wrong. That this was his reality still stung. It was just that the initial honeymoon with the biting astonishment was over. "My nigga! You don't know how good it is to see you up, boy. They told me you were gone pull through, but they didn't know exactly when." He had already seen the missing foot, so he didn't think to play into Redd's understandable sense of agony. "Damn, yo. You know you my boy. I'm glad you up."

The doctor and nurse team decided to back away for a moment and allow the reunion to play out.

"Man, what happened to you? Where is your freakin' arm, man?" Redd asked, still not sure whether to be happy or concerned.

"Same place your foot is." He was only one who could have slid in such a joke.

"What the hell?"

The doctor sensed this was an appropriate time to interject. Confidentiality was not really an issue since both may as well had been brothers. Jerome was already privy to the story but listened again. "Both of you had infections spreading in your foot and arm, so we had to act fast to prevent continuance. Although you have no family here that would have granted us permission to go through with the surgery, our standard practice for military personnel is to use our professional judgment in cases like this. The short version is that both of you would not have made it if we didn't make the tough call."

"Yo, I hear what you saying, doc," admitted Redd, "but it's gone take me a minute to process this." Jerome still sat on Redd's bed, agreeing. As much as he could, he helped the nurse resume her efforts in getting him to the scale. As least he wouldn't weigh as much as before, in theory, Jerome joked. Redd's chuckle was forced.

"One eighty-two," noted Nurse Ghattas.

"Wow. I haven't weighed that in a while." His mind became a little more sober. "So how many of us made it? What actually happened? How long are we gone be here? Anybody contact our families?"

"Well, there were a total of seven casualties. Quite a few from your platoon, the bombers, Kabir."

"Kabir?" Redd became choked up. "No!"

"Yes, he didn't make it. Everybody else sustained some kind of injury from the blast. Seems like the couple that came in after you all started your session wasn't really interested in poetry at all. And it turns out that the baby in their crib wasn't a baby at all. The embassy here is making sure that all families are contacted. We generally are required to do it within a week of any incidents. Rest assured, they'll be contacted. Speaking of rest, you guys have had enough excitement for today. Take the remainder of the day to relax and get yourselves together mentally. We'll get some dinner in to you in about an hour and also some more meds."

After the experts excused themselves, there was nothing else for the maimed duo to do other than think, talk. Jerome made his way back over to his bed after grabbing the remote.

Afghan channels offered very few shows that were engaging, just basic news and war stuff. That was why he stopped to watch a semi-comedic show. That was different, a show of laughs. The audience, the male holding the microphone, and the laughter were the signs. Although he couldn't understand anything being said, he chuckled a little since the audience hinted that the guy was funny.

"I just don't know about this new normal," confessed Redd. "This one gone be a tough one to get through, dawg. Why you ain't trippin'?"

"I did, man. You know I did. Ain't but so much fresh shock you can keep having. You just get used to it each day. I'm sure I'll have some more days where I get pissed off, but I'll just deal with it one day at a time."

"I can only hope I get to that place, kid. I got to get in touch with Jamay and my boy. They gotta know I'm alright."

"They contact your families for you, remember."

"Yeah, but it ain't the same. This right here make you slow down and appreciate life. I need to talk to them, tell 'em I love 'em."

"I feel you, getting all mushy mushy."

"Damn right, yo. Life's short." Redd canvassed the quarters as best he could in a reclining mode. The light teal wall. Some psychologist thought it would be a calming color for patients. Fresh chrysanthemums alongside both beds. A spinning globe, a portrait of President Ghani, a leather sofa chair for a would-be visitor. For those who made it to the chair, they'd be able to thumb through back issues of *Gellara* and all of its most recent edginess. Everything in the room appeared to have a woman's touch, for sure. "I guess this place ain't half bad if you just stop and look at it."

"Yeah, it's decent. It's a step up from the USO, just minus the entertainment."

"Bruh, what you talkin' 'bout!" It was indeed a statement and not a question. "I miss those USO days. They used to treat us like royalty. A home away from home. Good memories. But for real though, playa, where do we go from here? We spend all this time fighting for our home turf and end up like this. Black men going to war for America, and we still getting shot down like dogs at home, number one, and then, number two, we come over here and we still a target. Bad thing is, out of all the training we doing to help these soldiers fight for themselves, we wind up getting blown up at some innocent poetry event. That's effed up, yo."

"Nah, it ain't 'effed up.' It's fucked up."

Gabriel would have to relocate soon to another assignment, so he figured that he'd go ahead and go get the lady to force the reveal.

"I'm not sure how things are going to go for now," said Redd, "but I guess we'll have to keep it in the Lord's hands for him to make some sense out of. Not having no foot gone be a bitch, yo. I'm just keeping it as real as real can be kept."

The room door opened, and a middle-aged, petite white woman entered. "Special delivery!" she announced.

"Nurse Barb!" responded Jerome. He knew why she was there.

Toward Redd, she celebrated, "Well, looks like our other sleepyhead has finally awakened." Redd seemed quite confused.

"I've got it right here for both of you," continued the nurse. With both arms behind her back, she approached both beds. "Here you go," she said. She revealed two slices of red velvet cake with icing and pecans. "It's your pre-dinner dessert. We do things a little backward here. You eat the sweets first and then the main course."

"Well damn!" chirped an excited Redd. "That's what I'm talkin' 'bout. How the hell y'all over here know how to make red velvet?" He reached out for it.

"Now, now, now. We have a policy. You only get it if I call you by your nickname. Everything is so serious around here that this is our only way of keeping things light and playful."

Jerome added, "Yeah, playa. I had to tell her my nickname from when I was a snotty-nosed kid. How I used to be real fat and always ate candy bars and potato chips all day. Man, I did it so much, they gave me a name that just stuck, but I ain't tell y'all niggas because it ain't none of your business."

That cake looked scrumptious, so Redd obliged. "Well, Ms. Nurse, if you just got to have my nickname, you can just call me 'Middie' because I used to be shy growing up. So it's just a play on the word 'timid.' There you have it." He couldn't believe he told them this. Nobody but his family back in Vegas knew of it. "I can't believe I just told you that."

"Middie, Middie, Middie, Middie." Jerome, amused, couldn't resist. "Out of all of these years we been serving, I never knew you to be no shy or timid."

"Well, now you know."

The nurse, needing to make her way to the rest of the rooms, made her usual dramatic cake presentation to the guys. "And so we have a succulent slide of red velvet cake for you, Middie." He grabbed it and the fork, tearing into it one morsel at a time.

"Damn. This good."

Making her way over to Jerome, she extended her hand, bearing the final gift. "And last, we have one irresistible slice of red sugary happiness for the one and only, the uniquely designed, the bold, the courageous . . . Krunchy."

28

UMBRELLA TALK

RAIN PITTER-PATTERED against the metal trash can beside the coffee shop. They enjoyed cups of coffee and cool water with lemon. They convened at a table outside but under the awning, keeping them dry. A refreshing mix. He agreed to meet with her at Garnet's prodding since Davida appeared to be a little down. She sat pensively, listening to Pastor Castillo and attempting to make sense out of his logic. She knew he was right but was in her feelings because of Tario's dilemma. "I know," she said, "but it's just not fair. They profiled them guys and took him in for no reason. If they were white, they wouldn't be going through none of this stuff."

"Davida, trust me. I get the frustration. I been living in the Vegas area for a long time, and I see how cops treat minorities. We just have to keep praying and trust the Lord will make a change."

"No disrespect, Pastor C, but we been praying long enough. We need some action." Her half-militant stance even surprised her. Since Tario's was the life hanging in the balance, she had discovered in herself a newfound activist. "If you ask me, along with all our protesting, we need to lead a serious campaign to get rid of a certain term in the dictionary, 'cause it ain't ever gone have no meaning."

Taken aback but intrigued, he pressed in. "Term? What term?" He was normally the one providing these so-called provocative moments.

"Post-racial. There's no such thing as post-racial."

"I guess I never thought of that. Interesting observation, though." He laughed at how right she appeared to be.

"There ain't never gone be a time where that term gone be appropriate, at least not in America. We'll never truly be able to say it and mean it as long as we keep being guilty of DWWB."

"Dare I even ask?" inquired the clergyman.

"Doing Whatever While Black. We always get approached and antagonized about doing simple stuff, and it always blows up into something unnecessary. We can't do nothing. We can't rent an Airbnb. We can't sit in a lobby at a hotel or a white college. We can't barbeque. We can't sit in Starbucks. We can't sell water, use a coupon at CVS, cash a paycheck, or cut somebody's grass. We can't play golf, swim in our clubhouse pools, enter our own condo building, ask for directions, or ride in a car with our white grandmother."

"Right."

"We can't do our job in real estate and inspect a home. We can't try to get a refund, babysit a white child, shop for prom clothes, walk through a bodega with a backpack. And on and on and on. I'm sick of it. They always calling the cops on Black people for dumb stuff. That's why it ain't never gone be a time where we live in a post-racial society. White people gone always feel like they got to keep Black folk in check.

It's always gone be a part of how they think. I don't care how many laws change; they ain't gone change. I'm not trying to be pessimistic, but it's just the way it is and the way it's gone be, Pastor C."

"I know. It's tough. It can tug at the core of your belief system." He understood her point exactly. Even as a pastor, he understood this complexity, what was supposed to be versus what was. He didn't preach much about it over the pulpit directly but tried to incorporate it from as much of a spiritual perspective as possible. His soapbox would never be political. The most he was allowed to do was encourage the people to vote. The Lord forbade him to promote a Democratic-or-bust philosophy. Or to turn the current events of the day into sermon fodder. Rather, he would preach holiness and hope hearts would turn for the better.

"It's just hard to know what to do in times like this. You want to trust that the system is gonna work, but then you keep hearing about this BS that ain't fair. I don't want to turn into somebody I'm not, just to make sure we get treated right. How do you not let them change you into somebody else?"

The pastor sat ruminating, letting the question simmer a bit. The Lord dropped a thought in his heart that would hopefully help her put her response to the recent drama in perspective. "What's that?" He pointed to the left of her chair.

"This?"

"Yes."

She picked it up. "It's what it looks like. It's my umbrella."

"What do you use it for?"

She hadn't yet experienced one of these classic Castillo moments and was caught off guard somewhat. "Um, I use it for the same reason everybody else uses it for. To keep me dry on days like this. I use it for what it's supposed to be used for."

She thought she'd beat him at whatever game he was playing, even though she didn't know the rules.

"Are you sure?"

"Am I sure about what?" she answered, confused.

"That that's what it's supposed to be used for."

"Pastor, everybody knows what an umbrella is used for."

"But is that what it's supposed to be used for?"

"Okay, where are you going with this?"

"What if I told you that the original purpose of an umbrella wasn't to keep you dry? What if I told you that this wasn't the reason it was designed or created? Is it possible that people have changed the purpose of the umbrella to fit their own needs and desires?"

She wasn't quite sure what he meant. "Okay."

"In the same vein, you can't let other people or situations deter you from who you are and what you represent. The pressures of life will try to get you to act out of character and compromise who you are at your core. But you can't let others use you for a purpose different than what the Lord created you for, even if it seems like you're fulfilling something necessary and worthwhile based on who they think you should be. Ultimately, if you allow them to change your function and essence, they win. If it's not the need you were created to fill, then you're wasting your time and your life. Be you. Stay true to yourself and His principles. Let Him work out the rest."

Her light bulb went off. "Do you always teach lessons this way?"

"I try to. I'm trying to follow His example in that regard. I still have a ways to go to outdo the pearl parable or the one with the unjust judge. One day."

Five minutes gave way to less philosophical banter and enjoyment of the outdoor elements. The rain subsided as they prepared to vacate. Somewhat surprised that she had to ask, she eventually inquired about the obvious. "So you just gone leave me hanging regarding this umbrella thing, huh?"

He almost told her directly but was of the opinion that it would stick better if she researched it on her own. This was his specialty in driving points home, making listeners participate in discovering punchlines. He'd give her one final hint.

"Do a little searching. Google is your friend. The actual word has Latin roots, and its original meaning has absolutely nothing to do with rain." He finished his cup of coffee, placed it on the table for bussing, and made his way out, smiling. "When you find out, send me a text and let me know."

Curiosity piqued, she watched the teacher exit and requested more hot water for her used tea bag.

GOD'S LAUGHTER

"GIRL, WAIT, TURN that up!" hurled Giselle.

"Looks like they releasing him. And you gone get enough of calling me that."

"Chile, boo. You gotta give me a minute. You know this different for me," she joked.

"Yes, that's him. They letting him go from the precinct."

Nieko and Giselle were watching Tario on television being released. All of the media coverage had shone too much light on his situation over the last forty-eight hours for there to be any further mishandling. Much to Officer Schmidt's disappointment, the detainee would only be issued a citation for noise violation and fined. A smaller but no-less-woke crowd had gathered once again outside to usher the man toward his freedom. It was done in the early morning while the majority of the rabble-rousers would more than likely be asleep.

"That's a shame," noted Giselle. "Just wonder what woulda happened if he didn't have all them cameras out there. He probably woulda ended up missing just like a whole lot of the other not-so-lucky ones."

"It's a sad day. Let's just be happy he got out alive."

The court TV show resumed after being interrupted and the two continued the small talk. Giselle, born Ardrick, was one of Nieko's friends that he didn't feel compelled to sever ties with while on his new journey. For one, Giselle didn't pressure him not to follow where his heart was leading him. Two, she was just a good-hearted genuine person who kept it real. But she was who she was and didn't see herself as an aberration.

"You ain't never lied. Consider him to be one of the lucky ones."

"Gets under my skin that cops just feel like they can do anything to us nowadays. It's not gone become an issue, though, until stuff like this start happening to white folks. Just like with crack. As long as black folk were dying from it, it wasn't a story. When it started affecting Ms. Sally in the upscales, then it was time to stop the presses."

"Yes, honey, crack is still wack," joked Giselle.

They laughed. "So how are things going down at the House of Givenchy? I miss that place."

"Well, you know you can come back any time, Ms. Thing. I mean, Mr. Thing. I mean, whatever. This gone take me a minute to adjust my speech with you. You know that, right? We miss you, too, though. Everybody is steady asking about you. They don't understand this transformation thing you going through."

"It is what it is. I don't really expect everybody to under-stand. It's just the road that I feel is the right one for me to be on."

"My son, don't forget to throw away those panties and heels," the Holy Spirit reminded Nieko. It was such a weird time for

that to be brought up. Out of the blue. He had been feeling the prompting lately but heard the Lord clearly this time. He'd get around to it.

"Everybody just saying that your decision seems so drastic. They keep trying to get me to explain what you feeling. Some of them think you just trying to be shady. Other ones think they did something to you to make you want to leave." She put her feet on the couch and lay in a curling position with a blanket covering her lower body. "So where is this coming from? I mean, when did you start thinking about all of this? I mean, like, are you straight now? Do you find women attractive sexually? I'm sorry for all the questions, hun, but I'm just confused."

"That's a lot of questions," he joked. "Believe it or not, I'm not sure that I know all the answers to them. Nah, nobody did anything to me to make me do this. I been thinking about it for a minute. I just haven't talked with nobody about it. I'm just me. I don't know if I fit into a category, straight, gay, or whatever. Like, I wasn't molested as a child or nothing. I just clicked better with guys in my teens, and I just went with it. We've all heard of straight people who eventually come to terms with being gay. For me, I feel like it's happening in reverse. Maybe I'm just evolving. I don't know if I'll marry or not. I may just stay single. Who knows?"

Confused, Giselle just said, "Oh, okay. I guess. I just want you to be happy, Nieko. I don't want you to get to the end of your life and regret not being yourself and end up alone."

"Yeah, I get it. A few people have told me that. I'm okay with being alone. I actually love it. It's the lonely thing people gotta watch out for. I know a lot of people who are with somebody, and they're still lonely. It's a big façade. Ain't nothin' that says just because you got somebody, you're happy. Some married folk are wracking their brain, trying to figure out a way they can get single. Single folk are wracking their brain, trying to figure out a way they can get with somebody. Ain't nobody happy. I'm over it with thinking you can't be single and content."

"Mm."

"The best way you can explain it to them is by thinking about your own transformation. You decided to make a change based on what you felt was right for you. You didn't decide to transition to a woman because you thought the whole male species was bad. It was about following your own path."

"Yeah, I guess so. These hormone pills are a bitch, though. I don't know if the thick thighs and bubble ass that come with it are worth the mood swings and this weight gain. I done gained five more pounds in the last two weeks."

"Boohoo. I'm sure you did your research to find out what the side effects of all that was gone be, though, before you went through with it."

"Yeah, but research ain't the same as going through it in person."

"And just like you got to think about the ups and downs that go along with being a new woman, I got to think about the good and bad that come along with living my new life. And it's not so new anymore. I been on this path for almost ten months now, so it's not exactly a honeymoon period anymore. It's getting real."

"Well, you know me. Ardrick's been gone for three years. Giselle's been handling shit for a minute now, so there you go." She pulled out a wallet-sized baby picture of the cutest five-year-old boy with two missing front teeth. She stared half-sad, half-relieved. Maybe it was the effect of the hormones, but she felt extra sensitive today while looking at the image. "Sometimes, I wonder what advice I woulda gave that little badass back then to let him know it would it was gone be alright. He would have no idea what he would have to go through later."

Nieko snatched the picture. "Aw, look at you. You were so cute."

"Were?"

"You know what I mean. For real for real, though, you should come with me to church sometimes."

"No thank you, bitch. I'll pass. Not the way they judged me there the last time I went. I can't count how many times I got the side-eye. And that's when I was going as Ardrick. You yourself know I was a little ole' feminine thang. Girl, how they was looking at me sitting with my legs crossed at the knees and my leg dangling."

"That's hilarious."

"I just don't have time for it. All the fakitude."

"Our church is a little different. It's hard to explain, but it just is. They challenge you to do better in life, but you never feel attacked."

"How 'bout I just keep watching you to see if you change from the mean bitch you used to be. If I see you change, then I'll know your so-called religion is for real. Other than that, I'm good."

A text came through Nieko's phone. *What's good.* "This boy just keeps on trying."

"Lemme guess. Mr. Mo!"

"Who else? He still tryin' it."

"Now *that's* the thing that would make me come to your church. You used to be head over heels about that fool, and now you not giving him the time o' day. That's a *real* miracle." They both shook their heads. "Anyway, girl, lemme get outta here. I mean boy. You know what I mean. You just gotta keep giving me a minute." He gathered his keys, phone, purse, and made his way to the door eventually, after grabbing something from the kitchen that was easy to eat.

"Alright, Zelly. Stay out of trouble. Take care of yourself. I'm praying for you."

"Thanks, girl."

Mo texted again. *Yo, Neek.* It was ignored just the same.

The streets of Toronto were abuzz with excitement nowadays. With World War II recently over, the demand for new vehicles for soldiers arriving home was a car manufacturer's dream. These, the Fabulous Fifties, saw a rise in interest for several types of automobiles, especially the Chevrolet, a stiff competitor with the all-too-popular Ford. Those who didn't care for the big-ticket item in cars were afforded another luxury in the newly constructed subway system for the city. After five years of planning, drilling, digging, and executing, the new transportation mode was now up and running, providing a viable option for those who couldn't afford the new rides or who chose to keep them parked. Jasper and his family fell in neither of those categories. He was saving to buy his own set of wheels to avoid unnecessary interest and happily settled on the underground alternative. Today, they were headed to church, as they did every Sunday.

"Let's go, darling," he voiced to his honey. She grabbed the three kids, and they were soon on their way to their Sunday meeting. Of course, she made sure the youngest had her usual coloring book in hand so that she would be more distracted and less distracting.

Theirs was a church that had recently joined the Pentecostal Assemblies, which had been making many a wave in the community with its radical nature of Christianity. Its flavor was a pre-Azusa type. The laying on of hands, the fiery preaching, the new limbs being grown, and yes, once, an elderly lady lifting herself from a wheelchair to walk. Even her doctor had to marvel at her new normal.

"Come, children," nudged the mother. Jasper would sit with the other deacons in the front section. He had kissed his wife and kids shortly after parking.

Once settled, it would be two hours of singing, worshiping, testifying, and preaching. Today, though, would be slightly different. The children only paid attention to the degree that something other than the regular displays would occur, other than the normal miracles. After the praise service had ended and hands were lifted throughout the edifice, Elder Orr, a fixed figure on the pulpit and one of the pastor's key parishioners, began speaking with other tongues as the Spirit gave utterance. It must have gone on for a minute straight with particular stress of one of the Romance languages, some cross between Romanian and Catalan.

There was dead silence. The congregation was up on their scripture. Such a display, if authentic, needed to be followed by interpretation for the sake of harmony, according to 1 Corinthians 14. It was so quiet that one could hear the proverbial rat piss on cotton. After about thirty seconds in this state of awkwardness, the pastor decided he'd approach the mic and make some type of transition. He wasn't one to play with the Lord, as his comrade had just apparently did. Right as he began to speak, a little girl hopped onto the pew for height. She was a tiny thing. What was more shocking than what she was about to say was her appearance.

She had been born special. Her parents thought it somewhat strange since they were both pecan brown. Nobody could really explain the phenomenon, although doctors gave it the old college try. Here she was, totally colorless, whiter than the average white person. Hair, skin, fingernails, eyelashes, underarms, little feet—all white. Flag-surrender white, dove white, Chinese-funeral white. Her brothers toughened her up by default. They bullied, taunted, shrugged aside, encouraged, loved her like anyone else's younger brat of a sister. So by the time she started school, the smirks and stares had zero effect on her esteem.

The congregation had gotten used to the family unit and her ghostly, almost ghastly, appearance; it had, however, never witnessed this teeny vessel being used of the Lord in the fashion that was about to unfold, neither had her kinfolk. The tiny albino girl leapt onto the pew and allowed herself to be the Lord's mouthpiece.

> "'Know that in this day, I stand ready and able to intervene in the lives of My people. I see, know, and love you. It is I who have allowed the enemy to triumph over you but only for a season. Nothing gets past Me without My approval. Rest in the fact that nothing is a shock to Me. Nothing has Me biting My nails. And neither should you. I am the God Who walks on water. I am the God Who tells the waves to calm down. I am the God Who looks at the wind to shut it up. Rest in Me, My children. And know that in time, I shall bring you out with a strong, steady hand,' saith God."

Her brothers watched her in amazement as she placed her knees on the pew and slid back down on the floor to get back to her kiddy assignment. Jasper's ears had perked up during her interpretive monologue. He had turned while the child spoke. His eyes confirmed what his ears already knew. His baby girl was not only unique; she was unforgettable. She was somewhat oblivious to what had just happened. She picked up her coloring book and started back at her artistic challenge of trying not to color outside the lines. But she'd discover that coloring within the lines would just not be her lot in life.

Services for today at The Alive Christ Church would be bitter-sweet. Castillo had received word yesterday that McElroy had succumbed to the pressures of the journey. He'd left his wife and kids because he said he needed some space to breathe, to gather himself. And this was not too long after the Lord had used him mightily in the services at Alive recently with signs and wonders following. Something was in the air and appeared to be tugging at the hearts of the faithful. Castillo promised himself he wouldn't be moved as much as it hurt seeing others evacuate. Come what may, he'd hang until the end.

The praise service was halfway done, so he'd have to masquerade the pain of the news and put on his smile so he could feed the flock its portion of soul food for the day. Carl sat in the office waiting for his boss to start making a move to leave. Castillo grabbed his hankie, while his assistant reached for the laptop. Carl almost bumped into the pastor, who had stopped briefly at the door to utter a short prayer for protection. Not an unusual occurrence but not a consistent one either. Carl never knew which Sunday Castillo would be led to offer a last-minute prayer. Sometimes, neither did Castillo. They headed quietly down the hall.

They made their way to rest in their pulpit chairs. There were a few more preliminaries, like announcements, the offering, and another song or two. The pastor would soon assume his position at the podium after Carl went before him and placed his laptop in its normal reachable location. Castillo worked the message in a way that gave the Lord leeway to talk to the people's hearts. He taught himself how to shape his presentation using technology. He had often gotten lost turning pages in a heavy Bible while he preached. The laptop allowed him to quickly find scriptures during his message; he could also view any notes he needed to reference during his anointed presentations. As usual, he started by reading the scripture backdrop for the message and then would often take a peek at his notes. Before long, he had slid into his rhythm of exhorting, admonishing, rebuking, comforting. No notes needed.

And he was extremely passionate about his message today. He wanted to remind the people that they weren't to look to man to validate their faith. Members were on their feet in agreement but weren't quite ready for where Castillo would take them next. In fact, a few of them took their seats as he continued because it made them reassess if they could be so committed.

> "And as Joshua said, 'As for me and my house, we will serve the Lord.' But be careful, we're living in a day where the *house* may decide to quit and walk out and throw in the towel. So, you gotta get radically selfish and be willing to say, 'As for me, *I* will serve the Lord.' Hopefully, the house will come along, but if the house turns back, if your family chooses not to serve Him, if your best friend walks away, what's gone become of *your* faith?"

A strong sense of sobriety swept over the congregation. This journey was real, and the pastor was quite aware of his charge to remind them of such. He mesmerized listeners as he weaved into his message further thoughts on Israel's becoming a nation again, wars and rumors of them, advances in technology, and of a great falling away. His preaching texts came from Luke 12:54–56 and I Corinthians 15:52. This day, as he preached on the current challenges of the day, the rapture, and the Great Tribulation, he spoke from the title, "Earth, Wind, and Fire." He'd finished up with the "earth" portion by discussing Joshua and his house. Now, everyone listened intently as he wrapped up the "wind" portion.

"It's true. No man knows the day nor the hour when the Lord will reappear. But according to our text, we *do* know the season. And the season is now! The wind will blow soon and take us up out here so that we can be with the Lord forever. ¡Gloria a su nombre!"

"Shut the hell up!" Heads turned and eyes watched the hillbilly ease his way from his chair in the back and make his way to the front. Ushers would have detained him, but his twenty-two-caliber derringer was a great deterrent. It was much better than his old-school shotgun, but he hoped it would be just as effective. Although as different as night and day, both guns shared the double barrel feature. And this miniature terror machine was actually kind of cute. Silver and cute. What wasn't cute was just how easy it was to purchase online. No background or criminal check, no ID verification, nothing. He just forked over the half of a grand, and it was his, especially not knowing the ins and outs of computers and the internet. "Just shut your immigrant ass up!"

Strange silence won out as Rusty made his way closer to the pulpit slowly, making sure his piece was steady in hand. Ashtoreth glided beside him. Gabriel sat on the pulpit, stoically looking away. Some faithful members prayed silently. They would have been louder and didn't themselves know why they weren't. Castillo refused to back down. He continued preaching, praying, lifting his hands, and ignoring the obvious. He preached with all his heart, admonishing the congregation to place faith in the One Almighty God. He quoted relevant scripture and stared at Rusty, who had come within eight feet of the pulpit. The pastor shouted his famous refrain again. "¡Gloria a su nombre!"

This tended to irk Rusty even more. "Who the hell is Gloria, you fake preacher? You just in here leading all these minds to hell. Us real Christians get sick and tired of fake preachers like you who just wanna come in our good communities and take the people money. You are destroying this community."

Unfazed, the faith man continued. He'd moved on to the final "fire" part of his message.

> "For this is a day where your faith will be tried with fire. Will you stand? Will He say to you, 'Well done, thou good and faithful servant'? Only you will determine whether He does or not."

Ashtoreth was somewhat confused because Gabriel remained seated, but she didn't let that distract her mission. She whispered a few more suggestions Rusty's way. "And all of you stupid fools ain't got no mind of yo' own." He waved his gun, pointing it at random people by mistake. His anger toward them was only incidental. His issue alone was with this perceived charlatan. "Following a man who don't mean none of you no good. The blind leading the blind." He inched closer to the pulpit, close enough that he could have been mistaken for a possible convert coming to the alter to surrender. Actually, he stood directly in front of Gabriel, who still sat and let the scene unfold. He looked up at the preacher, who vehemently continued to declare the good news on the raised platform. Rusty aimed upward, not particularly at any body part. Either one would do. "Sometimes, you just gotta take justice into your own hand or else this city, this town, this state, this country gone go to shit."

Pastor Castillo ignored him yet again, focusing on the troubled eyes of the flock. This was his mission, his chance to prove his steady conviction. He was no fan of martyrdom but stood his ground and dug deeper into the preached Word. This was what Jesus must have felt, a performance under pressure.

"And he who is a friend of the world is an enemy of God. Either he will hate the one and love the other; or else he will hold to the one, and des—"

The single bullet entered the pastor's stomach and exited through his back. One shot, perfectly delivered. It almost shocked Rusty himself at how on target he was. Even those in the rear heard the thud. Castillo could still see his people but only through sideways eyes, and someone seemed to be turning the light dimmer switch more and more to the left.

Ashtoreth backed her way out of the church, looking around and anticipating a bum's rush from a heavenly host. Nothing. She forced a smile and skedaddled. She couldn't wait to tell her compatriots of the victory. Gabriel wept. Unperceived by everyone, including Gabriel, God Himself was laughing.

THE FIERY
RED CONVERTIBLE

THE THREE-YEAR old had already tossed eight pennies into the fountain but continued to whine since her mom refused to give her any more to waste. The fountain at Meadows Mall was huge and provided casual sport for those kids and some adults who still found some merit in making a wish. Inconsolable, the kid admitted defeat as she was guided away with a promise of an ice cream cone from the food court.

Jim sat about fifteen feet away in one of those individual metal chairs. It made no sense how heavy they were, perhaps an impediment for theft. As he sat, he read some article in yesterday's *L.A. Times*. He wasn't really as engrossed in the story as others might have believed. He kept staring in the vicinity of the fountain, making his own wish without the coin toss. He only looked with his eyes and kept his head facing down toward the newspaper. His short-sleeved, buttoned shirt, paired with his sandals and khaki, knee-length shorts, made it easier for him to blend in with the mall's natural surroundings. His pulled-down cap, however, suggested something more mystique-based, questionable, nefarious. The time for his appointment was upon him, and he wanted to make sure he wasn't the cause for delay.

He looked around more conspicuously this time. Anxiety set in, and he almost got up until he thought he saw R.J. in the distance. He smiled and waited until the kid got closer. Thankfully, he was by himself. This was the only factor in the equation that always complicated his operation, not knowing where the parents would be. He trusted that children were able to convince their way to solitude. It was a gamble he didn't mind taking because he had become quite skilled at disappearing if the time came to do so.

R.J. appeared slightly tense and concerned. He robotically moved, veering neither to the left nor right. He had gotten within ten feet of the fountain and resisted the urge to look behind him. He was regretting that he even started the ball rolling in this direction, but he was learning a valuable lesson. He reached the fountain and looked around awaiting Emily's arrival.

That was Jim's sign, that look of *What next?* from the child. He folded the newspaper and left it on his table. Adjusting his hat, he rose and ambled his way to the meeting point. The kid, he thought, was cuter in person that in his avatar. His red hair popped with a vibrance that seemed retouched. That was a good thing. He casually approached the fountain, hands in pocket, and tried to appear as if he reached it by happenstance.

"Well, what are you doing here by yourself?" he asked.

"Hello. I am just waiting for Emily."

"Oh, wow. Is she your girlfriend?" He tossed a nickel into the water so as not to appear suspicious.

"No, she's just a friend."

"Oh, that's nice. It's always good to have friends." He stalled a bit. "I can't believe your parents left you out here alone. Are they in one of the stores out here? They probably let you come to the fountain by yourself all the time, huh?" He acted concerned.

"Well, we don't come here that much. When we do, they let me come and play at the fountain as long as I come back to them in twenty minutes."

"What does she look like?"

"I'm not sure. She said she would see me and get my attention. I met her when I was playing Fortnite. You can play the game and talk with your friends on there, too. It's like you can play against each other. And they even have dances your characters do and you can join in, dances like the Carlton and the Floss."

"Yes, the Floss! My daughter tries to get me to do that dance all the time. That sounds so cool." Though married, he had no children. "I'll have to learn how to do that. I'm just an old fogey. I can't keep up with all these dances and technology things." He hesitated and started back in. "Well, looks like Emily's running a little late. Maybe we can go grab some ice cream and meet back here. By the time we get back, she'll probably be waiting. My treat. What do you think?"

"Um, I don't know. I don't wanna miss her."

"You won't. I promise. I just have a taste for a nice milkshake. Don't you?"

"Well, kinda. That *would* be nice."

Both headed in the direction of the food court. Both looked nervous but for different reasons. Jim masked his angst the most. This wasn't his first rodeo. R.J. was providing the usual innocence that he was so used to preying upon. He would become victim number six. They sauntered into Chick-fil-A to grab a couple of treats.

"Hello, may I help the next guest?" The two approached. "Welcome to Chick-fil-A. May I have a name for your order."

"That would be Jim."

"Hello, Jim. How may I be of service to you today."

"Me and my man here will get a coupla milkshakes. We'll do the strawberry one for me and . . . why don't we do the chocolate one for this fellow right here." R.J. was looking a little concerned that the twenty minutes would be up soon. Ashtoreth, who was already in the restaurant before they entered, hovered in the air over in the corner, observing, smiling.

After a minute or so, the cashier returned with order in hand.

"Thank you, Jenae. I know these'll be great." He had read her nametag.

"My pleasure."

Right before they sat, Jim acted worried and stared back in the direction of the fountain. "That's weird, R.J. I still don't see her at the fountain yet. Maybe we can just take a second and hang out here and enjoy these milkshakes."

"How did you know my name?"

Caught unawares, he still thought on his feet. "Yes, you told me back at the fountain when we first saw each other." He knew he was lying but was a master manipulator like no other.

"Oh, I did?" reacted a partially convinced R.J.

"Don't you worry. We'll have you back to the fountain in no time. Oh, my gosh. This strawberry milkshake is splendiferous. They must use Breyers ice cream in this. How's yours?"

R.J. forced himself to drink, although he didn't really want to. His stomach was doing its best to give him the red-flag warning. Way down in the pit of his being, he knew this was not normal. "It's okay," he offered.

"Enough of the small chat. Get his punk ass to the damn car," whispered Ashtoreth into his ear. Her fangs began to protrude. Her wings expanded, revealing six talons and a hairy tail three meters long. *"Just hurry and get him to the car, you fuckin' perv. Now!"*

"Wow, this is so great! Oh . . . have you ever seen a convertible?" asked the trickster.

"On TV."

"No way! You have to see one up close, in person."

"You have one?"

"Yes. It's a fiery red 1994 Ford Mustang GT. It's my baby. Come on, let's go check it out." He touched R.J.'s shoulder. "We can look to see if Emily got to the fountain yet first, just to be sure."

"Okay."

They looked toward the fountain's direction one final time, and no sign existed of any girl that appeared to be R.J.'s age. "I don't see anybody, do you?"

"I don't think so," replied R.J.

"Well, it won't take long. The convertible's right out here. I'll let you take a look at it, but you have to come right back. Your parents are gonna wonder where you are once it gets past twenty minutes. You don't wanna disobey them and be late. It's just right out here. Let's hurry!" He knew that once he made it to the car, it would be over. The goal was to snatch and grab and get the kid away from the mall. He just had to lead him away, one step at a time.

"Are you sure we're gonna be back in time? I think it's already twenty minutes now."

"Yes, I know. That's what I'm saying. We need to run

so you can see the car, and then we'll hurry and run back. Let's go."

They walked fast and headed toward the mall's exit. Jim walked briskly, encouraging R.J. to speed it up, trot even. They finally made it outside. As they got closer, there it was. It really was a Ford convertible sitting there. He hadn't lied about that. He could finally sense victory. He was surprised at just how gullible the child was. The convertible was the gift that kept on giving. The afternoon sunlight bounced off the car, almost making it appear otherworldly, unnatural. If Jim's eyes could have pierced through the invisible barrier, he would have seen Ashtoreth hovering above the red machine. And if his ears were able, he would have heard this same Ashtoreth, who saw Raphaela approaching with entourage, say, *"That BITCH!"*

"Mr. Brewer, how are you?" A stranger's voice came from nowhere.

"Excuse me?" Jim answered.

"I'll need you to come with me, please." The stranger's voice belonged to Sergeant Atkinson. He and his fellow officer were beginning to apprehend the low-life suspect. "Could you place your hands behind your back for me, sir?"

"This has got to be some kind of mistake, officers. I'm just showing the kid my convertible and then I was gone take him back to meet his parents."

"Hm, I think the tap will reveal a little more information. Milkshakes? Really? You couldn't come up with one better than that? And the convos online leading up to this? How would you explain those, Mr. Brewer? Or shall I call you 'Emily'?"

"You bitch! You set me up!" Ashtoreth growled at Raphaela.

"That fuckin' kid set me up!" Jim angrily exclaimed.

"Ahh, now we see the real Ashtoreth, fangs and all!" chuckled Raphaela.

"Ahh, now we see the real Mr. Brewer, attitude and all!" They guided him away from his prized ride. "Looks like we're gonna have to impound this humdinger of a car, huh? Maybe sell it, get a few grand for some of the parts? She stands to rake in a buncha dough, don't she, Mr. Brewer? A real winner." Shoppers were starting to become privy of the drama. A few had begun recording.

Agitated, Ashtoreth blindsided Raphaela and knocked her to the ground. She pounced on top of the cherub, throwing all her weight on her and wrapping her tail around her neck to choke. They tussled and rolled a bit. Before Raphaela realized it, her own wings expanded and the hugest glow emanated from her being, knocking Ashtoreth to the ground. In a nano-second, Raphaela's foot rested on Ashtoreth's scaly neck. The gargoyle's struggles to free herself were futile. The catfight was in full effect.

"You have no right to impound my car!" Jim roared. Agi-tated, he blindsided Officer Atkinson and knocked him to the ground, though he was still handcuffed. Jim pounced on top of the officer, throwing all his weight on him and initi-ated what he thought was an effective chokehold. They tussled and rolled a bit. In an instant, the other officer grabbed him, turned him over, and placed his knee on Jim's neck. Strug-gles to free himself were futile. Officer Atkinson got himself together, brushed himself off, and proceeded to the squad car.

"Calm down!" Raphaela said to her ruffled nemesis. *"Calm down. You don't want to make things worse on yourself. You're fighting a losing battle. You are no match when the saints of the Most High are praying."*

"Just calm down, Mr. Brewer! Calm down," said the offi-cer. "You don't want to make it worse on yourself. You're fighting a losing battle. You're no match against the law."

Raphaela raised her foot, and Ashtoreth darted a safe distance away. Her wings were noticeably disheveled. She fumed and stared hotly at her opponent. She knew not to try it again. She knew her limits. Raphaela's strength, reinforced by Garnet's prayers, was too formidable. *"This isn't the last you've heard from me, damn it! You just wait and see! I'll be in contact with my backup."* Perturbed, she flew into the distance, leaving a trail of sulfur behind.

The officer lifted his knee. Jim's appearance was noticeably disheveled. Jim fumed and stared hotly at the officer. He knew not to try it again. He knew his limits. The officer's own strength, reinforced by his taser and billy club, was too formidable. "This isn't the last you've heard from me, damn it! You just wait and see! I'll be in contact with my lawyer." Perturbed, Jim ducked and entered the cop car, leaving a trail of fear behind in R.J.'s little world.

Officer Young escorted Garnet to where the action was happening. They had been watching the whole scenario unfold on a screen from an undisclosed location in the mall. If she could, she would have jumped through that screen to go rescue her small, innocent lamb. But she had to stand back, so that the authorities would get all the information they needed to seize the culprit. She held tightly to R.J., who was teary-eyed and sniffling. He had pulled off the biggest acting performance of his short life and had earned his Oscar nomination. But this was no Hollywood. It was as real as real could get. "You did well, son," reassured Young. "You were very brave."

R.J. did not feel comfortable enough to talk yet. He just hugged his grandmother and would not let go. So Garnet did the talking. "We were happy to help, sir. I thank the Lord it turned out okay."

"Yes, ma'am. We've been monitoring Jim Brewer for quite a

while. We've been intercepting his online activity here recently and thought we were ready to set up a sting here at the mall. Thank you for giving us permission to follow through with it. I know the kid's a bit shaken up, but we couldn't have done it without you or him."

"Thank you for contacting me and letting me know about the chats. I try as best I can to stay on top of that boy, but I just don't know that much about the internet and computers. But God keeps helping me raise this child while his daddy is away." She raised her hands and said hallelujah right in the middle of the mall. A *"Thank you, Jesus"* would soon follow.

All the officers whisked Jim away and called for the truck to impound the vehicle. Whether others understood or agreed with it or not, Garnet knew her prayers revealed this plot of the enemy. Hell had lost again. Discerning that this was no time for scolding, Garnet, saying nothing, walked with her arm around the kid's shoulder. And Raphaela walked with her invisible arm around Garnet's. The scolding, the love, the concern was all implied in Garnet's silence. She finally said what she thought would be comforting to hear to the young fellow. "How about some of grandma's favorite pasta tonight?"

31

You Wanna Be a Man?

"BABY, THAT'S WHY you can't trust strangers. Everybody is not nice. Some people want to hurt you."

"I thought it was a girl my age," replied R.J.

"I don't know too much about this chatting stuff, so I have to depend on the Lord to help me raise you. He keeps you protected even when things that you do like this blindside me. I praise Him so much."

R.J. remained quiet and accepted her subtle rebuke.

Night lights provided an escort for the two as they made their way into the grocery store's entrance. It had begun getting darker earlier, making it feel as though it was later than it actually was. They'd focus on picking up necessary ingredients for tonight's feast. Although R.J. wasn't a cook, he knew all of the components needed to make her famous concoction. He could almost gather all the materials and the proper amounts of them without looking. So he figured that he'd let her gather herself and cool off while he continued to assess what just happened back at the mall. "Gramma, I'll get the tomatoes and garlic and mozzarella."

"Okay, baby. Just find me when you finish."

They went down their separate aisles, and Garnet continued to thank the Lord under her breath for His faithfulness. *"You know, Lord, I need help raising this child. I don't say it much, but I don't really know what I'm doing. This day is different than his mother's day when she was a little girl. I can't see everything he does, so I thank you for looking after him. Help me, Lord. Keep helping me."*

"Hi there, Garnet."

Reaching for the Barilla lasagna noodles, she hadn't noticed Marjorie sneaking up beside her.

"Hey there," answered Garnet. "I didn't know you shop in these parts."

"Yeah, I don't stay too far from here . . . about a mile south. Off of Nylo."

"What?" Garnet joked. "The MacArthur hopeful actually does her own food shopping by herself with no assistance?"

"Speaking of which, I found out I'm a finalist."

"Marge, that is so fantastic. Those things are hard to get."

"Thanks. That process is so hellish." In somewhat of a facetious disposition, she responded, "And I wouldn't exactly say that I'm shopping all alone." Almost on cue, a gorgeous, short-haired brunette approached. She didn't say a word, didn't have to. She just locked her right arm in Marjorie's left. Garnet remembered her likeness with that in the tuxedo photo she had seen earlier in her colleague's office. "I thought you were supposed to be getting some Brussels sprouts and green tea," Marjorie directed toward the woman. In a gotcha kind of way, the woman held up both items in her left hand to prove Marjorie wrong.

"This is Darcy," Marjorie offered. Both were mature enough to know that no formal introduction was needed regarding the extent and scope of their association.

"Hi," said Darcy.

"Hello," responded Garnet.

Like clockwork, R.J. happened upon the group, relaying to his grandmother that he had gathered all the items she had requested. He had mildly complained about needing a small cart to carry them in.

"Oh, R.J., please. You don't need nothing to put them in. You're a big boy. You're big and strong enough to carry these things." To the rest, she continued, "Everyone, this is my whippersnapper of a grandson, R.J. Say hello, R.J."

"Hi."

"We better get outta here," said Garnet. "We've had a long and eventful day. Time to get this meal going before my grandson accuses me of neglect and not feeding him. I'll see you all later. Let's go, man."

Fortunately, the express checkout lane was empty. No inconsiderate customer had brought her thirty-something items into that line. It would have been smooth sailing to get out of there, but Garnet had forgotten to grab something.

"Oh, no. R.J., do grandma a quick favor. Run and get a firm white onion. I don't know how I forgot that. I think it's on aisle–"

"It's against the wall on the far end, aisle one," Fran, the clerk, interjected.

Just what R.J. wanted. Permission to bolt through the store like Usain. As he made the turn at the aisle, he came to an abrupt stop, not because he had reached the requested onion section. He stared in awe, as the spectacle caught him completely by surprise. He tried not to stare but there was no way he could turn his eyes away. No way that he could unsee it. As if the fountain incident was not enough, this would have to be a close second at forcing him to grow up and become an adult before he wanted to. He managed to grab an onion and make his way back to his grandmother, who chided him for taking too long.

"Come on, R.J. You know we're in the checkout line, and there's people behind us." She grabbed the onion quickly while the cashier weighed it and provided the final total. R.J. continued staring back at the general aisle area, not quite knowing what to think. To the cashier, Garnet gave a "Have a good night, Fran," and headed out.

The other two eventually pushed their cartful of items to Fran's lane as well. They'd gotten it down to a science, the amount of stuff to get that would carry them a good week. If they continued with only eating out on Wednesdays, they'd be set for a while.

"It's not *that* farfetched of an idea to build a wall. There's got to be some way to control crossing the border. However you feel about him, you can't really criticize the fact that he's trying to make them do it the right way." Marjorie supported the whole idea of restricting entry into the States if it was not done the proper way.

"Indeed, I can. That's not all his platform is based on. The wall is just a smokescreen. That part's not so bad. It's all the deportation he wants to do along with it. He already said he's okay with breaking up families. So the parents would be forced to leave the U.S. while the children stay. What kind of crap is that? It's a complicated problem, and you can't solve it by simply 'returning them to sender' and wishing them well."

They rarely discussed politics, especially in public. It engendered too many emotions. The president had brought both of them out of their shells when it came to certain topics, and they didn't mind discussing when they felt the urge, even in the checkout line.

"One twelve, sixteen," said Fran. She knew already to place their groceries in their reusable shopping bags.

"Well, I'm just saying I see both sides. If we shipped *everybody* back to their country, nobody'll be left here except Native Americans. If the country does nothing, it'll just be an open-door, free-for-all." Marjorie swiped her card. "We have to find a way to stop people from coming in illegally. Suppose you were standing in line in this grocery store waiting to check out and people just kept skipping in front of you to pay for their stuff. Don't tell me you wouldn't get upset and feel slighted. It's the same argument with immigrants who are coming in the right way while others skip the line ahead of them."

They grabbed the bags and stepped into the path of the automatic door. They'd almost walked right up to the door before it sensed their presence. It needed to be fixed.

"Yeah, I can see that. I still just don't know if a wall is the answer. How tall? How wide? And for how long? I just feel like it needs some more thought. Plus, all people gone do is find a way under it or over it. If they want to get past that wall, they're going to find a way."

There would not be enough time to settle the matter now, in the cover of night. Several customers wondered why mart owners hadn't invested more in placing lights more strategically in the parking lot area. Certain parts gave off an alley feel. Parking there in the day was fine, but there was something sinister about navigating through the night. The only reason the two ended up parking there was that they thought they'd be gone by now. They hadn't anticipated bumping into Garnet and company. No biggie, though.

"I just hope something gets figured out. It's kinda sad all the way around."

What else was sad was their obliviousness of what was unfolding right before their eyes.

"You bitch!"

Someone had cold-cocked Marjorie across the back of the head, so hard that her bags fell to the ground. So did she.

"What the hell!" exclaimed Darcy. Her small frame made it impossible to intervene in any significant way. Her voice had to make up for what her stature lacked. "STOP! STOP IT!" She stared unnervingly at this random fool, dressed in a regular tee, jeans, and blue ski mask. How dare he not show his respect by at least wearing the typical robber's uniform. She'd soon discover, however, that it wasn't money that had driven him to launch the attack.

Indeed, the perpetrator had tunnel vision. He continued to beat, kick, brutalize. Marjorie would have fought back, but the element of surprise had served its purpose well. All she could do was use herself to semi-shield herself from the attacker's consistency.

Darcy tried to dial 911, but her shaking kept getting in the way. The three numbers felt like ten. She hoped somebody, anybody was close. "HELP! SOMEBODY, PLEASE HELP!"

"You bulldagger!" yelled the attacker. "You wanna munch carpets, huh? Munch on these!" He kept hitting, aiming for the face. Making bruises on the face was key, he thought. She would remember this incident every time she mustered the courage in the future to glance in a mirror. "All these men out here, and you want to grab on some titties. You want what you already got!" The assault relentlessly continued. They were grown-man kicks, like the ones in those extreme fighting matches. "You wanna be a man, then take this ass-whippin' like a man."

Although she didn't want to, Darcy convinced herself that running to get help was the only solution. Even if she didn't manage to find somebody, the assailant wouldn't know it. She ran full speed in an out-of-body type of way, toward the grocery entrance. She was just debating politics a minute ago. As she looked back, all she saw was a slavery-like beating and a blur on the ground. From where she was, she couldn't see the damage occurring to the arm, the legs, the head. She just saw a blur getting pummeled. "PLEASE HELP! PLEASE HELP!"

Strange it was. It ended just as quickly as it began. His stealthy disappearance into the darkness was only outmatched by his covert arrival. Before anyone knew it, this unknown had mounted his motorcycle and sped into the distance.

Back behind them, Marjorie writhed in pain, feeling swollen in the face and hoping nothing had happened to her petite partner. Little did she know, her other half had become a beast, screaming, shouting, coaxing, until some dyad took her lead and headed back with her to see if there was still a fighting chance.

32
No Guarantee

CAMPUS LIFE WAS quiet since students weren't around after summer school; the three-week gap between the end of the summer session and the beginning of fall classes proved needful for all who kept the school's engine running smoothly. Staff generally had Fridays off, and faculty enjoyed the benefits of not having to come in at all for the entire summer. A few of the latter often popped in unannounced with their new tans and new tales of their summer travels. Although Garnet went nowhere since finishing the teaching of her summer course, she had been rather busy with her own drama. A drop by the office would be a fresh change of pace. Plus, she figured she'd come in and get her thoughts together for her *U.S. Era of Civil War and Reconstruction* syllabus for the fall.

"Hi, Opal. Is you done lost a few pounds, girl?" That southern part of Garnet had come alive again with no notice.

"Hi, Professor Gibbs. Yes, a few. Just a few."

"Girl, hush. If you lose one pound, that's more than enough.

Everybody knows how hard it is to get results when it comes to that."

"I just told myself I wouldn't stop until I saw some progress. I started doing Zumba. The less it felt like exercise, the more I stuck with it. Amazing how much you can lose when you're convinced that all you're doing is dancing for an hour."

"I heard that," interjected Celeste. "I remember I used to do that. Until I didn't. My instructor was more on the hood side. She was just using class as an excuse to make us twerk. I was so embarrassed. People was staring through the glass, watching us like we were crazy. I asked her, 'So what part of the body does this work for?' Girl, she said, 'All of it.' And that wasn't the worst. She had a nerve to make us get on our knees like a dog and lift one leg like we were peeing on a fire hydrant and still tryna twerk at the same time. I finally got up and told her, I said, 'I'm sorry, ma'am. I don't have enough insurance to cover what you tryna make us do.' I grabbed my water bottle and towel so fast and limped my butt up outta there. And I did *not* look back."

Garnet and Opal became undone with laughter. "I didn't even hear you come in," confessed Garnet. "You know you is a fool. I don't know why I put up with you."

"I decided I would just stick to the treadmill and stationary bike. What I don't lose that way, it's not meant for me to lose."

After making her way into Garnet's office, she plopped into a chair. "Nette, I got some good news. I got transferred to Records and Registration. And can you say, 'eight percent salary increase'?"

"Celeste, that is so wonderful."

"I guess that's what you call favor from the Lord."

Garnet hadn't really heard Celeste talk this way, using this Christian vernacular. "Alrighty, lady. Look who's giving glory to

God." She placed her hand on Celeste's forehead and pretended to take her temperature.

"Yes. I'm learning not just to count my blessings but to give credit to where they're coming from."

"No objections here."

"Anyway, I just wanted to stop by. I'll be using the rest of my personal time and taking a little time away. Use it or lose it."

"Wow, good for you. Where are you going?"

"Professor Gibbs, Mr. Zimmerman's on the line," Opal interrupted. "Should I send the call through?"

"One sec," responded Garnet.

Celeste continued. "I'm headed to Miami for a little rest and then home to Memphis to check on my mother."

"Is she okay?"

"She's fine. She just claims I never get back to see her, especially since I'm single, which she never fails to remind me about."

"Be happy whether you single or married. Neither one is better than the other. Just be happy either way."

"Well, maybe I'll get my groove back when I get to Miami. I ain't gettin' no younger." She gave Garnet a hug and headed out.

"Enjoy yourself, girl. Just be safe. You know I love you and happy that you're getting away to get some time for yourself. It's always going to be plenty to do around here. Always remember to refresh and rejuvenate yourself." She realized she should've been taking her own advice, as she'd had no real vacation since summer school ended. She'd change that soon.

After hugging Celeste and bidding her farewell, she gave Opal the okay to transfer the call.

"Tell me some good news, Cason."

"Jesus is Lord."

"Uh oh. Whenever that's the default, I know something else is not going right. What's the deal?"

"Well, looks like LCU's going to be losing their federal funding. The court gave them an ultimatum, but the school's Board of Trustees decided to stick by its guns and not change their mission statement. They just thought making it all-inclusive would compromise too much of its standards."

"What's their backup plan regarding finances? Are they gonna just let their doors close?"

"They're appealing to alumni and explaining the situation. They're hoping that will sustain them for about two years. They'll have to figure out something else after that to maintain a steady endowment. Not looking too promising, though."

Uriel listened in and knew Cason was right. The handwriting was on the wall. He knew the school would fold in three years because the college was not going to take their financial matters into its own hand.

"What a changing world! Who would have thought these private Christian schools would be in a place where they had to make choices like this? I said it once and I'll say it again. You have to be in a situation where you can finance your own vision. Otherwise, you'll always be in position where you have to bend according to somebody else's rules."

"Yeah. They're continuing their funding for another year to allow for them to make changes. After that, the shoe's going to fall."

"We'll see what happens. You gave it your all, so you should feel proud. As long as you feel like you gave it a good go, that's all you can ask for. It just seems that the conservative agenda is being pushed aside more and more."

"Anyway, gotta run. Wanted to get back with you, though, as promised. Taking on some civil rights case now dealing with discrimination between Airbnb rentals. Seems like some owners are only renting to whites. They're telling those with black profiles there are no vacancies but telling those with white profiles that there is space available, all for the same dates."

"Your work is never done, sir."

"Yeah, that's what I'm afraid of."

"Alright, well thanks for getting back with me, Cason. I appreciate the follow-up. I'll keep you lifted up. Stay on the front line, my brother. Keep fighting the good fight."

"Love ya, Garnet."

Belial overheard the discussion, too. He was ecstatic, not necessarily because the college would eventually close but because of the college administration's laziness and lack of any substantive action to confirm the faith it said it had.

She hung up, shook her head, and perused her syllabus. She'd probably change percentage allocations for the different grade categories this semester.

"R.J., please get these shoes and put them in your room. Sometimes, I think you do this on purpose to make me mad."

"Alright, mom." He responded quickly, surprisingly. In a jiffy, the shoes disappeared. He even let a "Yes, ma'am" slip out. The experience at the mall did its part in growing him up. The close call was making the idea of family more of a concrete notion to him. His father's awayness had already begun the adulting process for him, but this most recent episode was his and his alone. Maybe obeying wouldn't be such a bad idea.

"Thank you," said Jamay. She honestly thought she'd have to go several rounds with the youngster and was a bit thrown off when he readily complied. "Thank you."

"Don't know what to say, huh?" joked Davida. She sat in the living room, ankles crossed and flipping channels.

"And had a nerve to say, 'Thank you' twice." Tario joined in on the fun. He rested one of his legs across Davida's.

"You two lovebirds gone leave me alone, yeah mon," answered Jamay, adding a bit of Jamaican humor. "Seriously, though, he's being forced to grow up quick. It's just a reality with this young generation. Ain't no need in thinking you gone raise them in no bubble. And if you do, get ready for it to get popped."

"I know that's right," added Davida.

"I saw how quiet and subdued he was this morning and figured he was thinking about something, so I asked him if he was thinking about Redd. You know, when the military people called us and told us about his foot, I wasn't sure what to do, how to explain it to the child, how he would take it. So I just thought he was sad about that. But turns out it wasn't that at all he was thinking about."

"Really? What was it, then?"

"To my surprise, he said he kept thinking about something he saw the last time he was at the grocery store with mama. He said he ran to one of the aisles, and when he turned the corner, he saw a lady who mama knows kissing another lady on the lips. He ain't never seen nothing like that before, so it just threw him for a loop."

"Yo, Jamay, I ain't no parent," started Tario, "but I know you don't think you gone be able to shield that boy from the world. This a new millennium. If you don't tell him about it, he gone see it on TV, or he's going to hear other kids talk about it in school. And it ain't got nothing to do with whether his daddy's here or in Afghanistan. He just gone see stuff."

"Listen at you, trying to be all rational and logical," praised Davida.

"I'm just saying. You gotta let kids know what's out here. Ain't like you tellin' them to do it or not. They just gotta know. You see what happened with him down at the mall. If the cops didn't give you guys heads up on it a couple of days before the meeting, God only knows what could have happened to li'l man. You owe it to him to be real with him." Realizing what he said, he joked, "And I'm the one that got the nerve to be giving props to any kind of police, with all the crap they put me through."

"Yeah, a part of me knows that, but another part of me wants to protect him as long as I can."

"So what did you tell him about what he saw? Or what else did he say?" inquired Davida.

"I just basically asked him what he felt about it."

"He said he was shocked. Said it made him feel weird. That's why he went back into the checkout line and didn't say nothing about it to mama. So I told him what we believe about it and told him to pray and ask the Lord to help him process what he saw. That's about the only thing I could think of in the moment. Wish mama woulda been around. I'm sure she woulda known what to say. She still don't know, and I probably won't tell her. Maybe this is just for me to learn how to handle as a mother. I got a feeling it's gone be more things he gone see, the older he gets. Mama ain't gone always be around, and tell you the truth, it really ain't her responsibility. I'm the one who gotta be prepared."

Davida turned toward Tario and cuddled up next to him. "I'm just glad my boo is finally free, in spite of what the cops had up their sleeve. He doesn't know how much we were praying for him. If you don't believe the Lord is real by now, you ain't never gone believe. That was straight up terrible."

"I know, baby. Shit got real up in there. People be talking 'bout what they would do if it was them, until it ends up being them. It just be you and them dumb officers in there. That's it."

"And the Lord," said Jamay.

"I'm just glad y'all had my back. That main cop was corrupter than a mug. Called me a coon, and nigger, and everything in between. Hell, I even started telling him about the Lord, anything to get him to think about what he was doing."

"Pressure and the will to survive will make you do some strange things," Davida concluded."

"Did I hear him say he started preaching in jail?" No one had heard Garnet sneak in. She'd overheard the conversation from his curse word. "Cursing one minute. Preaching the next. So you grabbing a page from Peter's playbook now, huh?"

Tario didn't understand the reference. Jamay and Davida did and chuckled. "Hey, Dr. G."

"You know, that should have been enough to give you a wake-up call, sonny boy. The Lord's hand was protecting you. You may not know that people have been interceding for you for a long time, Tario. The Lord is calling for you. There's no guarantee that you'll get another chance to give him your life. Time is fleeing, and tomorrow's not promised. Not trying to scare you or nothing, but you never know when your time will be up. And you ain't got to wait until you get to nobody's church. You can give him your heart right now."

"Yeah, I hear you, Dr. G. I hear you." But he wasn't quite willing to make it official yet. But it *would* happen soon.

She placed her hand on his shoulder as she walked by and let the blinds down a little. "It is sweltering out there. Good Lord."

"You went to work today, mama?"

"No, I wouldn't call it that. Just went in to get some things straight before the fall semester rolls around. It'll be here before you know it."

"I'm gone have to sit in on one of your classes one day," commented Tario. "I bet you be threatening them like nobody's business."

"You're more than welcome. Come, if you dare."

"Look at this." Davida stopped on the local news station. The reporter was standing in front of a cordoned-off area with something resembling steam rising far in the distance behind her. Her accompanying camera crew panned to her left, revealing a line of cars evacuating the area. Broadcasting from Hawaii's Big Island should have been a fun assignment, but the recent summer developments were causing much upheaval and tons of panic.

Everyone watched and listened, shaking heads or making other gestures signifying disbelief. "Well, I guess there goes your once-in-a-lifetime trip to Hawaii," joked Tario.

"Not really," Davida said. "Most tourists don't go to Big Island that much anyway. Most of the people go to Oahu or Maui."

"Especially the vets," said Garnet. "They go to Pearl Harbor over on the main island."

"What's all that smoke from?" R.J. asked. He'd made his way back into the room and was wondering why everyone hung on the reporter's every word.

"From the lava," said Jamay. "The lava is coming up from the ground. Now, all those people have to move and get out of the way. It's a mix of earthquakes and volcanoes at the same time."

"So why is the reporter still there? Can't it come up from the ground where she standing at?"

"Because reporters are dumb," chimed in Tario. "That's

probably the stupidest job you could have. They the only ones that run toward something that's dangerous while everybody else running the other way. Don't be a reporter, R.J. Make me that promise."

"Tario, leave him alone," said Davida. "If he wants to become a reporter, let him do it."

"I don't want to be no reporter," the child uttered. "But has it always been there? Why is the lava just starting to come through the ground now?"

Garnet hopped on it. "Signs of the time, baby. Signs of the time."

"What does that exactly mean, Dr. G?" Tario inquired. "Seems like I hear that all the time. Signs of what? Signs pointing to what?"

Garnet heard him but didn't hear him. Everybody listened and waited for her response, including R.J. Still focused on the TV, she came off as ignoring him and provided no further explanation. In fact, she said it again, oblivious that all were interested in her take. "Signs of the time." She remembered an appointment scheduled for today. "Oh, baby, I won't be around for dinner," Garnet mentioned. "I need to stop by UMC tonight. I'll pick up something while I'm out."

"You gotta go by the hospital? Anything wrong?" inquired Jamay.

"No, I just need to stop by there. If I don't do it tonight, I won't get around to it until next week."

Through the tube, lava continued to do its damage, starting fires and uprooting residents, who never imagined that such a tranquil place would be transformed to a hotbed of destruction.

DE UN ALBINA

TRAVELING BACK TO the Jalalabad camp proved to be as uneventful as one might have guessed. A full two weeks had passed before Redd and Jerome were able to make the journey home. It was amazing how they adapted to being handicapped. Their ability to bounce back had been epic, the stuff of Hollywood. But time would tell in the long run. Two weeks still qualified as too early to assess how the reality would change their worlds. Merciless were PTSD and its offshoots, the effects of which started off innocuously but often morphed into a death grip that knew well how to suffocate and maim. No one knew what the guys' emotions would do two months from now, or a year, or over the course of a lifetime. The renowned one-day-at-a-time admonition would have to be enough. And this day felt like a win. At least in part.

Life at the base still felt the sting of the others' passing. The absence of Chaz and Jones was palatable. Especially Jones. She had learned to hold her own amongst the guys' taunts and shenanigans. Although she was a gorgeous woman when she fixed herself up, the fellows never crossed the #metoo line with her. She was their sister, a true sister with all the rights, privileges, and responsibilities that pertained thereto, like the arguments, scoldings, and other mainstays indicative of strong sibling rivalries and relationships. Now, she and all of her jokes were gone, just like that.

All they were supposed to be doing was trying to train Afghan soldiers to defend their own territory. Fate, thus, orchestrated circumstances in such a way that they weren't even able to defend themselves. It was time to go home. It wasn't worth being blown to pieces for no apparent reason. They knew the chances of it happening were there. But now, the chances weren't just there anymore. They were here. Theory had transformed to reality. At this point, Redd was keenly aware of what was necessary.

"I'm going back to Vegas, yo."

"Not much you can do for soldiers here. Me neither, truth be told," agreed Jerome.

"This just brings everything into perspective, man. My son almost lost his father at a poetry reading. Of all places. Not on the battlefield, not dressed up in camouflage, hiding in the woods. But at a damn poetry reading."

"It won't be hard to plead your case, bruh. If they deny your request, ain't no hope for none of us."

"Not even about pleading, though. I just physically don't have the capacity to carry out what they sent me here to do. It won't be considered AWOL."

Each had learned to be what the other missed. Jerome did stuff that was better to do with two feet. Redd, with two hands. Other mates chipped in where necessary.

Maybe without this devastation, Redd would not have considered his return so strongly. Maybe there would be some bonding with R.J. after all, before time got away too far and fast. Who knew? It seemed to be a sure step one in the process. One of those strange answers to somebody's prayers. One of those answers that hurt first but made sense later, one of those crucifixion answers. In Redd's mind, it wasn't that deep, per se. He simply wished for it to be America outside again. And he made a vow that he wouldn't stop until it happened.

Pensively, Rusty sat in the precinct. He didn't demand his one phone call or nothing. Just sat and smirked. He'd reached his limit concerning this immigration and minority nonsense. Who were the ones looking out for his kind? Everybody was playing the victim in America, but white folk were the ones who kept getting overlooked. Out of all they'd done for this country, this was the thanks they got. Nothing. It didn't matter about the Native Americans, and he wished assholes would quit bringing that up; it wasn't like they had a *real* civilization no how, just making clothes, creating pottery all day, and sharpening arrows for bows. Didn't even have no real stuff that made a country a country. No machinery, no smallpox to help advance medicine, no guns. Just a bunch of backward-ass tribes singing and cajoling. Thank goodness for Columbus and 'nem to bring some order to all of the uncultured chaos.

So offing one spic wasn't much, but it was a start. Too bad it had to be a preacher. Just got caught in the mental crossfire. Besides, being a preacher would go a long way. His followers would get the point that America couldn't stand for this anymore. Somebody had to do something about it, so Rusty was willing to take a stand and do something. It didn't matter what the repercussions were. Who cared how it affected those around him, including his wife? Times were changin' and he did what he had to do. Oh, how he longed for the halcyon days of the '50s!

Ashtoreth, fresh from her recent shaming at the hands of Raphaela, was happy to place this victory in the win column. This was the ultimate victory because the dumb pastor wouldn't be around to lead all the gullible folk down a senseless and hopeless rabbit hole of hope. There was nothing good coming out of this one.

"Here's some lunch, sir," said the warden. In part, he was sympathetic to the old man. Hence, the respect shown.

Rusty grabbed it and nibbled on the pear. "How long do you think it'll be 'til my trial?"

"No one knows, sir. It's a long road before then."

"Looks like I'll be in for it pretty bad, huh?"

"Who knows? It all depends on the system." He seemed to be giving Rusty advice on the sly. "I done seen a lot of stuff in my day. Some stuff that *won't* supposed to happen happened and some stuff that *was* supposed to didn't. If you get you a good lawyer, ain't no telling what might happen."

"This whole world's screwed to shit. Ain't nobody speaking up for the little man no more. I myself don't see how it's gone survive if don't nobody level-headed come in and say somethin' 'bout it. The only one seem to be speaking up about it is Trump. Thank God for him. He such a good man."

The steel door of the prison entrance swung open, giving way to a petite older woman who had eventually been holding out on how physically strong she was. She bolted to the dilapidated front desk. "Russ! I need to speak to my husband, Russ!"

"No visitors until about an hour or so, ma'am," responded the desk officer.

"No, you don't understand. I need to speak to my husband."

Without further confrontation, the officer shook his head

and granted her her white privilege. He led her back to the visitor's area and had her husband brought out. No handcuffs, no
nothing. Musta been nice.

"Rusty, what the hell were you thinking?" Martha Jo frantically asked.

"Not too loud, honey. They might be recording. We don't
want to jeopardize our chances." He called himself taking the
officer's advice. "It may not be over."

"The hell it ain't, Rusty! Don't you know churches today
have cameras? You not making no sense. What the hell were
you thinking?"

"You just don't get it, Mart. You just don't get it."

"The hell I don't. I know damn well what's going on in the
world." She didn't really curse, so Rusty knew she was upset.
"You act like this world supposed to revolve around you and
what you think. Well, I got news for ya. The world's changing
and you better get with it. I knew you had your ways about
ya, but I never thought it would come down to this. Sure, you
complain from the couch about stuff, but you actin' like that
book title about a cuckoo's nest."

He had no clue about what she was referring to.

"One day," she continued, "you gone realize that this ain't
the '60s no more. That old way of thinking is dying, Russ. I
don't know how I married you in the first place, thinking you
would grow out of your racist self."

"Oh, Mart, it ain't no racism."

"Yes, it is! Just that you don't see it. Everybody else can see
it but you. I don't see how you can go this far to try to prove
your senseless point."

"You wouldn't, Mart. You wouldn't understand."

"I got just as much white in my blood as you do, prolly
more white than red. But it's more to life than just being white.

You gotta live with everybody. And not just live with and tolerate 'em. But respeck 'em and treat 'em like the human beings they is. Not go around shootin' and killin' 'em like dogs."

"*Supposably* shootin' and killin' 'em. Ain't nobody proved nothin' yet."

She stared at him in a shaking-my-head manner, realizing that none of what she said was penetrating. "You're pathetic." She had stood up to him before, but this was different. Her resolve was set, scarily so. "And you're on your own. I'm not fightin' this one with ya. I wouldn't be surprised if you rotted in hell for this."

He pounded the table and stood up. "Martha Jo, you just shut your mouth!"

"No, you shut yours!" They were each other's mirror image. They both stood, staring in the other's face. Deep down, it threw Rusty for a loop because he had never seen her in this light before. Sure, she had been a voice of reason for him to consider before, but never had she stood toe to toe with him, challenging his core the way she did now. "I'm just lettin' you know you on your own on this one. You on your own." The alpha she-wolf had spoken.

"Mart!"

She grabbed her keys and her pocket book and threw it over her shoulder. As she got to the door, she turned around and looked back at him with disgust before bolting out. Neither Rusty nor she, for that matter, knew that Gabriel had been by her side, giving her strength that she didn't know she needed to stand up to her husband and tell him what he didn't want to hear. Things were shaping up according to the Plan, despite all the reprehensible theatrics.

When Dr. Varras entered room 1006, he knew this would be no run-of-the-mill matter. His patient was asleep, absorbing the IV's nutrients. Her visitor sat inaudibly. Aside from the occasional beeping of the bedside machine, the turning of the visitor's flimsy Bible pages created the only noise in the room. The UMC doctor acknowledged her and told her that he'd be back in ten minutes or so to check on her.

"Okay."

Soon, the silence gave way to a stirring in the patient's bed. She moved around a bit, trying to find the least irritable position. Less acute was the pain from facial swelling, but the throbbing continued. She managed to open her eyes and tried to make out who silently kept her company. She figured it was no one other than who it was supposed to be. "Baby?"

"I haven't been called that in quite some time." Laughing, she said, "Hi, Marjorie. It's Garnet."

"Oh." She coughed a bit. "What a surprise."

"Don't force a conversation, Marge. You don't have to say anything. I know you're in pain, girl. Do you need anything. The doctor left a few minutes ago. Said she'll be back." She grabbed a paper towel, wet it, and placed it across her friend's forehead.

"Ole' Doctor Varras. She's good. Helps me a lot."

"My God, Marge. I am so sorry this happened. I don't know how we could have missed seeing anything. R.J. and I weren't that much ahead of you. Where did you guys park?"

Her voice was firm but obviously not as strong. The speech was slow. "Around the side of the grocery store. The lights weren't that bad. I could tell it was planned, though. They must have been stalking me the whole time. Before I knew it, I was waylaid pretty badly. They threw punches and personal insults my way." The beating had been rather intense, so much so that she seemed to be convinced that there was more than one assailant. Throbbing in her lower right jaw was keen. Her doctor would chastise her if she knew how much she was talking. But she had to talk for sanity.

Garnet shook her head in disgust, still dabbing Marjorie's face gently. Healing would be a long journey. Odds were low that she'd return to the classroom in the fall. Disability checks would have to sustain her for a while. No one doubted her resolve to bounce back. It would just take time. After shifting a little to her left side, she paused and noticed the room's elephant. "Honestly, I'm actually a little shocked that you visited."

"Really? Why?"

"I didn't think you really liked me all that much. Especially after that heated conversation between me and Leigh at the diversity meeting."

"Oh yeah, that. I was a little embarrassed at how that went. I had a conversation with Leigh myself. It was a doozy." She walked around the room, peeking out of the windows and adjusting the covers some. She then sat back down in her own chair, reclining. "Leigh is a work of art."

"I just know how much you don't necessarily care for the way I live."

"Come on, Marge. I disagree with a lot of stuff that a lot of people do. As I'm sure you disagree with some things others do. We both have that right. But that doesn't mean I don't value you as a person, a human being. God knows, nobody deserves what happened to you."

Marjorie grunted an "I see" grunt. "Yeah, it's the typical 'hate-the-sin, love-the-sinner' speech."

"Oh, Marge, stop now. Ain't nobody giving no speech. The only reason I'm bringing any of this up is because you brought it up indirectly. Nobody's against *you*. We can fundamentally disagree with each other on principal. It's life. It's America. We get to do that." She got up and handed her some water after seeing her struggle to reach it on her own.

She coughed again. Realizing this was really not a time to engage in such an argument, the patient relented. "Either way, I'm glad you decided to stop by. Shocked but glad. Thank you, girl."

Dr. Varras and Darcy walked in. Darcy pecked Marjorie on the cheek and shook Garnet's hand. She sat on the other edge of the bed, making sure the exposed feet were covered. The doctor approached the bed and informed of the need to get updated readings. Garnet knew to back away. "You haven't been doing a lot of talking, have you Ms. West? You have to give yourself ample time to heal." He placed the thermometer in her mouth.

"No, she's been pretty good, doctor. Hasn't been talking much. I've been doing most of the talking." Garnet thought she'd intervene. She felt a little guilty for urging her to go against doctor's speaking orders. She caught Marjorie's eyes, offering a coy smile.

This was the best time to sneak out, thought Garnet. The gang back home would begin to wonder where she was. Plus, now she was starving. A pit stop at El Sarape would, no doubt, do wonders at satisfying her Mexican food craving. Grabbing her purse, she made her way out, turning one final time to confront a trio of goodbyes.

No one really knew the restaurant's secret ingredients, especially in the alambres and tlayudas. Rumor had it that a unique mixture of Aleppo flakes, vanilla beans, and epazote was the spice concoction that kept 'em coming back. Gerardo, the owner, had relocated to the area from Oaxaca ten years ago and had found his sweet spot in the community. He got the everyday downtown workers and the locals from the Arthur McCants and Mi Casa en el Sol neighborhoods. He even got the transients on I-515 who needed hunger breaks as they traveled to wherever. Garnet was closer to the second group, often finding herself there at least twice a month. She could taste the cuisine already, summoned by its alluring and aromatic woos. With no shame, she allowed herself a slight trot to the entrance. The leaving couple held the door for her more out of curiosity than politeness. They discussed among themselves after clearing her presence. As usual, she paid no attention to their ignorance and kept it moving.

"Hey, Garnet," greeted Gerardo. "The usual?"

She was slightly embarrassed that he knew what her usual was, but she guessed that was the reason the business thrived. "Yes, Gerardo. Thank you. I was gonna grab it and run, but I think I'll sit and eat. I'll get a pineapple Jarritos out the fridge, so add that to the bill."

"One sincronizada and a shrimp ranchero combo coming up. The Jarritos is on me."

Sinking in a booth next to a Mexican couple, she decompressed a bit, still mulling over the hospital visit. Marjorie's prognosis was gloomy but positive. She couldn't feel what Marjorie felt but hoped to provide whatever support was necessary to get her up and back to her old self. She stared at the couple and how blissful they seemed. Stars seemed to populate the sky in their eyes. Even with a baby that refused to be ignored. Cries seeming to demand food or a changing or who knows what permeated the restaurant but were forgiven. Garnet was only able to view the back of the stroller since the front was turned toward the father, who tended to the little one. The mother glanced over at Garnet and gave her a familiar smile, a hopeful one. The husband's face lit up too once he stared over toward her way. Garnet returned the gesture, relieved that some stranger acknowledged her for who she was and not what she looked like.

"Two more minutes, Garnet," announced Geraldo.

"No problem. No rush."

The loud mouth's cries died down, and soon she was overcome with sleep, finally. The mother wished to check on her and reached for the stroller, repositioning it to face her direction. And Garnet's.

Garnet gasped almost an audible gasp, which the couple naturally heard. Transfixed, she rose from her booth and made her way to the couple's table, not caring that she didn't know them from Adam. She simply stood admiring, staring, loving, reminiscing. The Mexican couple smiled back. There she stood, looking at the most beautiful, tiny albino that ever graced the face of the earth. Eyes closed, breathing fast, remnant tears that had escaped her pea-like ducts, pacifier stuck in mouth. Garnet could do nothing but smile, so the couple broke the silence.

"Hello, ma'am," the wife uttered.

"Hi," Garnet answered. "I'm sorry. I don't mean to—"

"I know. No worries."

"Sabía que la amarías tan pronto como te vi entrar," said the husband, who knew English but used it only when necessary. In situations like this, he knew his wife would interpret for him.

Garnet was a little shocked at first but would soon flow with it.

"He says that he had a feeling you would be drawn to her when he saw you come in."

"Oh, really. I wonder why." Garnet chuckled.

"It's not every day this happens."

"This is true, especially in Vegas. Maybe it's time for me to start gambling. Looks like the odds are in our favor." Everyone laughed.

Garnet stared down again at the infant. "She's as cute as a button."

"¿Eres de la zona?"

"Are you from here?" She continued providing the translation after each of his questions. Garnet didn't miss a beat.

"No, I'm from Canada . . . Toronto. I've been in the area for a while. I work over at UNLV."

"¿Eres una profesora?"

"Yes. I teach history to a bunch of spoiled brats. Summers off make it worth it, I guess. How long have you guys been here?"

"We've only been here for four months. We relocated from Phoenix to find better job opportunities. Plus, we feel like we're under less scrutiny. We can't afford to let anything threaten our family. The government, politicians, nobody."

Garnet was keen. She heard what the wife didn't say. She guessed it was an issue of immigration status, probably related to her husband. "Well, there are great opportunities here."

Unprompted, the baby awoke and stirred. Her eyes opened and looked about. She saw her mother, her father, and then Garnet. She lit up once she locked eyes with Garnet and started squirming.

"May I?" Garnet asked. The two looked so drained from catering to the bundle of joy's every need. Garnet could sense the tail had been wagging the dog and thought that providing a respite, however brief, would help.

"Sí. Por favor."

The little one levitated with Garnet's help. She smiled,

showing all five of her teeth. R.J. was the last person she had held this intimately. It brought back so many memories.

"She loves you," the wife observed.

"Aww. You're a gorgeous thing," she said to the baby. "You don't know me, precious, but you're gonna turn many heads in your wonderful life. Your life is going to be so successful." She sensed the Holy Spirit speaking through her and continued. "Stay sweet, and keep loving everyone, no matter what anybody does to you. Don't worry about people staring at you. It's not you. It's them. It's their insufficiency. Hold your head up, sweet pea, because you are fearfully and wonderfully made."

The poor little thing stared at her, staring at her with turned and cocked head like a confused puppy.

"Order's ready, Garnet," voiced Gerardo. "Are you sitting over here?"

"Yes, right over by the purse. I'll be there in a minute. I'm starving." She gently placed the cutie back into the stroller and bid one final farewell to the couple. "Anyway, it was nice meeting you. I'm sure I'll see you around, especially if you come here regularly. Looks like we have a lot in common." She shook their hands and accepted their warm reciprocation.

More pep filled her step as she made it back to her table. Famished but revived, she was noticeably tickled pink. Literally. She kept laughing to herself. Never would she have thought that she'd run into someone like that beautiful child in this restaurant of all places.

"What a nice lady!" mouthed the wife. "She seemed so relieved. And what she said was so sweet and kind."

He agreed. "De un albina a otro." He casually stated what was blatantly obvious to anyone who happened to be in the restaurant during the interchange.

"Indeed, honey. Indeed."

34

TOMORROW

IGNORING OLD FRIENDS' texts had become par for the course for Nieko. Not even Maurice's antics and attempts threw him off as easily nowadays. It was a decision he stuck with, despite all the cultural shifts and pressure from old friends, who just didn't seem to get him. Fighting to make his flesh behave was tough, but it paled in comparison to what he thought he'd gain from abstaining. His periodic wrestling matches with pleasuring himself was the last part of this he'd have to conquer fully. He managed to maintain victory over it for the most part. It overcame him only twice a month now. But when it did, it was ugly. It was a battle like no other. He wanted no one to be privy to how depraved things could get, this his vice.

After he'd climax, his feelings often straddled between embarrassing and dejected. That constant death grip, thinking you were cured and having it come back with a vengeance, was a beast. It should not have been named among those who named the name of Christ like he did. But, believe it or not, this was progress, given that it used to be a nightly occurrence during his time of getting over Mo. Constant episodes of unprotected sex with him had made their mark into his psyche and established a vicious tie of the soul. There he would be again at the moment of the cycle, asking the Lord for forgiveness, strength, and power to shake away from this stubborn hold. *"Next time, My son, ask Me for strength and power while the attack is happening so that you don't have to fall,"* the Holy Spirit suggested. *"You are forgiven, and you're still My boy."*

His friends knew he'd be back to kick it with them, probably later rather than sooner. They'd just wait it out and welcome his crazy, voguing self back. *What's the point?* they'd often text him. They frequently ended their texts with the yolo hashtag, hoping he'd come to his senses soon. He knew he wouldn't, though. Outside of Garnet and the gang and Giselle, he learned how to exist each day inside a wall of protective fire that the Holy Spirit seemed to keep around him. Something deep within him seemed to be steering him in a different direction. This seemed to be a call to come away, a wooing, a nudging. He couldn't get out, and no one could really get in. When they somehow got in, they somehow ended up out. It was a situation that Nieko had come to accept. A part of him was in a quandary, but he'd rationalized it as being good confusion—a confusion the butterfly must have experienced during its awkward and time-intensive metamorphosis, he thought. Most perplexing was that there was no direct and obvious cause for this new journey—no hell-fire-and-brimstone sermon about it from Pastor Castillo, no subtle ostracism from his family, nothing particularly that Mo did. It was just as mysterious as what precipitated his involvement initially—no molestation, no inducement from society's ever-emerging sense of liberalism, no missing father.

It just happened; and it was just happe*ning*. When he inquired of the Lord, the Lord only answered by placing 1 Corinthians 13:12 in his spirit. So that's what he went with week by week, month by month. And it almost was about to be a year.

Noticeably different was the mood in the service. Pastor Castillo's absence was weird in a word. Still shocked, the congregation still wrestled with the why of it all. Why him? Why now? Why during the service? Why in the way it did? Why didn't the Lord stop it? No answers, just questions. His homegoing service was phenomenal, but that didn't take away from its vitriolic sting. Elders and associate ministers filled in the gap each week to make weekly Sunday meetings happen, but it just wasn't the same; no one had been set aside as his successor. Pastors didn't really plan in this fashion. They generally thought they'd be around until a ripe old age. Now, there was a scramble for service sanity. Thankfully, Jamay and the gang handled praise and worship service. Outside of that, though, the only constant appeared to be change.

Some of everybody showed up today. Of course, there were Garnet and the other regulars. Celeste. Nieko. Davida. Tario. Yes, Tario. Gabriel. Yes, Gabriel, who had a special mission to make sure Tario showed up. It was a packed house. Randi and her new fiancée were in the mix. Kemal's passing was a mere afterthought, although it had only occurred a little while ago. She was bouncing back well, considering. Admittedly, it was taking her a while to get her sea legs back with respect to marriage. Things weren't forced but did happen at a rather speedy pace. She'd given so much with Kemal, only for things to veer the way they did. But she remained optimistic and steered clear of making the new man pay for the sins of the old. Or at least she tried to. She, Garnet, and Celeste managed to squeeze in small talk before service began.

"You look great, Randi." They hugged and stared victoriously at each other.

"Thanks, Nette. One day at a time. Things are shaping up rather well, thank the Lord. This is Badou."

"Ba-who?" joked Celeste. She was too unpredictable.

"Badou," he himself clarified, offering a deep Senegalese accent. Catching the joke, he declared, "I've pretty much heard all the different variations of my name, so there you have it. Nice to meet you ladies."

Shaking her head at Celeste, Garnet completed the greeting rounds. "Glad to meet you, Badou. You must be a special man because you're engaged to a special woman."

"This I know," confessed the six-foot-five specimen. "She's a special lady, a gift from God. I am grateful that she came into my life."

Where can I get me one of those? thought Celeste. She stared at Garnet and smiled. Garnet immediately knew what was brewing in that mind of Celeste's.

Without saying a word, she looked at Celeste and mentally transmitted her response with eyes squinting, *"Mind outta the gutter, girl. We in church. Come up higher."*

"Well, let us get our seats. Hopefully, I'll see you all at the church banquet tomorrow," Randi mentioned. "Sounds like it's gonna be a good time of fellowship."

"Yes, we'll definitely be there. I've been asked to be the emcee for it, so I'm praying that it will go well. As much as I stand in front of college students, I still get a bit nervous when I have to preside over functions like this."

"Oh Garnet, stop. You're a natural," encouraged Randi.

"Let the Lord use you. I'll see you guys tomorrow. Stay blessed." She scurried to her seat.

"Later, ladies," Badou thickly added.

Minister Boyd had the responsibility of delivering today's message. He preached from a subject weirdly and simply titled, "Mañana." Gabriel walked and whispered in ears. The Holy Spirit prepared hearts for the altar call. An urgency filled the air for those to come to the Lord. Boyd was at the part where he was quoting from Romans 5, where he was attempting to justify why everybody, rich or poor, educated or illiterate, conservative or liberal, needed Christ. The recent murder didn't hurt his momentum either. That seemed to keep the fleeting nature of life front and center. He quoted from the English Standard translation.

> "For if, because of one man's trespass (Adam), death reigned through that one man, much more will those who receive the abundance of grace and the free gift of righteousness reign in life through the one man Jesus Christ. So, as one trespass led to condemnation for all men, so one act of righteousness leads to justification and life for all men."

He continued as he made his altar call, his appeal for those to come forward to give their life to the Lord. The Holy Spirit did His job at convicting those present of their shortcomings and gently prodding them to surrender. Condemnation wasn't His modus operandi. He reminded and offered the alternative. He swept over the entire congregation, encouraging nonbelievers to surrender. Some visitors even seemed to feel a slight nudging, a tugging.

That job was actually Gabriel's for today's service. He

darted about, to and fro, literally pulling on the arms of some of the attendees to move them forward. Castillo's shooting, the ways of the world, and the pressures of life all seemed to converge upon today's moment and serve as fodder for winning some over. Strangers began trickling to the altar and standing, quizzically wondering what was next. Applause erupted as Boyd, Gabriel, and the Holy Spirit worked as a trio to accomplish the hour's purpose.

In particular, Gabriel had two specific assignments. He had been whispering in the ear of the first target for ten seconds and tugging at her arm to approach the altar. She made nothing of it because she sat inconspicuously in the rear. In fact, she only came to pay her respects to Castillo and his passing. She had felt so guilty and thought a trip to the church would serve as penance of a sort. If she'd have to describe her religion before, it would have probably been a mix between being a Catholic and a good-willed, old-school Baptist. This seemed to be different, though. This wooing just felt like love, simple love. Maybe this was one of the reasons for the recent tragedy, one of the few silver linings. If anything good could have come from it, this made sense as to one of the things that would. A life for a life, a divine circle. She had stalled long enough. At Gabriel's last nudging, Martha Jo stepped into the aisle, moving her way toward destiny. The distance between her and the altar shrank with each second, eventuating to zero. She couldn't figure if her tears were for Castillo's death, her husband's plight, or her new lease on life. Either way, tears seemed to be just the cleansing agent needed to wash away the old and welcome the new. They flowed. They just flowed. Once Ashtoreth would find out, she would indeed become furious.

The second prey would prove more of a challenge. Tario

even surprised himself with just how obdurate he was. Today, though, it would all come to a head. With him, the Holy Spirit's job was easy. The Spirit reminded him of Garnet's casual words, in which she nearly persuaded him herself to give his heart to the Master. Also, it didn't take a rocket scientist for him to remember the incident with the cops and how his life almost expired under their watch. The many conversations with Davida over the last two years had contributed greatly to helping him prioritize what was important and what wasn't. The Holy Spirit worked tirelessly to remind him of such interactions and how the Lord had spared his life for this moment. Gabriel pulled, tugged, whispered. At one point, Tario thought Davida was pulling him and looked toward her way.

She mistook his glance as a gesture for support. "I can go down there with you if you want me to."

Tario hesistated and thought, thought and hesitated. He moved his right foot toward the aisle but stopped there. The war in his mind raged intensely. What would this mean? He didn't see himself as becoming no monk. This was absurd. Why was he feeling this sense of pressure and urgency to walk to the front? Life had its challenges, but it wasn't that bad. His intellect and smooth-talking got him out of the jail incident. Dr. G was just tripping on those occasions when he was over at her house. And Davida was just a mini-version of Dr. G. Besides, what would his Que dog brothers think? If there was an opportunity now, there would be one later. "Nah, I'm good," he responded to Davida's invitation.

"Is there anyone else?" asked Boyd. The flow of walking traffic had died down, and this appeal would be the final one. "Anyone else?" This was really Raphaela's assignment, this Tario. But Gabriel agreed to stand in her stead on this one since he'd be in attendance already. More and more, he observed why mortal and immortal alike dubbed that Tario as stubborn. Gabriel tried one final time, reminding, urging, pulling, convincing. He didn't think it would be this tough, given the course of Tario's life. After a few more attempts, Gabriel regrettably capitulated. The Spirit lifted and stopped convicting, guiding, revealing, and bearing witness. Tario no longer felt the nagging. That inexplicable invisible yanking on his soul had subsided. It was probably just his imagination and a mixture of the clapping, the loud noise, the music, and the celebration, he thought.

"Let's thank those who made the choice to give their hearts to the Lord. The angels are up in heaven rejoicing at your decision to come in to the fold." All but one. Gabriel stood at the altar, somewhat saddened at his inability to deliver on that obstinate man. He wouldn't fail the next time. He'd see to it. From this point, it would be hardball. Time wouldn't necessarily be on Tario's side, so he might not be so fortunate the next time. He'd work to make sure Garnet's prayers would not be in vain. For sure, he'd have success the next time.

Those remaining in the congregation sat and gloated at the number of souls who made their way forward, a total of eight. Half-confused, half-disheartened, Davida leaned her head on Tario's shoulder and placed her hand on his knee, rubbing it in a comforting manner.

35
KARLA'S BABY

WORKER ANTS HAD labored so tirelessly to build the ant hill in the crack of Garnet's driveway. She'd seen it in its infancy but this completed work happened just last night. The queen had apparently instructed her underlings to hop to it, to finish the work, almost as if she knew something. It was just like those myths that purported dogs' ability to sense P-waves before a real earthquake hit, causing them to act frantically as a pre-warning predictor. The ants were sunken within by now, though, feeling rather accomplished with their own manufactured sense of security and shade. That was until R.J. noticed it and stomped it in his tracks. The sweeping motion of his foot destroyed the mound and spared his grandmother the hassle of eradicating it herself. He'd have to take a few more science lessons to discover that he'd only razed the outer structure. Much like the tip of an iceberg, the visible part was dwarfed by what lay underneath it. The dirt tunnel must have stretched ten feet beneath the soil's surface, shielding its occupants from any major harm. The entrance would probably be built back again in another day or so.

"That darn ant hill outside's finally gone," Garnet declared. "Seems like it just popped up outta nowhere. But my big, strong man took care of it for me."

R.J. smiled with pride.

Jamay took a surprising turn. "The Lord's presence in service yesterday was super strong. He was definitely in the building."

"It *was* good. It was terrific seeing so many people give their hearts to the Lord," Garnet agreed. "I just knew I would see Tario coming down, though. It felt to me like he was finally at the point of surrender. Guess not, as least not yet."

"Well, it just takes some people a little longer than others. Just gotta keep praying for him." Looking at her clock, she realized they were a little behind schedule. "We better get dressed. They'll be here soon." They'd all agreed to meet at Garnet's and drive to the banquet together. "I got to get dolled up and get R.J. ready."

"I still can't believe they asked me to preside. The fifteenth anniversary of the church is no small accomplishment. I wish Castillo could be there, but I know he'd want us to carry on and keep holding up the blood-stained banner."

"Maybe you should say that tonight, mom."

"I will, in some form or another."

"I knew you'd look good in that dress when I saw it. Was a no-brainer. I knew it would be the best Mother's Day gift . . . well . . . the second best."

"Yeah, gramma. That dress is lit."

"Lit? And where did you learn that from, sir?" Jamay asked.

"They just be saying it."

"Okay, but you better watch what they just be saying."

Garnet had become a little confused at Jamay's earlier correction. She inquired, "What you mean by second best?" She was trying to process the last comment. "I think that dress is the best of them all. What other dress you thinking of?"

"Mama, sit down." Once she did, Jamay opened up. "I know I haven't really said that much about my trip to Jamaica but just wanted to say thank you."

"Thank you? For what, Jamay?"

"Everything."

Garnet looked puzzled.

"For everything," she restated. "After I came back from Jamaica, I finally understood how blessed I am. I met Miss Eralia, and she gave me the address to where my birth mom stays. Well, stayed."

"Was she not there?"

"Mom, she's not living anymore. I met her brother, and he shared all he knew about her with me." She went to the drawer and retrieved the photo. "He gave me this."

Garnet stared for a while. "Aw, you're so pretty, and so is she. And there's Miss Eralia." She got teary. "Is she still as feisty as ever?"

"You know it. She was stretching and everything while we were there. She's a whirlwind." Both giggled.

"I only wanted to make sure you were taken care of, Jamay. Sometimes, good things can come out of tragedy. I was scared myself, wondering what gave me the gall to think I could raise somebody else's child. But things just kept on workin' out and gettin' better and better. I hoped you wouldn't grow up and become upset or leave me in the dust after finding out whatever you would find out."

"Ma, you know I'd never do that. I'm glad I went, though. When I was a little girl, I think I always had questions about the adoption. I mean, I'm glad you were honest with me, but a part of me kept asking myself, 'Why didn't they want me?' I just kinda always thought it was something I did to make them not want me. What did I do so bad to make them not want me? As a grown lady, I know now that life is a complicated beast, but a small child doesn't relate to all of that." She began to tear up, and so did Garnet. "But it was a necessary journey, my trip there. It was an eye-opening experience. It's making me more appreciative of how I raise this one right here." She pulled R.J. over to herself and kissed his forehead. He pretended not to like it.

"Thank the Lord," said Garnet. "There are so many people who are adopted, and nobody ever knows. It's a secret they'd rather keep secret, and it affects who they are and how they interact with people. It haunts them in their relationships, and they never really get over it. I'm glad you're rising to the challenge and letting the Lord help you through it. You may always have to deal with those feelings that try to make you feel like you're not worthy or you don't measure up, but He'll help you get through those. You are complete in Him, nothing lacking. Maybe you can help somebody else who's going through it. The Lord never puts us on a haphazard journey. You never know who you'll inspire with your story."

"I love you, ma."

Garnet walked over and hugged her and the grandson. That gesture said it all.

Becoming more focused, Jamay got back into mommy mode. "Come on to the back, R.J., so we can get our clothes on. We got a banquet to get dressed for."

Just then, the doorbell rang. "Mama, get that since you already dressed. Let us get on back here so we can get ready."

Garnet motioned the door open.

"Heyy, Dr. G," Tario exclaimed.

"Hey, Ms. Gibbs," stated Davida.

"Nette!" Celeste greeted.

Three different people, three different salutations. She was no Wonder Woman, but her impact on others was undeniable. "Well, hello everybody. Don't you all look phenomenal."

"Whoa, Dr. G, you tryna go on *The Bachelorette* or something?" joked the male prankster.

"Oh hush, Tario. You 'bout worse than them students who give me gifts at the end of the year to get a good grade."

"Turn around, Nette. Lemme look at ya. You is go'geous."

"Well, it's not 'cause I picked it out. Jamay got it from somewhere in Nordstrom this past Mother's Day. I'd say she has pretty good taste. These Tracy Reese dresses make you feel elegant but comfy. Anyway, Jamay and R.J. will be out in a minute. They're finishing up getting themselves together. Just have a seat and make yourselves at home. Let me get you all something to drink."

"Nah, Dr. G, I'm good. Just rest and relax. It's just us."

Suddenly, a loud screeching sound from the back room startled them. It was loud enough to draw all parties from the front to the rear. Thankfully, Garnet's heels were off, so she was able to arrive first with all others in tow. They turned the corner to the back room to discover the shrieks were sounds of joy. Jamay was still jumping up and down, and R.J. was a bit awkward in expressing his excitement but was elated, nonetheless. The home computer was left on, and they happened to hear the call coming through. R.J. answered; he remembered how it functioned from the last time.

"He's coming home! He's coming home!" All of Jamay's anxiety, depression, excitement, and hope had been rolled into one big expressive ball. "Redd's coming home!"

The gang couldn't believe it. Garnet kept saying, *"Thank you, Jesus"* while everyone else contributed to the celebration. Tario's *"That's what's up"* mixed in with the rest of the celebratory congratulations. It was the happy before tonight's happy. The Lord was indeed The Big Orchestrator. His timing was second to none. Redd was still on the screen and smiled ear to ear. "Hi, good people. Jamay's right. I'm coming home for good next month. Thought about it for a minute, and I miss my baby and my boy. Life is short. You never know when the end gone be the end. I ain't willing to miss out no more on life with my family."

R.J. had become infatuated with staring at Redd's missing foot. "Bring it closer, daddy. I can't really see it."

"Son, you can't see what ain't there." But he held his leg up anyway for all to see. "Hey, the foot might be gone, but I'm still here!" He appeared to be adjusting well, and it confirmed in R.J.'s mind that he really was the superhero that his grandmother had alluded to over the years.

Folks chatted with Redd for about ten more minutes before they realized they'd better be getting to the Bellagio. "Okay, baby, we on our way to the church banquet tonight. We'll be back in touch. Probably will call when we get back if you gone be up," Jamay suggested.

"Oh, I'll be up. I'll have the computer on. It'll wake me up if I'm sleep. Love you all."

"Love you, daddy."

"Love you, too, R.J."

Everyone at Garnet's, especially R.J., had a noticeable pep in the step. He'd finally be getting his father back. It was something he'd long for for such a long time but never really talked about. Now, it was real. No more having to wonder when. When was now, in just a month. Finally.

They poured out into various cars, heading eastward. Garnet felt pumped up to preside. This new news was just the fuel she needed to extol the Lord and encourage the people to do the same. She was no preacher, but if the Lord anointed her, she stood with the best of them. No need for a script. That only held her back. With her, it had to be hot off the Lord's press. From His mouth to and through hers. She entered the car with Jamay, who was crying a bit. All she could do was look out her window, smile, and observe the clouds forming in the distance. To herself, she uttered, *"Thank you for the rain, Lord. Thank you for the rain."*

Gabriel, Raphaela, and Uriel were at the throne receiving further instructions. After tonight's banquet, they were given specific commands to be carried out over the course of the next week. The Lord stressed protecting Redd from any more harm on foreign soil. In two days, Celeste would get into a car accident and would get thrown through the windshield if they did not intervene. In four days, R.J. would nearly drown at the public swimming pool at the hands of Belial, who would hang out at the bottom of the pool and grab the kid's legs. They were to make sure it didn't go down as planned. On the same day, Nieko would become slightly depressed and text Maurice to see how he was fairing. Stumbling blocks were needed to thwart the impending meeting, which would lead to sex. And other situations would require divine interference, or they would go bust. As long as the saints were praying, nothing would go awry, hopefully. The Lord was always steps ahead of the enemy and his wiles. His human remnant was always poised to intercede; his angels were always positioned to strong-arm opposing forces.

"Yes, Master, we will make sure your children are protected this week. Hosanna! Hosanna! Hosanna! You are the Ruler of the universe and are worthy to be praised!" They departed from the throne of grace and headed back to the Lord's footstool, still lifting up the name of Jehovah as they went.

It was an hour until the official start of the banquet. They'd arrived an hour early to be assured of parking and to find the room where the event would take place. Valet parking was a fortune at the Bellagio, so they thought an early arrival would increase their chances at getting one of the few self-parking spaces that was available. Fortunately, they were right. Entering through the basement hallway, they meandered past a security desk and a few restaurants.

"This is a little eerie. This area reminds me of the same area where all that stuff happened in Chicago, you know where that girl ended up in the hotel freezer," recalled Davida.

"Stop, Davida," responded Tario. "All hotels have that same general look. We ain't got time to be thinking like that. We supposed to be going to have fun."

"Yeah, they was, too."

"Anyhow," interrupted Garnet, "we're here to celebrate the Lord and how far He's brought us and the ministry such a long way." Looking about, she figured she'd ask security for directions. "We're trying to find the banquet for The Alive Christ Church. Any idea where it might be?"

"You can check with the concierge up the way, ma'am. They have a master list of which functions are in which rooms."

"Thank you, sir."

They discovered it would be in the Grand Patio. They were given a discount rate since they were a church but probably because it was rumored that they'd probably be a loud bunch. Being in an outside space would allow them to be them without disturbing too many others. Granted, it was the Bellagio, so no fingers could be pointed at any one group in particular about raucousness and noise. Gamblers and other revelers did their part in contributing to the hotel's reputation in that regard. At any rate, the Patio was great. The view of the pools and courtyards provided extra benefit to what already promised to be a wonderful space catch.

"This is beautiful, absolutely beautiful," exclaimed Garnet. The podium stood over by the glass window. "Look at all the people outside. You would think I would have been in here before, but I haven't. I never come to the Bellagio for anything."

"Whoa, gramma! Look at the pools down there and all those people swimming. Can I go swimming?" R.J. was enamored of the view.

"Maybe one day, R.J., not today. We'll have to come one day and get a room so we can go swimming. Besides, they're probably not even open."

Room chairs began filling. Kids ran around the luxurious space, almost bumping into the tables. Parents chided and chastised. Church leaders located Garnet and made sure she was aware of the agenda for the night. Video tributes were to be a part of the night's festivities, so the hotel's AV team were completing the taping of cords to the floor to prevent inadvertent slips, trips, and falls.

Hotel waitstaff had set up drink stations throughout. Their main efforts would be needed with dish disappearance after the main and dessert courses, so drink efficiency would have to run on auto-pilot. Almost on cue, Nieko walked in and greeted Garnet.

"So look who gets to *be* served this time as opposed to serving," she joked. "Probably makes you feel funny, huh?"

"Not one bit, Sister Gibbs. I put in my fair share of wearing my black tux and hard-bottomed black shoes. Today, I sit, eat, and enjoy."

"Well, you look dapper." He donned a light blue and white seer-sucker suit, a white Oxford, and red bowtie with matching hanky. The brown Versace belt, blue and brown designer socks, and a pair of brown ECCO sneaker shoes rounded out his ensemble.

"Thank you. I hardly ever get to wear my glad rags, so I had to hit 'em hard today."

"Hittin' 'em is definitely what you doin'." They laughed. "You can sit over at our table, if you want."

"Okay, thanks."

Tario had managed to get a glass of wine in another area of the hotel and brought it over to where the family gathered. He knew they wouldn't be serving such at the function and felt it okay to partake before the function started.

"Wine, Tario?" Davida voiced. "You know this is a church function. It's a banquet, but it's still a church function."

He placed the glassful on the table. "That's why I'm gone finish it before the program starts. By the way, I heard Jesus drank."

"See, now you bordering on blasphemy. No, He did not."

"He did something with wine. Brought it in for a party like we having today."

"You need to read, Rio. It won't no party. It was a wedding. And He didn't bring wine in from nowhere. He turned water into wine."

"Well, there you go. Same thing. Can't be too bad if He thought it was okay to use his magic to create some." He had another joke brewing. "And it can make you do some off-the-wall craziness. See, look at this." He wrote something on a sheet of paper. "What this say?" he asked Davida.

Looking at it, she rolled her eyes and said, "Liquor store."

"Say it faster."

"Liquor store."

"Faster."

"Liquor store. Tario, stop playing. Why you got me saying this foolishness?"

"Now, say it slower."

"Liquor store."

"Slower."

"Liquor store."

"And by the time you finish doing all that drinking," he stated, "that's what it's gone turn into by the time you get home to your boo. A lick her store!"

"You know what! I'm not fooling with you. You play too much!" She rolled her eyes again, this time much slower and longer. Just know that sometimes, He'll give you what you want if you keep asking for it, good *or* bad. They were feening for some wine, and, guess what, they got just what they wanted. Just because He made some wine don't mean he . . . I'm not doing this with you today. Sometimes, talking to you is like talking to a kindergartener." He laughed. She sighed.

With thirty minutes left until the function began, Garnet made her way over to the table where her family and friends sat. Karla joined them, along with her bubbly five-month old, who had just finished drinking dinner. She had joined the church within the last month and was encouraged to attend the banquet to meet various families within the fold. Outgoing as she was, she plopped herself and the baby beside the

Gibbses and company. All were engaged in small talk when Garnet approached.

"Hey mom," Jamay started. "This is Karla and her baby."

"Hi, Karla. Pleased to meet you. Are my people over here talking your head off and embarrassing the church?"

"No, no. They are being very nice to me."

"How are you enjoying Alive?"

"So far, so good. Everyone is so nice. Spirit's there. I'm sure I'll grow if I keep coming."

"You will. You will." Spotting the little one, she inquired. "Oh, and who is this little angel? What's your name?"

Realizing the question was really directed to her, Karla responded, "Say, 'My name is little Chablis.'" The mother lifted her from the crib and shook her side to side in a playful manner. The child had just awakened and grinned ear to ear.

Tario realized the baby was named after some wine and repeated sarcastically in Davida's ear, "Speaking of wine . . ."

She hit his leg under the table. "Stop!" she whispered back. "That's also a region in France."

"Yeah, okay. We'll go with that. She was named after a region in France."

"Isn't she beautiful?" interjected Garnet. With no hesitation, she reached out to hold her. The mother yielded and handed her over. "Oh," continued the emcee, "she is such a doll." Holding her close, she patted her little back in adoration and love. It was a feeling that reminded her of what she felt when she held Jamay, R.J., and the sweet girl at the Mexican restaurant. Excited, the bundle of joy did quite a bit of squirming in Garnet's arms, prompting Garnet to grab a seat.

"Whoa! Somebody's a little squirm machine, isn't she?" Before Garnet could comfortably situate Chablis in her hands, the baby somehow managed to reach the table. Her tiny but strong legs reached Tario's glass, causing it to topple. Its red contents soaked the tablecloth and Garnet's white dress. "Oh, dear! Oh, my Lord!"

Nieko instantly reached for the glass and set it aright. Karla hurried and grabbed Chablis from Garnet, who looked for napkins or anything close that would erase the wine's color before it settled. Unfortunately, nothing did.

"Yo, my bad!" belted Tario. He felt it was his fault since he brought it over.

"I've got to hurry and get home to change. I can't preside with this all over me."

"Come on, mom, let's go," rushed Jamay. I'll drive you home. We have a few minutes. We'll just tell them you had a little accident. Thank goodness we don't stay too far."

"No, I'll drive her," interjected Tario. "It's my fault this happened. It's the least I can do. Plus, Jamay, I rode with you before. You drive too slow. We need to be back in thirty minutes tops."

"Not a bad idea. I can't wait. Jamay, explain to the minister what happened. See if they'll let you and a few others have a short praise service, just until I get back. It shouldn't take long." She started trotting toward the entrance, attempting to cover as much of the stain as possible. More people began streaming in. "Come on, Tario. Let's go!"

"I'm here, Dr. G. I'm right here!"

Tario came to a rolling stop and then stepped on it. He knew better, but he was rushing to get her home and then back to the Bellagio before the festivities started.

"That was a stop sign, baby, slow down! I'll get there when I get there." Deep down, though, Garnet was actually happy he was flooring it. She didn't subscribe to Murphy's Law, but there didn't seem to be another explanation for what had transpired over the last hour. "God bless that li'l Chablis." They both laughed. "But it ain't no need in dyin' trying to get back to the hotel. Jamay and the others will keep 'em occupied until I get back. Just be careful."

"Dr. G, I'm good. You in good hands." He made a right from W. Tropicana onto Van Carol and continued until it became Mt. Nido. He parked alongside the curb and turned on his flashers. There was no need to pull into the driveway. Hopefully, she wouldn't take all day.

"Okay, I'll be right back. Gimme ten minutes. I already know which dress I'll put on." Realizing she was being a bit rude, she caught herself. "You can come in and wait inside if you want."

"Naw, go 'head. I'm just gone marinate and relax out here 'til you get back."

"Well, don't have too much fun marinatin'," she jokingly retorted. "I can't keep up at all with y'all young folk talk." She swung the door open and started a fast trot toward the house. All day today from the moment her eyes opened, she had been feeling a little different. She couldn't explain it, but her spirit felt troubled. Not in a particularly bad way. And not in a way as though she thought she needed to intercede for somebody. Just a constant and quiet churning in her inner heart.

Much to her surprise, it had begun drizzling. The sun also shone through the clouds. The devil was beating his wife. As she made her way to the door, she looked up to assess the gathering of clouds to see if she needed to bring her umbrella back with her. *"Jesus, hold the rain,"* she uttered to Him softly. She glanced over at the forget-me-nots that she planted last year and observed their making an effort to rebloom. Maybe a little rain wouldn't be too bad.

Outside, Tario had watched Garnet through the water-checkered passenger door window as she made her way inside. "No she ain't tryin' to run," he kidded to himself. "That's prolly the first time she done ran in years." After laughing at his own joke, he switched the radio station to 97.5. Out of respect for Garnet, he had the radio set so she could listen to her gospel music. She didn't demand it, but he knew she wouldn't take too well to the latest urban beats and references enjoyed by the modern day's twentysomething crowd. He wasn't about to listen to no gospel music today, though, which he whispered to himself. He'd now have a few minutes to revel in hip-hop heaven. The radio personalities were playing Nipsey Hussle, which made him bop his head back and forth and back and forth.

After unlocking the door, Garnet barreled in and headed straight for her room. She was moving so fast that she had to double-back to disarm the alarm system. The umbrella would be necessary given the developing weather, so she grabbed it from the coat closet and placed it by the door. She entered the bathroom and turned on the faucet so that she could rewash her face and apply some of her makeup again. She smirked again at Chablis and slithered out of her soiled dress, walking to the kitchen in her slip and bare feet. She grabbed a quick drink of water in the kitchen and returned to the bathroom.

Ten minutes would fly by, so Tario would enjoy all of the moment by reclining his seat all the way back. He was completely horizontal. The treble and bass were kicking. He closed his eyes and rapped the "Last Time That I Checc'd" lyrics along with the artist. He turned his head a little in the direction of his Samsung to see if anyone had texted him. Nobody had. He noticed that it was 6:56 p.m. He saw that the rain had picked up and was assaulting the windshield like it had a vendetta against it.

He made sure all four windows were rolled up, closed his eyes again, and just waited, urging, "Don't take all night, Dr. G. Time is tickin'. Time is tickin'."

12:00

36
MIDNIGHT

HE WAS SHAKEN awake coincidentally. It didn't have anything to do with the fact that he really *was* up against the
clock. He hadn't even felt himself dozing off, let alone dwelling in the deep trenches of sleepville. The car's soothing
interior and the sound of the deafening rain must have been
the tag-teaming culprits, lulling him into that Sandman-ushered space. And now, they were late. When she exited the car,
she said she'd be right back and that she already had an idea
about what she'd change into. So the amount of time this was
taking was absurd. Even if she had to steam the dress, this was
taking way too long; ten minutes had become twenty. "What
in the hell is she doing in there?" Tario stated to himself. He
shot Davida a text, claiming that they were six minutes away.
But the truth was that they hadn't even left yet. Now that the
downpour had calmed to a drizzle, he'd just make his way
inside to see what the holdup was. Soon, the car's engine was
off, and he performed unequal jump-strides from the curb to
the front door, careful to avoid the patches of water.

He cracked open the front door. "Dr. G?" After a short silence, he repeated. "Dr. G?" As he entered the house, she still didn't answer. The floor creaked. Making his way through the hallway, he noticed the umbrella propped against the wall. The hallway fed into the living room. Nothing there either. A quick transition into the kitchen revealed nothing but an empty glass in the sink. Nothing too out of the ordinary, except for the slip on the kitchen floor. *Yo, Dr. G trippin',* he thought. *I know we in a rush, but she just throwing stuff everywhere.* Other than that, the kitchen was spick and span.

Finally, his ears saved him. He heard water running in her bathroom. He'd never laid eyes on her bedroom before, so the thought of entering naturally made him feel guilty and like he was trespassing. He called for her louder, now that he stood right next to her door. "Dr. G?" He had to walk softly so that he didn't see anything he wasn't supposed to, especially if she was sitting on the toilet or praying. Or worse, sitting on the toilet and praying. "Dr. G?"

Filled with consternation, he inched toward the bathroom door and touched it, preparing to turn. In an instant, the knob turned and the door swung open away from him.

Garnet was rushing as fast as she could when she was startled. "Tario, sweetie, what are you doing in here? I thought you were going to wait in the car."

Embarrassed, he said what he thought made sense. "It was getting late, and I just wanted to come in and make sure you were alright. I called your name I don't know how many times, and you didn't say nothing. I was hoping didn't nothing bad happen."

A text from Davida popped up on Tario's phone: *So wya? Jmy and them still doing praise. Tell Ms Gibbs Jmy need her to brng trunks 4 RJ. Hotel gone let him swim in pool. Hurry!*

"Bad? What do you mean 'bad'? I got to hurry and get back. It's quarter past." She turned off the faucet and virtually ran throughout the house, picking up the slip, the soiled dress, and even managed to wash the used glass.

"You look very nice, Dr. G. Can I help with anything?" She had changed into a light blue cocktail dress by Zac Posen, sleeveless. This and the wine-stained one were the only real formal pieces she had in that closet of hers. Slipping into her silver heels, she grabbed a navy scarf to offset any possible cold temperatures in the hotel, along with her earrings. She hated when hotels turned their air on Alaska, thinking they were offsetting temperatures outside. She'd put the earrings on in the car.

"No, just grab the umbrella on the way out. Let's go." She grabbed her keys. "Close the door so I can set the alarm."

With the countdown in motion, he opened the door, and she scurried through the hall toward him, only a few feet behind. Grabbing the umbrella, he half-stepped outside but remembered. Turning back around, he stated, "Oh, Dr. G, I forgot. Jamay wants you to–"

Never in a million years would he ever forget the image that his eyes were trying to make him believe was real.

He stared, simply stared, wondering what this mass on the floor behind him was: a dress, a scarf, shoes, earrings, keys. It was a strange mound, some strange heap. Stuck half-inside, half-outside the door, he looked at the pouring rain bouncing off his car to his front and that puddle of clothing behind him. And then back around. Baffled. He relaxed his hold on the umbrella slightly, musing, brooding, still staring at the mostly blue mass. Struggling to get his mental bearings straight, he decided to follow his gut instinct but changed his mind. What was this joke, this untimely ruse? "Dr. G?"

As each mysterious second arrived and crept away, he slowly realized that the only sound louder than the alarm's steady beeps was this stealthy, liberating, promised, selective silence.

TWO 'TIL MIDNIGHT

1. Some of the action in the novel is framed as war between angels and demons. In other parts, the Holy Spirit interacts with and speaks to several characters. What is your position on whether the supernatural can influence occurrences in real life? Discuss any situations in which you have interacted with or observed the supernatural.

2. R.J. is forced to deal with the absence of his father because of patriotic duties. The troops get creative and use technology to help bridge the Redd-R.J. gap, making their separation more bearable. What other measures could be taken to help children of troops deal better with life when their mother and/or father is serving the country overseas?

3. After the diversity meeting, Leigh chides Garnet because of her failure to speak up and voice her opinion about the hot topic of discussion. While Leigh believes that, in a secular world, Christians should "say more and speak up more" (page 283), Garnet feels that they do not "have to be so vocal about everything. People have to see your lifestyle and see that you care before they start hearing anything about the Lord" (page 283). Whose perspective do you tend to agree with more? Why?

4. What's eating Rusty becomes clear in the novel, which hints at the fact that he was around during the unrest of the turbulent 1960s. One could argue that, since people

like Rusty have been set in their ways for so long on issues regarding race, there is no need to attempt to change their viewpoint; they will never change how and what they think about any race other than theirs. How valid do you think this argument is?

5. Nieko suggests to Giselle that there is a possibility that he may remain single for the rest of his life. Giselle responds, "I just want you to be happy . . . I don't want you to get to the end of your life and . . . end up alone" (page 303). Discuss whether or not you think society places equal value on singlehood as it does on marriage. What factors do you think contribute to how society views being single and/or being married?

6. In the diversity meeting, the conversation becomes quite heated. Marjorie believes gay peoples' struggle should be equated with that of African-Americans. Leigh states, "Oh, Lord! I knew it would just be a matter of time before someone would go there and bring that up. That's what's called a fallacy of false equivalence" (page 227). Discuss whether there is any merit in Leigh's claim.

7. Because of interaction on social media, R.J. puts himself in a precarious situation when he decides to meet Emily at the fountain in the mall. What strategies can parents and guardians employ to monitor their children's online activity and reduce the likelihood that they end up in potentially dangerous predicaments?

8. When Jamay visits the adoption agency, Miss Eralia encourages her to keep a certain perspective on her journey to find out information about her birth parents. She

says, "Dat's what everybody dat come back 'ere wonder. Deep down, dat's what they travel all dem miles fuh. Just to see if they loved. Well, even if yuh didn' or don' find out nothin' spectacula', yuh livin' and got a chance to make someting out yuhself. Out of everyting that 'appened, yuh got a life to be able to do someting wit'" (page 179). Discuss whether or not Miss Eralia's words should be sufficient for any adoptees who wish to search for their biological parents.

9. George converses with his wife about how he felt responsible to speak up and confront Officer Schmidt, a fellow white cop, when Tario was being roughed up. He states, "My gut feeling is that things aren't gone change until white people start speaking up . . . I'm not saying we gotta be the 'Great White Hopes,' but we gotta make sure our voices are heard right along with theirs" (page 277). What responsibility should non-participatory white cops show toward fellow white cops who seem to abuse their power? What responsibility do white people have in general as it relates to other white people's unfair treatment of minority groups?

10. At the end, Tario turns around and sees an intriguing spectacle. Discuss what you think is going on. What do you think the author means by the phrase "stealthy, liberating, promised, selective silence" (page 382)?

In *Lemonade: Inspired by Actual Events*, Dillard narrates his own coming-of-age story from boy to man. Exposed to the goods, the bads, and the uglies of Dillard's world, readers can't help but sympathize with, cheer for, and laugh out loud at a man who is trying his best to find the most stable path that leads to becoming a man. Simply, it is a tale of triumph amid opposition. Dillard stands in life's kitchen, gathers his ingredients, and shows us what to make when all there seems to be is a basket full of lemons.

Lemonade: Inspired by Actual Events
$14.98

"An engaging read from first page to last, *Lemonade* is an articulate, candid, inherently fascinating, true-life story that marks Dillard as an accomplished writer able to draw his readers into his personal memoir with an intimacy rarely encountered."
—*Midwest Book Review*

"Anyone reading this book will empathize with Bernard, feel his pain, and rejoice in his victories as he moves from being a child to becoming a man in his own right."
—*AAMBC Book Reviews*

CPSIA information can be obtained
at www.ICGtesting.com
Printed in the USA
FFHW020447090819
54109777-59844FF

9 780578 45